北京外国语大学王佐良外国文学高等研究院出品
北 京 外 国 语 大 学“双 一 流”建 设 项 目 成 果

外国文学研究文库 · 第三辑

A History of Literary Criticism in the Renaissance

文艺复兴时期文学批评史

乔尔·伊莱亚斯·斯平加恩 著
Joel Elias Spingarn
马海良 导读

外语教学与研究出版社
FOREIGN LANGUAGE TEACHING AND RESEARCH PRESS
北京 BEIJING

图书在版编目(CIP)数据

文艺复兴时期文学批评史 = A History of Literary Criticism in the Renaissance ：英文 /（美）乔尔·伊莱亚斯·斯平加恩（Joel Elias Spingarn）著 ；马海良导读. -- 北京 ：外语教学与研究出版社，2020.9

（外国文学研究文库. 第三辑）

ISBN 978-7-5213-2049-7

Ⅰ. ①文… Ⅱ. ①乔… ②马… Ⅲ. ①文艺复兴 - 文学批评史 - 西方国家 - 英文 Ⅳ. ①I561.093

中国版本图书馆 CIP 数据核字 (2021) 第 141875 号

出 版 人　徐建忠
项目负责　姚　虹　徐　宁
责任编辑　徐　宁
责任校对　都楠楠
封面设计　奇文云海
出版发行　外语教学与研究出版社
社　　址　北京市西三环北路 19 号（100089）
网　　址　http://www.fltrp.com
印　　刷　三河市北燕印装有限公司
开　　本　650×980　1/16
印　　张　24
版　　次　2021 年 8 月第 1 版　2021 年 8 月第 1 次印刷
书　　号　ISBN 978-7-5213-2049-7
定　　价　59.00 元

购书咨询：（010）88819926　电子邮箱：club@fltrp.com
外研书店：https://waiyants.tmall.com
凡印刷、装订质量问题，请联系我社印制部
联系电话：（010）61207896　电子邮箱：zhijian@fltrp.com
凡侵权、盗版书籍线索，请联系我社法律事务部
举报电话：（010）88817519　电子邮箱：banquan@fltrp.com
物料号：320490001

前　言

由北京外国语大学王佐良外国文学高等研究院策划、外语教学与研究出版社出版的“外国文学研究文库”就要与读者见面了。近年来，我国外国文学学界同仁一直在积极探索有效途径，引进国外学者的学术著作，以提升我国的学术研究水平，增强我国学者的国际学术话语权。但由于国外文学研究领域发展迅猛，以及国内出版经费缺乏等一系列问题，国外文学研究领域许多经典的和最新的研究成果无法得到及时传播与出版。为了弘扬我国老一辈学者外国文学研究的优秀传统，促进我国外国文学研究的深入开展，我们组织策划了这套“外国文学研究文库”，旨在将国外文学学界的学术成果及时引进和介绍给我国外国文学学者、学生及爱好者，反映外国文学研究领域在世界范围的发展趋势与前沿探索，使我国学界更好地与国际学界接轨与对话，以此推进我国外国文学研究的发展。

“外国文学研究文库”定位于对国外文学研究重要成果展开的

引介，将采用购买原作版权、组织国内该领域有影响的学者撰写导读的方式进行。这些导读将有助于读者把握作品的脉络，掌握其思想要点，更全面、更深入地理解作品要义。鉴于英语之外其他语种作品的受众问题，除以英语撰写的著作以原文的形式出版之外，我们拟将其他语种的国外学者著作翻译成汉语，并附以专家导读。该“文库”是一套开放性的系列丛书，我们将陆续推出国外具有影响力的学术著作，内容范围包括以下四个方向：外国文学理论、外国文学批评、比较文学理论与批评，以及文化批评研究。

北京外国语大学王佐良外国文学高等研究院邀请到了我国重要学者参加编委会，推荐挑选国外学界具有影响力的研究著作。国内这一领域的资深学者将为著作撰写导读，并为非英语著作确定译者。我们希望通过这套“文库”，为拓展和深化我国的外国文学研究，为帮助我国外国文学学者拓宽批评视野、开拓研究思路，尽我们的微薄之力。

这套“文库”的出版，得到了我国外国文学研究领域众多学者的鼎力相助和大力支持，也得到了外语教学与研究出版社的全力配合，特此表示衷心感谢！

金莉
北京外国语大学教授
王佐良外国文学高等研究院院长

导 读

马海良
北京外国语大学英语学院

欧洲的“文艺复兴”（the Renaissance）被普遍看作“现代”的起点，自然也会成为现代性话语的重要源头，那么作为一个学科的文学批评与文艺复兴有着怎样的关联？对于外国文学研究者来说，这无疑是个分量非凡的大问题，对这个问题的探究不仅具有学术史和知识史的价值，而且有助于在更为开阔而深厚的历史维度下，认识文学批评的本质和发展轨迹，从而提高文学研究所必需的理论自觉和批评内涵。一百多年前，确切地说，1899 年出版的这本《文艺复兴时期文学批评史》仍然让今天的读者充满期待。

按照一般的社会文化史分期，“文艺复兴”是指 14—16 世纪始于意大利，后来逐渐扩展到整个欧洲，推动神权至上的西欧地区转变为各个世俗的民族国家的思想文化运动。不过，《文艺复兴时期文学批评史》并不是囊括整个文艺复兴时期的通史，而是选择 16 世纪意大利、法国和英国的文学批评活动展开重点考察，因为作者认为 16 世纪是文艺复兴的高潮阶段，而意法英则是文艺复兴时期文学批评活动的主要场地且具有足够的代表性；当然出于语境的考虑，作者有时会简要述及其他国家文艺复兴的情况，时间上也会进入16世纪之前或之后。全书分三个部分依次呈现意大利、法国及英国的文学批评状况和成就，这个顺序对应着文艺复兴时期文学批评在三个国家中发生和展开的实际时序，即现代批评最早出现于意大利，确切时间应该是1535年，因为这一年贺拉斯（Horace）《诗艺》的意大利文译本正式出版；十年之后的1545年法国出版了《诗艺》的法文译本，而英文版《诗艺》则出版于1567年，也就是说，现代批评在英国出现的时间比在意大利晚了三十多年。把现代批评的历史起点这一宏大的事件与贺拉斯的一部作品译入不同民族语言的具体年份联结起来，如此精细的描述反映出作者一丝不苟的学术意趣，也增强了整个研究的可靠性，不过对于我们来说，更为突出的似乎是作者斯平加恩[1]着意强调贺拉斯所代表的古典主义（classicalism）在现代批评产生过程中发挥的不可或缺的作用。

意大利是文艺复兴的发源地，文艺复兴时期的代表人物包括但丁（Dante）、彼特拉克（Petrarch）、薄伽丘（Boccaccio）等伟大作家，其中但丁提出了著名的“四义”说，即字面义、譬喻义、道德义、寓言义，这些知识今天的文学研究者大都耳熟能详。然而把文学视为独立范畴进行深入考察，对其性质、内涵、构成、

---

1 斯平加恩（Joel Elias Spingarn, 1875—1939），出生在纽约市一个犹太裔家庭，1899年获得美国哥伦比亚大学博士学位后，留校担任比较文学教授；1903年发起创办《比较文学》（*Comparative Literature*）杂志；1916年设立了以自己的名字命名的斯平加恩奖章（the Spingarn Medal），每年授予做出杰出贡献的非裔美国人；1930—1939年担任美国全国有色人种协进会（National Association for the Advancement of Colored People, NAACP）主席。斯平加恩的主要作品还有三卷本编著《17世纪批评文集》（*Critical Essays of the Seventeenth-Century*, 1908）、编著《正义的呐喊：社会抗议文学选集》（*The Cry for Justice: An Anthology of the Literature of Social Protest*, 1915）、《创造性批评文集》（*Creative Criticism and Other Essays*, 1931）和几部诗集。

功能等基本属性作出系统论述，或者说文学批评的明显成型，还需要等待 16 世纪的到来。现代意义上的文学自觉还需要希腊罗马古典文化来唤醒和催生，这一状况符合“复兴”的本义，即“再生”“重生”古希腊罗马的学术和文化，颇有“继绝学”（the Revival of Learning）的意味。

欧洲漫长的中世纪唯神学独尊，所有的精神活动和文化形式都必须为上帝服务，必须从神学中获得合法性。按照这样的文化制度，文学自然不可能有独立的地位，而且总体来说，文学不被宗教所信任，一举一动都被置于宗教神学的监督之下。在神学主流看来，文学背负着许多原罪，譬如文学离不开虚构和说谎，所以文学远离真实，扭曲真理；文学沉溺于情感，甚至不遗余力地鼓动激情，使人丧失节制和自我约束，有害于人的健康成长；文学作品里充斥着诲淫诲盗的描写，败坏风气，腐蚀社会。总之，文学的本质似乎就是有毒的，最好像柏拉图（Plato）设想的那样，从宗教的理想国中驱赶出去。中世纪的作家们也尝试为文学的正能量辩护，指出文学虚构不等于撒谎，虚构是为了更有效地表达道德含义；文学作品不能只看字面意义，而是应该读懂深层的教化寓意；退一步说，不是诗或文学本身有问题，而是对文学形式的误用和滥用造成了神学指控的那些遗憾，如果运用得当，文学就能发挥独特的积极作用，例如《圣经》里就有大量优美的诗歌。但是在神学独大的宗教社会里，人们只能从服务和辅助价值的角度为文学作一些辩护，无法从本质属性上论述文学的合法独立地位。

但丁曾经偶尔提及贺拉斯，对亚里士多德（Aristotle）却似乎一无所知。到了 16 世纪，随着希腊罗马古典文献纷纷译入欧洲主要语言，西欧好古之风兴盛，西欧学界已经是言必称希腊罗马了。在文学领域，古希腊罗马思想同样为人们提供了丰富而得力的资源，尤其是贺拉斯的《诗艺》和亚里士多德的《诗学》成了文人们的《圣经》，“书里的几乎每个段落都有不计其数的评论家和批评家推敲讨论”。贺拉斯用热情洋溢的诗句把诗人尊奉为人类的第一位老师，他教育人类辨识万物，走出混沌，创设制度，守护人伦；诗人的本性是神圣的。达尼埃洛（Daniello, 1536）的《诗学》几乎就是贺拉斯《诗艺》的翻版。他像贺拉斯一样，把诗赞誉为最古老而高贵的艺术，诗人以悦耳动听、华美绚烂的语言诉说上帝和自然的所有秘密和人类的全部知识；诗人发明和传授生活的艺术，从来不会像哲学家那样进行枯燥乏味的说教；实际上，最早的诗歌就是人类所有的哲学。明图尔诺（Minturno, 1559）效仿达尼埃洛，在《论诗人》里把诗看作人类全部知识的总和，这个世界是先有诗人，然后才有了各门知识，因此之故，即使一个野蛮民族，也不会排斥诗歌。诗人竟然被赋予了神圣的崇高地位，这对于中世纪的人们来说颇为惊世骇俗，无异于对上帝的亵渎，好在贺拉斯等人本来就是“异教徒”，要惩罚他们，实在是鞭长莫及。

如果说贺拉斯为文艺复兴时期批评家的文学合法性辩护提供了主要的感性和情感支持，那么亚里士多德则给了他们一套现成的、相当系统的文学理论，同时也启发他们以理性思辨、严密论证的方式进行理论建构。亚里士多德《诗学》的拉丁文译本和希腊文版本分别在 15 世纪末和 16 世纪初才进入意大利。不过，意大利文艺复兴经过长时间的酝酿和发展在 16 世纪进入巅峰，亚里士多德的出现恰逢其时，自然会激起批评家的强烈共鸣和响应。1536 年达尼埃洛论及亚里士多德的《诗学》，1543 年《诗学》已经进入大学，用作戏剧课程的教材。1549 年，塞尼（Bernardo Segni）把《诗学》译成意大利文，一方面反映了学界对这部经典的重视达到了新的高度，另一方面也使它得到更加广泛的传播。亚里士多德提出了著名的“诗比历史更真实”的命题，认为诗人与历史学家的区别关键不在于一个用韵文体写作，一个用散文体写作，而在于诗人的功能并非讲述已经发生的事实，而是讲出可能发生的情况，即按照可然律或必然律将会发生的事情；也就是说，诗表达普遍性，而历史关注的是特殊性，因此诗比历史更像哲学。达尼埃洛在其《诗学》中也对诗人与历史学家作了区分，指出历史学家必须如实描述事物，诗人则不受事实的约束，而是按照事物应该有的样子来模仿生活。这种关于“理想的模仿”（ideal imitation）的说法显然直接来自亚里士多德，而且据斯平加恩考证，这是现代批评中最早出现的对亚里士多德理论的征引。当然，达尼埃洛在亚里士多德的基础上也作了一些引申和补充，指出诗人与历史学家也有一些共同点，譬如他们都要描写人物、地点，反映善恶，出现一定程度的放大、缩小或偏离，寓教于乐，等等。罗博泰利（Robortelli）在他为1548年拉丁文版《诗学》作的评论中对亚里士多德理论进行了具体的拓展，认为诗人既可以占用已然事实，也可以独创自己的材料，不过关键在于叙述已然事实时，应该按照可能是或应该是的样子去呈现，而独创材料时，须按照可能律、可然律或必然律来呈现。进一步看，独创事物分为两类，即合乎自然之事和超越自然之事，前者是按照可然律或必然律产生的，而后者是按照人类已知法则或规律，合乎逻辑地演绎出来的。关于另外一个与亚里士多德有关的问题，即用散文体进行模仿者能否称为诗人，罗博泰利的答案是最优秀的诗作总是模仿与韵文的完美结合，显示出重视形式因素的倾向。大致与此同时，瓦尔基（Varchi）在系列演讲中对亚里士多德的模仿说作了更为确切的阐述，认为模仿是诗的本质属性，诗即模仿；模仿的对象包括行动、情感、心灵。至于模仿以韵文体为首选，乃是源于人对和谐感的本能喜好，和谐感让人愉悦喜乐。比瓦尔基更强调韵文体重要性的是斯卡利杰（Julius Cæsar Scaliger），他坚持韵文是诗之为诗的根本因素之一，诗人的工作便是“用韵文进行模仿”（imitation in verse）。卡斯特尔韦特罗（Castelvetro）在1570年评论《诗学》时为韵文体之所以重要的原因作了解释，认为散文体不适合模仿或想象之事，因为按照人们的一般预期，散文体是用来描写确切事实的。尽管韵文并非诗之为诗的决定因素，但它是诗的衣饰外表；因此诗不能用散文来写，历史不能用韵文来写，正如男女不能穿上对方的衣服。斯平加恩认为，卡斯特尔韦特罗的这番话比文艺复兴时期的大部分作家都更贴近亚里士多德的本意。

诗的功能或目的向来是批评理论要回答的一个重要问题，甚至是首要问题，因为事物合法性的基石是有用性，由此可以理解为什么贺拉斯的《诗艺》即使在中世纪也能得到一定程度的关注。从功用角度讲，《诗艺》提出的“寓教于乐”更容易打动依然习惯于神学教条的中世纪读者。既然诗歌能够以愉悦的方式表达宗教思想，弘扬上帝之光，实现道德教化的目的，那么何不顺势而为积极利用文学的这种独特优势呢？当然细绎之下，可以发现“寓教于乐”看上去是一个浅显而诱人的策略，实际上蕴含着巨大的转换能量，“乐”在不经意间被堂而皇之地界定为文学的根本属性之一，为后来以审美愉悦为最高追求，从而独立自主的文学范畴作了铺垫。“寓教于乐”理论在 16 世纪的意大利得到进一步挖掘和阐发，达尼埃洛紧跟贺拉斯，坚持认为诗人的本分就是“亦教亦乐”（teach and delight）；不过，鉴于最终目的是让受众接受所教，因此应该加上一项“亦化”，即成功感化和教化受众。也有人提出更为明确具体的目标，钦齐奥（Giraldi Cintio）认为诗人致力于针砭罪恶，褒扬美德；马吉（Maggi）主张诗人的最高追求是有益于人的心灵，因为愉悦来自道德的进步；瓦尔基认为诗人的职责是帮助人们实现灵魂的完美和幸福，属于道德范畴。斯卡利杰指出，固然诗即模仿，但是模仿并非诗的旨归，检视诗品的主要参照要看它是否作了“令人愉悦的教诲”（delightful instruction）。明图尔诺在此基础上添加了第三项：感人——感动并感化。一首诗仅仅塑造出英雄形象是不够的，还必须让读者开始心悦诚服地崇拜这个英雄。这一思想代表了文艺复兴时期的普遍观念，即哲学家用警句进行指导，诗人用样板作出示范。打铁须得自身硬，被捧到圣人地位的诗人似乎必须自己先成为全能的完人，才有资格教诲众生，这一要求不能说没有逻辑。事实上，文艺复兴时期的批评家们对诗人几乎无所不包的能力作了充分的设想。利奥纳尔迪（Alessandro Lionardi）要求诗人既是优秀的演说家，亦是优秀的历史学家、自然哲学家和道德哲学家；贝尔纳多·塔索（Bernardo Tasso）认为，要习得诗艺，不仅要熟读亚里士多德，还要熟悉艺术、科学以及整个世界；明图尔诺提出，诗人须掌握各种知识，了解所有美德，因此从根本上说，诗人是智者兼贤者，是一个有能力驾驭语言、从事模仿的好人，也可以说，坏人写不出好诗。总体来看，文艺复兴时期对文学功用的论述主要承接了贺拉斯的资源，并且在此基础上进行了更广泛的拓展，集中体现为对伦理道德价值的重视、对实际教化成效的追求，以及对诗人自身完美高度的要求。不过也要看到，有人从亚里士多德那里出发，走向对“乐”或“愉悦”的最终选择，例如卡斯特尔韦特罗，而托尔夸托·塔索（Torquato Tasso，贝尔纳多·塔索之子）则更进一步，指出艺术的使命就是再现本真之美（real beauty）或自在之美，它让所有人愉悦，却与任何实际的用处无关。这一看法已经非常接近后来的康德美学了。从修辞逻辑的角度看，这个命题既表述功能，也表述性质。

在希腊罗马古典文献的复兴和引领下，16 世纪意大利批评家对文学的基本问题作了系统的考察和论述，除此之外，也对悲剧、喜剧、史诗等具体文类作了深入的阐发，使整个批评理论的建构呈现出相当可观的规模。

亚里士多德对悲剧的定义是意大利批评家们扩展和深化工作的基础：“悲剧是对一个严肃、完整而规模可观的行动的模仿。”达尼埃洛认为，所谓“严肃”（serious or illustrious）的行动是指重大的或严重的事情（grave matters），譬如国王驾崩或帝国灭亡。悲剧以那些重大事情为本色主题，而喜剧呈现的是日常生活，二者绝不可以混合。由于悲剧表现重要人物和重大事件，所以舞台上不能出现轻浮低俗、残暴血腥、不合情理的场面。达尼埃洛的这些观点对16世纪及其后的批评理论影响甚大。不过，钦齐奥认为悲剧行动的“重大”或“重要”与伦理价值无关，而是主要指行动中的人物来自社会最高层级，因此悲剧与喜剧分界的真正参照是人物的社会地位。罗博泰利主张悲剧中的人物应该来自社会高层，因为只有非凡人物的颓败才能震撼观众，激荡起他们的同情。马吉认同罗博泰利的悲剧观，但是对喜剧的人物身份作了更具体的安排，主张那些奴隶、生意人、女佣、小丑等下层人（low people）是喜剧角色。斯卡利杰的戏剧理论对后来的新古典主义戏剧（neo-classical drama）产生了重要影响，他认为悲剧是对某个结局不幸的重大事件（illustrious event）的模仿，风格须庄重，文体宜用韵文。卡斯特尔韦特罗的悲剧理论比其前辈更加系统，对后世的影响也更大。他的特殊贡献在于把舞台条件视为重要的参考因素。剧场的大小以观众能够听清楚为标准，韵文台词要考虑到演员的声音特点；主题及语言不能高深冷僻，因为观众前来看戏是为了娱乐，而且他们的文化程度参差不齐；剧场里人声嘈杂，如果无法充分理解剧情和主题，就不可能产生激情。卡斯特尔韦特罗戏剧论述最突出的地方是在钦齐奥、罗博泰利、塞尼、特里西诺（Trissino）、马吉、斯卡利杰等其他批评家的研究基础上提出了时间－地点－剧情合一论（unities of time, place and action），即无论悲剧或喜剧，都应该呈现一个行动，剧情时间不超过一个白天或12小时，剧情发生地点的数量越少越好，地点之间的距离越近越好，这些规则成为后来法国戏剧三一律的直接基础。关于戏剧的功能，意大利批评家们着力的重点是亚里士多德的净化说（katharsis）的伦理意义。钦齐奥提出，所有的戏剧都旨在弘扬美德，只是喜剧的途径是讪笑和快乐，悲剧则通过恐惧和怜悯来清除恶念，固守善心。斯卡利杰纯粹从伦理角度阐述戏剧的功能，认为戏剧劝人弃恶向善。意大利像整个西欧一样，直到18世纪末之前都以伦理阐发为主流，甚至要求戏剧能够执行惩恶扬善的诗之正义（poetic justice）的功能，然而16世纪还是有一些意大利批评家在申明伦理功用的同时，也重视愉悦效果。明图尔诺认为悲剧具有教化伦理之用，不过其实现途径仍然是愉悦，亦即寓教于乐；观众从人物的失败中学到教训，从优美的戏剧语言和舞台形式中获得愉悦。罗博泰利、韦托里（Vettori）和卡斯特尔韦特罗都认为“净化”是指观众逐渐适应令人震撼的悲剧情节不断激起的恐惧和怜悯之情，从而降低甚至消除恐惧和怜悯，达到心理情感的和谐宁静。

虽然亚里士多德认为悲剧是诗的最高形式，但是文艺复兴时期很多人却把史诗（epic poetry）奉为诗中之诗。特里西诺就指出，维吉尔（Virgil）和荷马（Homer）是迄今最伟大的诗人。斯平加恩推测，这种现象是中世纪遗绪所致，维吉尔是中世纪人最尊重的诗人。在这一传统的助力下，史诗便成为批评家们侧重的文学形式。特里西诺首次把亚里士多德的史诗理论引入现代文学批评，他的《诗艺》第六部分几乎全部用来探讨史诗。他认为史诗像悲剧一样，讲述重要人物的重大行动，而行动以单一为佳。明图尔诺同样也采用亚里士多德的悲剧－史诗理论，但是指出了二者的差异，即史诗中没有音乐和舞蹈。卡斯特尔韦特罗认为史诗乃想象的历史，因此史诗能够做许多历史所不能做或做不到的事情。历史记述已经发生之事，史诗可以讲述实际从未发生但完全可能发生的事情。历史只能呈现一个人的所有行状，而史诗既可以讲述一个人物的许多故事，也可以讲述许多人的许多事迹，或一个民族的一件事情。关于史诗的行动合一性的讨论往往与传奇（romance）联系在一起。钦齐奥指出，在亚里士多德的时代还没有传奇这一文类，因此他的理论并不适合传奇；传奇在语言、精神、宗教情感等诸多方面与希腊文学不同，因此无法且无须追随希腊规则，而是应该遵循自身的发展规律和传统。史诗讲述一人一事，传记讲述一人多事，传奇讲述多人多事。钦齐奥认为传奇高于史诗，因为传奇具有更宏大的伦理教化效果。受钦齐奥影响，贝尔纳多·塔索也由史诗的辩护者转而推崇传奇。其子托尔夸托尝试将史诗与传奇糅合折中，指出传奇的骑士生活主题及故事的多样性（variety）是阅读快感的重要来源，但是荷马和维吉尔的史诗所具有的完美的合一性（unity）结构也不可或缺。传奇成为重要议题，表明意大利批评家们已经开始处理当代文学中的新现象和民族文学传统，他们已经能够不囿于希腊罗马古典，拥有自己的独立判断和理论阐述。

从时间表上看，法国文艺复兴比意大利晚了近二百年。意大利文艺复兴经过14—15世纪两百余年的发展，到16世纪进入高潮，而法国在16世纪之前仍然处于中世纪时期。1494年，查理八世（Charles VIII）入侵意大利，让法国文人看到了一道完全不同的文化景观，他们把轰轰烈烈的意大利文艺复兴称为“新学”（the New Learning），并且在经过一段时间准备后，开始模仿意大利文艺复兴，或者说向希腊罗马古典学习。斯平加恩认为1545年贺拉斯《诗艺》的法文译本出版，尤其是1549年杜贝莱（Du Bellay）《法语辩例》的问世，是法国走出中世纪，开始文艺复兴的确定标志。16世纪的前半个世纪里，法国文人撰写了数量有限的文学研究著作，而且大部分旨在总结和指导创作实践，属于文体学、修辞学、语言学范畴，例如法布里（Pierre Fabri, 1521）的《真正伟大的完满修辞艺术》、杜邦（Gracien du Pont, 1539）的《格律修辞》等。这些著作列出一套具体方法和技巧，辅以大量作品例证，指导作家们如何写出一篇好作品，有点像“写作手册”“创作秘笈”之类。不过，在讲授关于谋篇布局、格律音韵、章法节奏、辞藻文体等技法时，不免显示出以前人为师的理念。

到了16世纪中期，意大利文艺复兴的影响愈益浓厚。杜贝莱的《法语辩例》呼吁诗人废寝忘食地学习古典，指出诗人的天分需要博学的支持才能创作出优秀作品。佩尔蒂埃（Jacques

Pelletier du Mans, 1555）的《诗艺》像贺拉斯的作品一样，热情洋溢地赞誉诗人能够化腐朽为神奇，点铁成金，洞幽烛微。龙萨（Ronsard, 1565）在《法语诗艺概略》一书里表达了七星诗社（the Pléiade）的思想，他们像亚里士多德和意大利批评家们一样，认为韵文不等于诗歌，最早的诗实际上就是神学寓言，真诗人的灵魂中只有善、圣洁和美德。诗人的创造力既源于自然之美，也来自师法古人。诗人模仿、发明和再现古人已经判定为正确的事物。这些说法中显然能看到意大利批评家斯卡利杰和明图尔诺的影子。沃克兰（Vauquelin de la Fresnaye, 1605）的《法语诗艺》这部耗时三十余年的鸿篇巨制可谓16世纪法国文学批评的集大成者，作者在书里向亚里士多德、贺拉斯、明图尔诺等人给自己的启发致以衷心感谢。沃克兰认为，诗是模仿的艺术。正如演说家的使命是说服听众，医生的职责是治病救人，诗人的任务是使人愉悦，否则就有违本分。不过还须谨记，愉悦说到底并非目的，而是手段。通过愉悦来完善道德，在意大利文艺复兴先行者那里已经耳熟能详的这种以伦理诉求为终极目标的观念，是整个欧洲文艺复兴时期诗学的基本立场。

法国批评文献中最早提到亚里士多德的著作的是西比莱（Thomas Sibilet, 1548）的《诗艺》，作者指出悲剧是对一个严肃重大行动的模仿；悲剧中的行动可以取自真实历史，也可以按照历史逻辑演义而成；悲剧的效果在于灾变引起的强烈情感反应；悲剧的功能是改良生活风尚。几年后，佩尔蒂埃的《诗艺》系统地阐述了戏剧理论。鉴于中世纪法国一直只有道德剧（morality）和滑稽剧（farce），他号召人们尝试悲剧和喜剧。他指出，悲剧与喜剧在题材、人物、结局、文体以及用语等方面差异甚大，二者唯一的共同点也许只是它们都由五幕组成。喜剧的人物来自社会底层，语言和文体通俗如口语，而悲剧里的人物是王侯将相，语言庄重；喜剧的结局是欢乐的，而悲剧的结尾则令人伤心欲绝。死亡、流放、命运多舛是悲剧的主题，而喜剧则表现青年男女的爱情和激情、无限的母爱、不诚实的奴隶以及劳累的仆人。这些观点对法国戏剧产生了明显的影响，格雷万（Grévin）在为自己的剧作《凯撒之死》写的序言中自豪地说，即使按照亚里士多德的标准来衡量，法国悲剧也已经做到了完美。而拉塔耶（Jean de la Taille）则持完全相反的观点，认为法国从未有过真正的悲剧。然而无论如何，亚里士多德诗学已经成为法国戏剧理论的一部分，这是确定无疑的。

应该特别关注的是戏剧合一性理论在法国的历史演化，因为一般文学史都以戏剧三一律为法国标志性的文学概念。据斯平加恩考察，法国历史上的第一部悲剧是若代尔（Jodelle, 1552）创作的《克莉奥佩特拉》，剧中提到情节时间不宜超过一个白天。龙萨和沃克兰也提及戏剧的时间限度不超过一天。卡斯特尔韦特罗于1570年提出的较为具体的时间－地点合一理论两年后就传到了法国，拉塔耶（1572）在《悲剧艺术》中在卡斯特尔韦特罗的基础上作出更为简洁明确的说明：“故事或剧情应该发生在一天之内，始终保持同一时间、同一地点。”尽管也有反对这种合一理论的声音，但是到16世纪末，时间－地点合一理论已经成为主流，直到17世纪终于在法国确立为牢固的戏剧法条。

英国历史中的16世纪也是一个浓墨重彩的时代，前半个世纪是亨利八世时代（1509—1547年在位），发生了著名的宗教改革运动；后半个世纪是伊丽莎白女王时代（1558—1603年在位），1588年英国战胜西班牙无敌舰队，夺得海上霸权。虽然莎士比亚的大半生属于16世纪，但是斯平加恩认为英国文艺复兴时期的文学批评在影响上不及意大利，在丰富性上不及法国，而且总体来说，这个时期的英国批评没有什么创新，基本上是消化、吸收意大利文艺复兴的遗产，主旨是为创作实践提供可以操作的技法、规范和示例。考克斯（Leonard Coxe, 1524）的《修辞艺术或技法》是为年轻学生讲解修辞技巧的手册，威尔逊（Wilson, 1553）

的《修辞艺术》是一部更为系统全面的写作指导读本。帕特纳姆（William Puttenham, 1589）的《英诗艺术》对诗的形式、题材和修辞格作了系统的分类，韦布（Webbe, 1586）的《话说英诗》首次把古典格律全面介绍给英国读者。虽然这些著作主要关注具体的语言、修辞和格律等形式议题，但是由于参照了意大利和法国学者的文献，因此文艺复兴批评精神还是深刻地进入了英国诗学，改变了人们的文学观念。威尔逊吸收了彼特拉克和薄伽丘等人的观点，指出诗是一种寓言形式，通过曲折的情节、生动的形象和优美的语言，表达深层的伦理道德诉求，例如荷马史诗《奥德赛》表面讲的是尤利西斯的漂泊故事，实际上表达的是人生必须经历的各种考验。韦布指出，诗具有一种"怜爱的权威"（loving authority），能够和颜悦色地教育人们弃恶从善。帕特纳姆的诗人观直接来自意大利批评家斯卡利杰，认为诗人的本质是发明或创造，在这个意义上说，诗人与上帝无异。

综观 16 世纪的英国文坛，最重要且最具影响力的批评家当推锡德尼（Sir Philip Sidney）。锡德尼（1595）的《为诗一辩》对诗或文学的性质、构成和功能作了空前系统的理论阐发，集中体现了英国文艺复兴批评的成就。《为诗一辩》指出，诗把光明带到世界，是一切知识的源头，诗人是人类最早的哲学家和历史学家，因此古希腊罗马人把诗人尊奉为圣贤和先知。锡德尼对诗的定义综合了亚里士多德和贺拉斯的思想，"诗是模仿的艺术 [……] 是有声的画，亦教亦乐"。锡德尼特别提醒人们，诗不等于合辙押韵的表达，擅长韵文写作的人未必就是诗人，用散文体写作的人可能是真正的诗人，柏拉图的《对话集》就是一首优美的诗。显然，锡德尼是抓住某种深层的、本质的东西来界定诗，表明他在把文学视为具有特殊品质的独立范畴。关于诗的独特性，锡德尼指出，哲学家通过精警的语言指导人生，历史学家通过举例来引导人生，而诗人则能够将二者结合起来，实现美德教化的目的，因此诗是人类智慧的最高形式。这种关联明显受到亚里士多德理论的影响，斯平加恩认为锡德尼是受亚里士多德影响最为深刻和全面的16世纪英国批评家。还应该看到，锡德尼在亚里士多德的基础上进行了重要的拓展，他提出所有的艺术都以自然为对象并遵从自然之道，就像演员必须照着剧本进行演出，但是唯有诗人能够不受自然的约束，克服自然的缺陷，创造出高于自然的另一个自然。锡德尼也是英国戏剧批评的开创者，《为诗一辩》像意大利批评理论一样，指出悲剧是对一个高贵行动的模仿，目的是激发崇敬和同情。悲剧应该再现重大事件、重要人物，风格应该庄严典雅，而当时英国舞台上的悲剧并不符合这个标准。喜剧是“对常见的生活谬误的模仿”，应该以嘲讽的方法去表现，从而提醒观众避免犯下类似错误，但是英国的喜剧作者偏重逗笑，嘲讽不足，因此削弱了教育意义。《为诗一辩》还提到时间－地点合一问题，斯平加恩认为，锡德尼基本上完整转述了卡斯特尔韦特罗的观点，即行动应该限制在同一地点，不超过一天，意在提醒英国戏剧家不要触犯这一原则。

锡德尼诗学一方面表现出强烈的古典主义倾向和亚里士多德的影响，体现出鲜明的文艺复兴批评特征，另一方面也显示出英国文学传统中有一些独特之处，是古典理论难以周全地涵盖汇通的，法国也存在类似的问题，例如“传奇”的特殊性就很难照搬古典理论得到通达的解释。可贵的是，文艺复兴批评家们清楚意识到不能完全用古典理论来裁剪民族文学，各民族文学都因其特殊历史路径而形成各自的传统，因此在学习希腊罗马古典文献时，应该抱持拿来主义的态度，应该以“我”为中心，为“我”所用；学习古典的现实动机和最终目标是建设和促进自己的文学文化。事实上，文艺复兴时期回荡着一个非常高亢的声音，那就是赞美自己的民族语言，把法语或英语称为世界上最完美的语言，换言之，文艺复兴在标明与神学对立的所谓“普世价值”的人本主义的同时，也毫不遮掩地吹响了民族觉醒的号角；联想到但丁的那篇名作《论俗语》，人们有理由相信作为现代事件的民族意识的觉醒和民族国家的形成是文艺复兴的重要内涵，而文学批评积极参与了这一现代事件，同时也是这一现代事件的产物。

《文艺复兴时期文学批评史》这本书值得一读的地方除了提出并论证了西方现代批评诞生于文艺复兴，提供了特别丰富的文艺复兴时期西欧主要国家的批评文献线索，还在于这本厚重的专著为今天的读者了解和体认一百多年前的文学理论状态提供了一个价值独特的样本，让我们看到“批评现代性”的关键标识为文学的自觉意识这一观念早在19世纪末就已然确立，俄国形式主义和英美新批评的理论端倪似乎可以推回到20世纪伊始，甚至更早一些——事实上，早在1910年3月9日，年轻的斯平加恩教授就在哥伦比亚大学作了题目为“The New Criticism”的专题演讲，明确主张对艺术作品的意义解读应该限制在审美范畴内进行。我们还看到，“批评理论”（critical theory）早在一百多年前就已经进入文学学科的寻常词汇；按照斯平加恩的用法，“批评”（criticism）与“文学批评”（literary criticism）是同义词，而且包含三层含义，可以指针对创作实践的“实用或具体批评”（applied or concrete criticism），也可以指“诗学”（poetics）或文学理论，第三层意思是指“批评文献”（critical literature）；这样的用法与今天几无区别。这部专著实际上是作者斯平加恩刚刚完成的博士学位论文，现在通读这部老书，可以窥见19世纪末的文学知识状况和文学学科面貌，一百多年前的文学观念和表述语言对于当今读者来说竟然毫不陌生，这真是一种奇妙的体验！当然，今天的读者也非常清楚，斯平加恩严格地以“创造”“想象”“审美”等概念来界定文学的本质，无论是反映了当年的主流观念，还是表达了他自己坚持的主张，在后来的批评场域中，已经遭遇到不同程度的质疑和挑战。

PREFACE TO THE SECOND EDITION

SOME few years ago, when an Italian translation of this work was being prepared for the press, I made a thorough revision of the text and incorporated a large mass of additional material. I have neither the leisure nor the inclination to undertake so complete a revision at the present time, and much of the material added in the Italian version would scarcely be likely to interest the English reader. In this second edition I have corrected all specific inaccuracies and misstatements which have come to my notice, and I have added a new Conclusion of twenty pages which in part reproduces an article on "The Origins of Modern Criticism" in *Modern Philology* for April, 1904.

When this book first appeared, the poet Carducci noted with patriotic regret that no one in Italy had taken the trouble to read the important body of criticism with which this work is concerned. Since then the critics and theorists of the Cinquecento have been the object of considerable study, in England as well as in Italy; and their signifcance as the real founders of modern criticism is no longer open to question.

J. E. S.

COLUMBIA UNIVERSITY,
January, 1908.

PREFACE TO THE FIRST EDITION

THIS essay undertakes to treat the history of literary criticism in the Renaissance. The three sections into which the essay is divided are devoted, respectively, to Italian criticism from Dante to Tasso, to French criticism from Du Bellay to Boileau, and to English criticism from Ascham to Milton; but the critical activity of the sixteenth century has been the main theme, and the earlier or later literature has received treatment only in so far as it serves to explain the causes or consequences of the critical development of this central period. It was at this epoch that modern criticism began, and that the ancient ideals of art seemed once more to sway the minds of men; so that the history of sixteenth-century criticism must of necessity include a study of the beginnings of critical activity in modern Europe and of the gradual introduction of the Aristotelian canons into modern literature.

This study has been made subservient, more particularly, to two specific purposes. While the critical activity of the period is important and even interesting in itself, it has been here studied primarily for the purpose of tracing the origin and causes of the classic spirit in modern letters and of discovering the sources of the rules and theories embodied in the neo-classic literature of the seventeenth and eighteenth centuries. How did the classic spirit arise? Whence did it come, and how did it develop? What was the origin of the principles and precepts of neo-classicism? These are some of the questions I have attempted to answer in this essay; and, in answering them, I have tried to remember that this is a history, not of critical literature, but of literary criticism. For this reason I have given to individual books and authors less prominence than some of them perhaps deserved, and have confined myself almost exclusively to the origin of principles, theories, and rules, and to the general temper of classicism. For a similar reason I have been obliged to say little or nothing of the methods and results of applied, or concrete, criticism.

This, then, has been the main design of the essay; but furthermore, as is indicated in the title, I have attempted to point out the part played by Italy in the growth of this neo-classic spirit and in the formulation of these neo-classic principles. The influence of the Italian Renaissance in the development of modern science, philosophy, art, and creative literature has been for a long time the subject of much study. It has been my more modest task to trace the indebtedness of the modern world to Italy in the domain of literary criticism; and I trust that I have shown the Renaissance influence to be as great in this as in the other realms of study. The birth of modern criticism was due to the critical activity of Italian humanism; and it is in sixteenth-century Italy that we shall find, more or less matured, the general spirit and even the specific principles of French classicism. The second half of the design, then, is the history of the Italian influence in literary criticism; and with Milton, the last of the humanists in England, the essay naturally closes. But we shall find, I think, that the influence of the Italian Renaissance in the domain of literary criticism was not even then all decayed, and that Lessing and Shelley, to mention no others, were the legitimate inheritors of the Italian tradition.

The bibliography at the end of the essay indicates sufficiently my obligations to preceding writers. It has been prepared chiefly for the purpose of facilitating reference to works cited in the text and in the foot-notes, and should be consulted for the full titles of books therein mentioned; it makes no pretence of being a complete bibliography of the subject. It will be seen that the history of Italian criticism in the sixteenth century has received scarcely any attention from modern scholars. The most complete lists of the critical works of the Renaissance are to be found in Crescimbeni's *Istoria della Volgar Poesia* (Rome, 1698) and in Blankenburg's *Litterarische Zusätze zu Sulzer's Allgemeiner Theorie der schönen Künste* (Leipzig, 1796—98). In regard to Aristotle's *Poetics*, I have used the text, and in general followed the interpretation, given in Professor S. H. Butcher's

Aristotle's Theory of Poetry and Fine Art, a noble monument of scholarship vivified by literary feeling. I desire also to express my obligations to Professor Butcher for an abstract of Zabarella, to Mr. P. O. Skinner of Harvard for an analysis of Capriano, to my friend, Mr. F. W. Chandler, for summaries of several early English rhetorical treatises, and to Professor Cavalier Speranza for a few corrections; also to my friends, Mr. J. G. Underhill, Mr. Lewis Einstein, and Mr. H. A. Uterhart, and to my brother, Mr. A. B. Spingarn, for incidental assistance of some importance.

But, above all, I desire to acknowledge my indebtedness to Professor George E. Woodberry. This book is the fruit of his instruction; and in writing it, also, I have had recourse to him for assistance and criticism. Without the aid so kindly accorded by him, the book could hardly have been written, and certainly would never have assumed its present form. But my obligations to him are not limited to the subject or contents of the present essay. Through a period of five years the inspiration derived from his instruction and encouragement has been so great as to preclude the possibility of its expression in a preface. *Quare habe tibi quidquid hoc libelli.*

NEW YORK,

March, 1899.

CONTENTS

PART FIRST

LITERARY CRITICISM IN ITALY

PART SECOND

LITERARY CRITICISM IN FRANCE

PART THIRD

LITERARY CRITICISM IN ENGLAND

Part First

LITERARY CRITICISM IN ITALY

LITERARY CRITICISM IN ITALY

CHAPTER I

THE FUNDAMENTAL PROBLEM OF RENAISSANCE CRITICISM

THE first problem of Renaissance criticism was the justification of imaginative literature. The existence and continuity of the æsthetic consciousness, and perhaps, in a less degree, of the critical faculty, throughout the Middle Ages, can hardly be denied; yet distrust of literature was keenest among the very class of men in whom the critical faculty might be presupposed, and it was as the handmaid of philosophy, and most of all as the vassal of theology, that poetry was chiefly valued. In other words, the criteria by which imaginative literature was judged during the Middle Ages were not literary criteria. Poetry was disregarded or contemned, or was valued if at all for virtues that least belong to it. The Renaissance was thus confronted with the necessity of justifying its appreciation of the vast body of literature which the Revival of Learning had recovered for the modern world; and the function of Renaissance criticism was to reëstablish the æsthetic foundations of literature, to reaffirm the eternal lesson of Hellenic culture, and to restore once and for all the element of beauty to its rightful place in human life and in the world of art.

I. *Mediæval Conceptions of Poetry*

The mediæval distrust of literature was the result of several coöperating causes. Popular literature had fallen into decay, and in its contemporary form was beneath serious consideration. Classical literature was unfortunately pagan, and was moreover but imperfectly known. The mediæval Church from its earliest stages had regarded pagan culture with suspicion, and had come to look upon the development of popular literature as antagonistic to its own supremacy. But beyond this, the distrust of literature went deeper, and was grounded upon certain theoretical and fundamental objections to all the works of the imagination.

These theoretical objections were in nowise new to the Middle Ages. They had been stated in antiquity with much more directness and philosophical efficacy than was possible in the mediæval period. Plato had tried imaginative literature by the criteria of reality and morality, both of which are unæsthetic criteria, although fundamentally applicable to poetry. In respect to reality, he had shown that poetry is three removes from the truth, being but the imitation, by the artist, of the imitation, in life, of an idea in the mind of God. In respect to morality, he had discovered in Homer, the greatest of poets, deviations from truth, blasphemy against the gods, and obscenity of various sorts. Furthermore, he had found that creative literature excites the emotions more than does actual life, and stirs up ignoble passions which were better restrained.

These ideas ran throughout the Middle Ages, and indeed persisted even beyond the Renaissance. Poetry was judged by these same criteria, but it was natural that mediæval writers should substitute more practical reasons for the metaphysical arguments of Plato. According to the criterion of reality, it was urged that poetry in its very essence is untrue, that at bottom it is fiction, and therefore false. Thus Tertullian said that "the Author of truth hates all the false; He regards as adultery all that is unreal.... He never will approve pretended loves, and wraths, and groans, and tears;" [1] and he affirmed that in place of these pagan works there was in the Bible and the Fathers, a vast body of Christian literature and that this is "not fabulous, but true, not tricks of art, but plain realities." [2] According to the criterion of morality, it was urged that as few works of the imagination were entirely free from obscenity and blasphemy, such blemishes are inseparable from the poetic art; and accordingly, Isidore of Seville says that a Christian is forbidden to read the figments of the poets, "quia per oblectamenta inanium fabularum mentem excitant ad incentiva libidinum." [3]

The third, or psychological objection, made by Plato, was similarly emphasized. Thus Tertullian

1 *De Spectac.* xxiii. 2 *Ibid.* xxii. 3 *Differentiæ*, iii. 13, 1.

pointed out that while God has enjoined us to deal calmly and gently and quietly with the Holy Spirit, literature, and especially dramatic literature, leads to spiritual agitation. [1] This point seemed to the mediæval mind fundamental, for in real beauty, as Thomas Aquinas insisted, desire is quieted. [2] Furthermore, it was shown that the only body of literary work worthy of serious study dealt with pagan divinities and with religious practices which were in direct antagonism to Christianity. Other objections, also, were incidentally alluded to by mediæval writers. For example, it was said, the supreme question in all matters of life is the question of conduct, and it was not apparent in what manner poetry conduces to action. Poetry has no practical use; it rather enervates men than urges them to the call of duty; and above all, there are more profitable occupations in which the righteous man may be engaged.

These objections to literature are not characteristically mediæval. They have sprung up in every period of the world's history, and especially recur in all ages in which ascetic or theological conceptions of life are dominant. They were stock questions of the Greek schools, and there are extant treatises by Maximus of Tyre and others on the problem whether or not Plato was justified in expelling Homer from his ideal commonwealth. The same objections prevailed beyond the Renaissance; and they were urged in Italy by Savonarola, in Ger-

1 *De Spectac.* xv. *Cf.* Cyprian, *Epist. ad Donat.* viii.

2 *Cf.* Bosanquet. *Hist. of Æsthetic*, p. 148.

many by Cornelius Agrippa, in England by Gosson and Prynne, and in France by Bossuet and other ecclesiastics.

II. *The Moral Justification of Poetry*

The allegorical method of interpreting literature was the result of the mediæval attempt to answer the objections just stated. This method owed its origin to the mode of interpreting the popular mythology first employed by the Sophists and more thoroughly by the later Stoics. Such heroes as Hercules and Theseus, instead of being mere brute conquerors of monsters and giants, were regarded by the Stoic philosophers as symbols of the early sages who had combated the vices and passions of mankind, and they became in the course of time types of pagan saints. The same mode of interpretation was later applied to the stories of the Old Testament by Philo Judæus, and was first introduced into Occidental Europe by Hilary of Poitiers and Ambrose, Bishop of Milan. [1] Abraham, Adam, Eve, Jacob, became types of various virtues, and the biblical stories were considered as symbolical of the various moral struggles in the soul of man. The first instance of the systematic application of the method to the pagan myths occurs in the *Mythologicon* of Fulgentius, who probably flourished in the first half of the sixth century; and in his *Virgiliana Continentia*, the *Æneid* is

1 *Cf.* St. Augustine, *Confess.* v. 14, vi. 4; Clemens Alex, *Stromata*, v. 8.

treated as an image of life, and the travels of Æneas as the symbol of the progress of the human soul, from nature, through wisdom, to final happiness.

From this period, the allegorical method became the recognized mode of interpreting literature, whether sacred or profane. Petrarch, in his letter, *De quibusdam fictionibus Virgilij*, [1] treats the *Æneid* after the manner of Fulgentius; and even at the very end of the Renaissance Tasso interpreted his own romantic epics in the same way. After the acceptance of the method, its application was further complicated. Gregory the Great ascribes three meanings to the Bible, — the literal, the typical or allegorical, and the moral. Still later, a fourth meaning was added; and Dante distinctly claims all four, the literal, the allegorical, the moral or philosophical, and the anagogical or mystical, for his *Divine Comedy*. [2]

This method, while perhaps justifying poetry from the standpoint of ethics and divinity, gives it no place as an independent are; thus considered, poetry becomes merely a popularized form of theology. Both Petrarch and Boccaccio regarded allegory as the warp and woof of poetry; but they modified the mediæval point of view by arguing conversely that theology itself is a form of poetry, — the poetry of God. Both of them insist that the Bible is essentially poetical, and that Christ himself spoke largely in poetical images. This point

1 *Opera*, p. 867.
2 *Cf.* Dante, *Epist.* xi. 7; *Convito*, ii. 1, 1.

was so emphasized by Renaissance critics that Berni, in his *Dialogo contra i Poeti* (1537), condemns the poets for speaking of God as Jupiter and of the saints as Mercury, Hercules, Bacchus, and for even having the audacity to call the prophets and the writers of the Scriptures poets and makers of verses.[1]

The fourteenth and fifteenth books of Boccaccio's treatise, *De Genealogia Deorum*, have been called "the first defence of poesy in honor of his own art by a poet of the modern world;" but Boccaccio's justification of imaginative literature is still primarily based on the usual mediæval grounds. The reality of poetry is dependent on its allegorical foundations; its moral teachings are to be sought in the hidden meanings discoverable beneath the literal expression; pagan poetry is defended for Christianity on the ground that the references to Greek and Roman gods and rituals are to be regarded only as symbolical truths. The poet's function, for Boccaccio, as for Dante and Petrarch, was to hide and obscure the actual truth behind a veil of beautiful fictions — *veritatem rerum pulchris velaminibus adornare.*[2]

The humanistic point of view, in regard to poetry, was of a more practical and far-reaching nature than that of the Middle Ages. The allegorical interpretation did indeed continue throughout the Renaissance, and Mantuan, for example, can only

1 Berni, p. 226 *sq.*

2 Petrarch, *Opera*, p. 1205; *cf.* Boccaccio, *Gen. degli Dei*, p. 250, v.

define a poem as a literary form which is bound by the stricter laws of metre, and which has its fundamental truths hidden under the literal expressions of the fable. For still later writers, this mode of regarding literature seemed to present the only loophole of escape from the moral objections to poetry. But in employing the old method, the humanists carried it far beyond its original application. Thus Lionardo Bruni, in his *De Studiis et Literis* (c. 1405), after dwelling on the allegorical interpretation of the pagan myths, argues that when one reads the story of Æneas and Dido, he pays his tribute of admiration to the genius of the poet, but the matter itself is known to be fiction, and so leaves no moral impression.[1] By this Bruni means that fiction as such, when known to be fiction, can leave no moral impression, and secondly, that poetry is to be judged by the success of the artist, and not by the efficacy of the moralist. Similarly, Battista Guarino, in his *De Ordine Docendi et Studendi* (1459), says that we are not disturbed by the impieties, cruelties, horrors, which we find in poetry; we judge these things simply by their congruity with the characters and incidents described. In other words, "we criticise the artist, not the moralist."[2] This is a distinct attempt at the æsthetic appreciation of literature, but while such ideas are not uncommon about this time, they express isolated sentiments, rather than a doctrine strictly coördinated with an æsthetic theory of poetry.

1 Woodward, *Vittorino da Feltre*, p. 132. 2 *Ibid.* p. 175.

The more strict defence of poetry was attempted for the most part on the grounds set forth by Horace in his *Ars Poetica*. At no period from the Augustan Age to the Renaissance does the *Ars Poetica* seem to have been entirely lost. It is mentioned or quoted, for example, by Isidore of Seville [1] in the sixth century, by John of Salisbury [2] in the twelfth century, and by Dante [3] in the fourteenth. Horace insists on the mingled instructiveness and pleasurableness of poetry; and beyond this, he points out the value of poetry as a civilizing factor in history, regarding the early poets as sages and prophets, and the inventors of arts and sciences: —

> "Orpheus, inspired by more than human power,
> Did not, as poets feigned, tame savage beasts,
> But men as lawless and as wild as they,
> And first dissuaded them from rage and blood.
> Thus when Amphion built the Theban wall,
> They feigned the stones obeyed his magic lute;
> Poets, the first instructors of mankind,
> Brought all things to their proper native use;
> Some they appropriated to the gods,
> And some to public, some to private ends:
> Promiscuous love by marriage was restrained,
> Cities were built, and useful laws were made;
> So ancient is the pedigree of verse,
> And so divine the poet's function." [4]

This conception of the early poet's function was an old one. It is to be found in Aristophanes; [5] it runs through Renaissance

1 *Etymologiæ*, viii. 7, 5. 2 *Policraticus*, i. 8.
3 Moore, *Dante and his Early Biographers*, London, 1890, pp. 173, 174.
4 *Ars Poet.* 391 (Roscommon). 5 *Frogs*, 1030 *sq.*

criticism; and even in this very century, Shelley [1] speaks of poets as "the authors of language, and of music, of the dance, and architecture, and statuary, and painting," as "the institutors of laws, and the founders of civil society, and the inventors of the arts of life." To-day the idealist takes refuge in the same faith: "The tree of knowledge is of equal date with the tree of life; nor were even the tamer of horses, the worker in metals, or the sower, elder than those twin guardians of the soul, — the poet and the priest. Conscience and imagination were the pioneers who made earth habitable for the human spirit." [2]

It was this ethical and civilizing function of poetry which was first in the minds of the humanists. Action being the test of all studies,[3] poetry must stand or fall in proportion as it conduces to righteous action. Thus, Lionardo Bruni [4] speaks of poetry as "so valuable an aid to knowledge, and so ennobling a source of pleasure"; and Æneas Sylvius Piccolomini, in his treatise *De Liberorum Educatione* (1450), declares that the crucial question is not, Is poetry to be contemned? but, How are the poets to be used? and he solves his own question by asserting that we are to welcome all that poets can render in praise of integrity and in condemnation of vice, and that all else is to be left unheeded. [5] Beyond this, the humanists urged in

1 *Defence of Poetry*, ed. Cook, p. 5.
2 Woodberry, "A New Defence of Poetry," in *Heart of Man*, New York, 1899, p. 76.
3 Woodward, p. 182 *sq.* 4 *Ibid.* p. 131. 5 *Ibid.* p. 150.

favor of poetry the fact of its antiquity and divine origin, and the further fact that it had been praised by great men of all professions, and its creators patronized by kings and emperors from time immemorial.

There were then at the end of the Middle Ages, and the beginning of the Renaissance, two opposing tendencies in regard to the poetic art, one representing the humanistic reverence for ancient culture, and for poetry as one of the phases of that culture, and the other representing not only the mediæval tradition, but a purism allied to that of early Christianity, and akin to the ascetic conceptions of life found in almost every period. These two tendencies are expressed specifically in their noblest forms by the great humanist Poliziano, and the great moral reformer Savonarola. In the *Sylvœ*, written toward the close of the fifteenth century, Poliziano dwells on the divine origin of poetry, as Boccaccio had done in his *Vita di Dante*; and then, after the manner of Horace, he describes its ennobling influence on man, and its general influence on the progress of civilization. [1] He then proceeds to survey the progress of poetry from the most ancient times, and in so doing may be said to have written the first modern history of literature. The second section of the *Sylvœ* discusses the bucolic poets; the third contains that glorification of Virgil which began during the Middle Ages, and, continued by Vida and others, became in

1 Pope, *Selecta Poemata*, ii. 108; *cf. Ars Poet.* 398.

Scaliger literary deification; and the last section is devoted to Homer, who is considered as the great teacher of wisdom, and the wisest of the ancients. Nowhere does Poliziano exhibit any appreciation of the æsthetic value of poetry, but his enthusiasm for the great poets, and indeed for all forms of ancient culture, is unmistakable, and combined with his immense erudition marks him as a representative poet of humanism. [1]

On the other hand, the puristic conception of art is elaborated at great length by Savonarola in an apology for poetry contained in his tractate, *De Divisione ac Utilitate Omnium Scientarum*, [2] written about 1492. After classifying the sciences in true scholastic fashion, and arranging them according to their relative importance and their respective utility for Christianity, he attacks all learning as superfluous and dangerous, unless restricted to a chosen few. Poetry, according to the scholastic arrangement, is grouped with logic and grammar; and this mediæval classification fixes Savonarola's conception of the theory of poetic art. He expressly says that he attacks the abuse of poetry and not poetry itself, but there can be no doubt that, at bottom, he was intolerant of creative literature. Like Plato, like moral reformers of all ages, he feared the free play of the imaginative faculty; and in connecting poetry with logic he was tending toward the elimination of the imagination in art. The basis of his æsthetic system, such as it is,

1 *Cf.* Gaspary, ii. 220.

2 Villari, p. 501 *sq.*, and Perrens, ii. 328 *sq.*

rests wholly on that of Thomas Aquinas; [1] but he is in closer accord with Aristotle when he points out that versification, a merely conventional accompaniment of poetry, is not to be confounded with the essence of poetry itself. This distinction is urged to defend the Scriptures, which he regards as the highest and holiest form of poetry. For him poetry is coördinate with philosophy and with thought; but in his intolerance of poetry in its lower forms, he would follow Plato in banishing poets from an ideal state. The imitation of the ancient poets especially falls under his suspicion, and in an age given up to their worship he denies both their supremacy and their utility. In fine, as a reformer, he represents for us the religious reaction against the paganization of culture by the humanists. But the forces against him were too strong. Even the Christianization of culture effected during the next century by the Council of Trent was hardly more than temporary. Humanism, which represents the revival of ancient pagan culture, and rationalism, which represents the growth of the modern spirit in science and art, were currents too powerful to be impeded by any reformer, however great, and, when combined in classicism, were to reign supreme in literature for centuries to come. But Savonarola and Poliziano serve to indicate that modern literary criticism had not yet begun. For until some rational answer to the objections urged against poetry in

1 *Cf.* Cartier, *L'Esthétique de Savonarole*, in Didron's *Annales Archéologiques*, 1847, vii. 255 *sq.*

antiquity and in the Middle Ages was forthcoming, literary criticism in any true sense was fundamentally impossible; and that answer came only with the recovery of Aristotle's *Poetics*.

III. *The Final Justification of Poetry*

The influence of Aristotle's *Poetics* in classical antiquity, so far as it is possible to judge, was very slight; there is no apparent reference to the *Poetics* in Horace, Cicero, or Quintilian, [1] and it was entirely lost sight of during the Middle Ages. Its modern transmission was due almost exclusively to Orientals. [2] The first Oriental version of Aristotle's treatise appears to have been that made by Abu-Baschar, a Nestorian Christian, from the Syriac into Arabic, about the year 935. Two centuries later, the Moslem philosopher Averroës made an abridged version of the *Poetics*, which was translated into Latin in the thirteenth century, by a certain German, named Hermann, and again, by Mantinus of Tortosa in Spain, in the fourteenth century. Hermann's version seems to have circulated considerably in the Middle Ages, but it had no traceable influence on critical literature whatsoever. It is mentioned and censured by Roger Bacon, but the *Poetics* in any form was probably unknown to Dante, to Boccaccio, and beyond a single obscure reference, to Petrarch. Some of the humanists, such as Benvenuto da Imola in his commentary on Dante, cite the

1 Egger, 209 *sq.* 2 *Ibid.* 555 *sq.*

version of Averroës; but the critical ideas of the period show slight indication of Aristotelian influence, and during the sixteenth century itself there seems to have been a well-defined impression that the *Poetics* had been recovered only after centuries of oblivion. Thus, Bernardo Segni, who translated the *Poetics* into Italian in 1549, speaks of it as "abandoned and neglected for a long time"; [1] and Bernardo Tasso, some ten years later, refers to it as "buried for so long a time in the obscure shadows of ignorance." [2]

It was then as a new work of Aristotle that the Latin translation by Giorgio Valla, published at Venice in 1498, must have appeared to Valla's contemporaries. Though hardly successful as a work of scholarship, this translation, and the Greek text of the *Poetics* published in the Aldine *Rhetores Grœci* in 1508, had considerable influence on dramatic literature, but scarcely any immediate influence on literary criticism. Somewhat later, in 1536, Alessandro de' Pazzi published a revised Latin version, accompanied by the original; and from this time, the influence of the Aristotelian canons becomes manifest in critical literature. In 1548, Robortelli produced the first critical edition of the *Poetics*, with a Latin translation and a learned commentary, and in the very next year the first Italian translation was given to the world

1 Segni, p. 160.

2 B. Tasso, *Lettere*, ii. 525. See also, Robortelli, 1548, "Jacuit liber hic neglectus, ad nostra fere haec usque tempora."

by Bernardo Segni. From that day to this the editions and translations of the *Poetics* have increased beyond number, and there is hardly a single passage in Aristotle's treatise which has not been discussed by innumerable commentators and critics.

It was in Aristotle's *Poetics* that the Renaissance was to find, if not a complete, at least a rational justification of poetry, and an answer to every one of the Platonic and mediæval objections to imaginative literature. As to the assertion that poetry diverges from actual reality, Aristotle [1] contended that there is to be found in poetry a higher reality than that of mere commonplace fact, that poetry deals not with particulars, but with universals, and that it aims at describing not what has been, but what might have been or ought to be. In other words, poetry has little regard for the actuality of the specific event, but aims at the reality of an eternal probability. It matters not whether Achilles or Æneas did this thing, or that thing, which Homer or Virgil ascribes to either, but if Achilles or Æneas was such a man as the poet describes, he must necessarily act as Homer or Virgil has made him do. It is needless to say that Aristotle is here simply distinguishing between ideal truth and actual fact, and in asserting that it is the function of poetry to imitate only ideal truth he laid the foundations, not only of an answer to mediæval objections, but also of modern æsthetic criticism.

Beyond this, poetry is justified on the grounds of morality, for while not having a distinctly moral aim, it is

1 *Poet.* ix.

essentially moral, because it is this ideal representation of life, and an idealized version of human life must necessarily present it in its moral aspects. Aristotle distinctly combats the traditional Greek conception of the didactic function of poetry, but it is evident that he insists fundamentally that literature must be moral, for he sternly rebukes Euripides several times on grounds that are moral, rather than purely æsthetic. In answer to the objection that poetry, instead of calming, stirs and excites our meanest passions, that it "waters and cherishes those emotions which ought to wither with drought, and constitutes them our rulers, when they ought to be our subjects," [1] Aristotle taught those in the Renaissance who were able to understand him, that poetry, and especially dramatic poetry, does not indeed starve the emotions, but excites them only to allay and to regulate them, and in this æsthetic process purifies and ennobles them. [2] In pointing out these things he has justified the utility of poetry, regarding it as more serious and philosophic than history, because it universalizes mere fact, and imitates life in its noblest aspects.

These arguments were incorporated into Renaissance criticism; they were emphasized, as we shall see, over and over again, and they formed the basis of the justification of poetry in modern critical literature. At the same time, this purely æsthetic conception of art did not prevail by itself in the sixteenth century, even in those for whom Aristotle meant most, and who best understood his meaning;

1 Plato, *Rep.* x. 660. 2 *Poet.* vi. 2; *Pol.* viii. 7.

the Horatian elements, also, as found in the early humanists, were elaborated and discussed. In the *Poetica* of Daniello (1536), these Horatian elements form the basis for a defence of poetry [1] that has many marked resemblances to various passages in Sir Philip Sidney's *Defence of Poesy*. After referring to the antiquity and nobility of poetry, and affirming that no other art is nobler or more ancient, Daniello shows that all things known to man, all the secrets of God and nature, are described by the poets in musical numbers and with exquisite ornament. He furthermore asserts, in the manner of Horace, that the poets were the inventors of the arts of life; and in answer to the objection that it was the philosophers who in reality did these things, he shows that while instruction is more proper to the philosopher than to the poet, poets teach too, in many more ways, and far more pleasantly, than any philosopher can. They hide their useful teachings under various fictions and fabulous veils, as the physician covers bitter medicine with a sweet coating. The style of the philosopher is dry and obscure, without any force or beauty by itself; and the delightful instruction of poetry is far more effective than the abstract and harsh teachings of philosophy. Poetry, indeed, was the only form of philosophy that primitive men had, and Plato, while regarding himself as an enemy of poets, was really a great poet himself, for he expresses all his ideas in a wondrously harmonious rhythm, and with great splendor of words and images. This defence of

1 Daniello, p. 10 *sq*.

Daniello's is interesting, as anticipating the general form of such apologies throughout the sixteenth century.

Similarly, Minturno in his *De Poeta* (1559), elaborates the Horatian suggestions for a defence of poetry. He begins by pointing out the broad inclusiveness of poetry, which may be said to comprehend in itself every form of human learning, and by showing that no form of learning can be found before the first poets, and that no nation, however barbarous, has ever been averse to poetry. The Hebrews praised God in verse; the Greeks, Italians, Germans, and British have all honored poetry; the Persians have had their Magi and the Gauls their bards. Verse, while not essential to poetry, gives the latter much of its delightful effectiveness, and if the gods ever speak, they certainly speak in verse; indeed, in primitive times it was in verse that all sciences, history, and philosophy were written.[1]

To answer the traditional objections against imaginative literature which had survived beyond the Middle Ages seemed to the Renaissance a simpler task, however, than to answer the more philosophical objections urged in the Platonic dialogues. The authority of Plato during the Renaissance made it impossible to slight the arguments stated by him in the *Republic*, and elsewhere. The writers of this period were particularly anxious to refute, or at least to explain away, the reasons for which Plato had banished poets from his ideal commonwealth.

1 *De Poeta*, p. 13 *sq*.

Some critics, like Bernardo Tasso [1] and Daniello, [2] asserted that Plato had not argued against poetry itself, but only against the abuse of poetry. Thus, according to Tasso, only impure and effeminate poets were to be excluded from the ideal state, and according to Daniello, only the more immoral tragic poets, and especially the authors of obscene and lampooning comedies. Other Renaissance writers, like Minturno [3] and Fracastoro, [4] answered the Platonic objections on more philosophical grounds. Thus Fracastoro answers Plato's charge that, since poetry is three removes from ideal truth, poets are fundamentally ignorant of the realities they attempt to imitate, by pointing out that the poet is indeed ignorant of what he is speaking of, in so far as he is a versifier and skilled in language, just as the philosopher or historian is ignorant of natural or historical facts in so far as he, too, is merely skilled in language, but knows these facts in so far as he is learned, and has thought out the problems of nature and history. The poet, as well as the philosopher and the historian, must possess knowledge, if he is to teach anything; he, too, must learn the things he is going to write about, and must solve the problems of life and thought; he, too, must have a philosophical and an historical training. Plato's objection, indeed, applies to the philosopher, to the orator, to the historian, quite as much as to the poet. As to Plato's second charge, that

1 *Lettere*, ii. 526.

2 *Poetica*, p. 14 *sq.*

3 *De Poeta*, p. 30 *sq.*

4 *Opera*, i. 361 *sq.*

imagination naturally tends toward the worst things, and accordingly that poets write obscenely and blasphemously, Fracastoro points out that this is not the fault of the art, but of those who abuse it; there are, indeed, immoral and enervating poets, and they ought to be excluded, not only from Plato's, but from every commonwealth. Thus various Aristotelian and Horatian elements were combined to form a definite body of Renaissance criticism.

CHAPTER II

THE GENERAL THEORY OF POETRY IN THE ITALIAN RENAISSANCE

In the first book of his *Geography* Strabo defines poetry as "a kind of elementary philosophy, which introduces us early to life, and gives us pleasurable instruction in reference to character, emotion, action." This passage sounds the keynote of the Renaissance theory of poetry. Poetry is therein stated to be a form of philosophy, and, moreover, a philosophy whose subject is life, and its object is said to be pleasurable instruction.

I. *Poetry as a Form of Scholastic Philosophy*

In the first place, poetry is a form of philosophy. Savonarola had classed poetry with logic and grammar, and had asserted that a knowledge of logic is essential to the composing of poetry. The division of the sciences and the relative importance of each were a source of infinite scholastic discussion during the Middle Ages. Aristotle had first placed dialectic or logic, rhetoric, and poetics in the same category of efficient philosophy. But Averroës was probably the first to confuse the function of poetics with that of logic, and to make the former a subdivision, or form, of the latter; and this classification appears to have been accepted by the scholastic philosophers of the Middle Ages.

This conception of the position of poetry in the body of human knowledge may be found, however, throughout the Renaissance. Thus, Robortelli, in his commentary on Aristotle's *Poetics* (1548), gives the usual scholastic distinctions between the various forms of the written or spoken word (*oratio*): the demonstrative, which deals with the true; the dialectic, which deals with the probable; the rhetorical, with the persuasive; and the poetic, with the false or fabulous.[1] By the term "false" or "fabulous" it is meant merely that the subject of poetry is not actual fact, but that it deals with things as they ought to be, rather than as they are. Varchi, in his public lectures on poetry (1553), divides philosophy into two forms, real and rational. Real philosophy deals with things, and includes metaphysics, ethics, physics, geometry, and the like; while rational philosophy, which includes logic, dialectic, rhetoric, history, poetry, and grammar, deals not with things, but with words, and is not philosophy proper, but the instrument of philosophy. Poetry is therefore, strictly speaking, neither an art nor a science, but an instrument or faculty; and it is only an art in the sense that it has been reduced to rules and precepts. It is, in fact, a form of logic, and no man, according to Varchi, can be a poet unless he is a logician; the better logician he is,

1 Robortelli, p. 1 *sq*.

the better poet he will be. Logic and poetry differ, however, in their matter and their instruments; for the subject of logic is truth, arrived at by means of the demonstrative syllogism, while the subject of poetry is fiction or invention, arrived at by means of that form of the syllogism known as the example. Here the enthymeme, or example, which Aristotle has made the instrument of rhetoric, becomes the instrument of poetry.

This classification survived in the Aristotelian schools at Padua and elsewhere as late as Zabarella and Campanella. Zabarella, a professor of logic and later of philosophy at Padua from 1564 to 1589, explains at length Averroës's theory that poetics is a form of logic, in a treatise on the nature of logic, published in 1578. [1] He concludes that the two faculties, logic and poetics, are not instruments of philosophy in general, but only of a part of it, for they refer rather to action than to knowledge; that is, they come under Aristotle's category of efficient philosophy. They are not the instruments of useful art or of moral philosophy, the end of which is to make one's self good; but of civil philosophy, the end of which is to make others good. If it be objected that they are *τιῶν εὐαντίων*, that is, of both good and evil, it may be answered that their proper end is good. Thus, in the *Sympo-*

1 This analysis of Zabarella, *Opera Logica*, *De Natura Logicæ*, ii. 13-23, I owe to the kindness of Professor Butcher of Edinburgh. Zabarella probably derived his knowledge of Aristotle's *Poetics* from Robortelli, under whom he studied Greek. *Cf.* Bayle, *Dict.* s. v. Zabarella.

sium, the true poet is praised; while in the *Republic* the poets who aim at pleasure and who corrupt their audiences are censured; and Aristotle in his definition of tragedy says that the end of tragedy is to purge the passions and to correct the morals of men (*affectiones animi purgare et mores corrigere*).

Even later than Zabarella, we find in the *Poetica* of Campanella a division of the sciences very similar to that of Savonarola and Varchi. Theology is there placed at the head of all knowledge, in accordance with the mediæval tradition, while poetics, with dialectic, grammar, and rhetoric, is placed among the logical sciences. Considering *poetica* as a form of philosophy, another commentator on Aristotle, Maggi (1550), takes great pains to distinguish its various manifestations. *Poetica* is the art of composing poetry, *poesis*, the poetry composed according to this art, *poeta*, the composer of poetry, and *poema*, a single specimen of poetry.[1] This distinction is a commonplace of classical criticism, and appears in Varro, Plutarch, Hermogenes, and Aphthonius.

II. *Poetry as an Imitation of Life*

In the second place, according to the passage from Strabo cited at the beginning of this chapter, poetry introduces us early to life, or, in other words, its subject is human action, and it is what Aristotle calls it, an imitation of human life. This raises

1 Maggi, p. 28 *sq*. *Cf.* B. Tasso, *Lettere*, ii. 514; Scaliger, *Poet.* i. 2; Castelvetro, *Poetica*, p. 7; Salviati, Cod. Magliabech. ii. ii. 11, fol. 384 v.; B. Jonson, *Timber*, p. 74.

two distinct problems. First, what is the meaning of imitation? and what in life is the subject-matter of this imitation?

The conception of imitation held by the critics of the Renaissance was that expressed by Aristotle in the ninth chapter of the *Poetics*. The passage is as follows: —

> "It is evident from what has been said that it is not the function of the poet to relate what has happened, but what may happen, — what is possible according to the law of probability or necessity. The poet and the historian differ not by writing in verse or in prose. The work of Herodotus might be put into verse, and it would still be a species of history, with metre no less than without it. The true difference is that one relates what has happened, the other what may happen. Poetry, therefore, is a more philosophical and a higher thing than history; for poetry tends to express the universal, history the particular. The universal tells us how a person of given character will on occasion speak or act, according to the law of probability or necessity; and it is this universality at which poetry aims in giving expressive names to the characters."

In this passage Aristotle has briefly formulated a conception of ideal imitation which may be regarded as universally valid, and which, repeated over and over again, became the basis of Renaissance criticism.

In the *Poetica* of Daniello (1536), occurs the first allusion in modern literary criticism to the Aristotelian notion of ideal imitation. According to Daniello, the poet, unlike the historian, can mingle fictions with facts, because he is not obliged, as is the historian, to describe things as they actually are or have been, but rather as they ought to be; and it is in this that the poet most differs from the historian, and not in the writing of verses; for even if Livy's works were versified, they would still be histories as before. [1] This is of course almost a paraphrase of the passage in Aristotle; but that Daniello did not completely understand the ideal element in Aristotle's conception is shown by the further distinction which he draws between the historian and the poet. For he adds that the poet and the historian have much in common; in both there are descriptions of places, peoples, laws; both contain the representation of vices and virtues; in both, amplification, variety, and digressions are proper; and both teach, delight, and profit at the same time. They differ, however, in that the historian, in telling his story, recounts it exactly as it happened, and adds nothing; whereas the poet is permitted to add whatever he desires, so long as the fictitious events have all the appearance of truth.

Somewhat later, Robortelli treats the question of æsthetic imitation from another point of view. The poet deals with things as they ought to be, but he can either appropriate actual fact, or he can invent his material. If he does the former, he narrates the truth not as it really happened, but as it might or ought to happen; while if he invents his material, he must do so in accordance with the law of possibility, or necessity, or probability and veri-

1 Daniello, p. 41 *sq*.

similitude.[1] Thus Xenophon, in describing Cyrus, does not depict him as he actually was, but as the best and noblest king can be and ought to be; and Cicero, in describing the orator, follows the same method. From this it is evident that the poet can invent things transcending the order of nature; but if he does so, he should describe what might or ought to have been.

Here Robortelli answers a possible objection to Aristotle's statement that poets deal only with what is possible and verisimilar. Is it possible and verisimilar that the gods should eat ambrosia and drink nectar, as Homer describes, and that such a being as Cerberus should have several heads, as we find in Virgil, not to mention various improbable things that occur in many other poets? The answer to such an objection is that poets can invent in two ways. They can invent either things according to nature or things transcending nature. In the former case, these things must be in keeping with the laws of probability and necessity; but in the latter case, the things are treated according to a process described by Aristotle himself, and called paralogism, which means, not necessarily false reasoning, but the natural, if quite inconclusive, logical inference that the things we know not of are subject to the same laws as the things we know. The poets accept the existence of the gods from the common notion of men, and then treat all that relates to these deities in accordance with this system of paralogism. In tragedy and comedy

1 Robortelli, p. 86 *sq.*

men are described as acting in accordance with the ordinary occurrences of nature; but in epic poetry this is not entirely the case, and the marvellous is therefore admitted. Accordingly, this marvellous element has the widest scope in epic poetry; while in comedy, which treats of things nearest to our own time, it ought not to be admitted at all.

But there is another problem suggested by the passage from the *Poetics* which has been cited. Aristotle says that imitation, and not metre, is the test of poetry; that even if a history were versified, it would still remain history. The question then arises whether a writer who imitates in prose, that is, without verse, would be worthy of the title of poet. Robortelli answers this question by pointing out that metre does not constitute the nature, force, or essence of poetry, which depends entirely on the fact of imitation; but at the same time, while one who imitates without verse is a poet, in the best and truest poetry imitation and metre are combined. [1]

In Fracastoro's *Naugerius, sive de Poetica Dialogus* (1555), there is the completest explanation of the ideal element in the Aristotelian conception of imitation. The poet, according to Aristotle, differs from other writers in that the latter consider merely the particular, while the poet aims at the universal. He is, in other words, attempting to describe the simple and essential truth of things, not by depicting the nude thing as it is, but the idea of things clothed in all their beauties. [2] Here

1 Robortelli, p. 90 *sq*. 2 Fracastoro, i. 340.

Fracastoro attempts to explain the Aristotelian conception of the type with the aid of the Platonic notion of beauty. There were, in fact, in the Renaissance, three conceptions of beauty in general vogue. First, the purely objective conception that beauty is fixed or formal, that it consists in approximating to a certain mechanical or geometrical form, such as roundness, squareness, or straightness; secondly, the Platonic conception, ethical rather than æsthetic, connecting the beautiful with the good, and regarding both as the manifestation of divine power; and, thirdly, a more purely æsthetic conception of beauty, connecting it either with grace or conformity, or in a higher sense with whatever is proper or fitting to an object. This last idea, which at times approaches the modern conception that beauty consists in the realization of the objective character of any particular thing and in the fulfilment of the law of its own being, seems to have been derived from the *Idea* of the Greek rhetorician Hermogenes, whose influence during the sixteenth century was considerable, even as early as the time of Filelfo. It was the celebrated rhetorician Giulio Cammillo, however, who appears to have popularized Hermogenes in the sixteenth century, by translating the *Idea* into Italian, and by expounding it in a discourse published posthumously in 1544.

As will be seen, Fracastoro's conception of beauty approximates both to the Platonic and to the more purely æsthetic doctrines which we have mentioned; and he expounds and elaborates this æsthetic notion in the following manner. Each art has its own rules of proper expression. The historian or the philosopher does not aim at all the beauties or elegancies of expression, but only such as are proper to history or philosophy. But to the poet no grace, no embellishment, no ornament, is ever alien; he does not consider the particular beauty of any one field, — that is, the singular, or particular, of Aristotle, — but all that pertains to the simple idea of beauty and of beautiful speech. Yet this universalized beauty is no extraneous thing; it cannot be added to objects in which it has no place, as a golden coat on a rustic; all the essential beauty of each species is to be the especial regard of the poet. For in imitating per-sons and things, he neglects no beauty or elegance which he can attribute to them; he strives only after the most beautiful and most excellent, and in this way affects the minds of men in the direction of excellence and beauty.

This suggests a problem which is at the very root of Aristotle's conception of ideal imitation; and it is Fracastoro's high merit that he was one of the first writers of the Renaissance to explain away the objection, and to formulate in the most perfect manner what Aristotle really meant. For, even granting that the poet teaches more than others, may it not be urged that it is not what pertains to the thing itself, but the beauties which he adds to them, — that it is ornament, extraneous to the thing itself (*extra rem*), and not the thing itself, — which seems to be the chief regard of the poet? But after all, what is *extra rem*? Are beautiful columns, domes, peristyles *extra rem*, because a thatched roof will protect us from rain and frost; or is noble raiment *extra rem*, because a rustic garment would suffice? The poet, so far from adding anything extraneous to the things he imitates, depicts them in their very essence; and it is because he alone finds the true beauty in things, because he attributes to them their true nobility and perfection, that he is more useful than any other writer. The poet does not, as some think, deal with the false and the unreal.[1] He assumes nothing openly alien to truth, though he may permit himself to treat of old and obscure legends which cannot be verified, or of things which are regarded as true on account of their appearance, their allegorical signification (such as the ancient myths and fables), or their common acceptance by men. So we may conclude that not every one who uses verse is a poet, but only he who is moved by the true beauty of things — by their simple and essential beauties, not merely apparent ones. This is Fracastoro's conclusion, and it contains that mingling of Platonism and Aristotelianism which may be found somewhat later in Tasso and Sir Philip Sidney. It is the chief merit of Fracastoro's dialogue, that even while emphasizing this Platonic element, he clearly distinguishes and defines the ideal element in æsthetic imitation.

About the same time, in the public lectures of Varchi (1553), there was an attempt to formulate a more explicit

1 Fracastoro, i. 357 *sq*.

definition of poetry on the basis of Aristotle's definition [1] of tragedy. Poetry, according to Varchi, is an imitation of certain actions, passions, habits of mind, with song, diction, and harmony, together or separately, for the purpose of removing the vices of men and inciting them to virtue, in order that they may attain their true happiness and beatitude. [2] In the first place, poetry is an imitation. Every poet imitates, and any one who does not imitate cannot be called a poet. Accordingly, Varchi follows Maggi in distinguishing three classes of poets, — the poets *par excellence*, who imitate in verse; the poets who imitate without using verse, such as Lucian, Boccaccio in the *Decameron*, and Sannazaro in the *Arcadia*; and the poets, commonly but less properly so called, who use verse, but who do not imitate. Verse, while not an essential attribute of poetry, is generally required; for men's innate love of harmony, according to Aristotle, was one of the causes that gave rise to poetic composition. Certain forms of poetry however, such as tragedy, cannot be written without verse; for "embellished language," that is, verse, is included in the very definition of tragedy as given by Aristotle.

The question whether poetry could be written in prose was a source of much discussion in the Renaissance; but the consensus of opinion was overwhelmingly against the prose drama. Comedy in prose was the usual Italian practice of this period, and various scholars [3] even sanction the

1 *Poet.* vi. 2. 2 Varchi, p. 578. 3 *E.g.* Piccolomini, p. 27 *sq.*

practice on theoretical grounds. But the controversy was not brought to a head until the publication of Agostino Michele's *Discorso in cui si dimostra come si possono scrivere le Commedie e le Tragedie in Prosa* in 1592; and eight years later, in 1600, Paolo Beni published his Latin dissertation, *Disputatio in qua ostenditur præstare Comœdiam atque Tragœdiam metrorum vinculis solvere.* [1] The language of Beni's treatise was strong — its very title speaks of liberating the drama from the shackles of verse; and for a heresy of this sort, couched as it was in language that might even have been revolutionary enough for the French romanticists of 1830, the sixteenth century was not yet fully prepared. Faustino Summo, answering Beni in the same year, asserts that not only is it improper for tragedy and comedy to be written in prose, but that no form of poetry whatever can properly be composed without the accompaniment of verse. [2] The result of the whole controversy was to fix the metrical form of the drama throughout the period of classicism. But it need not be said that the same conclusion was not accepted by all for every form of poetry. The remark of Cervantes in *Don Quixote*, that epics can be written in prose as well as in verse, is well known; and Julius Cæsar Scaliger [3] speaks of Heliodorus's romance as a model epic.

Scaliger, however, regards verse as a fundamental part of poetry. For him, poetry and history have the forms of narration and ornament in common, but differ

1 Tiraboschi, vii. 1331.
2 Summo, pp. 61-69.
3 *Poet.* iii. 95.

in that poetry adds fictions to the things that are true, or imitates actual things with fictitious ones, — *majore sane apparatu*, that is, among other things, with verse. As a result of this notion, Scaliger asserts that if the history of Herodotus were versified, it would no longer be history, but historical poetry. Under no circumstances, theoretically, will he permit the separation of poetry from mere versification. He accordingly dismisses with contempt the usual argument of the period that Lucan was an historian rather than a poet. "Take an actual history," says Scaliger; "how does Lucan differ, for example, from Livy? He differs in using verse. Well, then he is a poet." Poetry, then, is imitation in verse; [1] but in imitating what ought to be rather than what is, the poet creates another nature and other fortunes, as if he were another God. [2]

It will be seen from these discussions that the Renaissance always conceived of æsthetic imitation in this ideal sense. There are scarcely any traces of realism, in anything like its modern sense, in the literary criticism of this period. Torquato Tasso does indeed say that art becomes most perfect as it approaches most closely to nature; [3] and

1 *Poet.* i. 1.

2 Another critic of the time, Vettori, 1560, pp. 14, 93, attacks poetic prose on the ground that in Aristotle's definition of the various poetic forms, verse is always spoken of as an essential part. It is interesting to note that the phrase "poetic prose" is used, perhaps for the first time, in Minturno, *Arte Poetica*, 1564, p. 3, etc.

3 *Opere*, x. 254. *Cf.* Minturno, *Arte Poetica*, p. 33.

Scaliger declares that the dramatic poet must beyond all things aim at reproducing the actual conditions of life.[1] But it is the appearance of reality, and not the mere actuality itself, that the critics are speaking of here. With the vast body of mediæval literature before them, in which impossibilities follow upon impossibilities, and the sense of reality is continually obscured, the critical writers of the Renaissance were forced to lay particular stress on the element of probability, the element of close approach to the seeming realities of life; but the imitation of life is for them, nevertheless, an imitation of things as they ought to be — in other words, the imitation is ideal. Muzio says that nature is adorned by art: —

> "Suol far l' opere sue roze, e tra le mani
> Lasciarle a l' arte, che le adorni e limi;"[2]

and he distinctly affirms that the poet cannot remain content with exact portraiture, with the mere actuality of life: —

> "Lascia 'l vero a l' historia, e ne' tuoi versi
> Sotto i nomi privati a l' universo
> Mostra che fare e che non far si debbia."

In keeping with this idealized conception of art, Muzio asserts that everything obscene or immoral must be excluded from poetry; and this puristic notion of art is everywhere emphasized in Renaissance criticism. It was the *verisimile*, as has been said, that the writers of this period especially insisted upon. Poetry must have the appearance of

1 *Poet.* iii. 96. 2 Muzio, p. 69.

truth, that is, it must be probable; for unless the reader believes what he reads, his spirit cannot be moved by the poem. [1] This anticipates Boileau's famous line: —

> "L'esprit n'est point ému de ce qu'il ne croit pas." [2]

But beyond and above the *verisimile*, the poet must pay special regard to the ethical element (*il lodevole e l'onesto*). A poet of the sixteenth century, Palingenius, says that there are three qualities required of every poem: —

> "Atqui scire opus est, triplex genus esse bonorum,
> Utile, delectans, majusque ambobus honestum." [3]

Poetry, then, is an ideal representation of life; but should it be still further limited, and made an imitation of only human life? In other words, are the actions of men the only possible themes of poetry, or may it deal, as in the *Georgics* and the *De Rerum Natura*, with the various facts of external nature and of science, which are only indirectly connected with human life? May poetry treat of the life of the world as well as of the life of men; and if only of the latter, is it to be restricted to the actions of men, or may it also depict their passions, emotions, and character? In short, how far may external nature on the one hand, and the internal working of the human soul on the other hand, be regarded as the subject-matter of poetry? Aristotle says that poetry deals with the actions of

1 Giraldi Cintio, i. 61.
2 *Art Poét.* iii. 50. *Cf.* Horace, *Ars Poet.* 188.
3 *Zodiac. Vitæ*, i. 143.

men, but he uses the word "actions" in a larger sense than many of the Renaissance critics appear to have believed. His real meaning is thus explained by a modern writer: —

"Everything that expresses the mental life, that reveals a rational personality, will fall within this larger sense of action.... The phrase is virtually an equivalent for ἤθη (character), πάθη (emotion), πράξεις (action).... The common original from which all the arts draw is human life, — its mental processes, its spiritual movements, its outward acts issuing from deeper sources; in a word, all that constitutes the inward and essential activity of the soul. On this principle landscape and animals are not ranked among the objects of æsthetic imitation. The whole universe is not conceived of as the raw material of art. Aristotle's theory is in agreement with the practice of the Greek poets and artists of the classical period, who introduce the external world only so far as it forms a background of action, and enters as an emotional element into man's life and heightens the human interest." [1]

Aristotle distinctly says that "even if a treatise on medicine or natural philosophy be brought out in verse, the name of poet is by custom given to the author; and yet Homer and Empedocles have nothing in common except the material; the former, therefore, is properly styled poet, the latter, physicist rather than poet." [2]

The Aristotelian doctrine was variously conceived during the Renaissance. Fracastoro, for example, asserts that the imitation of human life alone is not of itself a test of poetry, for such a test would exclude Empedocles and Lucretius; it would make

1 Butcher, pp. 117, 118.

2 *Poet.* i. 8.

Virgil a poet in the *Æneid*, and not a poet in the *Georgics*. All matters are proper material for the poet, as Horace says, if they are treated poetically; and although the imitation of men and women may seem to be of higher importance for us who are men and women, the imitation of human life is no more the poet's end than the imitation of anything else. [1] This portion of Fracastoro's argument may be called apologetic, for the imitation of human actions as a test of poetry would exclude most of his own poems, [2] such as his famous *De Morbo Gallico* (1529), written before the influence of Aristotle was felt in anything but the mere external forms of creative literature. For Fracastoro, all things poetically treated become poetry, and Aristotle himself [3] says that everything becomes pleasant when correctly imitated. So that not the mere composition of verse, but the Platonic rapture, the delight in the true and essential beauty of things, is for Fracastoro the test of poetic power.

Varchi, on the other hand, is more in accord with Aristotle, in conceiving of "action," the subject-matter of poetry, as including the passions and habits of mind as well as the merely external actions of mankind. By passions Varchi means those mental perturbations which impel us to an action at any particular time (πάθη); while by manners, or habits of mind, he means those mental qualities which distinguish one man or one class of men from another (ἤθη). The exclusion of the

1 Fracastoro, i. 335 *sq.*

2 *Cf.* Castelvetro, *Poetica*, p. 27 *sq.*

3 *Rhet.* i. 11.

emotional or introspective side of human life would leave all lyric and, in fact, all subjective verse out of the realms of poetry; and it was therefore essential, in an age in which Petrarch was worshipped, that the subjective side of poetry should receive its justification.[1] There is also in Varchi a most interesting comparison between the arts of poetry and painting.[2] The basis of his distinction is Horace's *ut pictura poesis*, doubtless founded on the parallel of Simonides preserved for us by Plutarch; and this distinction, which regarded painting as silent poetry, and poetry as painting in language, may be considered almost the keynote of Renaissance criticism, continuing even up to the time of Lessing.

In Capriano's *Della Vera Poetica* (1555) poetry is given a preëminent place among all the arts, because it does not merely deal with actions or with the objects of any single sense. For Capriano, poetry is an ideal representation of life, and as such "vere nutrice e amatrice del nostro bene."[3] All sensuous or comprehensible objects are capable of being imitated by various arts. The nobler of the imitative arts are concerned with the objects of the nobler senses, while the ignobler arts are concerned with the objects of the senses of taste, touch, and smell. Poetry is the finest of all the arts, because it comprehends in itself all the faculties and powers of the other arts, and can in fact imitate anything, as, for example, the form of a lion, its color, its ferocity, its roar, and the like. It is also the highest form of art because it makes use of the most effi-

1 *Cf.* A. Segni, 1581, cap. i. 2 Varchi, p. 227 *sq.* 3 Capriano, cap. ii.

cacious means of imitation, namely, words, and especially since these receive the additional beauty and power of rhythm. Accordingly, Capriano divides poets into two classes: natural poets, who describe the things of nature, and moral poets (such as epic and tragic poets), who aim at presenting moral lessons and indicating the uses of life; and of these two classes the moral poets are to be rated above the natural poets.

But if all things are the objects of poetic imitation, the poet must know everything; he must have studied nature as well as life; and, accordingly, Lionardi, in his dialogues on poetic imitation (1554), says that to be a good poet, one must be a good historian, a good orator, and a good natural and moral philosopher as well; [1] and Bernardo Tasso asserts that a thorough acquaintance with the art of poetry is only to be gained from the study of Aristotle's *Poetics*, combined with a knowledge of philosophy and the various arts and sciences, and vast experience of the world. [2] The Renaissance, with its humanistic tendencies, never quite succeeded in discriminating between erudition and genius. Scaliger says that nothing which proceeds from solid learning can ever be out of place in poetry, and Fracastoro (1555) and Tomitano (1545) both affirm that the good poet and the good orator must essentially be learned scholars and philosophers. Scaliger therefore distinguishes three classes of poets, — first, the theological poets, such as Orpheus and Amphion; secondly, the philosophical

1 Lionardi, p. 43 *sq*. 2 *Lettere*, ii. 525.

poets, of two sorts, natural poets, such as Empedocles and Lucretius, and moral poets, who again are either political, as Solon and Tyrtæus, economic, as Hesiod, or common, as Phocyllides; and, thirdly, the ordinary poets who imitate human life. [1] The last are divided according to the usual Renaissance classification into dramatic, narrative, and common or mixed. Scaliger's classification is employed by Sir Philip Sidney; [2] and a very similar subdivision is given by Minturno. [3]

The treatment of Castelvetro, in his commentary on the *Poetics* (1570), is at times much more in accord with the true Aristotelian conception than most of the other Renaissance writers. While following Aristotle in asserting that verse is not of the essence of poetry, he shows that Aristotle himself by no means intended to class as poetry works that imitated in prose, for this was not the custom of Hellenic art. Prose is not suited to imitative or imaginative subjects, for we expect themes treated in prose to be actual facts. [4] "Verse does not distinguish poetry," says Castelvetro, "but clothes and adorns it; and it is as improper for poetry to be written in prose, or history in verse, as it is for women to use the garments of men, and for men to wear the garments of women." [5] The test of poetry therefore is not the metre but the material. This approximates to Aristotle's own view; since while imitation is what distinguishes the poetic art, Aris-

1 Scaliger, *Poet.* i. 2.
2 *Defense*, pp. 10, 11.
3 *De Poeta*, p. 53 *sq.*
4 Castelvetro, *Poetica*, p. 23 *sq.*
5 *Ibid.* p. 190.

totle, by limiting it to the imitation of human life was, after all, making the matter the test of poetry.

Castelvetro, however, arrives at this conclusion on different grounds. Science he regards as not suitable material for poetry, and accordingly such writers as Lucretius and Fracastoro are not poets. They are good artists, perhaps, or good philosophers, but not poets; for the poet does not attempt to discover the truth of nature, but to imitate the deeds of men, and to bring delight to his audience by means of this imitation. Moreover, poetry, as will be seen later, is intended to give delight to the populace, the untrained multitude, to whom the sciences and the arts are dead letters;[1] if we concede these to be fit themes for poetry, then poetry is either not meant to delight, or not meant for the ordinary people, but is intended for instruction and for those only who are versed in sciences and arts. Moreover, comparing poetry with history, Castelvetro finds that they resemble each other in many points, but are not identical. Poetry follows, as it were, in the footsteps of history, but differs from it in that history deals with what has happened, poetry with what is probable; and things that have happened, though probable, are never considered in poetry as probable, but always as things that have happened. History, accordingly, does not regard verisimilitude or necessity, but only truth; poetry must take care to establish the probability of its subject in verisimilitude and necessity, since it cannot regard truth. Castelvetro in common with

1 *Cf.* T. Tasso, xi. 51.

most of the critics of the Renaissance seems to misconceive the full meaning of ideal truth; for to the Renaissance — nay, even to Shakespeare, if we are to consider as his own various phrases which he has put into the mouths of his dramatic characters — truth was regarded as coincident with fact; and nothing that was not actual fact, however subordinated to the laws of probability and necessity, was ever called truth.

It is in keeping with this conception of the relations between history and poetry, that Castelvetro should differ not only from Aristotle, but from most of the critics of his own time, in asserting that the order of the poetic narrative may be the same as that of historical narrative. "In telling a story," he says, "we need not trouble ourselves whether it has beginning, middle, and end, but only whether it is fitted to its true purpose, that is, to delight its auditors by the narration of certain circumstances which could possibly happen but have not actually happened." [1] Here the only vital distinction between history and poetry is that the incidents recounted in history have once happened, while those recounted in poetry have never actually happened, or the matter will not be regarded as poetry. Aristotle's fundamental requirement of the unity of the fable is regarded as unessential, and is simply observed in order to show the poet's ingenuity. This notion of poetic ingenuity is constant throughout Castelvetro's commentary. Thus he explains Aristotle's statement that poetry is more philosophic

1 *Poetica*, p. 158.

than history — more philosophic, according to Castelvetro, in the sense of requiring more thought, more speculation in its composition — by showing that it is a more difficult and more ingenious labor to invent things that could possibly happen, than merely to repeat things that have actually happened. [1]

III. *The Function of Poetry*

According to Strabo, it will be remembered, the object or function of poetry is pleasurable instruction in reference to character, emotion, action. This occasions the inquiry as to what is the function of the poetic art, and, furthermore, what are its relations to morality. The starting-point of all discussions on this subject in the Renaissance was the famous verse of Horace: —

> "Aut prodesse volunt aut delectare poetæ." [2]

This line suggests that the function of poetry may be to please, or to instruct, or both to please and instruct; and every one of the writers of the Renaissance takes one or other of these three positions. Aristotle, as we know, regarded poetry as an imitation of human life, for the purpose of giving a certain refined pleasure to the reader or hearer. "The end of the fine arts is to give pleasure (*πρὸς ἡδονήν*), or rational enjoyment (*πρὸς διαγωγήν*)." [3] It has already been said that poetry, in so far as it is an imitation of human life, and

1 *Poetica*, p.191. 2 *Ars Poet.* 333. 3 Butcher, p. 185.

attempts to be true to human life in its ideal aspects, must fundamentally be moral; but to give moral or scientific instruction is in no way the end or function of poetry. It will be seen that the Renaissance was in closer accord with Horace than with Aristotle, in requiring for the most part the *utile* as well as the *dulce* in poetry.

For Daniello, one of the earliest critical writers of the century, the function of the poet is to teach and delight. As the aim of the orator is to persuade, and the aim of the physician to cure, so the aim of the poet is equally to teach and delight; and unless he teaches and delights he cannot be called a poet, even as one who does not persuade cannot be called an orator, or one who does not cure, a physician.[1] But beyond profitableness and beauty, the poet must carry with him a certain persuasion, which is one of the highest functions of poetry, and which consists in moving and affecting the reader or hearer with the very passions depicted; but the poet must be moved first, before he can move others.[2] Here Daniello is renewing Horace's

"Si vis me flere, dolendum est
Primum ipsi tibi," —

a sentiment echoed by poets as different as Vauquelin, Boileau, and Lamartine.

Fracastoro, however, attempts a deeper analysis of the proper function of the poetic art. What is the aim of the poet? Not merely to give delight, for the fields, the stars, men and women,

1 Daniello, p. 25. 2 *Ibid.* p. 40.

the objects of poetic imitation themselves do that; and poetry, if it did no more, could not be said to have any reason for existing. Nor is it merely to teach and delight, as Horace says; for the descriptions of countries, peoples, and armies, the scientific digressions and the historical events, which constitute the instructive side of poetry, are derived from cosmographers, scientists, and historians, who teach and delight as much as poets do. What, then, is the function of the poet? It is, as has already been pointed out, to describe the essential beauty of things, to aim at the universal and ideal, and to perform this function with every possible accompaniment of beautiful speech, thus affecting the minds of men in the direction of excellence and beauty. Portions of Fracastoro's argument have been alluded to before, and it will suffice here to state his own summing up of the aim of the poet, which is this, "Delectare et prodesse imitando in unoquoque maxima et pulcherrima per genus dicendi simpliciter pulchrum ex convenientibus." [1] This is a mingling of the Horatian and Platonic conceptions of poetic art.

By other critics a more practical function was given to poetry. Giraldi Cintio asserts that it is the poet's aim to condemn vice and to praise virtue, and Maggi says that poets aim almost exclusively at benefiting the mind. Poets who, on the contrary, treat of obscene matters for the corruption of youth, may be compared with infamous physicians who give their patients deadly poison

1 Fracastoro, i. 363.

in the guise of wholesome medicine. Horace and Aristotle, according to Maggi, are at one on this point, for in the definition of tragedy Aristotle ascribes to it a distinctly useful purpose, and whatever delight is obtainable is to be regarded as a result of this moral function; for Maggi and the Renaissance critics in general would follow the Elizabethan poet who speaks of "delight, the fruit of virtue dearly loved." Muzio, in his versified *Arte Poetica* (1555), regards the end of poetry as pleasure and profit, and the pleasurable aim of poetry as attained by variety, for the greatest poems contain every phase of life and art.

It has been seen that Varchi classed poetry with rational philosophy. The end of all arts and sciences is to make human life perfect and happy; but they differ in their modes of producing this result. Philosophy attains its end by teaching; rhetoric, by persuasion; history, by narration; poetry, by imitation or representation. The aim of the poet, therefore, is to make the human soul perfect and happy, and it is his office to imitate, that is, to invent and represent, things which render men virtuous, and consequently happy. Poetry attains this end more perfectly than any of the other arts or sciences, because it does so, not by means of precept, but by means of example. There are various ways of making men virtuous, — by teaching them what vice is and what virtue is, which is the province of ethics; by actually chastising vices and rewarding virtues, which is the province of law; or by example, that is, by the representation of virtuous men receiving suitable rewards for their virtue, and of vicious men receiving suitable punishments, which is the province of poetry. This last method is the most efficacious, because it is accompanied by delight. For men either can not or will not take the trouble to study sciences and virtues — nay, do not even like to be told what they should or should not do; but in hearing or reading poetic examples, not only is there no trouble, but there is the greatest delight, and no one can help being moved by the representation of characters who are rewarded or punished according to an ideal justice.

For Varchi, then, as for Sir Philip Sidney later, the high importance of poetry is to be found in the fact that it teaches morality better than any other art, and the reason is that its instrument is not precept but example, which is the most delightful and hence the most efficacious of all means. The function of poetry is, therefore, a moral one, and it consists in removing the vices of men and inciting them to virtue. This twofold moral object of poetry — the removal of vices, which is passive, and the incitement to virtue, which is active — is admirably attained, for example, by Dante in his *Divina Commedia*; for in the *Inferno* evil men are so fearfully punished that we resolve to flee from every form of vice, and in the *Paradiso* virtuous men are so gloriously rewarded that we resolve to imitate every one of their perfections. This is the expression of the extreme view of poetic justice; and while it is in keeping with the common sentiment of the Renaissance, it is of course entirely un-Aristotelian.

Scaliger's point of view is in accord with the common Renaissance tradition. Poetry is imitation, but imitation is not the end of poetry. Imitation for its own sake — that is, art for art's sake — receives no encouragement from Scaliger. The purpose of poetry is to teach delightfully (*docere cum delectatione*); and, therefore, not imitation, as Aristotle says, but delightful instruction, is the test of poetry. [1] Minturno (1559) adds a third element to that of instruction and of delight. [2] The function of poetry is not only to teach and delight, but also to move, that is, beyond instruction and delight the poet must impel certain passions in the reader or hearer, and incite the mind to admiration of what is described.[3] An ideal hero may be represented in a poem, but the poem is futile unless it excites the reader to admiration of the hero depicted. Accordingly, it is the peculiar office of the poet to move admiration for great men; for the orator, the philosopher, and the historian need not necessarily do so, but no one who does not incite this admiration can really be called a poet.

This new element of admiration is the logical consequence of the Renaissance position that philosophy teaches by precept, but poetry by example, and that in this consists its superior ethical efficacy. In Seneca's phrase, "longum iter per præcepta,

1 Scaliger, *Poet.* vi. ii. 2.

2 *De Poeta*, p. 102. *Cf.* Scaliger, *Poet.* iii. 96.

3 *De Poeta*, p. 11.

breve per exempla." If poetry, therefore, attains its end by means of example, it follows that to arrive at this end the poet must incite in the reader an admiration of the example, or the ethical aim of poetry will not be accomplished. Poetry is more than a mere passive expression of truth in the most pleasurable manner; it becomes like oratory an active exhortation to virtue, by attempting to create in the reader's mind a strong desire to be like the heroes he is reading about. The poet does not tell what vices are to be avoided and what virtues are to be imitated, but sets before the reader or hearer the most perfect types of the various virtues and vices. It is, in Sidney's phrase (a phrase apparently borrowed from Minturno), "that feigning notable images of virtues, vices, or what else, with that delightful instruction, which must be the right describing note to know a poet by." Dryden, a century later, seems to be insisting upon this same principle of admiration when he says that it is the work of the poet "to affect the soul, and excite the passions, and above all to move admiration, which is the delight of serious plays." [1]

But Minturno goes even further than this. If the poet is fundamentally a teacher of virtue, it follows that he must be a virtuous man himself; and in pointing this out, Minturno has given the first complete expression in modern times of the consecrated conception of the poet's office. As no form of knowledge and no moral excellence is foreign to the poet, so at bottom he is the truly wise

1 *Essay of Dramatic Poesy*, p. 104.

and good man. The poet may, in fact, be defined as a good man skilled in language and imitation; not only ought he to be a good man, but no one will be a good poet unless he is so. [1] This conception of the moral nature of the poet may be traced henceforth throughout modern times. It is to be found in Ronsard [2] and other French and Italian writers; it is especially noticeable in English literature, and is insisted on by Ben Jonson, [3] Milton, [4] Shaftesbury, [5] Coleridge, [6] and Shelley. [7] In this idea Plato's praise of the philosopher, as well as Cicero's and Quintilian's praise of the orator, was by the Renaissance transferred to the poet; [8] but the conception itself goes back to a passage in Strabo's *Geography*, a work well known to sixteenth-century scholars. This passage is as follows: —

"Can we possibly imagine that the genius, power, and excellence of a real poet consist in aught else than the just imitation of life in formed discourse and numbers? But how should he be that just imitator of life, whilst he himself knows not its measures, nor how to guide himself by judgment and understanding? For we have not surely the same notion of the poet's excellence as of the ordinary craftsman's, the subject of whose art is senseless stone or timber,

1 *De Poeta*, p. 79.
2 *Œuvres*, vii. 318.
3 *Works*, i. 333.
4 *Prose Works*, iii. 118.
5 *Characteristicks*, 1711, i. 207.
6 H. C. Robinson, *Diary*, May 29, 1812, "Coleridge talked of the impossibility of being a good poet without being a good man."
7 *Defence of Poetry*, p. 42.
8 Minturno plainly says as much, *De Poeta*, p. 105.

without life, dignity, or beauty; whilst the poet's art turning principally on men and manners, he has his virtues and excellence as poet naturally annexed to human excellence, and to the worth and dignity of man, insomuch that it is impossible he should be a great and worthy poet who is not first a worthy and good man." [1]

Another writer of the sixteenth century, Bernardo Tasso, tells us that in his poem of the *Amadigi* he has aimed at delight rather than profitable instruction.[2] "I have spent most of my efforts," he says, "in attempting to please, as it seems to me that this is more necessary, and also more difficult to attain; for we find by experience that many poets may instruct and benefit us very much, but certainly give us very little delight." This agrees with what one of the sanest of English critics, John Dryden (1668), has said of verse, "I am satisfied if it caused delight, for delight is the chief if not the only end of pocsie; instruction can be admitted but in the second place, for poesie only instructs as it delights." [3]

It is this same end which Castelvetro (1570) ascribes to poetic art. For Castelvetro, as in a lesser degree for Robortelli also, the end of poetry is delight, and delight alone. [4] This, he asserts, is the position of Aristotle, and if utility is to be conceded to poetry at all, it is merely as an accident, as in the tragic purgation of terror and compassion. [5]

1 *Geog*. i. ii. 5, as cited by Shaftesbury.
2 *Lettere*, ii. 195.
3 *Essay of Dramatic Poesy*, p. 104.
4 *Cf.* Piccolomini, p. 369.
5 Castelvetro, *Poetica*, p. 505. *Cf.* Twining, ii. 449, 450.

But he goes further than Aristotle would have been willing to go; for poetry, according to Castelvetro, is intended not merely to please, but to please the populace, in fact everybody, even the vulgar mob. [1] On this he insists throughout his commentary; indeed, as will be seen later, it is on this conception that his theory of the drama is primarily based. But it may be confidently asserted that Aristotle would have willingly echoed the conclusion of Shakespeare, as expressed in *Hamlet*, that the censure of one of the judicious must o'erweigh a whole theatre of others. At the same time, Castelvetro's conception is in keeping with a certain modern feeling in regard to the meaning of poetic art. Thus a recent writer regards literature as aiming "at the pleasure of the greatest possible number of the nation rather than instruction and practical effects," and as applying "to general rather than specialized knowledge." [2] There is, then, in Castelvetro's argument this modicum of truth, that poetry appeals to no specialized knowledge, but that its function is, as Coleridge says, to give a definite and immediate pleasure.

Torquato Tasso, as might be expected, regards poetry in a more highly ideal sense. His conception of the function of poets and of the poetic art may be explained as follows: The universe is beautiful in itself, because beauty is a ray from the Divine splendor; and hence art should seek to approach as closely as possible to nature, and to catch and

1 *Poetica*, p. 29.
2 Posnett, cited by Cook, p. 247.

express this natural beauty of the world. [1] Real beauty, however, is not so called because of any usefulness it may possess, but is primarily beautiful in itself; for the beautiful is what pleases every one, just as the good is what every one desires. [2] Beauty is therefore the flower of the good (*quasi un fiore del buono*); it is the circumference of the circle of which the good is the centre, and accordingly, poetry, as an expression of this beauty, imitates the outward show of life in its general aspects. Poetry is therefore an imitation of human actions, made for the guidance of life; and its end is delight, *ordinato al giovamento*. [3] It must essentially delight, either because delight is its aim, or because delight is the necessary means of effecting the ethical end of art. [4] Thus, for example, heroic poetry consists of imitation and allegory, the function of the former being to cause delight, and that of the latter to give instruction and guidance in life. But since difficult or obscure conceits rarely delight, and since the poet does not appeal to the learned only, but to the people, just as the orator does, the poet's idea must be, if not popular in the ordinary sense of the word, at least intelligible to the people. Now the people will not study difficult problems; but poetry, by appealing to them on the side of pleasure, teaches them whether they will or no; and this constitutes the true effectiveness of poetry, for it is the most delightful, and hence the most valuable, of teachers. [5]

1 *Opere*, viii. 26 *sq*.
2 *Ibid*. ix. 123.
3 *Ibid*. xii. 13.
4 *Ibid*. xi. 50.
5 *Ibid*. xii. 212.

Such, then, are the various conceptions of the function of poetry, as held by the critics of the Renaissance. On the whole, it may be said that at bottom the conception was an ethical one, for, with the exception of such a revolutionary spirit as Castelvetro, by most theorists it was as an effective guide to life that poetry was chiefly valued. Even when delight was admitted as an end, it was simply because of its usefulness in effecting the ethical aim.

In concluding this chapter, it may be well to say a few words, and only a few, upon the classification of poetic forms. There were during the Renaissance numerous attempts at distinguishing these forms, but on the whole all of them are fundamentally equivalent to that of Minturno, who recognizes three *genres*, — the lyric or melic, the dramatic or scenic, and the epic or narrative. This classification is essentially that of the Greeks, and it has lasted down to this very day. With lyric poetry this essay is scarcely concerned, for during the Renaissance there was no systematic lyric theory. Those who discussed it at all gave most of their attention to its formal structure, its style, and especially the conceit it contained. The model of all lyrical poetry was Petrarch, and it was in accordance with the lyrical poet's agreement or disagreement with the Petrarchan method that he was regarded as a success or a failure. Muzio's critical poem (1551) deals almost entirely with lyrical verse, and there are discussions on this subject in the works of Trissino, Equicola, Ruscelli,

Scaliger, and Minturno. But the real question at issue in all these discussions is merely that of external form, and it is with the question of principles, in so far as they regard literary criticism, that this essay is primarily concerned. The theory of dramatic and epic poetry, being fundamental, will therefore receive almost exclusive attention.

CHAPTER III

THE THEORY OF THE DRAMA

ARISTOTLE'S definition of tragedy is the basis of the Renaissance theory of tragedy. That definition is as follows: "Tragedy is an imitation of an action that is serious, complete, and of a certain magnitude; in language embellished with each kind of artistic ornament, the several kinds being found in separate parts of the play; in the form of action, not of narration; through pity and fear effecting the proper *katharsis* or purgation of these emotions." [1]

To expand this definition, tragedy, in common with all other forms of poetry, is the imitation of an action; but the action of tragedy is distinguished from that of comedy in being grave and serious. The action is complete, in so far as it possesses perfect unity; and in length it must be of the proper magnitude. By embellished language, Aristotle means language into which rhythm, harmony, and song enter; and by the remark that the several kinds are to be found in separate parts of the play, he means that some parts of tragedy are rendered through the medium of verse alone, while others receive the aid of song. Moreover, tragedy is dis-

1 *Poet.* vi. 2.

tinguished from epic poetry by being in the form of action instead of that of narration. The last portion of Aristotle's definition describes the peculiar function of tragic performance.

I. *The Subject of Tragedy*

Tragedy is the imitation of a *serious* action, that is, an action both grave and great, or, as the sixteenth century translated the word, illustrious. Now, what constitutes a serious action, and what actions are not suited to the dignified character of tragedy? Daniello (1536) distinguishes tragedy from comedy in that the comic poets "deal with the most familiar and domestic, not to say base and vile operations; the tragic poets, with the deaths of high kings and the ruins of great empires." [1] Whichever of these matters the poet selects should be treated without admixture of any other form; if he resolves to treat of grave matters, mere loveliness should be excluded; if of themes of loveliness, he should exclude all grave themes. Here, at the very beginning of dramatic discussion, the strict separation of themes or *genres* is advocated in as formal a manner as ever during the period of classicism; and this was never deviated from, at least in theory, by any of the writers of the sixteenth century. Moreover, according to Daniello, the dignified character of tragedy demands that all unseemly, cruel, impossible, or ignoble incidents should be excluded from the stage; while even comedy

1 Daniello, p. 34.

should not attempt to represent any lascivious act.[1] This was merely a deduction from Senecan tragedy and the general practice of the classics.

There is, in Daniello's theory of tragedy, no single Aristotelian element, and it was not until about a decade later that Aristotle's theory of tragedy played any considerable part in the literary criticism of the sixteenth century. In 1543, however, the *Poetics* had already become a part of university study, for Giraldi Cintio, in his *Discorso sulle Comedie e sulle Tragedie*, written in that year, says that it was a regular academic exercise to compare some Greek tragedy, such as the *Œdipus* of Sophocles, with a tragedy of Seneca on the same subject, using the *Poetics* of Aristotle as a dramatic text-book.[2] Giraldi distinguishes tragedy from comedy on somewhat the same grounds as Daniello. "Tragedy and comedy," he says, "agree in that they are both imitations of an action, but they differ in that the former imitates the illustrious and royal, the latter the popular and civil. Hence Aristotle says that comedy imitates the worse sort of actions, not that they are vicious and criminal, but that, as regards nobility, they are worse when compared with royal actions." Giraldi's position is made clear by his further statement that the actions of tragedy are called illustrious, not because they are virtuous or vicious, but merely because they are the actions of people of the highest rank.[3]

This conception of the serious action of tragedy,

1 *Cf.* Horace, *Ars Poet.* 182 *sq.*
2 Giraldi Cintio, ii. 6.
3 *Ibid.* ii. 30.

which makes its dignity the result of the rank of those who are its actors, and thus regards rank as the real distinguishing mark between comedy and tragedy, was not only common throughout the Renaissance, but even throughout the whole period of classicism, and had an extraordinary effect on the modern drama, especially in France. Thus Dacier (1692) says that it is not necessary that the action be illustrious and important in itself: "On the contrary, it may be very ordinary or common; but it must be so by the quality of the persons who act.... The greatness of these eminent men renders the action great, and their reputation makes it credible and possible."[1]

Again, Robortelli (1548) maintains that tragedy deals only with the greater sort of men (*prœstantiores*), because the fall of men of such rank into misery and disgrace produces greater commiseration (which is, as will be seen, one of the functions of tragedy) than the fall of men of merely ordinary rank. Another commentator on the *Poetics*, Maggi (1550), gives a slightly different explanation of Aristotle's meaning. Maggi asserts that Aristotle,[2] in saying that comedy deals with the worse and tragedy with the better sort of men, means to distinguish between those whose rank is lower or higher than that of ordinary men; comedy dealing with slaves, tradesmen, maidservants, buffoons, and other low people, tragedy with kings and heroes.[3] This explanation is defended on grounds similar to

1 Cited by Butcher, p. 220.

2 *Poet.* iv. 7.

3 Maggi, p. 64.

those given by Robortelli, that is, the change from felicity to infelicity is greater and more noticeable in the greatest men. [1]

This conception of the rank of the characters as the distinguishing mark between tragedy and comedy is, it need not be said, entirely un-Aristotelian. "Aristotle does undoubtedly hold," says Professor Butcher, "that actors in tragedy ought to be illustrious by birth and position. The narrow and trivial life of obscure persons cannot give scope for a great and significant action, one of tragic consequence. But nowhere does he make outward rank the distinguishing feature of tragic as opposed to comic representation. Moral nobility is what he demands; and this — on the French stage, or at least with French critics — is transformed into an inflated dignity, a courtly etiquette and decorum, which seemed proper to high rank. The instance is one of many in which literary critics have wholly confounded the teaching of Aristotle." [2] This distinction, then, though common up to the end of the eighteenth century, is not to be found in Aristotle; but the fact is, that a similar distinction can be traced, throughout the Middle Ages, throughout classical antiquity, back almost to the time of Aristotle himself.

The grammarian, Diomedes, has preserved the definition of tragedy formulated by Theophrastus, Aristotle's successor as head of the Peripatetic school. According to this definition, tragedy is "a change in the fortune

1 Maggi, p. 154.
2 Butcher, p. 220 *sq*.

of a hero." [1] A Greek definition of comedy preserved by Diomedes, and ascribed to Theophrastus also, [2] speaks of comedy as dealing with private and civil fortunes, without the element of danger. This seems to have been the accepted Roman notion of comedy. In the treatise of Euanthius-Donatus, comedy is said to deal with the common fortunes of men, to begin turbulently, but to end tranquilly and happily; tragedy, on the other hand, has only mighty personages, and ends terribly; its subject is often historical, while that of comedy is always invented by the poet. [3] The third book of Diomedes's *Ars Grammatica*, based on Suetonius's tractate *De Poetis* (written in the second century A.D.), distinguishes tragedy from comedy in that only heroes, great leaders, and kings are introduced in tragedy, while in comedy the characters are humble and private persons; in the former, lamentations, exiles, bloodshed predominate, in the latter, love affairs and seductions. [4] Isidore of Seville, in the seventh century, says very much the same thing: "Comic poets treat of the acts of private men, while tragic poets treat of public matters and the histories of kings; tragic themes are based on sorrowful affairs, comic themes on joyful ones." [5] In another place he speaks of tragedy as dealing with the ancient deeds and mis-

1 Butcher, p. 219, n. 1.——Müller, ii. 394, attempts to harmonize the definition of Theophrastus with that of Aristotle.

2 Egger, *Hist. de la Critique*, p. 344, n. 2.

3 Cloetta, i. 29. *Cf.* Antiphanes, cited by Egger, p. 72.

4 Cloetta, p. 30.

5 *Etymol.* viii. 7, 6.

deeds of infamous kings, and of comedy as dealing with the actions of private men, and with the defilement of maidens and the love affairs of strumpets. [1] In the *Catholicon* of Johannes Januensis de Balbis (1286) tragedy and comedy are distinguished on similar grounds: tragedy deals only with kings and princes, comedy with private citizens; the style of the former is elevated, that of the latter humble; comedy begins sorrowfully and ends joyfully, tragedy begins joyfully and ends miserably and terribly. [2] For Dante, any poem written in an elevated and sublime style, beginning happily and ending in misery and terror, is a tragedy; his own great vision, written as it is in the vernacular, and beginning in hell and ending gloriously in paradise, he calls a comedy. [3]

It appears, therefore, that during the post-classic period and throughout the Middle Ages, comedy and tragedy were distinguished on any or all of the following grounds: —

i. The characters in tragedy are kings, princes, or great leaders; those in comedy, humble persons and private citizens.

ii. Tragedy deals with great and terrible actions; comedy with familiar and domestic actions.

iii. Tragedy begins happily and ends terribly; comedy begins rather turbulently and ends joyfully.

1 *Etymol.* xviii. 45 and 46.

2 Cloetta. p. 28, and p. 31 *sq.*

3 *Epist.* xi. 10. *Cf.* Gelli's Lectures on the Divine Comedy, ed. Negroni, 1887, i. 37 *sq.*

iv. The style and diction of tragedy are elevated and sublime; while those of comedy are humble and colloquial.

v. The subjects of tragedy are generally historical; those of comedy are always invented by the poet.

vi. Comedy deals largely with love and seduction; tragedy with exile and bloodshed.

This, then, was the tradition that shaped the un-Aristotelian conception of the distinctions between comedy and tragedy, which persisted throughout and even beyond the Renaissance. Giraldi Cintio has followed most of these traditional distinctions, but he is in closer accord with Aristotle[1] when he asserts that the tragic as well as the comic plot may be purely imaginary and invented by the poet.[2] He explains the traditional conception that the tragic fable should be historical, on the ground that as tragedy deals with the deeds of kings and illustrious men, it would not be probable that remarkable actions of such great personages should be left unrecorded in history, whereas the private events treated in comedy could hardly be known to all. Giraldi, however, asserts that it does not matter whether the tragic poet invents his story or not, so long as it follows the law of probability. The poet should choose an action that is probable and dignified, that does not need the intervention of a god in the unravelling of the plot, that does not occupy much more than the space of a day, and that can be represented on the stage in three or

1 *Poet.* ix. 5-9.

2 Giraldi Cintio, ii. 14.

four hours.[1] In respect to the dénouement of tragedy, it may be happy or unhappy, but in either case it must arouse pity and terror; and as for the classic notion that no deaths should be represented on the stage, Giraldi declares that those which are not excessively painful may be represented, for they are represented not for the sake of commiseration but of justice. The argument here centres about Aristotle's phrase *ἐν τῷ φανερῷ θάνατοι*,[2] but the common practice of classicism was based on Horace's express prohibition: —

"Ne pueros coram populo Medea trucidet."[3]

Giraldi gives it as a universal rule of the drama that nothing should be represented on the stage which could not with propriety be done in one's own house.[4]

Scaliger's treatment of the dramatic forms is particularly interesting because of its great influence on the neo-classical drama. He defines tragedy as an imitation of an illustrious event, ending unhappily, written in a grave and weighty style, and in verse.[5] Here he has discarded, or at least disregarded, the Aristotelian definition of tragedy, in favor of the traditional conception which had come down through the Middle Ages. Real tragedy, according to Scaliger, is entirely serious; and although there are a few happy endings in ancient tragedy, the unhappy ending is most proper to the

1 Giraldi Cintio, ii. 20.
2 *Poet.* xi. 6.
3 *Ars Poet.* 182-188.
4 Giraldi Cintio, ii. 119.
5 Scaliger, *Poet.* i. 6.

spirit of tragedy itself. *Mortes aut exilia* — these are the fit accompaniments of the tragic catastrophe. [1] The action begins tranquilly, but ends horribly; the characters are kings and princes, from cities, castles, and camps; the language is grave, polished, and entirely opposed to colloquial speech; the aspect of things is troubled, with terrors, menaces, exiles, and deaths on every hand. Taking as his model Seneca, whom he rates above all the Greeks in majesty, [2] he gives as the typical themes of tragedy "the mandates of kings, slaughters, despairs, executions, exiles, loss of parents, parricides, incests, conflagrations, battles, loss of sight, tears, shrieks, lamentations, burials, epitaphs, and funeral songs." [3] Tragedy is further distinguished from comedy on the ground that the former derives its argument and its chief characters from history, inventing merely the minor characters; while comedy invents its arguments and all its characters, and gives them names of their own. Scaliger distinguishes men, for the purposes of dramatic poetry, according to character and rank; [4] but it would seem that he regarded rank alone as the distinguishing mark between tragedy and comedy. Thus tragedy is made to differ from comedy in three things: in the rank of the characters, in the quality of the actions, and in their different endings; and as a result of these differences, in style also.

The definition of tragedy given by Minturno, in his treatise *De Poeta* (1559), is merely a paraphrase

1 Scaliger, i. 11; iii. 96.
2 *Ibid.* vi. 6.
3 *Ibid.* iii. 96.
4 *Ibid.* i. 13.

of Aristotle's. He conceives of tragedy as describing *casus heroum cuius sibi quisque fortunæ fuerit faber*, and it thus acts as a warning to men against pride of rank, insolence, avarice, lust, and similar passions. [1] It is grave and illustrious because its characters are illustrious; and no variety of persons or events should be introduced that are not in keeping with the calamitous ending. The language throughout must be grave and severe; and Minturno has expressed his censure in such matters by the phrase, *poema amatorio mollique sermone effœminat*, [2] a censure which would doubtless apply to a large portion of classic French tragedy.

In Castelvetro (1570) we find a far more complete theory of the drama than had been attempted by any of his predecessors. His work is by no means a model of what a commentary on Aristotle's *Poetics* should be. In the next century, Dacier, whose subservience to Aristotle was even greater than that of any of the Italians, accuses Castelvetro of lacking every quality necessary to a good interpreter of Aristotle. "He knew nothing," says Dacier, "of the theatre, or of character, or of the passions; he understood neither the reasons nor the method of Aristotle; and he sought rather to contradict Aristotle than to explain him." [3] The fact is that Castelvetro, despite considerable veneration for Aristotle's authority, often shows remark-

1 *De Poeta*, p. 43 *sq*.
2 *Ibid*. p. 173. *Cf*. Milton's phrase, "vain and amatorious poem."
3 Dacier, 1692, p. xvii.

able independence of thought; and so far from resting content, in his commentary, with the mere explanation of the details of the *Poetics*, he has attempted to deduce from it a more or less complete theory of poetic art. Accordingly, though diverging from many of the details, and still more from the spirit of the *Poetics*, he has, as it were, built up a dramatic system of his own, founded upon certain modifications and misconceptions of the Aristotelian canons. The fundamental idea of this system is quite modern; and it is especially interesting because it indicates that by this time the drama had become more than a mere academic exercise, and was actually regarded as intended primarily for representation on the stage. Castelvetro examines the physical conditions of stage representation, and on this bases the requirements of dramatic literature. The fact that the drama is intended for the stage, that it is to be acted, is at the bottom of his theory of tragedy, and it was to this notion, as will be seen later, that we are to attribute the origin of the unities of time and place.

But Castelvetro's method brings with it its own *reductio ad absurdum*. For after all, stage representation, while essential to the production of dramatic literature, can never circumscribe the poetic power or establish its conditions. The conditions of stage representation change, and must change, with the varying conditions of dramatic literature and the inventive faculty of poets, for truly great art makes, or at least fixes, its own conditions. Besides, it is with what is permanent and universal that the artist — the dramatic artist as well as the rest — is concerned; and it is the poetic, and not the dramaturgic, element that is permanent and universal. "The power of tragedy, we may be sure," says Aristotle, "is felt even apart from representation and actors;" [1] and again: "The plot [of a tragedy] ought to be so constructed that even without the aid of the eye any one who is told the incidents will thrill with horror and pity at the turn of events." [2]

But what, according to Castelvetro, are the conditions of stage representation? The theatre is a public place, in which a play is presented before a motley crowd, — *la moltitudine rozza*, — upon a circumscribed platform or stage, within a limited space of time. To this idea the whole of Castelvetro's dramatic system is conformed. In the first place, since the audience may be great in number, the theatre must be large, and yet the audience must be able to hear the play; accordingly, verse is added, not merely as a delightful accompaniment, but also in order that the actors may raise their voices without inconvenience and without loss of dignity. [3] In the second place, the audience is not a select gathering of choice spirits, but a motley crowd of people, drawn to the theatre for the purpose of pleasure or recreation; accordingly, abstruse themes, and in fact all technical discussions, must be eschewed by the playwright, who is thus limited, as we should say to-day, to the elemental

1 *Poet.* vi. 19. 2 *Poet.* xiv. 1.
3 Castelvetro, *Poetica,* p. 30.

passions and interests of man.[1] In the third place, the actors are required to move about on a raised and narrow platform; and this is the reason why deaths or deeds of violence, and many other things which cannot be acted on such a platform with convenience and dignity, should not be represented in the drama.[2] Furthermore, as will be seen later, it is on this conception of the circumscribed platform and the physical necessities of the audience and the actors, that Castelvetro bases his theory of the unities of time and place.

In distinguishing the different *genres*, Castelvetro openly differs with Aristotle. In the *Poetics*, Aristotle distinguishes men according as they are better than we are, or worse, or the same as we are; and from this difference the various species of poetry, tragic, comic, and epic, are derived. Castelvetro thinks this mode of distinction not only untrue, but even inconsistent with what Aristotle says later of tragedy. Goodness and badness are to be taken account of, according to Castelvetro, not to distinguish one form of poetry from another, but merely in the special case of tragedy, in so far as a moderate virtue, as Aristotle says, is best able to produce terror and pity. Poetry, as indeed Aristotle himself acknowledges, is not an imitation of character, or of goodness and badness, but of men acting; and the different kinds of poetry are distinguished, not by the goodness and badness, or the character, of the persons selected for imitation, but by their rank or condition alone. The great and all-pervading

1 Castelvetro, *Poetica*, pp. 22, 23.

2 *Ibid.* p. 57.

difference between royal and private persons is what distinguishes tragedy and epic poetry on the one hand from comedy and similar forms of poetry on the other. It is rank, then, and not intellect, character, action, — for these vary in men according to their condition, — that differentiates one poetic form from another; and the distinguishing mark of rank on the stage, and in literature generally, is the bearing of the characters, royal persons acting with propriety, and meaner persons with impropriety. [1] Castelvetro has here escaped one pitfall, only to fall into another; for while goodness and badness cannot, from any æsthetic standpoint, be made to distinguish the characters of tragedy from those of comedy, — leaving out of consideration here the question whether this was or was not the actual opinion of Aristotle, — it is no less improper to make mere outward rank or condition the distinguishing feature. Whether it be regarded as an interpretation of Aristotle or as a poetic theory by itself, Castelvetro's contention is, in either case, equally untenable.

II. *The Function of Tragedy*

No passage in Aristotle's *Poetics* has been subjected to more discussion, and certainly no passage has been more misunderstood, than that in which, at the close of his definition of tragedy, he states its peculiar function to be that of effecting through pity and fear the proper purgation

1 Castelvetro, *Poetica*, pp. 35, 36.

(κάθαρσις) of these emotions. The more probable of the explanations of this passage are, as Twining says, [1] reducible to two. The first of these gives to Aristotle's *katharsis* an ethical meaning, attributing the effect of the tragedy to its moral lesson and example. This interpretation was a literary tradition of centuries, and may be found in such diverse writers as Corneille and Lessing, Racine and Dryden, Dacier and Rapin. According to the second interpretation, the purgation of the emotions produced by tragedy is an emotional relief gained by the excitement of these emotions. Plato had insisted that the drama excites passions, such as pity and fear, which debase men's spirits; Aristotle in this passage answers that by the very exaltation of these emotions they are given a pleasurable outlet, and beyond this there is effected a purification of the emotions so relieved. That is, the emotions are clarified and purified by being passed through the medium of art, and by being, as Professor Butcher points out, ennobled by objects worthy of an ideal emotion. [2] This explanation gives no direct moral purpose or influence to the *katharsis*, for tragedy acts on the feelings and not on the will. While the ethical conception, of course, predominates in Italian criticism, as it does throughout Europe up to the very end of the eighteenth century, a number of Renaissance critics, among them Minturno and Speroni, even if they failed to elaborate the further æsthetic meaning of Aristotle's definition, at least perceived that Aristotle ascribed

1 Twining, ii. 3. 2 Butcher, ch. vi.

to tragedy an emotional and not an ethical purpose. It is unnecessary to give a detailed statement of the opinions of the various Italian critics on this point; but it is essential that the interpretations of the more important writers should be alluded to, since otherwise the Renaissance conception of the function of the drama could not be understood.

Giraldi Cintio points out that the aim of comedy and of tragedy is identical, viz. to conduce to virtue; but they reach this result in different ways; for comedy attains its end by means of pleasure and comic jests, while tragedy, whether it ends happily or unhappily, purges the mind of vice through the medium of misery and terror, and thus attains its moral end. [1] Elsewhere, [2] he affirms that the tragic poet condemns vicious actions, and by combining them with the terrible and the miserable makes us fear and hate them. In other words, men who are bad are placed in such pitiable and terrible positions that we fear to imitate their vices; and it is not a purgation of pity and fear, as Aristotle says, but an eradication of all vice and vicious desire that is effected by the tragic *katharsis*. Trissino, in the fifth section of his *Poetica* (1563), cites Aristotle's definition of tragedy; but makes no attempt to elucidate the doctrine of *katharsis*. His conception of the function of the drama is much the same as Giraldi's. It is the office of the tragic poet, through the medium of imitation, to praise and admire the good, while that of the comic poet is to mock and vituperate the bad; for tragedy,

1 Giraldi Cintio, ii. 12. 2 *Ibid.* i. 66 sq.

as Aristotle says, deals with the better sort of actions, and comedy with the worse.[1]

Robortelli (1548), however, ascribes a more æsthetic function to tragedy. By the representation of sad and atrocious deeds, tragedy produces terror and commiseration in the spectator's mind. The exercise of terror and commiseration purges the mind of these very passions; for the spectator, seeing things performed which are very similar to the actual facts of life, becomes accustomed to sorrow and pity, and these emotions are gradually diminished.[2] Moreover, by seeing the sufferings of others, men sorrow less at their own, recognizing such things as common to human nature. Robortelli's conception of the function of tragedy is, therefore, not an ethical one; the effect of tragedy is understood primarily as diminishing pity and fear in our minds by accustoming us to the sight of deeds that produce these emotions. A similar interpretation of the *katharsis* is given by Vettori (1560) and Castelvetro (1570).[3] The latter compares the process of purgation with the emotions which are excited by a pestilence. At first the infected populace is crazed by excitement, but gradually becomes accustomed to the sight of the disease, and the emotions of the people are thus tempered and allayed.

A somewhat different conception of *katharsis* is that of Maggi. According to him, we are to under-

1 Trissino, ii. 93 *sq.*

2 Robortelli, p. 52 *sq.*

3 Vettori, p. 56 *sq.*, and Castelvetro, *Poetica*, p. 117 *sq.*

stand by purgation the liberation through pity and fear of passions similar to these, but not pity and fear themselves; for Maggi cannot understand how tragedy, which induces pity and fear in the hearer, should at the same time remove these perturbations. [1] Moreover, pity and fear are useful emotions, while such passions as avarice, lust, anger, are certainly not. In another place, Maggi, relying on citations from Plato, Aristotle, and Alexander of Aphrodisias, explains the pleasure we receive from tragedy, by pointing out that we feel sorrow by reason of the human heart within us, which is carried out of itself by the sight of misery; while we feel pleasure because it is human and natural to feel pity. Pleasure and pain are thus fundamentally the same. [2] Varchi [3] is at one with Maggi in interpreting the *katharsis* as a purgation, not of pity and fear themselves, but of emotions similar to them.

For Scaliger (1561) the aim of tragedy, like that of all poetry, is a purely ethical one. It is not enough to move the spectators to admiration and dismay, as some critics say Æschylus does; it is also the poet's function to teach, to move, and to delight. The poet teaches character through actions, in order that we should embrace and imitate the good, and abstain from the bad. The joy

1 Maggi, p. 97 *sq*.

2 *Cf*. Shelley, *Defence of Poetry*, p. 35, "Tragedy delights by affording a shadow of that pleasure which exists in pain," etc.

3 *Lezzioni*, p. 660.

of evil men is turned in tragedy to bitterness, and the sorrow of good men to joy. [1] Scaliger is here following the extreme view of poetic justice which we have found expressed in so many of the Renaissance writers. In the last century, Dr. Johnson, in censuring Shakespeare for the tragic fate meted out to Cordelia and other blameless characters, showed himself an inheritor of this Renaissance tradition, just as we shall see that Lessing was in other matters. For Scaliger the moral aim of the drama is attained both indirectly, by the representation of wickedness ultimately punished and virtue ultimately rewarded, and more directly by the enunciation of moral precepts throughout the play. With the Senecan model before him, such precepts (*sententiœ*) became the very props of tragedy, — *sunt enim quasi columnœ aut pilœ quœdam universœ fabricœ illius*, — and so they remained in modern classical tragedy. Minturno points out that these *sententiœ* are to be used most in tragedy and least in epic poetry. [2]

Minturno also follows Scaliger in conceiving that the purpose of tragedy is to teach, to delight, and to move. It teaches by setting before us an example of the life and manners of superior men, who by reason of human error have fallen into extreme unhappiness. It delights us by the beauty of its verse, its diction, its song, and the like. Lastly, it moves us to wonder, by terrifying us and exciting our pity, thus purging our minds of such matters. This process of purgation is likened by Minturno

1 Scaliger, *Poet.* vii. i. 3; iii. 96. 2 *Arte Poetica*, p. 287.

to the method of a physician: "As a physician eradicates, by means of poisonous medicine, the perfervid poison of disease which affects the body, so tragedy purges the mind of its impetuous perturbations by the force of these emotions beautifully expressed in verse." [1]

According to this interpretation of the *katharsis*, tragedy is a mode of homœopathic treatment, effecting the cure of one emotion by means of a similar one; and we find Milton, in the preface to *Samson Agonistes*, explaining the *katharsis* in much the same manner: —

> "Tragedy, as it was anciently composed, hath been ever held the gravest, moralest, and most profitable of all other poems; therefore said by Aristotle to be of power, by raising pity and fear, or terror, to purge the mind of those and such like passions; that is, to temper and reduce them to just measure with a kind of delight, stirred up by reading or seeing those passions well imitated. Nor is nature wanting in her own effects to make good his assertion; for so in physic, things of melancholic hue and quality are used against melancholy, sour against sour, salt to remove salt humours."

This passage has been regarded by Twining, Bernays, and other modern scholars as a remarkable indication of Milton's scholarship and critical insight; [2] but after all, it need hardly be said, he was merely following the interpretation of the Italian commentators on the *Poetics*. Their writings he had studied and knew thoroughly, had imbibed all the critical ideas of the Italian Renaissance, and in the very preface from which we have just quoted,

1 *Arte Poetica*, p. 77.

2 Butcher, pp. 229, 230.

filled as it is with ideas that may be traced back to Italian sources, he acknowledges following "the ancients and Italians," as of great "authority and fame." Like Milton, Minturno conceived of tragedy as having an ethical aim; but both Milton and Minturno clearly perceived that by *katharsis* Aristotle had reference not to a moral, but to an emotional, effect.

One of the most interesting discussions on the meaning of the *katharsis* is to be found in a letter of Sperone Speroni [1] written in 1565. His explanation of the passage itself is quite an impossible one, if only on philological grounds; but his argument is very interesting and very modern. He points out that pity and fear may be conceived of as keeping the spirit of men in bondage, and hence it is proper that we should be purged of these emotions. But he insists that Aristotle cannot refer to the complete eradication of pity and fear — a conception which is Stoic rather than Peripatetic, for Aristotle does not require us to free ourselves from emotions, but to regulate them, since in themselves they are not bad.

III. *The Characters of Tragedy*

Aristotle's conception of the ideal tragic hero is based on the assumption that the function of tragedy is to produce the *katharsis*, or purgation, of pity and fear, — "pity being felt for a person who, if not wholly innocent, meets with suffering

1 *Opere*, v. 178.

beyond his deserts; fear being awakened when the sufferer is a man of like nature with ourselves." [1] From this it follows that if tragedy represents the fall of an entirely good man from prosperity to adversity, neither pity nor fear is produced, and the result merely shocks and repels us. If an entirely bad man is represented as undergoing a change from distress to prosperity, not only do we feel no pity and no fear, but even the sense of justice is left unsatisfied. If, on the contrary, such a man entirely bad falls from prosperity into adversity and distress, the moral sense is indeed satisfied, but without the tragic emotions of pity and fear. The ideal hero is therefore morally between the two extremes, neither eminently good nor entirely bad, though leaning to the side of goodness; and the misfortune which falls upon him is the result of some great flaw of character or fatal error of conduct. [2]

This conception of the tragic hero was the subject of considerable discussion in the Renaissance; in fact, the first instance in Italian criticism of the application of Aristotelian ideas to the theory of tragedy is perhaps to be found in the reference of Daniello (1536) to the tragic hero's fate. Daniello, however, understood Aristotle's meaning very incompletely, for he points out that tragedy, in order to imitate most perfectly the miserable and the terrible, should not introduce just and virtuous men fallen into vice and injustice through the adversity of fortune, for this is more wicked than it is miser-

1 Butcher, p. 280 *sq.*

2 *Poet.* xiii. 2, 3.

able and terrible, nor should evil men, on the contrary, be introduced as changed by prosperity into good and just men.[1] Here Daniello conceives of tragedy as representing the change of a man from vice to virtue, or from virtue to vice, through the medium of prosperity or misfortune. This is a curious misconception of Aristotle's meaning. Aristotle refers, not to the ethical effect of tragedy, but to the effect of the emotions of pity and terror upon the mind of the spectator, although of course he does not wish the catastrophe to shock the moral sense or the sense of justice.

Giraldi Cintio, some years after Daniello, follows Aristotle more closely in the conception of the tragic hero; and he affirms, moreover, that tragedy may end happily or unhappily so long as it inspires pity and terror. Now, Aristotle has expressly stated his disapprobation of the happy ending of tragedy, for in speaking of tragedies with a double thread and a double catastrophe, that is, tragedies in which the good are ultimately rewarded and the bad punished, he shows that such a conclusion is decidedly against the general tragic effect.[2] Scaliger's conception of the moral function of the tragic poet as rewarding virtue and punishing vice is therefore inconsistent with the Aristotelian conception; for, as Scaliger insists that every tragedy should end unhappily, it follows that only the good must survive and only the bad suffer. Another critic of this time, Capriano (1555), points out that the fatal ending of tragedy is due to the inability

1 Daniello, p. 38. 2 *Poet.* xiii. 7.

of certain illustrious men to conduct themselves with prudence; and this is more in keeping with Aristotle's true meaning. [1]

It has been seen that Aristotle regarded a perfectly good man as not fitted to be the ideal hero of tragedy. Minturno, however, asserts that tragedy is grave and illustrious because its characters are illustrious, and that therefore he can see no reason, despite Aristotle, why the lives of perfect men or Christian saints should not be represented on the stage, and why even the life of Christ would not be a fit subject for tragedy. [2] This is, indeed, Corneille's opinion, and in the *examen* of his *Polyeucte* he cites Minturno in justification of his own case. As regards the other characters of tragedy, Minturno states a curious distinction between characters fit for tragedy and those fit for comedy. [3] In the first place, he points out that no young girls, with the exception of female slaves, should appear in comedy, for the reason that the women of the people do not appear in public until marriage, and would be sullied by the company of the low characters of comedy, whereas the maidens of tragedy are princesses, accustomed to meet and converse with noblemen from girlhood. Secondly, married women are always represented in comedy as faithful, in tragedy as unfaithful to their husbands, for the reason that comedy concludes with friendship

1 *Della Vera Poetica,* cap. iii.

2 *De Poeta,* p. 182 *sq.*

3 *Arte Poetica,* p. 118 *sq.*; also in Scaliger and Giraldi Cintio.

and tranquillity, and unfaithful relations could never end happily, while the love depicted in tragedy serves to bring about the tragic ruin of great houses. Thirdly, in comedy old men are often represented as in love, but never in tragedy, for an amorous old man is conducive to laughter, which comedy aims at producing, but which would be wholly out of keeping with the gravity required in tragedy. These distinctions are of course deduced from the practice of the Latin drama — the tragedies of Seneca on the one hand, and the comedies of Plautus and Terence on the other.

In a certain passage of Aristotle's *Poetics* there is a formulation of the requirements of character-drawing in the drama. [1] In this passage Aristotle says that the characters must be good; that they must be drawn with propriety, that is, in keeping with the type to which they belong; that they must be true to life, something quite distinct either from goodness or propriety; and that the characters must be self-consistent. This passage gave rise to a curious conception of character in the Renaissance and throughout the period of classicism. According to this, the conception of *decorum*, it was insisted that every old man should have such and such characteristics, every young man certain others, and so on for the soldier, the merchant, the Florentine or Parisian, and the like. This fixed and formal mode of regarding character was connected with the distinction of rank as the fundamental difference between the characters of

1 *Poet.* xv. 1-5.

tragedy and comedy, and it was really founded on a passage in Horace's *Ars Poetica*, —

> "Ætatis cujusque notandi sunt tibi mores," [1]

and on the rhetorical descriptions of the various characteristics of men in the second book of Aristotle's *Rhetoric*.

The explanation of the Renaissance conception of *decorum* may start from either of two points of view. In the first place, it is to be noted that Horace, and after him the critics of the Renaissance, set about to transpose to the domain of poetry the tentative distinctions of character formulated by Aristotle, in the *Rhetoric*, simply for the purposes of rhetorical exposition. These distinctions, it must be repeated, were rhetorical and not æsthetic, and they are therefore not alluded to by Aristotle in the *Poetics*. The result of the attempt to transpose them to the domain of poetry led to a hardening and crystallization of character in the classic drama. But the æsthetic misconception implied by such an attempt is only too obvious. In such a system poetry is held accountable, not to the ideal truth of human life, but to certain arbitrary, or at best merely empirical, formulæ of rhetorical theory. The Renaissance was in this merely doing for character what was being done for all the other elements of art. Every such element, when once discriminated and definitely formulated, became fixed as a necessary and inviolable substitute for the reality which had thus been analyzed.

1 *Ars Poet.* 154 sq.

But we may look at the principle of *decorum* from another point of view. A much deeper question — the question of social distinctions — is here involved. The observance of *decorum* necessitated the maintenance of the social distinctions which formed the basis of Renaissance life and of Renaissance literature. It was this same tendency which caused the tragedy of classicism to exclude all but characters of the highest rank. Speaking of narrative poetry, Muzio (1551), while allowing kings to mingle with the masses, considers it absolutely improper for one of the people, even for a moment, to assume the sceptre. [1] Accordingly, men as distinguished by the accidents of rank, profession, country, and not as distinguished by that only which art should take cognizance of, character, became the subjects of the literature of classicism; and in so far as this is true, that literature loses something of the profundity and the universality of the highest art.

This element of *decorum* is to be found in all the critics of the Renaissance from the time of Vida [2] and Daniello. [3] So essential became the observance of *decorum* that Muzio and Capriano both considered it the most serious charge to be made against Homer, that he was not always observant of it. Capriano, comparing Virgil with Homer, asserts that the Latin poet surpasses the Greek in eloquence, in dignity, in grandeur of style, but beyond everything in *decorum*. [4] The seeming vulgarity

1 Muzio, p. 80.
2 Pope, i. 165.
3 *Poetica*, p. 36 sq.
4 Capriano, *op. cit.*, cap. v.

of some of Homer's similes, and even of the actions of some of his characters, appeared to the Renaissance a most serious blemish; and it was this that led Scaliger to rate Homer not only below Virgil, but even below Musæus. In Minturno and Scaliger we find every detail of character minutely analyzed. The poet is told how young men and old men should act, should talk, and should dress; and no deviations from these fixed formulæ were allowed under any circumstances. As a result of this, even when the poet liberated himself from these conceptions, and aimed at depicting character in its true sense, we find character, but never the development of character, portrayed in the neo-classic drama. The character was fixed from the beginning of the play to the end; and it is here that we may find the origin of Ben Jonson's conception of "humours." In one of Salviati's lectures, *Del Trattato della Poetica,* [1] Salviati defines a humour as "a peculiar quality of nature according to which every one is inclined to some special thing more than to any other." This would apply very distinctly to the sense in which the Elizabethans used the word. Thus Jonson himself, in the Induction of *Every Man out of his Humour,* after expounding the medical notion of a humour, says: —

> "It may, by metaphor, apply itself
> Unto the general disposition:
> As when some one peculiar quality
> Doth so possess a man, that it doth draw
> All his effects, his spirits, and his powers,

1 Cod. Magliabechiano, vii. 7, 715.

In their conflictions, all to run one way,
This may be truly said to be a humour."

The origin of the term "humour," in Jonson's sense, has never been carefully studied. Jonson's editors speak of it as peculiar to the English language, and as first used in this sense about Jonson's period. It is not our purpose to go further into this question; but Salviati's definition is close enough to Jonson's to indicate that the origin of this term, as of all other critical terms and critical ideas throughout sixteenth-century Europe, must be looked for in the æsthetic literature of Italy. [1]

IV. *The Dramatic Unities*

In his definition of tragedy Aristotle says that the play must be complete or perfect, that is, it must have unity. By unity of plot he does not mean merely the unity given by a single hero, for, as he says, "infinitely various are the incidents in one man's life which cannot be reduced to unity; and so, too, there are many actions of one man out of which we cannot make one action. Hence the error, as it appears, of all poets who have composed a Heracleid, a Theseid, or other poems of the kind. They imagine that as Heracles was one man, the story of Heracles ought also to be a unity." [2] This is Aristotle's statement of the unity of action. But

1 Another expression of Jonson's, " small Latin and less Greek," may perhaps be traced to Minturno's "poco del Latino e pochissimo del Greco," *Arts Poetica*, p. 158.

2 *Poet.* viii. 1-4.

what is the origin of the two other unities, — the unities of time and place? There is in the *Poetics* but a single reference to the time-limit of the tragic action and none whatsoever to the so-called unity of place. Aristotle says that the action of tragedy and that of epic poetry differ in length, "for tragedy endeavors, so far as possible, to confine itself to a single revolution of the sun, or but slightly to exceed this limit; whereas the epic action has no limits of time." [1] This passage is the incidental statement of an historical fact; it is merely a tentative deduction from the usual practice of Greek tragedy, and Aristotle never conceived of it as an inviolable law of the drama. Of the three unities which play so prominent a part in modern classical drama, the unity of action was the main, and, in fact, the only unity which Aristotle knew or insisted on. But from his incidental reference to the general time-limits of Greek tragedy, the Renaissance formulated the unity of time, and deduced from it also the unity of place, to which there is absolutely no reference either in Aristotle or in any other ancient writer whatever. It is to the Italians of the Renaissance, and not to the French critics of the seventeenth century, that the world owes the formulation of the three unities. The attention of scholars was first called to this fact about twenty years ago, by the brochure of a Swiss scholar, H. Breitinger, on the unities of Aristotle before Corneille's *Cid*; but the gradual development and formulation of the three unities have

1 *Poet.* v. 4.

never been systematically worked out. We shall endeavor here to trace their history during the sixteenth century, and to explain the processes by which they developed.

The first reference in modern literature to the doctrine of the unity of time is to be found in Giraldi Cintio's *Discorso sulle Comedie e sulle Tragedie*. He says that comedy and tragedy agree, among other things, in the limitation of the action to one day or but little more; [1] and he has thus for the first time converted Aristotle's statement of an historical fact into a dramatic law. Moreover, he has changed Aristotle's phrase, that tragedy limits itself "to a single revolution of the sun," into the more definite expression of "a single day." He points out that Euripides, in the *Heraclidœ*, on account of the long distance between the places in the action, had been unable to limit the action to one day. Now, as Aristotle must have known many of the best Greek dramas which are now lost, it was probably in keeping with the practice of such dramas that their actions were not strictly confined within the limits of one day. Aristotle, therefore, intentionally allowed the drama a slightly longer space of time than a single day. The unity of time, accordingly, becomes a part of the theory of the drama between 1540 and 1545, but it was not until almost exactly a century later that it became an invariable rule of the dramatic literature of France and of the world.

In Robortelli (1548) we find Aristotle's phrase,

1 Giraldi Cintio, ii. 10 *sq*.

"a single revolution of the sun," restricted to the artificial day of twelve hours; for as tragedy can contain only one single and continuous action, and as people are accustomed to sleep in the night, it follows that the tragic action cannot be continued beyond one artificial day. This holds good of comedy as well as tragedy, for the length of the fable in each is the same. [1] Segni (1549) differs from Robortelli, however, in regarding a single revolution of the sun as referring not to the artificial day of twelve hours, but to the natural day of twenty-four hours, because various matters treated in tragedy, and even in comedy, are such as are more likely to happen in the night (adulteries, murders, and the like); and if it be said that night is naturally the time for repose, Segni answers that unjust people act contrary to the laws of nature. [2] It was about this time, then, that there commenced the historic controversy as to what Aristotle meant by limiting tragedy to one day; and three-quarters of a century later, in 1623, Beni could cite thirteen different opinions of scholars on this question.

Trissino, in his *Poetica* (1563), paraphrases as follows the passage in Aristotle which refers to the unity of time: "They also differ in length, for tragedy terminates in one day, that is, one period of the sun, or but little more, while there is no time determined for epic poetry, as indeed was the custom with tragedy and comedy at their be-

1 Robortelli, pp. 50, 275, and appendix, p. 45. *Cf.* Luisino's Commentary on Horace's *Ars Poetica*, 1554, p. 40.

2 B. Segni, p. 170 v.

ginning, and is even to-day among ignorant poets." [1] Here for the first time, as a French critic remarks, the observance of the unity of time is made a distinction between the learned and the ignorant poet. [2] It is evident that Trissino conceives of the unity of time as an artistic principle which has helped to save dramatic poetry from the formlessness and chaotic condition of the mediæval drama. So that the unity of time became not only a dramatic law, but one the observation of which distinguished the dramatic artist from the mere ignorant compiler of popular plays.

There is in none of the writers we have mentioned so far any reference to the unity of place, for the simple reason that there is no allusion to such a requirement for the drama in Aristotle's *Poetics*. Maggi's discussion of the unity of time, in his commentary on the *Poetics* (1550), is of particular interest as preparing the way for the third unity. Maggi attempts to explain logically the reason for the unity of time. [3] Why should tragedy be limited as to time, and not epic poetry? According to him, this difference is to be explained by the fact that the drama is represented on the stage before our eyes, and if we should see the actions of a whole month performed in about the time it takes to perform the play, that is, two or three hours, the performance would be absolutely incredible. For example, says Maggi, if in a tragedy we should send a messenger to Egypt, and he would return in an hour, would not the spectator

1 Trissino, ii. 95.

2 Brunetière, i. 69.

3 Maggi, p. 94.

regard this as ridiculous? In the epic, on the contrary, we do not see the actions performed, and so do not feel the need of limiting them to any particular time. Now, it is to be noted here that this limitation of time is based on the idea of representation. The duration of the action of the drama itself must fairly coincide with the duration of its representation on the stage. This is the principle which led to the acceptance of the unity of place, and upon which it is based. Limit the time of the action to the time of representation, and it follows that the place of the action must be limited to the place of representation. Such a limitation is of course a piece of realism wholly out of keeping with the true dramatic illusion; but it was almost exclusively in the drama that classicism tended toward a minuter realism than could be justified by the Aristotelian canons. In Maggi the beginnings of the unity of place are evident, inasmuch as he finds that the requirements of the representation do not permit a messenger or any character in the drama to be sent very far from the place where the action is being performed. The closer action and representation coincide, the clearer becomes the necessity of a limitation in place as well as in time; and it was on this principle that Scaliger and Castelvetro, somewhat later, formulated the three unities.

There is, indeed, in Scaliger (1561) no direct statement of the unity of time; but the reference to it is nevertheless unmistakable. First of all, Scaliger requires that the events be so arranged and disposed that they approach nearest to actual truth (*ut quam proxime accedant ad veritatem*). [1] This is equivalent to saying that the duration of the action, its place, its mode of procedure, must correspond more or less exactly with the representation itself. The dramatic poet must aim, beyond all things, at reproducing the actual conditions of life. The *verisimile*, the *vraisemblable*, in the etymological sense of these words, must be the final criterion of dramatic composition. It is not sufficient that the spectator should be satisfied with the action as typical of similar actions in life. An absolutely perfect illusion must prevail; the spectator must be moved by the actions of the play exactly as if they were those of real life.

This notion of the *verisimile*, and of its effect of perfect illusion on the spectator's mind, prevailed throughout the period of classicism, and was vigorously defended by no less a critic than Voltaire himself. Accordingly, as Maggi first pointed out, if the playwright, in the few hours it takes to represent the whole play, requires one of his characters to perform an action that cannot be done in less than a month, this impression of actual truth and perfect illusion will not be left on the spectator's mind. "Therefore," says Scaliger, "those battles and assaults which take place about Thebes in the space of two hours do not please me; no sensible poet should make any one move from Delphi to Thebes, or from Thebes to Athens, in a mo-

1 Scaliger, iii. 96. So Robortelli, p. 53, speaks of tragedy as representing things *quæ multum accedunt ad veritatem ipsam*.

ment's time. Agamemnon is buried by Æschylus after being killed, and Lichas is hurled into the sea by Hercules; but this cannot be represented without violence to truth. Accordingly, the poet should choose the briefest possible argument, and should enliven it by means of episodes and details.... Since the whole play is represented on the stage in six or eight hours, it is not in accordance with the exact appearance of truth (*haud verisimile est*) that within that brief space of time a tempest should arise and a shipwreck occur, out of sight of land."

The observance of the unity of time could not be demanded in clearer or more forcible terms than this. But it is a mistake to construe this passage into a statement of the unity of place. [1] When Scaliger says that the poet should not move any one of the characters from Delphi to Thebes, or from Thebes to Athens, in a moment's time, he is referring to the exigencies, not of place, but of time. In this, as in many other things, he is merely following Maggi, who, as we have seen, says that it is ridiculous for a dramatist to have a messenger go to Egypt with a message and return in an hour. The characters, according to Scaliger, should not move from Delphi to Thebes in a moment, not because the action need necessarily occur in one single place, but because the characters cannot with any appearance of truth go a great distance in a short space of time. This is an approach to the unity of place, and had Scaliger followed his

1 *E.g.* Lintilhac, *De Scal. Poet.* p. 32.

contention to its logical conclusion, he must certainly have formulated the three unities. But by requiring the action to be disposed with the greatest possible approach to the actual truth, or, in other words, by insisting that the action must coincide with the representation, Scaliger helped more than any of his predecessors to the final recognition of the unity of place.

In Minturno [1] and in Vettori [2] we find a tendency to restrict the duration of the epic as well as the tragic action. It has been seen that Aristotle distinctly says that while the action of tragedy generally endeavors to confine itself within a period of about one day, that of epic poetry has no determined time. Minturno, however, alludes to the unity of time in the following words: "Whoever examines well the works of the most esteemed ancient writers, will find that the action represented on the stage is terminated in one day, or does not pass beyond the space of two days; while the epic has a longer period of time, except that its action cannot exceed one year in duration." [3] This limitation Minturno deduces from the practice of Homer and Virgil.[4] The action of the *Iliad* begins in the tenth year of the Trojan war, and lasts one year; the action of the *Æneid* begins in the seventh year after the departure of Æneas from Troy, and also lasts one year.

Castelvetro, however, was the first theorist to formulate the unity of place, and thus to give the

1 *De Poeta*, pp. 185, 281.
2 Vettori, p. 250.
3 *Arte Poet.* pp. 71, 117.
4 *Ibid.* p. 12.

three unities their final form. We have seen that Castelvetro's theory of the drama was based entirely upon the notion of stage representation. All the essentials of dramatic literature are thus fixed by the exigencies of the stage. The stage is a circumscribed space, and the play must be performed upon it within a period of time limited by the physical necessities of the spectators. It is from these two facts that Castelvetro deduces the unities of time and place. While asserting that Aristotle held it as *cosa fermissima e verissima* that the tragic action cannot exceed the length of an artificial day of twelve hours, he does not think that Aristotle himself understood the real reason of this limitation. [1] In the seventh chapter of the *Poetics* Aristotle says that the length of the plot is limited by the possibility of its being carried in the memory of the spectator conveniently at one time. But this, it is urged, would restrict the epic as well as the tragic fable to one day. The difference between epic and dramatic poetry in this respect is to be found in the essential difference between the conditions of narrative and scenic poetry. [2] Narrative poetry can in a short time narrate things that happen in many days or months or even years; but scenic poetry, which spends as many hours in representing things as it actually takes to do them in life, does quite otherwise. In epic poetry words can present to our intellect things distant in space and time; but in dramatic poetry the whole action occurs before our eyes, and is accordingly limited to what we can

1 Castelvetro, *Poetica*, pp. 157, 170. 2 *Ibid*. pp. 57, 109.

actually see with our own senses, that is, to that brief duration of time and to that small amount of space in which the actors are occupied in acting, and not any other time or place. But as the restricted place is the stage, so the restricted time is that in which the spectators can at their ease remain sitting through a continuous performance; and this time, on account of the physical necessities of the spectators, such as eating, drinking, and sleeping, cannot well go beyond the duration of one revolution of the sun. So that not only is the unity of time an essential dramatic requirement, but it is in fact impossible for the dramatist to do otherwise even should he desire to do so — a conclusion which is of course the *reductio ad absurdum* of the whole argument.

In another place Castelvetro more briefly formulates the law of the unities in the definitive form in which it was to remain throughout the period of classicism: "La mutatione tragica non può tirar con esso seco se non una giornata e un luogo." [1] The unities of time and place are for Castelvetro so very important that the unity of action, which is for Aristotle the only essential of the drama, is entirely subordinated to them. In fact, Castelvetro specifically says that the unity of action is not essential to the drama, but is merely made expedient by the requirements of time and place. "In comedy and tragedy," he says, "there is usually one action, not because the fable is unfitted to contain more than one action, but because

1 Castelvetro, *Poetica*, p. 534. *Cf.* Boileau, *Art Poét.* iii. 45.

the restricted space in which the action is represented, and the limited time, twelve hours at the very most, do not permit of a multitude of actions." [1] In a similar manner Castelvetro applies the law of the unities to epic poetry. Although the epic action can be accomplished in many places and at diverse times, yet as it is more commendable and pleasurable to have a single action, so it is better for the action to confine itself to a short time and to but few places. In other words, the more the epic attempts to restrict itself to the unities of place and time, the better, according to Castelvetro, it will be. [2] Moreover, Castelvetro was not merely the first one to formulate the unities in their definitive form, but he was also the first to insist upon them as inviolable laws of the drama; and he refers to them over and over again in the pages of his commentary on the *Poetics*. [3]

This then is the origin of the unities. Our discussion must have made it clear how little they deserve the traditional title of Aristotelian unities, or as a recent critic with equal inaccuracy calls them, the Scaligerian unities (*unités scaligériennes*). [4] Nor were they, as we have seen, first formulated in France, though this was the opinion of the seventeenth and eighteenth centuries. Thus Dryden says that "the unity of place, however it might be

1 Castelvetro, *Poetica*, p. 179.

2 *Ibid.* pp. 534, 535.

3 Other allusions to the unities, besides those already mentioned, will be found in Castelvetro, *Poetica*, pp. 163-165, 168-171, 191, 397, 501, 527, 531-536, 692, 697, etc.

4 Lintilhac, in the *Nouvelle Revue*, lxiv. 541.

practised by the ancients, was never one of their rules: we neither find it in Aristotle, Horace, or any who have written of it, till in our age the French poets first made it a precept of the stage."[1] It may be said, therefore, that just as the unity of action is *par excellence* the Aristotelian unity, so the unities of time and place are beyond a doubt the Italian unities. They enter the critical literature of Europe from the time of Castelvetro, and may almost be said to be the last contributions of Italy to literary criticism. Two years after their formulation by Castelvetro they were introduced into France, and a dozen years after this formulation, into England. It was not until 1636, however, that they became fixed in modern dramatic literature, as a result of the *Cid* controversy. This is approximately a hundred years after the first mention of the unity of time in Italian criticism.

V. *Comedy*

The treatment of comedy in the literary criticism of this period is entirely confined to a discussion and elaboration of the little that Aristotle says on the subject of comedy in the *Poetics*. Aristotle, it will be remembered, had distinguished tragedy from comedy in that the former deals with the nobler, the latter with the baser, sort of actions. Comedy is an imitation of characters of a lower type than those of tragedy, — characters of a lower type indeed, but not in the full sense of the word bad.

1 *Essay of Dramatic Poesy*, p. 31.

"The ludicrous is merely a subdivision of the ugly. It may be defined as a defect or ugliness which is not painful or destructive. Thus, for example, the comic mask is ugly and distorted, but does not cause pain." [1] From these few hints the Italian theorists constructed a body of comic doctrine. There is, however, in the critical literature of this period no attempt to explain the theory of the indigenous Italian comedy, the *commedia dell' arte*. The classical comedies of Plautus and Terence were the models, and Aristotle's *Poetics* the guide, of all the discussions on comedy during the Renaissance. The distinction between the characters of comedy and tragedy has already been explained in sufficient detail. All that remains to be done in treating of comedy is to indicate as briefly as possible such definitions of it as were formulated by the Renaissance, and the special function which the Renaissance understood comedy to possess.

According to Trissino (1563), the comic poet deals only with base things, and for the single purpose of chastising them. As tragedy attains its moral end through the medium of pity and fear, comedy does so by means of the chastisement and vituperation of things that are base and evil. [2] The comic poet, however, is not to deal with all sorts of vices, but only such as give rise to ridicule, that is, the jocose actions of humble and unknown persons. Laughter proceeds from a certain delight or pleasure arising from the sight of objects of ugliness.

1 *Poet.* v.1. *Cf. Rhet.* iii. 18.
2 Trissino, ii. 120. *Cf.* Butcher, p. 203 *sq.*

We do not laugh at a beautiful woman, a gorgeous jewel, or beautiful music; but a distortion or deformity, such as a silly speech, an ugly face, or a clumsy movement, makes us laugh. We do not laugh at the benefits of others; the finder of a purse, for example, arouses not laughter but envy. But we do laugh at some one who has fallen into the mud, because, as Lucretius says, it is sweet to find in others some evil not to be found in ourselves. Yet great evils, so far from causing us to laugh, arouse pity and fear, because we are apprehensive lest such things should happen to us. Hence we may conclude that a slight evil which is neither sad nor destructive, and which we perceive in others but do not believe to be in ourselves, is the primary cause of the ludicrous. [1] In Maggi's treatise, *De Ridiculis*, appended to his commentary on the *Poetics*, the Aristotelian conception of the ridiculous is accepted, with the addition of the element of *admiratio*. Maggi insists on the idea of suddenness or novelty; for we do not laugh at painless ugliness if it be very familiar or long continued. [2]

According to Robortelli (1548), comedy, like all other forms of poetry, imitates the manners and actions of men, and aims at producing laughter and

1 Trissino, ii. 127-130. Trissino seems to follow Cicero, *De Orat.* ii. 58 *sq.* It is to these Italian discussions of the ludicrous that the theory of laughter formulated by Hobbes, and after him by Addison, owes its origin. For Renaissance discussions of wit and humor before the introduction of Aristotle's *Poetics*, *cf.* the third and fourth books of Pontano's *De Sermone*, and the second book of Castiglione's *Cortigiano*.

2 Maggi, p. 307. *Cf.* Hobbes, *Human Nature*, 1650, ix. 13.

light-heartedness. But what produces laughter? The evil and obscene merely disgust good men; the sad and miserable cause pity and fear. The basis of laughter is therefore to be found in what is only slightly mean or ugly (*subturpiculum*). The object of comedy, according to the consensus of Renaissance opinion, is therefore to produce laughter for the purpose of rendering the minor vices ridiculous. Muzio (1551) indeed complains, as both Sidney and Ben Jonson do later, that the comic writers of his day were more intent on producing laughter than on depicting character or manners: —

"Intenta al riso
Più ch' a i costumi."

But Minturno points out that comedy is not to be contemned because it excites laughter; for by comic hilarity the spectators are kept from becoming buffoons themselves, and by the ridiculous light in which amours are placed, are made to avoid such things in future. Comedy is the best corrective of men's morals; it is indeed what Cicero calls it, *imitatio vitæ, speculum consuetudinis, imago veritatis*. This phrase, ascribed by Donatus to Cicero, runs through all the dramatic discussions of the Renaissance,[1] and finds its echo in a famous passage in *Hamlet*. Cervantes cites the phrase in *Don Quixote*; [2] and Il Lasca, in the prologue to *L'Arzigoglio*, berates the comic writers of his day after this fashion: "They take no account of the absurdities, the contradictions, the inequalities, and

1 *Cf.* B. Tasso, ii. 515; Robortelli, p. 2; etc.
2 *Don Quix.* iv. 21.

the discrepancies of their pieces; for they do not seem to know that comedy should be truth's image, the ensample of manners, and the mirror of life."

This is exactly what Shakespeare is contending for when he makes Hamlet caution the players not to "o'erstep the modesty of nature; for anything so overdone is from the purpose of playing, whose end, both at the first and now, was and is, to hold as 'twere the mirror up to nature; to show virtue her own feature, scorn her own image, and the very age and body of the time his form and pressure." [1]

The high importance which Scaliger (1561) gives to comedy, and in fact to satiric and didactic poetry in general, is one of many indications of the incipient formation of neo-classical ideals during the Renaissance. He regards as absurd the statement which he conceives Horace to have made, that comedy is not really poetry; on the contrary, it is the true form of poetry, and the first and highest of all, for its matter is entirely invented by the poet. [2] He defines comedy as a dramatic poem filled with intrigue (*negotiosum*), written in popular style, and ending happily. [3] The characters in comedy are chiefly old men, slaves, courtesans, all in humble station or from small villages. The action begins rather turbulently, but ends happily, and the

1 *Hamlet*, iii. 2

2 Scaliger, *Poet.* i. 2. Castiglione, in the second book of the *Cortigiano*, says that the comic writer, more than any other, expresses the true image of human life.

3 *Poet.* i. 5.

style is neither high nor low. The typical themes of comedy are "sports, banquets, nuptials, drunken carousals, the crafty wiles of slaves, and the deception of old men." [1]

The theory of comedy in sixteenth-century Italy was entirely classical, and the practice of the time agrees with its theory. There are indeed to be heard occasional notes of dissatisfaction and revolt, especially in the prologues of popular plays. Il Lasca, in the prologue to the *Strega*, defiantly protests against the inviolable authority of Aristotle and Horace, and in the prologue to his *Gelosia* reserves the right to copy the manners of his own time, and not those of Plautus and Terence. Cecchi, Aretino, Gelli, and other comic writers give expression to similar sentiments. [2] But on the whole these protests availed nothing. The authors of comedy, and more especially the literary critics, were guided by classical practice and classical theory. Dramatic forms like the improvised *commedia dell' arte* had marked influence on the practice of European comedy in general, especially in France, but left no traces of their influence on the literary criticism of the Italian Renaissance.

1 *Poet.* iii. 96.

2 Symonds, *Ren. in Italy*, v. 124 *sq.*, 533 *sq.* For Castelvetro's theory of comedy, see A. Fusco, *La Poetica di Lodovico Castelvetro*, Naples, 1904, p. 228 *sq.* Ben Jonson derived his theory of laughter in comedy from Daniel Heinsius; *cf.* my article in *Modern Philology*, 1905, ii. 451 *sq.*

CHAPTER IV

THE THEORY OF EPIC POETRY

Epic poetry was held in the highest esteem during the Renaissance and indeed throughout the period of classicism. It was regarded by Vida as the highest form of poetry, [1] and a century later, despite the success of tragedy in France, Rapin still held the same opinion. [2] The reverence for the epic throughout the Renaissance may be ascribed in part to the mediæval veneration of Virgil as a poet, and his popular apotheosis as prophet and magician, and also in part to the decay into which dramatic literature had fallen during the Middle Ages in the hands of the wandering players, the *histriones* and the *vagantes*. Aristotle [3] indeed had regarded tragedy as the highest form of poetry; and as a result, the traditional reverence for Virgil and Homer, and the Renaissance subservience to Aristotle, were distinctly at variance. Trissino (1561) paraphrases Aristotle's argument in favor of tragedy, but points out, notwithstanding this, that the whole world is unanimous in considering Virgil and Homer greater than any tragic poet before or after them. [4] Placed in

1 Pope, i. 133.

2 Rapin, 1674, ii. 2.

3 *Poet.* xxvi.

4 Trissino, ii. 118 *sq.*

this quandary, he concludes by leaving the reader to judge for himself whether epic or tragedy be the nobler form.

I. *The Theory of the Epic Poem*

Vida's *Ars Poetica*, written before 1520, although no edition prior to that of 1527 is extant, is the earliest example in modern times of that class of critical poems to which belong Horace's *Ars Poetica*, Boileau's *Art* Poétique, and Pope's *Essay on Criticism.* Vida's poem is entirely based on that of Horace; but he substitutes epic for Horace's dramatic studies, and employs the *Æneid* as the model of an epic poem. The incompleteness of the treatment accorded to epic poetry in Aristotle's *Poetics* led the Renaissance to deduce the laws of heroic poetry and of poetic artifice in general from the practice of Virgil; and it is to this point of view that the critical works on the *Æneid* by Regolo (1563), Maranta (1564), and Toscanella (1566) owe their origin. The obvious and even accidental qualities of Virgil's poem are enunciated by Vida as fundamental laws of epic poetry. The precepts thus given are purely rhetorical and pedagogic in character, and deal almost exclusively with questions of poetic invention, disposition, polish, and style. Beyond this Vida does not attempt to go. There is in his poem no definition of the epic, no theory of its function, no analysis of the essentials of narrative structure. In fact, no theory of poetry in any real sense is to be found in Vida's treatise.

Daniello (1536) deals only very cursorily with epic poetry, but his definition of it strikes the keynote of the Renaissance conception. Heroic poetry is for him an imitation of the illustrious deeds of emperors and other men magnanimous and valorous in arms,[1] — a conception that goes back to Horace's

> "Res gestae regumque ducumque et tristia bella."[2]

Trissino (1563) first introduced the Aristotelian theory of the epic into modern literary criticism; and the sixth section of his *Poetica* is given up almost exclusively to the treatment of heroic poetry. The epic agrees with tragedy in dealing with illustrious men and illustrious actions. Like tragedy it must have a single action, but it differs from tragedy in not having the time of the action limited or determined. While unity of action is essential to the epic, and is indeed what distinguishes it from narrative poems that are not really epics, the Renaissance conceived of vastness of design and largeness of detail as necessary to the grandiose character of the epic poem.[3] Thus Muzio says: —

> "Il poema sovrano è una pittura
> De l' universo, e però in sè comprende
> Ogni stilo, ogni forma, ogni ritratto."

Trissino regards *versi sciolti* as the proper metre for an heroic poem, since the stanzaic form impedes the continuity of the narrative. In this point he finds fault with Boccaccio, Boiardo, and Ariosto, whose romantic poems, moreover, he does not regard as epics, because they do not obey Aristotle's invio-

1 Daniello, p. 34. 2 *Ars Poet.* 73. 3 Trissino, ii. 112 *sq.*

lable law of the single action. He also finds fault with the romantic poets for describing the improbable, since Aristotle expressly prefers an impossible probability to an improbable possibility.

Minturno's definition of epic poetry is merely a modification or paraphrase of Aristotle's definition of tragedy. Epic poetry is an imitation of a grave and noble deed, perfect, complete, and of proper magnitude, with embellished language, but without music or dancing; at times simply narrating and at other times introducing persons in words and actions; in order that, through pity and fear of the things imitated, such passions may be purged from the mind with both pleasure and profit. [1] Here Minturno, like Giraldi Cintio, ascribes to epic poetry the same purgation of pity and fear effected by tragedy. Epic poetry he rates above tragedy, since the epic poet, more than any other, arouses that admiration of great heroes which it is the peculiar function of the poet to excite, and therefore attains the end of poetry more completely than any other poet. This, however, is true only in the highest form of narrative poetry; for Minturno distinguishes three classes of narrative poets, the lowest, or *bucolici*, the mediocre, or *epici*, who have nothing beyond verse, and the highest, or *heroici*, who imitate the life of a single hero in noble verse. [2] Minturno insists fundamentally on the unity of the epic action; and directly against Aristotle's statement, as we have seen, he restricts the duration of the action to one year. The license and prolixity

1 *Arte Poetica*, p. 9.

2 *De Poeta*, pp. 105, 106.

of the *romanzi* led the defenders of the classical epic to this extreme of rigid circumspection. According to Scaliger, the epic, which is the norm by which all other poems may be judged and the chief of all poems, describes *heroum genus, vita, gesta.* [1] This is the Horatian conception of the epic, and there is in Scaliger little or no trace of the Aristotelian doctrine. He also follows Horace closely in forbidding the narrative poet to begin his poem from the very beginning of his story (*ab ovo*), and in various other details.

Castelvetro (1570) differs from Aristotle in regard to the unity of the epic fable, on the ground that poetry is merely imaginative history, and can therefore do anything that history can do. Poetry follows the footsteps of history, differing merely in that history narrates what has happened, while poetry narrates what has never happened but yet may possibly happen; and therefore, since history recounts the whole life of a single hero, without regard to its unity, there is no reason why poetry should not do likewise. The epic may in fact deal with many actions of one person, one action of a whole race, or many actions of many people; it need not necessarily deal with one action of one person, as Aristotle enjoins, but if it does so it is simply to show the ingenuity and excellence of the poet. [2]

1 *Poet.* iii. 95.
2 Castelvetro, *Poetica*, p. 178 *sq*.

II. *Epic and Romance*

This discussion of epic unity leads to one of the most important critical questions of the sixteenth century, — the question of the unity of romance. Ariosto's *Orlando Furioso* and Boiardo's *Orlando Innamorato* were written before the Aristotelian canons had become a part of the critical literature of Italy. When it became clear that these poems diverged from the fundamental requirements of the epic as expounded in the *Poetics*, Trissino set out to compose an heroic poem which would be in perfect accord with the precepts of Aristotle. His *Italia Liberata*, which was completed by 1548, was the result of twenty years of study, and it is the first modern epic in the strict Aristotelian sense. With Aristotle as his guide, and Homer as his model, he had studiously and mechanically constructed an epic of a single action; and in the dedication of his poem to the Emperor Charles V. he charges all poems which violate this primary law of the single action with being merely bastard forms. The *romanzi*, and among them the *Orlando Furioso*, in seemingly disregarding this fundamental requirement, came under Trissino's censure; and this started a controversy which was not to end until the commencement of the next century, and in a certain sense may be said to remain undecided even to this day.

The first to take up the cudgels in defence of the writers of the *romanzi* was Giraldi Cintio, who in his youth had known Ariosto personally, and who wrote his *Discorso intorno al comporre dei Romanzi*, in April, 1549. The grounds of his defence are twofold. In the first place, Giraldi maintains that the romance is a poetic form of which Aristotle did not know, and to which his rules therefore do not apply; and in the second place, Tuscan literature, differing as it does from the literature of Greece in language, in spirit, and in religious feeling, need not and indeed ought not to follow the rules of Greek literature, but rather the laws of its own development and its own traditions. With Ariosto and Boiardo as models, Giraldi sets out to formulate the laws of the *romanzi*. The *romanzi* aim at imitating illustrious actions in verse, with the purpose of teaching good morals and honest living, since this ought to be the aim of every poet, as Giraldi conceives Aristotle himself to have said.[1] All heroic poetry is an imitation of illustrious actions, but Giraldi, like Castelvetro twenty years later, recognizes several distinct forms of heroic poetry, according as to whether it imitates one action of one man, many actions of many men, or many actions of one man. The first of these is the epic poem, the rules of which are given in Aristotle's *Poetics*. The second is the romantic poem, after the manner of Boiardo and Ariosto. The third is the biographical poem, after the manner of the *Theseid* and similar works dealing with the whole life of a single hero.

These forms are therefore to be regarded as three distinct and legitimate species of heroic poetry, the

1 Giraldi Cintio, i. 11, 64.

first of them being an epic poem in the strict Aristotelian sense, and the two others coming under the general head of *romanzi*. Of the two forms of *romanzi*, the biographical deals preferably with an historical subject, whereas the noblest writers of the more purely romantic form, dealing with many actions of many men, have invented their subject matter. Horace says that an heroic poem should not commence at the very beginning of the hero's life; but it is difficult to understand, says Giraldi, why the whole life of a distinguished man, which gives us so great and refined a pleasure in the works of Plutarch and other biographers, should not please us all the more when described in beautiful verse by a good poet. [1] Accordingly, the poet who is composing an epic in the strict sense should, in handling the events of his narrative, plunge immediately *in medias res*. The poet dealing with many actions of many men should begin with the most important event, and the one upon which all the others may be said to hinge; whereas the poet describing the life of a single hero should begin at the very beginning, if the hero spent a really heroic youth, as Hercules for example did. The poem dealing with the life of a hero is thus a separate *genre*, and one for which Aristotle does not attempt to lay down any laws. Giraldi even goes so far as to say that Aristotle [2] censured those who write the life of Theseus or Hercules in a single poem, not because they dealt with many actions of one man, but because they treated such a poem in exactly

1 Giraldi Cintio, i. 24.

2 *Poet.* viii. 2.

the same manner as those who dealt with a single action of a single hero, — an assertion which is of course utterly absurd. Giraldi then proceeds to deal in detail with the disposition and composition of the *romanzi*, which he rates above the classical epics in the efficacy of ethical teaching. It is the office of the poet to praise virtuous actions and to condemn vicious actions; and in this the writers of the *romanzi* are far superior to the writers of the ancient heroic poems. [1]

Giraldi's discourse on the *romanzi* gave rise to a curious dispute with his own pupil, Giambattista Pigna, who published a similar work, entitled *I Romanzi*, in the same year (1554). Pigna asserted that he had suggested to Giraldi the main argument of the discourse, and that Giraldi had adopted it as his own. Without entering into the details of this controversy, it would seem that the priority of Giraldi cannot fairly be contested. [2] At all events, there is a very great resemblance between the works of Giraldi and Pigna. Pigna's treatise, however, is more detailed than Giraldi's. In the first book, Pigna deals with the general subject of the *romanzi*; in the second he gives a life of Ariosto, and discusses the *Furioso*, point by point; in the third he demonstrates the good taste and critical acumen of Ariosto by comparing the first version of the *Furioso* with the completed and perfected copy. [3] Both

1 Giraldi, i. 66 *sq*.

2 *Cf*. Tiraboschi, vii. 947 *sq*., and Giraldi, ii. 153 *sq*. Pigna's own words are cited in Giraldi, i. p. xxiii.

3 Canello, p. 306 *sq*.

Pigna and Giraldi consider the *romanzi* to constitute a new *genre*, unknown to the ancients, and therefore not subject to Aristotle's rules. Giraldi's sympathies were in favor of the biographical form of the *romanzi*, and his poem, the *Ercole* (1557), recounts the whole life of a single hero. Pigna, who keeps closer to the tradition of Ariosto, regards the biographical form as not proper to poetry, because too much like history.

These arguments, presented by Giraldi and Pigna, were answered by Speroni, Minturno, and others. Speroni pointed out that while it is not necessary for the romantic poets to follow the rules prescribed by the ancients, they cannot disobey the fundamental laws of poetry. "The *romanzi*," says Speroni, "are epics, which are poems, or they are histories in verse, and not poems." [1] That is, how does a poem differ from a well-written historical narrative, if the former be without organic unity? [2] As to the whole discussion, it may be said here, without attempting to pass judgment on Ariosto, or any other writer of *romanzi*, that unity of some sort every true poem must necessarily have; and, flawless as the *Orlando Furioso* is in its details, the unity of the poem certainly has not the obviousness of perfect, and especially classical, art. A work of art without organic unity may be compared with an unsymmetrical circle; and, while the *Furioso* is not to be judged by any arbitrary or mechanical rules of unity, yet if it has not that internal unity which transcends all mere external form, it may be

1 Speroni, v. 521. 2 *Cf.* Minturno, *De Poeta*, p. 151.

considered, as a work of art, hardly less than a failure; and the farther it is removed from perfect unity, the more imperfect is the art. "Poetry adapts itself to its times, but cannot depart from its own fundamental laws." [1]

Minturno's answer to the defenders of the *romanzi* is more detailed and explicit than Speroni's, and it is of considerable importance because of its influence on Torquato Tasso's conception of epic poetry. Minturno does not deny — and in this his point of view is identical with Tasso's — that it is possible to employ the matter of the *romanzi* in the composition of a perfect poem. The actions they describe are great and illustrious, their knights and ladies are noble and illustrious, too, and they contain in a most excellent manner that element of the marvellous which is so important an element in the epic action. It is the structure of the *romanzi* with which Minturno finds fault. They lack the first essential of every form of poetry, — unity. In fact, they are little more than versified history or legend; and, while expressing admiration for the genius of Ariosto, Minturno cannot but regret that he so far yielded to the popular taste of his time as to employ the method of the *romanzi*. He approves of the suggestion of Bembo, who had tried to persuade Ariosto to write an epic instead of a romantic poem, [2] just as later, and for similar reasons, Gabriel Harvey attempted to dissuade Spenser from con-

1 Minturno, *Arte Poetica*, p. 31. For various opinions on the unity of the *Orlando Furioso*, *cf.* Canello, p. 106, and Foffano, p. 59 *sq.*

2 *Arte Poetica*, p. 31.

tinuing the *Faerie Queene*. Minturno denies that the Tuscan tongue is not well adapted to the composition of heroic poetry; on the contrary, there is no form of poetry to which it is not admirably fitted. He denies that the romantic poem can be distinguished from the epic on the ground that the actions of knights-errant require a different and broader form of narrative than do those of the classical heroes. The celestial and infernal gods and demi-gods of the ancients correspond with the angels, saints, anchorites, and the one God of Christianity; the ancient sibyls, oracles, enchantresses, and divine messengers correspond with the modern necromancers, fates, magicians, and celestial angels. To the claim of the romantic poets that their poems approximate closer to that magnitude which Aristotle enjoins as necessary for all poetry, Minturno answers that magnitude is of no avail without proportion; there is no beauty in the giant whose limbs and frame are distorted. Finally, the *romanzi* are said to be a new form of poetry unknown to Aristotle and Horace, and hence not amenable to their laws. But time, says Minturno, cannot change the truth; in every age a poem must have unity, proportion, magnitude. Everything in nature is governed by some specific law which directs its operation; and as it is in nature so it is in art, for art tries to imitate nature, and the nearer it approaches nature in her essential laws, the better it does its work. In other words, as has already been pointed out, poetry adapts itself to its times, but cannot depart from its own laws.

Bernardo Tasso, the father of Torquato, had originally been one of the defenders of the classical epic; but he seems to have been converted to the opposite view by Giraldi Cintio, and in his poem of the *Amadigi* he follows romantic models. His son Torquato, in his *Discorsi dell' Arte Poetica*, originally written one or two years after the appearance of Minturno's *Arte Poetica*, although not published until 1587, was the first to attempt a reconciliation of the epic and romantic forms; and he may be said to have effected a solution of the problem by the formulation of the theory of a narrative poem which would have the romantic subject-matter, with its delightful variety, and the epic form, with its essential unity. The question at issue, as we have seen, is that of unity; that is, does the heroic poem need unity? Tasso denies that there is any difference between the epic poem and the romantic poem as poems. The reason why the latter is more pleasing, is to be found in the fact of the greater delightfulness of the themes treated. [1] Variety in itself may be pleasing, for even a variety of disagreeable things may possibly please. But the perfect and at the same time most pleasing form of heroic poem would deal with the chivalrous themes of the *romanzi*, yet would possess that unity of structure which, according to the precepts of Aristotle and the practice of Homer and Virgil, is essential to every epic. There are two sorts of unity possible in art as in nature, — the simple unity of a chemical element, and the complex unity of an organism

1 T. Tasso, xii. 219 *sq.*

like an animal or plant, — and of these the latter is the sort of unity that the heroic poet should aim at.[1] Capriano (1555) had referred to this same distinction, when he pointed out that poetry ought not to be the imitation of a single act, such as a single act of weeping in the elegy, or a single act of pastoral life in the eclogue, for such a sporadic imitation is to be compared to a picture of a single hand without the rest of the body; on the contrary, poetry ought to be the representation of a number of attendant or dependent acts, leading from a given beginning to a suitable end.[2]

Having settled the general fact that the attractive themes of the *romanzi* should be employed in a perfect heroic poem, we may inquire what particular themes are most fitted to the epic, and what must be the essential qualities of the epic material.[3] In the first place, the subject of the heroic poem must be historical, for it is not probable that illustrious actions such as are dealt with in the epic should be unknown to history. The authority of history gains for the poet that semblance of truth necessary to deceive the reader and make him believe that what the poet writes is true. Secondly, the heroic poem, according to Tasso, must deal with the history, not of a false religion, but of the true one, Christianity. The religion of the pagans is absolutely unfit for epic material; for if the pagan deities are not introduced, the poem will lack the element of the marvellous, and if they are introduced it will lack

1 T. Tasso, xii. 234.

2 *Della Vera Poetica,* cap. iii.

3 T. Tasso, xii. 199 *sq.*

the element of probability. Both the marvellous and the *verisimile* must exist together in a perfect epic, and difficult as the task may seem, they must be reconciled. Another reason why paganism is unfit for the epic is to be found in the fact that the perfect knight must have piety as well as other virtues. In the third place, the poem must not deal with themes connected with the articles of Christian faith, for such themes would be unalterable, and would allow no scope to the free play of the poet's inventive fancy. Fourthly, the material must be neither too ancient nor too modern, for the latter is too well known to admit of fanciful changes with probability, and the former not only lacks interest but requires the introduction of strange and alien manners and customs. The times of Charlemagne and Arthur are accordingly best fitted for heroic treatment. Finally, the events themselves must possess nobility and grandeur. Hence an epic should be a story derived from some event in the history of Christian peoples, intrinsically noble and illustrious, but not of so sacred a character as to be fixed and immutable, and neither contemporary nor very remote. By the selection of such material the poem gains the authority of history, the truth of religion, the license of fiction, the proper atmosphere in point of time, and the grandeur of the events themselves. [1]

Aristotle says that both epic and tragedy deal with illustrious actions. Tasso points out that if the actions of tragedy and of epic poetry were both illustrious in the same way,

1 T. Tasso, xii. 208.

they would both produce the same results; but tragic actions move horror and compassion, while epic actions as a rule do not and need not arouse these emotions. The tragic action consists in the unexpected change of fortune, and in the grandeur of the events carrying with them horror and pity; but the epic action is founded upon undertakings of lofty martial virtue, upon deeds of courtesy, piety, generosity, none of which is proper to tragedy. Hence the characters in epic poetry and in tragedy, though both of the same regal and supreme rank, differ in that the tragic hero is neither perfectly good nor entirely bad, as Aristotle says, while the epic hero must have the very height of virtue, such as Æneas, the type of piety, Amadis, the type of loyalty, Achilles, of martial virtue, and Ulysses, of prudence.

Having formulated these theories of heroic poetry in his youth, Tasso set out to carry them into practice, and his famous *Gerusalemme Liberata* was the result. This poem, almost immediately after its publication, started a violent controversy, which raged for many years, and which may be regarded as the legitimate outcome of the earlier dispute in connection with the *romanzi*. [1] The *Gerusalemme* was in fact the centre of critical activity during the latter part of the century. Shortly after its publication, Camillo Pellegrino published a dialogue, en-

1 Accounts of this famous controversy will be found in Tiraboschi, Canello, Serassi, etc.; but the latest and most complete is that given in the twentieth chapter of Solerti's monumental *Vita di Torquato Tasso*, Torino, 1895.

titled *Il Caraffa* (1583), in which the *Gerusalemme* is compared with the *Orlando Furioso*, much to the advantage of the former. Pellegrino finds fault with Ariosto on account of the lack of unity of his poem, the immoral manners imitated, and various imperfections of style and language; and in all of these things, unity, morality, and style, he finds Tasso's poem perfect. This was naturally the signal for a heated and long-continued controversy. The Accademia della Crusca had been founded at Florence, in 1582, and it seems that the members of the new society felt hurt at some sarcastic remarks regarding Florence in one of Tasso's dialogues. Accordingly, the head of the academy, Lionardo Salviati, in a dialogue entitled *L' Infarinato*, wrote an ardent defence of Ariosto; and an acrid and undignified dispute between Tasso and Salviati was begun.[1] Tasso answered the Accademia della Crusca in his *Apologia*; and at the beginning of the next century, Paolo Beni, the commentator on Aristotle's *Poetics*, published his *Comparazione di Omero, Virgilio, e Torquato*, in which Tasso is rated above Homer, Virgil, and Ariosto, not only in dignity, in beauty of style, and in unity of fable, but in every other quality that may be said to constitute perfection in poetry. Before dismissing this whole matter, it should be pointed out that the defenders of Ariosto had absolutely abandoned the position of Giraldi and Pigna, that the *romanzi*

1 Nearly all the important documents of the Tasso controversy are reprinted in Rosini's edition of Tasso, *Opere*, vols. xviii.-xxiii.

constitute a *genre* by themselves, and are therefore not subject to Aristotle's law of unity. The question as Giraldi had stated it was this: Does every poem need to have unity? The question as discussed in the Tasso controversy had changed to this form: What is unity? It was taken for granted by both sides in the controversy that every poem must have organic unity; and the authority of Aristotle, in epic as in dramatic poetry, was henceforth supreme. It was to the authority of Aristotle that Tasso's opponents appealed; and Salviati, merely for the purpose of undermining Tasso's pretensions, wrote an extended commentary on the *Poetics*, which still lies in Ms. at Florence, and which has been made use of in the present essay. [1]

1 The question of unity was also raised in another controversy of the second half of the sixteenth century. A passage in Varchi's *Ercolano* (1570), rating Dante above Homer, started a controversy on the *Divine Comedy*. The most important outcome of this dispute was Mazzoni's *Difesa di Dante* (1573), in which a more or less novel theory of poetry is expounded in order to defend the great Tuscan poet.

CHAPTER V

THE GROWTH OF THE CLASSIC SPIRIT IN ITALIAN CRITICISM

THE growth of classicism in Renaissance criticism was due to three causes, — humanism, or the imitation of the classics, Aristotelianism, or the influence of Aristotle's *Poetics*, and rationalism, or the authority of the reason, the result of the growth of the modern spirit in the arts and sciences. These three causes are at the bottom of Italian classicism, as well as of French classicism during the seventeenth century.

I. *Humanism*

The progress of humanism may be distinguished by an arbitrary but more or less practical division into four periods. The first period was characterized by the discovery and accumulation of classical literature, and the second period was given up to the arrangement and translation of the works thus discovered. The third period is marked by the formation of academies, in which the classics were studied and humanized, and which as a result produced a special cult of learning. The fourth and last period is marked by the decline of pure erudition, and the beginning of æsthetic and stylistic scholarship. [1] The practical result of the revival of learning and the progress of humanism was thus the study and imitation of the classics. To this imitation of classical literature all that humanism gave to the modern world may be ultimately traced. The problem before us, then, is this: What was the result of this imitation of the classics, in so far as it regards the literary criticism of the Renaissance?

In the first place, the imitation of the classics resulted in the study and cult of external form. Elegance, polish, clearness of design, became objects of study for themselves; and as a result we have the formation of æsthetic taste, and the growth of a classic purism, to which many of the literary tendencies of the Renaissance may be traced. [2] Under Leo X. and throughout the first half of the sixteenth century, the intricacies of style and versification were carefully studied. Vida was the first to lay down laws of imitative harmony; [3] Bembo, and after him Dolce and others, studied the poetic effect of different sounds, and the onomatopœic value of the various vowels and consonants; [4] Claudio Tolomei attempted to introduce classical metres into the vernacular; [5] Trissino published subtle and systematic researches in Tuscan

1 Symonds, ii. 161, based on Voigt.

2 *Cf.* Woodward, p. 210 *sq.*

3 Hallam, *Lit. of Europe*, i. 8. 1. *Cf.* Pope, i. 182: " Omnia sed numeris vocum concordibus aptant," etc.

4 Bembo, *Le Prose*, 1525; Dolce, *Osservationi*, 1550, lib. iv.; etc.

5 *Versi e Regole de la Nuova Poesia Toscana*, 1539.

language and versification. [1] Later, the rhetorical treatises of Cavalcanti (1565), Lionardi (1554), and Partenio (1560), and the more practical manuals of Fanucci (1533), Equicola (1541), and Ruscelli (1559), all testify to the tremendous impulse which the imitation of the classics had given to the study of form both in classical and vernacular literatures.

In Vida's *Ars Poetica* there are abundant evidences of the rhetorical and especially the puristic tendencies of modern classicism. The mechanical conception of poetic expression, in which imagination, sensibility, and passion are subjected to the elaborate and intricate precepts of art, is everywhere found in Vida's poem. Like Horace, Vida insists on long preparation for the composition of poetry, and warns the poet against the indulgence of his first impulses. He suggests as a preparation for the composition of poetry, that the poet should prepare a list of phrases and images for use whenever occasion may demand. [2] He impresses upon the poet the necessity of euphemistic expressions in introducing the subject of his poem; for example, the name of Ulysses should not be mentioned, but he should be referred to as one who has seen many men and many cities, who has suffered shipwreck on the return from Troy, and the like. [3] In such mechanical precepts as these, the rhetoric of seventeenth-century classicism is antici-

1 Trissino, *Poética*, lib. i.-iv., 1529; Tomitano, *Della Lingua Toscana*, 1545; etc.
2 Pope, i. 134. *Cf.* De Sanctis, ii. 153 *sq.*
3 Pope, i. 152.

pated. Its restraint, its purity, its mechanical side, are everywhere visible in Vida. A little later, in Daniello, we find similar puristic tendencies. He requires the severe separation of *genres*, decorum and propriety of characterization, and the exclusion of everything disagreeable from the stage. In Partenio's *Della Imitatione Poetica* (1560), the poet is expressly forbidden the employment of the ordinary words in daily use, [1] and elegance of form is especially demanded. Partenio regards form as of superior importance to subject or idea; for those who hear or read poetry care more for beauty of diction than for character or even thought. [2]

It is on merely rhetorical grounds that Partenio distinguishes excellent from mediocre poetry. The good poet, unlike the bad one, is able to give splendor and dignity to the most trivial idea by means of adornments of diction and disposition. This conception seems to have particularly appealed to the Renaissance; and Tasso gives expression to a similar notion when he calls it the poet's noblest function "to make of old concepts new ones, to make of vulgar concepts noble ones, and to make common concepts his own." [3] In a higher and more ideal sense, poetry, according to Shelley, "makes familiar objects be as if they were not familiar." [4]

It is in keeping with this rhetorical ideal of classicism that Scaliger makes *electio et sui fastidium* the highest virtues of the poet. [5] All that is merely popular (*plebeium*)

1 Partenio, p. 80.
2 *Ibid.* p. 95.
3 *Opere*, xi. 51.
4 *Defence*, p. 13.
5 *Poet.* v. 3.

in thought and expression is to be minutely avoided; for only that which proceeds from solid erudition is proper to art. The basis of artistic creation is imitation and judgment; for every artist is at bottom somewhat of an echo. [1] Grace, decorum, elegance, splendor are the chief excellences of poetry and the life of all excellence lies in measure, that is, moderation and proportion. It is in the spirit of this classical purism that Scaliger minutely distinguishes the various rhetorical and grammatical figures, and carefully estimates their proper place and function in poetry. His analysis and systematization of the figures were immediately accepted by the scholars and grammarians of his time, and have played a large part in French education ever since. Another consequence of Scaliger's dogmatic teaching, the Latinization of culture, can only be referred to here in passing. [2]

A second result of the imitation of the classics was the paganization of Renaissance culture. Classic art is at bottom pagan, and the Renaissance sacrificed everything in order to appear classical. [3] Not only did Christian literature seem contemptible when compared with classic literature, but the mere treatment of Christian themes offered numerous difficulties in itself. Thus Muzio declares that the ancient fables are the best poetic materials, since they permit the introduction of the deities into poetry, and a poem, being something divine, should not dispense with the association of divinity. [4] To

1 *Poet.* v. 1; vi. 4.
2 *Cf.* Brunetière, p. 53.
3 Symonds, ii. 395 *sq.*
4 Muzio, p. 94.

bring the God of Israel into poetry, to represent him, as it were, in the flesh, discoursing and arguing with men, was sacrilege; and to give the events of poetic narrative divine authoritativeness, the pagan deities became necessities of Renaissance poetry. Savonarola, in the fifteenth century, and the Council of Trent, in the sixteenth, reacted against the paganization of literature, but in vain. Despite the Council of Trent, despite Tasso and Du Bartas, the pagan gods held sway over Parnassus until the very end of the classical period; and in the seventeenth century, as will be seen, Boileau expressly discourages the treatment of Christian themes, and insists that the ancient pagan fables alone must form the basis of neo-classical art.

A third result of the imitation of the classics was the development of applied, or concrete, criticism. If the foundations of literature, if the formation of style, can result only from a close and judicious imitation of classical literature, this problem confronts us: Which classical authors are we to imitate? An answer to this question involves the application of concrete criticism. A reason must be given for one's preferences; in other words, they must be justified on principle. The literary controversies of the humanists, the disputes on the subject of imitation, of Ciceronianism, and what not, all tended in this direction. The judgment of authors was dependent more or less on individual impressions. But the longer these controversies continued, the nearer was the approach to a literary criticism, justified by appeals to general principles, which became more and more fixed and determined; so that the growth of principles, or criteria of judgment in matters of literature, is in reality coterminous with the history of the growth of classicism.[1]

But one of the most important consequences of the imitation of the classics was that this imitation became a dogma of criticism, and radically changed the relations of art and nature in so far as they touch letters and literary criticism. The imitation of the classics became, in a word, the basis of literary creation. Vida, for example, affirms that the poet must imitate classical literature, for only by such imitation is perfection attainable in modern poetry. In fact, this notion is carried to such an extreme that the highest originality becomes for Vida merely the ingenious translation of passages from the classic poets: —

> "Haud minor est adeo virtus, si te audit Apollo,
> Inventa Argivûm in patriam convertere vocem,
> Quam si tute aliquid intactum inveneris ante."[2]

Muzio, echoing Horace, urges the poet to study the classics by day and by night; and Scaliger, as has been seen, makes all literary creation depend ultimately on judicious imitation: "Nemo est qui non aliquid de Echo." As a result, imitation gradually acquired a specialized and almost esoteric meaning, and became in this sense the starting-point of all the educational theories of the later

1 *Cf.* Dennis, *Select Works*, 1718, ii. 417 *sq.*
2 Pope, i. 167.

humanists. The doctrine of imitation set forth by John Sturm, the Strasburg humanist, was particularly influential.[1] According to Sturm, imitation is not the servile copying of words and phrases; it is "a vehement and artistic application of mind," which judiciously uses and transfigures all that it imitates. Sturm's theory of imitation is not entirely original, but comes through Agricola and Melanchthon from Quintilian.[2] Quintilian had said that the greater part of art consists in imitation; but for the humanists imitation became the chief and almost the only element of literary creation, since the literature of their own time seemed so vastly inferior to that of the ancients.

The imitation of the classics having thus become essential to literary creation, what was to be its relation to the imitation of nature? The ancient poets seemed to insist that every writer is at bottom an imitator of nature, and that he who does not imitate nature diverges from the purpose and principle of art. A lesson coming from a source so authoritative as this could not be left unheeded by the writers of the Renaissance, and the evolution of classicism may be distinguished by the changing point of view of the critics in regard to the relations between nature and art. This evolution may be traced in the neo-classical period through three distinct stages, and these three stages may be indicated by the doctrines respectively of Vida, Scaliger, and Boileau.

1 Laas, *Die Paedagogik des Johannes Sturm*, Berlin, 1872, p. 65 *sq.*

2 *Inst. Orat.* x. 2.

Vida says that it is the first essential of literary art to imitate the classics. This, however, does not prevent him from warning the poet that it is his first duty to observe and copy nature:—

> "Præterea haud lateat te, nil conarier artem,
> Naturam nisi ut assimulet, propiusque sequatur."

For Vida, however, as for the later classicists, nature is synonymous with civilized men, perhaps even further restricted to the men of the city and the court; and the study of nature was hardly more for him than close observation of the differences of human character, more especially of the external differences which result from diversity of age, rank, sex, race, profession, and which may be designated by the term *decorum.* [1] The imitation of nature even in this restricted sense Vida requires on the authority of the ancients. The modern poet should imitate nature because the great classical poets have always acknowledged her sway: —

> "Hanc unam vates sibi proposuere magistram."

Nature has no particular interest for Vida in itself. He accepts the classics as we accept the Scriptures; and nature is to be imitated and followed because the ancients seem to require it.

In Scaliger this principle is carried one stage farther. The poet creates another nature and other fortunes as if he were another God. [2] Virgil especially has created another nature of such beauty and perfection that the poet need not concern him

1 Pope, i. 165. 2 *Poet.* i. 1.

self with the realities of life, but can go to the second nature created by Virgil for the subject matter of his imitation. "All the things which you have to imitate, you have according to another nature, that is, Virgil." [1] In Virgil, as in nature, there are the most minute details of the foundation and government of cities, the management of armies, the building and handling of ships, and in fact all the secrets of the arts and sciences. What more can the poet desire, and indeed what more can he find in life, and find there with the same certainty and accuracy? Virgil has created a nature far more perfect than that of reality, and one compared with which the actual world and life itself seem but pale and without beauty. What Scaliger stands for, then, is the substitution of the world of art instead of life as the object of poetic imitation. This point of view finds expression in many of the theorists of his time. Partenio, for example, asserts that art is a firmer and safer guide than nature; with nature we can err, but scarcely with art, for art eradicates from nature all that is bad, while nature mingles weeds with flowers, and does not distinguish vices from virtues. [2]

Boileau carries the neo-classical ideal of nature and art to its ultimate perfection. According to him, nothing is beautiful that is not true, and nothing is true that is not in nature. Truth, for classicism, is the final test of everything, including beauty; and hence to be beautiful poetry must be founded on nature. Nature should therefore be the poet's

1 *Poet.* iii. 4.

2 Partenio, p. 39 *sq.*

sole study, although for Boileau, as for Vida, nature is one with the court and the city. Now, in what way can we discover exactly how to imitate nature, and perceive whether or not we have imitated it correctly? Boileau finds the guide to the correct imitation of nature, and the very test of its correctness, in the imitation of the classics. The ancients are great, not because they are old, but because they are true, because they knew how to see and to imitate nature; and to imitate antiquity is therefore to use the best means the human spirit has ever found for expressing nature in its perfection. [1] The advance of Boileau's theory on that of Vida and Scaliger is therefore that he founded the rules and literary practice of classical literature on reason and nature, and showed that there is nothing arbitrary in the authority of the ancients. For Vida, nature is to be followed on the authority of the classics; for Boileau, the classics are to be followed on the authority of nature and reason. Scaliger had shown that such a poet as Virgil had created another nature more perfect than that of reality, and that therefore we should imitate this more beautiful nature of the poet. Boileau, on the contrary, showed that the ancients were simply imitating nature itself in the closest and keenest manner, and that by imitating the classics the poet was not imitating a second and different nature, but was being shown in the surest way how to imitate the real and only nature. This final reconciliation

1 *Cf.* Brunetière, p. 102 *sq.*, and Lanson, *Hist. de le Litt. fr.*, p. 494 *sq.*

of the imitation of nature and the imitation of the classics was Boileau's highest contribution to the literary criticism of the neo-classical period.

II. *Aristotelianism*

The influence of Aristotle's *Poetics* is first visible in the dramatic literature of the early sixteenth century. Trissino's *Sofonisba* (1515), usually accounted the first regular modern tragedy, Rucellai's *Rosmunda* (1516), and innumerable other tragedies of this period, were in reality little more than mere attempts at putting the Aristotelian theory of tragedy into practice. The Aristotelian influence is evident in many of the prefaces of these plays, and in a few contemporary works of scholarship, such as the *Antiquæ Lectiones* (1516) of Cælius Rhodiginus, whom Scaliger called *omnium doctissimus præceptor noster*. At the same time, the *Poetics* did not immediately play an important part in the critical literature of Italy. From the time of Petrarch, Aristotle, identified in the minds of the humanists with the mediæval scholasticism so obnoxious to them, had lost somewhat of his supremacy; and the strong Platonic tendencies of the Renaissance had further contributed to lower the prestige of Aristotelianism among the humanists. At no time of the Renaissance, however, did Aristotle lack ardent defenders, and Filelfo, for example, wrote in 1439, "To defend Aristotle and the truth seems to me one and the same thing." [1] In the domain of philosophy the influence of Aristotle

1 *Lettres grecques*, ed. Legrand, 1892, p. 31.

was temporarily sustained by the liberal Peripateticism of Pomponazzi; and numerous others, among them Scaliger himself, continued the traditions of a modernized Aristotelianism. From this time, however, Aristotle's position as the supreme philosopher was challenged more and more; and he was regarded by the advanced thinkers of the Renaissance as the representative of the mediæval obscurantism that opposed the progress of modern scientific investigation.

But whatever of Aristotle's authority was lost in the domain of philosophy was more than regained in the domain of literature. The beginning of the Aristotelian influence on modern literary theory may be said to date from the year 1536, in which year Trincaveli published a Greek text of the *Poetics*, Pazzi his edition and Latin version, and Daniello his own *Poetica*. Pazzi's son, in dedicating his father's posthumous work, said that in the *Poetics* "the precepts of poetic art are treated by Aristotle as divinely as he has treated every other form of knowledge." In the very year that this was said, Ramus gained his Master's degree at the University of Paris by defending victoriously the thesis that Aristotle's doctrines without exception are all false.[1] The year 1536 may therefore be regarded as a turning-point in the history of Aristotle's influence. It marks the beginning of his supremacy in literature, and the decline of his dictatorial authority in philosophy.

1 " Quæcunque ab Aristotele dicta sint falsa et commentitia esse;" Bayle, *Dict.* s. v. Ramus, note C.

Between the year 1536 and the middle of the century the lessons of Aristotle's *Poetics* were being gradually learned by the Italian critics and poets. By 1550 the whole of the *Poetics* had been incorporated in the critical literature of Italy, and Fracastoro could say that "Aristotle has received no less fame from the survival of his *Poetics* than from his philosophical remains." [1] According to Bartolommeo Ricci, in a letter to Prince Alfonso, son of Hercules II., Duke of Ferrara, Maggi was the first person to interpret Aristotle's *Poetics* in public. [2] These lectures were delivered some time before April, 1549. As early as 1540, Bartolommeo Lombardi, the collaborator of Maggi in his commentary on the *Poetics*, had intended to deliver public lectures on the *Poetics* before a Paduan academy, but died before accomplishing his purpose. [3] Numerous public readings on the subject of Aristotle and Horace followed those of Maggi, — among them those by Varchi, Giraldi Cintio, Luisino, and Trifone Gabrielli; and the number of public readings on topics connected with literary criticism, and on the poetry of Dante and Petrarch, increased greatly from this time.

The number of commentaries on the *Poetics* itself, published during the sixteenth century, is really remarkable. The value of these commentaries in general is not so much that they add anything to the literary criticism of the Renaissance, but that their explanations of Aristotle's meaning

1 Fracastoro, i. 321.
2 Tiraboschi, vii. 1465.
3 Maggi, dedication.

were accepted by contemporary critics, and became in a way the source of all the literary arguments of the sixteenth century. Nor was their influence restricted merely to this particular period. They were, one might almost say, living things to the critics and poets of the classical period in France. Racine, Corneille, and other distinguished writers possessed copies of these commentaries, studied them carefully, cited them in their prefaces and critical writings, and even annotated their own copies of the commentaries with marginal notes, of which some may be seen in the modern editions of their works. In the preface to Rapin's *Réflexions sur l'Art Poétique* (1674) there is a history of literary criticism, which is almost entirely devoted to these Italian commentators; and writers like Chapelain and Balzac eagerly argued and discussed their relative merits.

Several of these Italian commentators have been alluded to already. [1] The first critical edition of the *Poetics* was that of Robortelli (1548), and this was followed by those of Maggi (1550) and Vettori (1560), both written in Latin, and both exhibiting great learning and acumen. The first translation of the *Poetics* into the vernacular was that by Segni (1549), and this was followed by the Italian commentaries of Castelvetro (1570) and Piccolomini (1575). Tasso, after comparing the works of these two commentators, concluded that while Castelvetro had greater erudition and invention,

1 In an appendix to this essay will be found an excerpt from Salviati's unpublished commentary on the *Poetics*, giving his judgment of the commentators who had preceded him.

Piccolomini had greater maturity of judgment, more learning, perhaps, with less erudition, and certainly learning more Aristotelian and more suited to the interpretation of the *Poetics.*[1] The two last sections of Trissino's *Poetica*, published in 1563, are little more than a paraphrase and transposition of Aristotle's treatise. But the curious excesses into which admiration of Aristotle led the Italian scholars may be gathered from a work published at Milan in 1576, an edition of the *Poetics* expounded in verse, Baldini's *Ars Poetica Aristotelis versibus exposita*. The *Poetics* was also adapted for use as a practical manual for poets and playwrights in such works as Riccoboni's brief *Compendium Artis Poeticœ Aristotelis ad usum conficiendorum poematum* (1591). The last of the great Italian commentaries on the *Poetics* to have a general European influence was perhaps Beni's, published in 1613; but this carries us beyond the confines of the century. Besides the published editions, translations, and commentaries, many others were written which may still be found in Ms. in the libraries of Italy. Reference has already been made to Salviati's (1586). There are also two anonymous commentaries dating from this period in Ms. at Florence, —one in the Magliabechiana and the other in the Riccardiana. The last work which may be mentioned here is Buonamici's *Discorsi Poetici in difesa d' Aristotele*, in which Aristotle is ardently defended against the attacks of his detractors.

1 Tasso, xv. 20.

It was in Italy during this period that the literary dictatorship of Aristotle first developed, and it was Scaliger to whom the modern world owes the formulation of the supreme authority of Aristotle as a critical theorist. Fracastoro had likened the importance of Aristotle's *Poetics* to that of his philosophical treatises. Trissino had followed Aristotle verbally and almost literally. Varchi had spoken of years of Aristotelian study as an essential prerequisite for every one who entered the field of literary criticism. Partenio, a year before the publication of Scaliger's *Poetics*, had asserted that everything relating to tragedy and epic poetry had been settled by Aristotle and Horace. But Scaliger went farther still. He was the first to regard Aristotle as the perpetual lawgiver of poetry. He was the first to assume that the duty of the poet is first to find out what Aristotle says, and then to obey these precepts without question. He distinctly calls Aristotle the perpetual dictator of all the arts: "Aristoteles imperator noster, omnium bonarum artium dictator perpetuus." [1] This is perhaps the first occasion in modern literature in which Aristotle is definitely regarded as a literary dictator, and the dictatorship of Aristotle in literature may, therefore, be dated from the year 1561.

But Scaliger did more than this. He was the first apparently to attempt to reconcile Aristotle's *Poetics*, not only with the precepts of Horace and the definitions of the Latin grammarians, but with the whole practice of Latin tragedy, comedy, and

1 *Poet.* vii. ii. 1.

epic poetry. It was in the light of this reconciliation, or concord of Aristotelianism with the Latin spirit, that Aristotle became for Scaliger a literary dictator. It was not Aristotle that primarily interested him, but an ideal created by himself, and founded on such parts of the doctrine of Aristotle as received confirmation from the theory or practice of Roman literature; and this new ideal, harmonizing with the Latin spirit of the Renaissance, became in the course of time one of the foundations of classicism. The influence of Aristotelianism was further augmented by the Council of Trent, which gave to Aristotle's doctrine the same degree of authority as Catholic dogma.

All these circumstances tended to favor the importance of Aristotle in Italy during the sixteenth century, and as a result the literary dictatorship of Aristotle was by the Italians foisted on Europe for two centuries to come. From 1560 to 1780 Aristotle was regarded as the supreme authority in letters throughout Europe. At no time, even in England, during and after that period, was there a break in the Aristotelian tradition, and the influence of the *Poetics* may be found in Sidney and Ben Jonson, in Milton and Dryden, as well as in Shelley and Coleridge. Lessing, even in breaking away from the classical practice of the French stage, defended his innovations on the authority of Aristotle, and said of the *Poetics*, "I do not hesitate to acknowledge, even if I should therefore be held up to scorn in these enlightened times, that I consider the work as infallible as the Elements of

Euclid."[1] In 1756, a dozen years before Lessing, one of the precursors of the romantic movement in England, Joseph Warton, had also said of the *Poetics*, "To attempt to understand poetry without having diligently digested this treatise would be as absurd and impossible as to pretend to a skill in geometry without having studied Euclid."[2]

One of the first results of the dictatorship of Aristotle was to give modern literature a body of inviolable rules for the drama and the epic; that is, the dramatic and heroic poets were restricted to a certain fixed form, and to certain fixed characters. Classical poetry was of course the ideal of the Renaissance, and Aristotle had analyzed the methods which these works had employed. The inference seems to have been that by following these rules a literature of equal importance could be created. These formulæ were at the bottom of classical literature, and rules which had created such literatures as those of Greece and Rome could hardly be disregarded. As a result, these rules came to be considered more and more as essentials, and finally, almost as the very tests of literature; and it was in consequence of their acceptance as poetic laws that the modern classical drama and epic arose. The first modern tragedies and the first modern epics were hardly more than such attempts at putting the Aristotelian rules into practice. The cult of form during the Renaissance had produced a reaction against the

1 *Hamburg. Dramat.* 101-104.
2 *Essay on Pope,* 3d ed., i. 171.

formlessness and invertebrate character of mediæval literature. The literature of the Middle Ages was infinitely inferior to that of the ancients; mediæval literature lacked form and structure, classical literature had a regular and definite form. Form then came to be regarded as the essential difference between the perfect literatures of Greece and Rome, and the imperfect and vulgar literature of the Middle Ages; and the deduction from this was that, to be classical, the poet must observe the form and structure of the classics. Minturno indeed says that "the precepts given of old by the ancient masters, and now repeated by me here, are to be regarded merely as common usage, and not as inviolable laws which must serve under all circumstances." [1] But this was not the general conception of the Renaissance. Muzio, for example, specifically says: —

"Queste legge ch' io scrivo e questi esempi
Sian, lettore, al tuo dir perpetua norma; "

and in another place he speaks of a precept he has given, as "vera, ferma, e inevitabil legge." [2] Scaliger goes still further than this; for, according to him, even the classics themselves are to be judged by these standards and rules. "It seems to me," says Scaliger, "that we ought not to refer everything back to Homer, just as though he were the norm, but Homer himself should be referred to the norm." [3] In the modern classical

1 *Arte Poetica*, p. 158.
2 Muzio, pp. 81 v., 76 v.
3 *Poet.* i. 5.

period somewhat later, these rules were found to be based on reason: —

> "These rules of old, discovered not devised,
> Are nature still, but nature methodized." [1]

But during the Renaissance they were accepted *ex cathedra* from classical literature.

The formulation of a fixed body of critical rules was not the only result of the Aristotelian influence. One of the most important of these results, as has appeared, was the rational justification of imaginative literature. With the introduction of Aristotle's *Poetics* into modern Europe the Renaissance was first able to formulate a systematic theory of poetry; and it is therefore to the rediscovery of the *Poetics* that we may be said to owe the foundation of modern criticism. It was on the side of Aristotelianism that Italian criticism had its influence on European letters; and that this influence was deep and widespread, our study of the critical literatures of France and England will in part show. The critics with whom we have been dealing are not merely dead provincial names; they influenced, for two whole centuries, not only France and England, but Spain, Portugal, and Germany as well.

Literary criticism, in any real sense, did not begin in Spain until the very end of the sixteenth century, and the critical works that then appeared were wholly based on those of the Italians. Rengifo's *Arte Poética Española* (1592), in so far as it

1 Pope, *Essay on Criticism*, 88.

deals with the theory of poetry, is based on Aristotle, Scaliger, and various Italian authorities, according to the author's own acknowledgment. Pinciano's *Philosophia Antigua Poética* (1596) is based on the same authorities. Similarly, Cascales, in his *Tablas Poéticas* (1616), gives as his authorities Minturno, Giraldi Cintio, Maggi, Riccoboni, Castelvetro, Robortelli, and his own countryman Pinciano. The sources of these and all other works written at this period are Italian; and the following passage from the *Egemplar Poético*, written about 1606 by the Spanish poet Juan de la Cueva, is a good illustration, not only of the general influence of the Italians on Spanish criticism, but of the high reverence in which the individual Italian critics were held by Spanish men of letters: —

> "De los primeros tiene Horacio el puesto,
> En numeros y estilo soberano,
> Qual en su Arte al mundo es manifesto.
> Escaligero [*i.e.* Scaliger] hace el paso llano
> Con general enseñamiento y guia,
> Lo mismo el docto Cintio [*i.e.* Giraldi Cintio] y Biperano. [1]
> Maranta [2] es egemplar de la Poesia,
> Vida el norte, Pontano [3] el ornamento,
> La luz Minturno qual el sol del dia....
> Acuden todos a colmar sus vasos

1 Viperano, author of *De Poetica libri tres*, Antwerp, 1579.

2 Maranta, author of *Lucullanæ Quæstiones*, Basle, 1564.

3 Three writers of the Renaissance bore this name: G. Pontano, the famous Italian humanist and Latin poet, who died in 1503; P. Pontano, of Bruges, the author of an *Ars Versificatoria*, published in 1520; and J. Pontanus, a Bohemian Jesuit, author of *Institutiones Poeticæ*, first published at Ingolstadt in 1594, and several times reprinted.

Al oceano sacro de Stagira [*i.e.* Aristotle],
Donde se afirman los dudosos pasos,
Se eterniza la trompa y tierna lira." [1]

The influence of the Italians was equally great in Germany. From Fabricius to Opitz, the critical ideas of Germany were almost all borrowed, directly or indirectly, from Italian sources. Fabricius in his *De Re Poetica* (1584) acknowledges his indebtedness to Minturno, Partenio, Pontanus, and others, but above all to Scaliger; and most of the critical ideas by which Opitz renovated modern German literature go back to Italian sources, through Scaliger, Ronsard, and Daniel Heinsius. No better illustration of the influence of the Italian critics upon European letters could be afforded than that given by Opitz's *Buch von der deutschen Poeterei.* [2]

The influence of Italian criticism on the critical literature of France and England will be more or less treated in the remaining portions of this essay. It may be noted here, however, that in the critical writings of Lessing there is represented the climax of the Italian tradition in European letters, especially on the side of Aristotelianism. Shelley represents a similar culmination of the Italian tradition in England. His indebtedness to Sidney and Mil-

1 Sedano, *Parnaso Español*, Madrid, 1774, viii. 40, 41.

2 *Cf.* Berghoeffer, *Opitz' Buch von der Poeterei*, 1888, and Beckherrn, *Opitz, Ronsard, und Heinsius*, 1888. The first reference to Aristotle's *Poetics*, north of the Alps, is to be found in Luther's *Address to the Christian Nobles of the German Nation*, 1520. Schosser's *Disputationes de Tragœdia*, published in 1559, two years before Scaliger's work appeared, is entirely based on Aristotle's *Poetics*.

ton, who represent the Italian influence in the Elizabethan age, and especially to Tasso, whom he continually cites, is very marked. The debt of modern literature to Italian criticism is therefore not slight. In the half century between Vida and Castelvetro, Italian criticism formulated three things: a theory of poetry, a rigid form for the epic, and a rigid form for the drama. These rigid forms for drama and epic governed the creative imagination of Europe for two centuries, and then passed away. But while modern æsthetics for over a century has studied the processes of art, the theory of poetry, as enunciated by the Italians of the sixteenth century, has not diminished in value, but has continued to pervade the finer minds of men from that time to this.

III. *Rationalism*

The rationalistic temper may be observed in critical literature almost at the very beginning of the sixteenth century. This spirit of rationalism is observable throughout the Renaissance; and its general causes may be looked for in the liberation of the human reason by the Renaissance, in the growth of the sciences and arts, and in the reaction against mediæval sacerdotalism and dogma. The causes of its development in literary criticism may be found not only in these but in several other influences of the period. The paganization of culture, the growth of rationalistic philosophies, with their all-pervading influence on arts and letters, and moreover the influence of Horace's *Ars Poetica,* with its ideal of "good sense," all tended to make the element of reason predominate in literature and in literary criticism.

In Vida the three elements which are at the bottom of classicism, the imitation of the classics, the imitation of nature, and the authority of reason, may all be found. Reason is for him the final test of all things: —

"Semper nutu rationis eant res." [1]

The function of the reason in art is, first, to serve as a standard in the choice and carrying out of the design, a bulwark against the operation of mere chance, [2] and secondly, to moderate the expression of the poet's own personality and passion, a bulwark against the morbid subjectivity which is the horror of the classical temperament. [3]

It has been said of Scaliger that he was the first modern to establish in a body of doctrine the principal consequences of the sovereignty of the reason in literature. [4] That was hardly his aim, and certainly not his attainment. But he was, at all events, one of the first modern critics to affirm that there is a standard of perfection for each specific form of literature, to show that this standard may be arrived at *a priori* through the reason, and to attempt a formulation of such standard for each literary form. "Est in omni rerum genere unum

1 Pope, i. 155.
2 *Loc. cit.*, beginning, "Nec te fors inopina regat."
3 Pope, i. 164, beginning, "Ne tamen ah nimium."
4 Lintilhac, in *Nouvelle Revue,* lxiv. 543.

primum ac rectum ad cuius tum normam, tum rationem cætera dirigenda sunt." [1] This, the fundamental assumption of Scaliger's *Poetics*, is also one of the basic ideas of classicism. Not only is there a standard, a norm, in every species of literature, but this norm can be definitely formulated and defined by means of the reason; and it is the duty of the critic to formulate this norm, and the duty of the poet to study and follow it without deviating from the norm in any way. Even Homer, as we have seen, is to be judged according to this standard arrived at through the reason. Such a method cuts off all possibility of novelty of form or expression, and holds every poet, ancient or modern, great or small, accountable to one and the same standard of perfection.

The growth and influence of rationalism in Italian criticism may be best observed by the gradual effect which its development had on the element of Aristotelianism. In other words, rationalism changed the point of view according to which the Aristotelian canons were regarded in the Italian Renaissance. The earlier Italian critics accepted their rules and precepts on the authority of Aristotle alone. Thus Trissino, at the beginning of the fifth section of his *Poetica*, finished in 1549, although begun about twenty years before, says, "I shall not depart from the rules and precepts of the ancients, and especially Aristotle." [2] Somewhat later, in 1553, Varchi says, "Reason *and* Aristotle are my *two* guides." [3] Here the element of the

1 Scaliger, *Poet.* iii. 11. 2 Trissino, ii. 92. 3 Varchi, p. 600.

reason first asserts itself, but there is no intimation that the Aristotelian canons are in themselves reasonable. The critic has two guides, the individual reason and the Aristotelian rules, and each of these two guides is to serve wherever the other is found wanting. This same point of view is found a decade later in Tasso, who says that the defenders of the unity of the epic poem have made "a shield of the authority of Aristotle, nor do they lack the arms afforded by the reason;" [1] and similarly, in 1583, Sir Philip Sidney says that the unity of time is demanded "both by Aristotle's precept and common reason." [2] Here both Tasso and Sidney, while contending that the particular law under discussion is in itself reasonable, speak of Aristotle's *Poetics* and the reason as separate and distinct authorities, and fail to show that Aristotle himself based all his precepts upon the reason. In Denores, a few years later, the development is carried one stage farther in the direction of the ultimate classical attitude, as when he speaks of "reason and Aristotle's *Poetics*, which is indeed founded on naught save reason." [3] This is as far as Italian criticism ever went. It was the function of neoclassicism in France, as will be seen, to show that such a phrase as "reason *and* Aristotle" is a contradiction in itself, that the Aristotelian canons and the reason are ultimately reducible to the same thing, and that not only what is in Aristotle will

1 Tasso, xii. 217.
2 *Defense of Poesy*, p. 48.
3 *Discorso*, 1587, p. 39 v.

be found reasonable, but all that reason dictates for literary observance will be found in Aristotle.

Rationalism produced several very important results in literature and literary criticism during the sixteenth century. In the first place, it tended to give the reason a higher place in literature than imagination or sensibility. Poetry, it will be remembered, was often classified by Renaissance critics as one of the logical sciences; and nothing could be in greater accord with the neo-classical ideal than the assertion of Varchi and others that the better logician the poet is, the better he will be as a poet. Sainte-Beuve gives Scaliger the credit of having first formulated this theory of literature which subordinates the creative imagination and poetic sensibility to the reason; [1] but the credit or discredit of originating it does not belong exclusively to Scaliger. This tendency toward the apotheosis of the reason was diffused throughout the sixteenth century, and does not characterize any individual author. The Italian critics of this period were the first to formulate the classical ideal that the standard of perfection may be conceived of by the reason, and that perfection is to be attained only by the realization of this standard.

The rationalistic spirit also tended to set the seal of disapprobation on extravagances of any sort. Subjectivity and individualism came to be regarded more and more, at least in theory, as out of keeping with classical perfection. Clearness, reasonableness, sociableness, were the highest requirements

1 *Causeries du Lundi*, iii. 44.

of art; and any excessive expression of the poet's individuality was entirely disapproved of. Man, not only as a reasonable being, but also as a social being, was regarded as the basis of literature. Boileau's lines: —

> "Que les vers ne soient pas votre éternel emploi;
> Cultivez vos amis, soyez homme de foi;
> C'est peu d'être agréable et charmant dans un livre,
> Il faut savoir encore et converser et vivre," [1]

were anticipated in Berni's *Dialogo contra i Poeti*, written in 1526, though not published until 1537. This charming invective is directed against the fashionable literature of the time, and especially against all professional poets. Writing from the standpoint of a polished and rationalistic society, Berni lays great stress on the fact that poetry is not to be taken too seriously, that it is a pastime, a recreation for cultured people, a mere bagatelle; and he professes to despise those who spend all their time in writing verses. The vanity, the uselessness, the extravagances, and the ribaldry of the professional poets receive his hearty contempt; only those who write verses for pastime merit approbation. "Are you so stupid," he cries, "as to think that I call any one who writes verses a poet, and that I regard such men as Vida, Pontano, Bembo, Sannazaro, as mere poets? I do not call any one a poet, and condemn him as such, unless he does nothing but write verses, and wretched ones at that, and is good for nothing else. But the men I have mentioned are not

1 *Art Poét.* iv. 121.

poets by profession." [1] Here the sentiments expressed are those of a refined and social age, — the age of Louis XIV. no less than that of Leo X.

The irreligious character of neo-classic art may also be regarded as one of the consequences of this rationalistic temper. The combined effect of humanism, essentially pagan, and rationalism, essentially sceptical, was not favorable to the growth of religious feeling in literature. Classicism, the result of these two tendencies, became more and more rationalistic, more and more pagan; and in consequence, religious poetry in any real sense ceased to flourish wherever the more stringent forms of classicism prevailed. In Boileau these tendencies result in a certain distinct antagonism to the very forms of Christianity in literature: —

> "C'est donc bien vainement que nos auteurs déçus,
> Bannissant de leurs vers ces ornemens reçus,
> Pensent faire agir Dieu, ses saints et ses prophètes,
> Comme ces dieux éclos du cerveau des poëtes;
> Mettent à chaque pas le lecteur en enfer;
> N'offrent rien qu'Astaroth, Belzébuth, Lucifer.
> De la foi d'un chrétien les mystères terribles
> D'ornemens égayés ne sont point susceptibles;
> L'Évangile à l'esprit n'offre de tous côtés
> Que pénitence à faire et tourmens mérités;
> Et de vos fictions le mélange coupable
> Même à ses vérités donne l'air de la fable." [2]

1 Berni, p. 249.
2 *Art Poét.* iii. 193. *Cf.* Dryden, *Discourse on Satire*, in *Works*, xiii. 23 *sq.*

CHAPTER VI

ROMANTIC ELEMENTS IN ITALIAN CRITICISM

In the Italian critical literature of the sixteenth century there are to be found the germs of romantic as well as classical criticism. The development of romanticism in Renaissance criticism is due to various tendencies, of ancient, of mediæval, and of modern origin. The ancient element is Platonism; the mediæval elements are Christianity, and the influence of the literary forms and the literary subject-matter of the Middle Ages; and the modern elements are the growth of national life and national literatures, and the opposition of modern philosophy to Aristotelianism.

I. *The Ancient Romantic Element*

As the element of reason is the predominant feature of neo-classicism, so the element of imagination is the predominant feature of romanticism; and according as the reason or the imagination predominates in Renaissance literature, there results neo-classicism or romanticism, while the most perfect art finds a reconciliation of both elements in the imaginative reason. According to the faculty of reason, when made the basis of literature, the poet is, as it were, held down to earth, and art becomes the mere reasoned expression of the truth of life. By the faculty of imagination, the poet is made to create a new world of his own, — a world in which his genius is free to mould whatever its imagination takes hold of. This romantic doctrine of the freedom of genius, of inspiration and the power of imagination, in so far as it forms a part of Renaissance criticism, owes its origin to Platonism. The influence of the Platonic doctrines among the humanists has already been alluded to. Plato was regarded by them as their leader in the struggle against mediævalism, scholasticism, and Aristotelianism. The Aristotelian dialectic of the Middle Ages appealed exclusively to the reason; Platonism gave opportunities for the imagination to soar to vague and sublime heights, and harmonize with the divine mysteries of the universe. As regards poetry and imaginative literature in general, the critics of the Renaissance appealed from the Plato of the *Republic* and the *Laws* to the Plato of the *Ion*, the *Phœdrus*, and the *Symposium*. Beauty being the subject-matter of art, Plato's praise of beauty was transferred by the Renaissance to poetry, and his praise of the philosopher was transferred to the poet.

The Aristotelian doctrine defines beauty according to its relations to the external world; that is, poetry is an imitation of nature, expressed in general terms. The Platonic doctrine, on the contrary, is concerned with poetry, or beauty, in so far as it concerns the poet's own nature; that is, the poet is divinely inspired and is a creator like God. Fracastoro, as has been seen, makes the Platonic rapture, the delight in the true and essential beauty of things, the true tests of poetic power. In introducing this Platonic ideal of poetic beauty into modern literary criticism, he defines and distinguishes poetry according to a subjective criterion; and it is according to whether the objective or the subjective conception of art is insisted upon, that we have the classic spirit or the romantic spirit. The extreme romanticists, like the Schlegels and their contemporaries in Germany, entirely eliminate the relation of poetry to the external world, and in this extreme form romanticism becomes identified with the exaggerated subjective idealism of Fichte and Schelling. The extreme classicists entirely eliminate the poet's personality; that is, poetry is merely reasoned expression, a perfected expression of what all men can see in nature, for the poet has no more insight into life — no more imagination — than any ordinary, judicious person.

The effects of this Platonic element upon Renaissance criticism were various. In the first place, it was through the Platonic influence that the relation of beauty to poetry was first made prominent. [1] According to Scaliger, Tasso, Sidney, another world of beauty is created by the poet, — a world that possesses beauty in its perfection as this world

1 De Sanctis, ii. 193 *sq.*

never can. The reason alone leaves no place for beauty; and accordingly, for the neo-classicists, art was ultimately restricted to moral and psychological observation. Moreover, Platonism raised the question of the freedom of genius and of the imagination. Of all men, only the poet, as Sidney and others pointed out, is bound down and restricted by no laws. But if poetry is a matter of inspiration, how can it be called an art? If genius alone suffices, what need is there of study and artifice? For the extreme romanticists of this period, genius alone was accounted sufficient to produce the greatest works of poetry; for the extreme classicists, studious and labored art unaided by genius fulfilled all the functions of poetic creation; but most of the critics of the sixteenth century seem to have agreed with Horace that genius, or an inborn aptitude, is necessary to begin with, but that it needs art and study to regulate and perfect it. Genius cannot suffice without restraint and cultivation.

Scaliger, curiously, reconciles both classic and romantic elements. The poet, according to Scaliger, is inspired, is in fact a creator like God; but poetry is an imitation (that is, re-creation) of nature, according to certain fixed rules obtained from the observation of the anterior expression of nature in great art. It is these rules that make poetry an art; and these rules form a distinct neo-classic element imposed on the Aristotelian doctrine.

II. *Mediæval Elements*

The Middle Ages contributed to the poetic ideal of the Renaissance two elements: romantic themes and the Christian spirit. The forms and subjects of mediæval literature are distinctly romantic. Dante's *Divine Comedy* is an allegorical vision; it is almost unique in form, and has no classical prototype. [1] The tendency of Petrarchism was also in the direction of romanticism. Its "conceits" and its subjectivity led to an unclassical extravagance of thought and expression; and the Petrarchistic influence made lyric poetry, and accordingly the criticism of lyric poetry, more romantic than any other form of literature or literary criticism during the period of classicism. It was for this reason that there was little lyricism in the classical period, not only in France, but wherever the classic temper predominated. The themes of the *romanzi* are also mediæval and romantic; but while they are mediæval contributions to literature, [2] they became contributions to literary criticism only after the growth of national life and the development of the feeling of nationality, both distinctly modern.

Some reference has already been made to the paganization of culture by the humanists. But with the growth of that revival of Christian sentiment which led to the Reformation, there were numerous attempts to reconcile Christianity with

1 *Cf.* Bosanquet, *Hist. of Æsthetic*, p. 152 *sq.*
2 *Cf.* Foffano, p. 151 *sq.*

pagan culture.[1] Such men as Ficino and Pico della Mirandola attempted to harmonize Christianity and Platonic philosophy; and under the great patron of letters, Pope Leo X., there were various attempts to harmonize Christianity with the classic spirit in literature. In such poems as Vida's *Christiad* and Sannazaro's *De Partu Virginis*, Christianity is covered with the drapery of paganism or classicism.

The first reaction against this paganization of culture was, as has been seen, effected by Savonarola. This reaction was reënforced, in the next century, by the influence and authority of the Council of Trent; and after the middle of the sixteenth century the Christian ideal plays a prominent part in literary criticism. The spirit of both Giraldi Cintio and Minturno is distinctly Christian. For Giraldi the *romanzi* are Christian, and hence superior to the classical epics. He allows the introduction of pagan deities only into epics dealing with the ancient classical subjects; but Tasso goes further, and says that no modern heroic poet should have anything to do with them. According to Tasso, the heroes of an heroic poem must be Christian knights, and the poem itself must deal with a true, not a false, religion. The subject is not to be connected with any article of Christian faith or dogma, because that was fixed by the Council of Trent; but paganism in any form is altogether unfit for a modern epic. Tasso even goes so far as to assert that piety shall be numbered among the virtues of the knightly heroes of epic poetry.

1 Symonds, ii. 470.

At the same time also, Lorenzo Gambara wrote his work, *De Perfecta Poeseos Ratione*, to prove that it is essential for every poet to exclude from his poems, not only everything that is wicked or obscene, but also everything that is fabulous or that deals with pagan divinities. [1] It was to this religious reaction that we owe the Christian poetry of Tasso, Du Bartas, and Spenser. But humanism was strong, and rationalism was rife; and the religious revival was hardly more than temporary. Neo-classicism throughout Europe was essentially pagan.

III. *Modern Elements*

The literature of the Middle Ages constitutes, as it were, one vast body of European literature; only with the Renaissance did distinctly national literatures spring into existence. Nationalism as well as individualism was subsequent to the Renaissance; and it was at this period that the growth of a national literature, of national life, — in a word, patriotism in its widest sense, — was first effected.

The linguistic discussions and controversies of the sixteenth century prepared the way for a higher appreciation of national languages and literatures. These controversies on the comparative merits of the classical and vernacular tongues had begun in the time of Dante, and were continued in the sixteenth century by Bembo, Castiglione, Varchi, Muzio, Tolomei, and many others; and in 1564 Salviati summed up the Italian side of the question in an

1 Baillet, iii. 70.

oration in which he asserted that the Tuscan, or, as he called it, the Florentine language and the Florentine literature are vastly superior to any other language or literature, whether ancient or modern. However extravagant this claim may appear, the mere fact that Salviati made such a claim at all is enough to give him a place worthy of serious consideration in the history of Italian literature. The other side of the controversy finds its extremest expression in a treatise of Celio Calcagnini addressed to Giraldi Cintio, in which the hope is expressed that the Italian language, and all the literature composed in that language, would be absolutely abandoned by the world. [1]

In Giraldi Cintio we find the first traces of purely national criticism. His purpose, in writing the discourse on the *romanzi*, was primarily to defend Ariosto, whom he had known personally in his youth. The point of view from which he starts is that the *romanzi* constitute a new form of poetry of which Aristotle did not know, and to which, therefore, Aristotle's rules do not apply. Giraldi regarded the romantic poems of Ariosto and Boiardo both as national and as Christian works; and Italian literature is thus for the first time critically distinguished from classical literature in regard to language, religion, and nationality. In Giraldi's discourse there is no apparent desire either to underrate or to disregard the *Poetics* of Aristotle; the fact was simply that Aristotle had not known the poems which deal with many actions of many men,

1 Tiraboschi, vii. 1559.

and hence it would be absurd to demand that such poems should conform to his rules. The *romanzi* deal with phases of poetry, and phases of life, which Aristotle could not be expected to understand.

A similar feeling of the distinct nationality of Italian literature is to be found in many of the prefaces of the Italian comedies of this period. Il Lasca, in the preface of the *Strega* (c. 1555), says that "Aristotle and Horace knew their own times, but ours are not the same at all. We have other manners, another religion, and another mode of life; and it is therefore necessary to make comedies after a different fashion." As early as 1534, Aretino, in the prologue of his *Cortegiana*, warned his audience "not to be astonished if the comic style is not observed in the manner required, for we live after a different fashion in modern Rome than they did in ancient Athens." Similarly, Gelli, in the dedication of the *Sporta* (1543), justifies the use of language not to be found in the great sources of Italian speech, on the ground that "language, together with all other natural things, continually varies and changes." [1]

Although there is in Giraldi Cintio no fundamental opposition to Aristotle, it is in his discourse on the *romanzi* that there may be found the first attempt to wrest a province of art from Aristotle's supreme authority. Neither Salviati, who had rated the Italian language above all others, nor Calcagnini, who had regarded it as the meanest of

1 Several similar extracts from Italian comic prologues may be found in Symonds, v. 533 *sq*.

all, had understood the discussion of the importance of the Tuscan tongue to be concerned with the question of Aristotle's literary supremacy. It was simply a national question — a question as to the national limits of Aristotle's authority, just as was the case in the several controversies connected with Tasso, Dante, and Guarini's *Pastor Fido.* [1] Castelvetro, in his commentary on the *Poetics*, differs from Aristotle on many occasions, and does not hesitate even to refute him. Yet his reverence for Aristotle is great; his sense of Aristotle's supreme authority is strong; and on one occasion, where Horace, Quintilian, and Cicero seem to differ from Aristotle, Castelvetro does not hesitate to assert that they could not have seen the passage of the *Poetics* in question, and that, in fact, they did not thoroughly understand the true constitution of a poet. [2]

The opposition to Aristotelianism among the humanists has already been alluded to. This opposition increased more and more with the development of modern philosophy. In 1536 Ramus had attacked Aristotle's authority at Paris. A few years later, in 1543, Ortensio Landi, who had been at the Court of France for some time, published his *Paradossi* in which it is contended that the works which pass under the name of Aristotle are not really Aristotle's at all, and that Aristotle himself was not only an ignoramus, but also the most villanous man of his age. "We have, of our own accord," he says, "placed our necks under the yoke,

1 Foffano, p. 154 *sq.*

2 *Poetica*, p. 32.

putting that vile beast of an Aristotle on a throne, and depending on his conclusions as if he were an oracle." [1] It is the philosophical authority of Aristotle that Landi is attacking. His attitude is not that of a humanist, for Cicero and Boccaccio do not receive more respectful treatment at his hands than Aristotle does. Landi, despite his mere eccentricities, represents the growth of modern free thought and the antagonism of modern philosophy to Aristotelianism.

The literary opposition and the philosophical opposition to Aristotelianism may be said to meet in Francesco Patrizzi, and, in a less degree, in Giordano Bruno. Patrizzi's bitter Antiperipateticism is to be seen in his *Nova de Universis Philosophia* (1591), in which the doctrines of Aristotle are shown to be false, inconsistent, and even opposed to the doctrines of the Catholic Church. His literary antagonism to Aristotle is shown in his remarkable work, *Della Poetica*, published at Ferrara in 1586. This work is divided into two parts, — the first historical, *La Deca Istoriale*, and the second controversial, *La Deca Disputata*. In the historical section he attempts to derive the norm of the different poetic forms, not from one or two great works as Aristotle had done, but from the whole history of literature. It is thus the first work in modern times to attempt the philosophical study of literary history, and to trace out the evolution of literary forms. The second or controversial section is directed against the *Poetics* of Aristotle, and in part

1 *Paradossi*, Venetia, 1545, ii. 29.

also against the critical doctrines of Torquato Tasso. In this portion of his work Patrizzi sets out to demonstrate — *per istoria, e per ragioni, e per autorità de' grandi antichi* — that the accepted critical opinions of his time were without foundation; and the *Poetics* of Aristotle himself he exhibits as obscure, inconsistent, and entirely unworthy of credence.

Similar antagonism to the critical doctrines of Aristotle is to be found in passages scattered here and there throughout the works of Giordano Bruno. In the first dialogue of the *Eroici Furori*, published at London in 1585, while Bruno was visiting England, he expresses his contempt for the mere pedants who judge poets by the rules of Aristotle's *Poetics*. His contention is that there are as many sorts of poets as there are human sentiments and ideas, and that poets, so far from being subservient to rules, are themselves really the authors of all critical dogma. Those who attack the great poets whose works do not accord with the rules of Aristotle are called by Bruno stupid pedants and beasts. The gist of his argument may be gathered from the following passage: —

"TANS. Thou dost well conclude that poetry is not born in rules, or only slightly and accidentally so; the rules are derived from the poetry, and there are as many kinds and sorts of true rules as there are kinds and sorts of true poets.

CIC. How then are the true poets to be known?

TANS. By the singing of their verses; in that singing they give delight, or they edify, or they edify and delight together.

CIC. To whom then are the rules of Aristotle useful?

TANS. To him who, unlike Homer, Hesiod, Orpheus, and others, could not sing without the rules of Aristotle, and who, having no Muse of his own, would coquette with that of Homer." [1]

A similar antagonism to Aristotle and a similar literary individualism are to be found in a much later work by Benedetto Fioretti, who under the pseudonym of Udeno Nisieli published the five volumes of his *Proginnasmi Poetici* between 1620 and 1639. [2] Just before the close of the sixteenth century, however, the *Poetics* had obtained an ardent defender against such attacks in the person of Francesco Buonamici, in his *Discorsi Poetici*; and three years later, in 1600, Faustino Summo published a similar defence of Aristotle. The attacks on Aristotle's literary dictatorship were of little avail; it was hardly necessary even to defend him. For two centuries to come he was to reign supreme on the continent of Europe; and in Italy this supremacy was hardly disturbed until the days of Goldoni and Metastasio.

1 *Opere*, ii. 315 (Williams's translation).

2 *Cf.* the diverse opinions of Tiraboschi, viii. 516, and Hallam, *Lit. of Europe*, pt. iii. ch. 7.

Part Second

LITERARY CRITICISM IN FRANCE

LITERARY CRITICISM IN FRANCE

CHAPTER I

THE CHARACTER AND DEVELOPMENT OF FRENCH CRITICISM IN THE SIXTEENTH CENTURY

LITERARY criticism in France, while beginning somewhat later than in Italy, preceded the birth of criticism in England and in Spain by a number of years. Critical activity in nearly all the countries of western Europe seems to have been ushered in by the translation of Horace's *Ars Poetica* into the vernacular tongues. Critical activity in Italy began with Dolce's Italian version of the *Ars Poetica* in 1535; in France, with the French version of Pelletier in 1545; in England, with the English version of Drant in 1567; and in Spain, with the Spanish versions of Espinel and Zapata in 1591 and 1592, respectively. Two centuries of literary discussion had prepared the way for criticism in Italy; and lacking this period of preparation, French criticism during the sixteenth century was necessarily of a much more practical character than that of Italy during the same age. The critical works of France, and of England also, were on the whole designed for those whose immediate intention it was to write verse themselves. The disinterested and philosophic treatment of æsthetic problems, wholly aside from all practical considerations, characterized much of the critical activity of the Italian Renaissance, but did not become general in France until the next century. For this reason, in the French and English sections of this essay, it will be necessary to deal with various rhetorical and metrical questions which in the Italian section could be largely disregarded. In these matters, as in the more general questions of criticism, it will be seen that sixteenth-century Italy furnished the source of all the accepted critical doctrines of western Europe. The comparative number of critical works in Italy and in France is also noteworthy. While those of the Italian Renaissance may be counted by the score, the literature of France during the sixteenth century, exclusive of a few purely rhetorical treatises, hardly offers more than a single dozen. It is evident, therefore, that the treatment of French criticism must be more limited in extent than that of Italian criticism, and somewhat different in character.

The literature of the sixteenth century in France is divided into two almost equal parts by Du Bellay's *Défense et Illustration de la Langue française*, published in 1549. In no other country of Europe is the transition from the Middle Ages to the Renaissance so clearly marked as it is in France by this single book. With the invasion of Italy by the army of Charles VIII. in 1494, the influence of Italian art, of Italian learning, of Italian poetry, had received its first impetus in France. But over half a century was to elapse before the effects of this influence upon the creative literature of France was universally and powerfully felt. During this period the activity of Budæus, Erasmus, Dolet, and numerous other French and foreign humanists strengthened the cause and widened the influence of the New Learning. But it is only with the birth of the Pléiade that modern French literature may be said to have begun. In 1549 Du Bellay's *Défense*, the manifesto of the new school, appeared. Ronsard's *Odes* were published in the next year; and in 1552 Jodelle inaugurated French tragedy with his *Cléopâtre*, and first, as Ronsard said,

> " Françoisement chanta la grecque tragédie."

The *Défense* therefore marks a distinct epoch in the critical as well as the creative literature of France. The critical works that preceded it, if they may be called critical in any real sense, did not attempt to do more than formulate the conventional notions of rhetorical and metrical structure common to the French poets of the later Middle Ages. The Pléiade itself, as will be more clearly understood later, was also chiefly concerned with linguistic and rhetorical reforms; and as late as 1580 Montaigne could say that there were more poets in France than judges and interpreters of poetry.[1] The creative reforms of the Pléiade lay largely in the direction of the formation of a poetic language, the introduction of new *genres*, the creation of new

1 *Essais*, i. 36.

rhythms, and the imitation of classical literature. But with the imitation of classical literature there came the renewal of the ancient subjects of inspiration; and from this there proceeded a high and dignified conception of the poet's office. Indeed, many of the more general critical ideas of the Pléiade spring from the desire to justify the function of poetry, and to magnify its importance. The new school and its epigones dominate the second half of the sixteenth century; and as the first half of the century was practically unproductive of critical literature, a history of French Renaissance criticism is hardly more than an account of the poetic theories of the Pléiade.

The series of rhetorical and metrical treatises that precede Du Bellay's *Défense* begins with *L'Art de dictier et de fere chançons, balades, virelais et rondeaulx*, written by the poet Eustache Deschamps in 1392, over half a century after the similar work of Antonio da Tempo in Italy. [1] Toward the close of the fifteenth century a work of the same nature, the *Fleur de Rhétorique*, by an author who refers to himself as L'Infortuné, seems to have had some influence on later treatises. Three works of this sort fall within the first half of the sixteenth century: the *Grand et vrai Art de pleine Rhétorique* of Pierre Fabri, published at Rouen in 1521; the *Rhétorique metrifiée* of Gracien du Pont, published at Paris in 1539; and the *Art Poétique* of Thomas Sibilet, published at Paris in 1548. The second

1 On these early works, see Langlois, *De Artibus Rhetoricæ Rhythmicæ*, Parisiis, 1890.

part of Fabri's *Rhétorique* deals with questions of versification — of rhyme, rhythm, and the complex metrical form of such poets as Crétin, Meschinot, and Molinet, in whom Pasquier found *prou de rime et équivoque, mais peu de raison.* As the *Rhétorique* of Fabri is little more than an amplification of the similar work of L'Infortuné, so the work of Gracien du Pont is little more than a reproduction of Fabri's. Gracien du Pont is still chiefly intent on *rime équivoquée, rime entrelacée, rime retrograde, rime concatenée*, and the various other mediæval complexities of versification. Sibilet's *Art Poétique* is more interesting than any of its predecessors. It was published a year before the *Défense* of Du Bellay, and discusses many of the new *genres* which the latter advocates. Sibilet treats of the sonnet, which had recently been borrowed from the Italians by Mellin de Saint-Gelais, the ode, which had just been employed by Pelletier, and the epigram, as practised by Marot. The eclogue is described as "Greek by invention, Latin by usurpation, and French by imitation." But one of the most interesting passages in Sibilet's book is that in which the French morality is compared with the classical drama. This passage exhibits perhaps the earliest trace of the influence of Italian ideas on French criticism; it will be discussed later in connection with the dramatic theories of this period.

It is about the middle of the sixteenth century, then, that the influence of Italian criticism is first visible. The literature of Italy was read with avidity in France. Many educated young Frenchmen travelled in Italy, and several Italian men of letters visited France. Girolamo Muzio travelled in France in 1524, and again in 1530 with Giulio Cammillo. [1] Aretino mentions the fact that a Vincenzo Maggi was at the Court of France in 1548, but it has been doubted whether this was the author of the commentary on the *Poetics*. [2] In 1549, after the completion of the two last parts of his *Poetica*, dedicated to the Bishop of Arras, Trissino made a tour about France. [3] Nor must we forget the number of Italian scholars called to Paris by Francis I. [4] The literary relations between the two countries do not concern us here; but it is no insignificant fact that the great literary reforms of the Pléiade should take place between 1548 and 1550, the very time when critical activity first received its great impetus in Italy. This Italian influence is just becoming apparent in Sibilet, for whom the poets between Jean le Maire de Belges and Clément Marot are the chief models, but who is not wholly averse to the moderate innovations derived by France from classical antiquity and the Italian Renaissance.

M. Brunetière, in a very suggestive chapter of his History of French Criticism, regards the *Défense* of Du Bellay, the *Poetics* of Scaliger, and the *Art Poétique* of Vauquelin de la Fresnaye as the most important critical works in France during

1 Tiraboschi, vii. 350.
2 *Ibid.* vii. 1465.
3 Morsolin, *Trissino*, p. 358.
4 Egger, *Hellénisme*, ch. vii.

the sixteenth century.[1] It may indeed be said that Du Bellay's *Défense* (1549) is not in any true sense a work of literary criticism at all; that Scaliger's *Poetics* (1561) is the work, not of a French critic, but of an Italian humanist; and that Vauquelin's *Art Poétique* (not published until 1605), so far as any influence it may have had is concerned, does not belong to the sixteenth century, and can hardly be called important. At the same time these three works are interesting documents in the literary history of France, and represent three distinct stages in the development of French criticism in the sixteenth century. Du Bellay's work marks the beginning of the introduction of classical ideals into French literature; Scaliger's work, while written by an Italian and in Latin, was composed and published in France, and marks the introduction of the Aristotelian canons into French criticism; and Vauquelin's work indicates the sum of critical ideas which France had gathered and accepted in the sixteenth century.

With Du Bellay's *Défense et Illustration de la Langue française* (1549) modern literature and modern criticism in France may be said to begin. The *Défense* is a monument of the influence of Italian upon French literary and linguistic criticism. The purpose of the book, as its title implies, is to defend the French language, and to indicate the means by which it can approach more closely to dignity and perfection. The fundamental contention of Du Bellay is, first, that the French

1 Brunetière, i. 43.

language is capable of attaining perfection; and, secondly, that it can only hope to do so by imitating Greek and Latin. This thesis is propounded and proved in the first book of the *Défense;* and the second book is devoted to answering the question: By what specific means is this perfection, based on the imitation of the perfection of Greek and Latin, to be attained by the French tongue? Du Bellay contends that as the diversity of language among the different nations is ascribable entirely to the caprice of men, the perfection of any tongue is due exclusively to the diligence and artifice of those who use it. It is the duty, therefore, of every one to set about consciously to improve his native speech. The Latin tongue was not always as perfect as it was in the days of Virgil and Cicero; and if these writers had regarded language as incapable of being polished and enriched, or if they had imagined that their language could only be perfected by the imitation of their own national predecessors, Latin would never have arrived at a higher state of perfection than that of Ennius and Crassus. But as Virgil and Cicero perfected Latin by imitating Greek, so the French tongue can only be made beautiful by imitating Greek, Latin, and Italian, all of which have attained a certain share of perfection. [1]

At the same time, two things must be guarded against. The French tongue cannot be improved by merely translating the classic and Italian tongues. Translation has its value in popularizing ideas; but by mere translation no language

1 *Cf.* Horace, *Ars Poet.* 53 *sq.*

or literature can hope to attain perfection. Nor is a mere bald imitation sufficient; but, in Du Bellay's oft-cited phrase, the beauties of these foreign tongues "must be converted into blood and nourishment." [1] The classics have "blood, nerves, and bones," while the older French writers have merely "skin and color." [2] The modern French writer should therefore dismiss with contempt the older poets of France, and set about to imitate the Greeks, Latins, and Italians. He should leave off composing rondeaux, ballades, virelays, and such *épiceries*, which corrupt the taste of the French language, and serve only to show its ignorance and poverty; and in their stead he should employ the epigram, which mingles, in Horace's words, the profitable with the pleasant, the tearful elegy, in imitation of Ovid and Tibullus, the ode, one of the sublimest forms of poetry, the eclogue, in imitation of Theocritus, Virgil, and Sannazaro, and the beautiful sonnet, an Italian invention no less learned than pleasing. [3] Instead of the morality and the farce, the poet should write tragedies and comedies; he should attempt another *Iliad* or *Æneid* for the glory and honor of France. This is the gist of Du Bellay's argument in so far as it deals in general terms with the French language and literature. The six or seven concluding chapters treat of more minute and detailed questions of language and versification. Du Bellay advises the adoption of classical words as a means of enriching the French tongue, and speaks with favor of the

1 *Défense*, i. 7. 2 *Ibid.* ii. 2. 3 *Ibid.* ii. 4.

use of rhymeless verse in imitation of the classics. The *Défense* ends with an appeal to the reader not to fear to go and despoil Greece and Rome of their treasures for the benefit of French poetry.[1]

From this analysis it will be seen that the *Défense* is really a philological polemic, belonging to the same class as the long series of Italian discussions on the vulgar tongue which begins with Dante, and which includes the works of Bembo, Castiglione, Varchi, and others. It is, as a French critic has said, a combined pamphlet, defence, and *ars poetica*;[2] but it is only an *ars poetica* in so far as it advises the French poet to employ certain poetic forms, and treats of rhythm and rhyme in a concluding chapter or two. But curiously enough, the source and inspiration of Du Bellay's work have never been pointed out. The actual model of the *Défense* was without doubt Dante's *De Vulgari Eloquio*, which, in the Italian version of Trissino, had been given to the world for the first time in 1529, exactly twenty years before the *Défense*. The two works, allowing for the difference in time and circumstance, resemble each other closely in spirit and purpose as well as in contents and design. Du Bellay's work, like Dante's, is divided into two books, each of which is again divided into about the same number of chapters. The first book of both works deals with language in general, and the relations of the vulgar tongue to the ancient and modern languages; the second book of both works deals with the particular practices of the

1 *Cf.* Vida, in Pope, i. 167.

2 Lanson, *op. cit.*, p. 274.

vulgar tongue concerning which each author is arguing. Both works begin with a somewhat similar theory of the origin of language; both works close with a discussion of the versification of the vernacular. The purpose of both books is the justification of the vulgar tongue, and the consideration of the means by which it can attain perfection; the title of *De Vulgari Eloquio* might be applied with equal force to either treatise. The *Défense*, by this justification of the French language on rational if not entirely cogent and consistent grounds, prepared the way for critical activity in France; and it is no insignificant fact that the first critical work of modern France should have been based on the first critical work of modern Italy. Thirty years later, Henri Estienne, in his *Précellence du Langage françois*, could assert that French is the best language of ancient or modern times, just as Salviati in 1564 had claimed that preëminent position for Italian.[1]

It is not to be expected that so radical a break with the national traditions of France as was implied by Du Bellay's innovations would be left unheeded by the enemies of the Pléiade. The answer came soon, in an anonymous pamphlet, entitled *Le Quintil Horatian sur la Défense et Illustration de la Langue françoise*. Until a very few years ago, this treatise was ascribed to a disciple of Marot, Charles Fontaine. But in 1883 an autograph letter of Fontaine's was discovered, in which he strenuously denies the authorship of the *Quintil Horatian*;

1 *Cf.* T. Tasso, xxiii. 97.

and more recent researches have shown pretty conclusively that the real author was a friend of Fontaine's, Barthélemy Aneau, head of the College of Lyons. [1] The *Quintil Horatian* was first published in 1550, the year after the appearance of the *Défense*. [2] The author informs us that he had translated the whole of Horace's *Ars Poetica* into French verse "over twenty years ago, before Pelletier or any one else," that is, between 1525 and 1530. [3] This translation was never published, but fragments of it are cited in the *Quintil Horatian*. The pamphlet itself takes up the arguments of Du Bellay step by step, and refutes them. The author finds fault with the constructions, the metaphors, and the neologisms of Du Bellay. Aneau's temperament was dogmatic and pedagogic; his judgment was not always good; and modern French critics cannot forgive him for attacking Du Bellay's use of such a word as *patrie*.

But it is not entirely just to speak of the *Quintil Horatian*, in the words of a modern literary historian, as full of futile and valueless criticisms. The author's minute linguistic objections are often hypercritical, but his work represents a natural reaction against the Pléiade. His chief censure of the *Défense* was directed against the introduction of classical and Italian words into the French language. "Est-ce là défense et illustration," he exclaims, "ou

1 H. Chamard, "Le Date et l'Auteur du Quintil Horatian," in the *Revue d'Histoire littéraire de la France*, 1898, v. 59 *sq*.

2 *Ibid*. v. 54 *sq*.

3 *Ibid*. v. 62; 63, n. 1.

plus tost offense et dénigration? " He charges the Pléiade with having contemned the classics of French poetry; the new school advocated the disuse of the complicated metrical forms merely because they were too difficult. The sonnet, the ode, and the elegy he dismisses as useless innovations. The object of poetry, according to Horace, is to gladden and please, while the elegy merely saddens and brings tears to the eyes. "Poetry," he says, "is like painting; and as painting is intended to fill us with delight, and not to sadden us, so the mournful elegy is one of the meanest forms of poetry." Aneau is unable to appreciate the high and sublime conception of the poet's office which the Pléiade first introduced into French literature; for him the poet is a mere versifier who amuses his audience. He represents the general reaction of the national spirit against the classical innovations of the Pléiade; and the *Quintil Horatian* may therefore be called the last representative work of the older school of poetry.

It was at about this period that Aristotle's *Poetics* first influenced French criticism. In one of the concluding chapters of the *Défense* Du Bellay remarks that "the virtues and vices of a poem have been diligently treated by the ancients, such as Aristotle and Horace, and after them by Hieronymus Vida." [1] Horace is mentioned and cited in numerous other places, and the influence of the general rhetorical portions of the *Ars Poetica* is very marked throughout the *Défense*; there are

1 *Défense*, ii. 9.

also many traces of the influence of Vida. But there is no evidence whatsoever of any knowledge of Aristotle's *Poetics*. Of its name and importance Du Bellay had probably read in the writings of the Italians, but of its contents he knew little or nothing. There is indeed no well-established allusion to the *Poetics* in France before this time. None of the French humanists seems to have known it. Its title is cited by Erasmus in a letter dated February 27, 1531, and it was published by him without any commentary at Basle in the same year, though Simon Grynæus appears to have been the real editor of this work. An edition of the *Poetics* was also published at Paris in 1541, but does not seem to have had any appreciable influence on the critical activity of France. Several years after the publication of the *Défense*, in the satirical poem, *Le Poëte Courtisan*, written shortly after his return from Italy in 1555, Du Bellay shows a somewhat more definite knowledge of the contents of the *Poetics*: —

> "Je ne veux point ici du maistre d'Alexandre [*i.e.* Aristotle],
> Touchant l'art poétic, les preceptes t'apprendre
> Tu n'apprendras de moy comment jouer il faut
> Les miseres des rois dessus un eschaffaut:
> Je ne t'enseigne l'art de l'humble comœdie
> Ni du Méonien la muse plus hardie:
> Bref je ne monstre ici d'un vers horacien
> Les vices et vertus du poëme ancien:
> Je ne depeins aussi le poëte du Vide." [1]

In 1555 Guillaume Morel, the disciple of Turnebus, published an edition of Aristotle's *Poetics* at Paris. It is interesting

1 Du Bellay, p. 120.

to note, however, that the reference in the *Défense* is the first allusion to the *Poetics* to be found in the critical literature of France; by 1549 the Italian Renaissance, and Italian criticism, had come into France for good. In 1560, the year before the publication of Scaliger's *Poetics*, Aristotle's treatise had acquired such prominence that in a volume of selections from Aristotle's works, published at Paris in that year, *Aristotelis Sententiœ*, the selections from the *Poetics* are placed at the head of the volume. [1] In 1572 Jean de la Taille refers his readers to what "the great Aristotle in his *Poetics*, and after him Horace though not with the same subtlety, have said more amply and better than I." [2]

The influence of Scaliger's *Poetics* on the French dramatic criticism of this period has generally been overestimated. Scaliger's influence in France was not inconsiderable during the sixteenth century, but it was not until the very end of the century that he held the dictatorial position afterward accorded to him. No edition of his *Poetics* was ever published at Paris. The first edition appeared at Lyons, and subsequent editions appeared at Heidelberg and Leyden. It was in Germany, in Spain, and in England that his influence was first felt; and it was largely through the Dutch scholars, Heinsius and Vossius, that his influence was carried into France in the next century. It is a mistake to say that he had any primary influence on

1 Parisiis, apud Hieronymum de Marnaf, 1560.
2 Robert, appendix iii.

the formulation and acceptance of the unities of time and place in French literature; there is in his *Poetics*, as has been seen, no such definite and formal statement of the unities as may be found in Castelvetro, in Jean de la Taille, in Sir Philip Sidney, or in Chapelain. At the same time, while Scaliger's *Poetics* did not assume during the sixteenth century the dictatorial supremacy it attained during the seventeenth, and while the particular views enunciated in its pages had no direct influence on the current of sixteenth-century ideas, it certainly had an indirect influence on the general tendency of the critical activity of the French Renaissance. This indirect influence manifests itself in the gradual Latinization of culture during the second half of the sixteenth century, and, as will be seen later, in the emphasis on the Aristotelian canons in French dramatic criticism. Scaliger was a personal friend of several members of the Pléiade, and there is every reason to believe that he wielded considerable, even if merely indirect, influence on the development of that great literary movement.

The last expression of the poetic theories of the Pléiade is to be found in the didactic poem of Vauquelin de la Fresnaye, *L'Art Poétique françois, où l'on peut remarquer la perfection et le défaut des anciennes et des modernes poésies*. This poem, though not published until 1605, was begun in 1574 at the command of Henry III., and, augmented by successive additions, was not yet complete by 1590. Vauquelin makes the following explicit acknowledgment of his indebtedness to the critical writers that preceded him: —

> "Pour ce ensuivant les pas du fils de Nicomache [*i.e.* Aristotle],
> Du harpeur de Calabre [*i.e.* Horace], et tout ce que remache
> Vide et Minturne aprés, j'ay cet œuvre apresté." [1]

Aristotle, Horace, Vida, and Minturno are thus his acknowledged models and sources. Nearly the whole of Horace's *Ars Poetica* he has translated and embodied in his poem; and he has borrowed from Vida a considerable number of images and metaphors. [2] His indebtedness to Aristotle and to Minturno brings up several intricate questions. It has been said that Vauquelin simply mentioned Minturno in order to put himself under the protection of a respectable Italian authority. [3] On the contrary, exclusive of Horace, Ronsard, and Du Bellay, the whole of whose critical discussions he has almost incorporated into his poem, Minturno is his chief authority, his model, and his guide. In fact, it was probably from Minturno that he derived his entire knowledge of the Aristotelian canons; it is not Aristotle, but Minturno's conception of Aristotle, that Vauquelin has adhered to. Many points in his poem are explained by this fact; here only one can be mentioned. Vauquelin's account, in the second canto of his *Art Poétique*, of the origin of

1 *Art Poét.* i. 63.
2 Pellissier, pp. 57-63.
3 Lemercier, *Étude sur Vauquelin*, 1887, p. 117, and Pellissier, p. 57.

the drama from the songs at the altar of Bacchus at the time of the vintage, is undoubtedly derived from Minturno. [1] It may have been observed that during the Renaissance there were two distinct conceptions of the origin of poetry. One, which might be called ethical, was derived from Horace, according to whom the poet was originally a lawgiver, or divine prophet; and this conception persists in modern literature from Poliziano to Shelley. The other, or scientific conception, was especially applied to the drama, and was based on Aristotle's remarks on the origin of tragedy; this attempt to discover some scientific explanation for poetic phenomena may be found in the more rationalistic of Renaissance critics, such as Scaliger and Viperano. Vauquelin de la Fresnaye, the disciple of Ronsard and the last exponent of the critical doctrines of the Pléiade, thus represents the incorporation of the body of Italian ideas into French criticism.

With Vauquelin de la Fresnaye and De Laudun Daigaliers (1598) the history of French criticism during the sixteenth century is at an end. The critical activity of this period, as has already been remarked, is of a far more practical character than that of Italy. Literary criticism in France was created by the exigencies of a great literary movement; and throughout the century it never lost its connection with this movement, or failed to serve it in some practical way. The poetic criticism was carried on by poets, whose desire it was to further

1 Minturno, *Arte Poetica*, p. 73; *De Poeta*, p. 252. *Cf.* Vauquelin, Pellissier's introduction, p. xliv.

a cause, to defend their own works, or to justify their own views. The dramatic criticism was for the most part carried on by dramatists, sometimes even in the prefaces of their plays. In the sixteenth century, as ever since, the interrelation of the creative and the critical faculties in France was marked and definite. But there was, one might almost say, little critical theorizing in the French Renaissance. Excepting, of course, Scaliger, there was even nothing of the deification of Aristotle found in Italian criticism. To take notice of a minute but significant detail, there was no attempt to explain Aristotle's doctrine of *katharsis*, the source of infinite controversy in Italy. There was no detailed and consistent discussion of the theory of the epic poem. All these things may be found in seventeenth-century France; but their home was sixteenth-century Italy.

CHAPTER II

THE THEORY OF POETRY IN THE FRENCH RENAISSANCE

It is in keeping with the practical character of the literary criticism of this period that the members of the Pléiade did not concern themselves with the general theory of poetry. Until the very end of the century there is not to be found any systematic poetic theory in France. It is in dramatic criticism that this period has most to offer, and the dramatic criticism is peculiarly interesting because it foreshadows in many ways the doctrines upon which were based the dramas of Racine and Corneille.

I. *The Poetic Art*

In Du Bellay's *Défense* there is no attempt to formulate a consistent body of critical doctrine; but the book exhibits, in a more or less crude form, all the tendencies for which the Pléiade stands in French literature. The fundamental idea of the *Défense* is that French poetry can only hope to reach perfection by imitating the classics. The imitation of the classics implies, in the first place, erudition on the part of the poet; and, moreover, it requires intellectual labor and study. The poet is born, it is true; but this only refers to the ardor and joyfulness of spirit which naturally excite him, but which, without learning and erudition, are absolutely useless. "He who wishes poetic immortality," says Du Bellay, "must spend his time in the solitude of his own chamber; instead of eating, drinking, and sleeping, he must endure hunger, thirst, and long vigils." [1] Elsewhere he speaks of silence and solitude as *amy des Muses*. From all this there arises a natural contempt for the ignorant people, who know nothing of ancient learning: "Especially do I wish to admonish him who aspires to a more than vulgar glory, to separate himself from such inept admirers, to flee from the ignorant people, — the people who are the enemies of all rare and antique learning, — and to content himself with few readers, following the example of him who did not demand for an audience any one beside Plato himself." [2]

In the *Art Poétique* of Jacques Pelletier du Mans, published at Lyons in 1555, the point of view is that of the Pléiade, but more mellow and moderate than that of its most advanced and radical members. The treatise begins with an account of the antiquity and excellence of poetry; and poets are spoken of as originally the *maîtres et réformateurs de la vie*. Poetry is then compared with oratory and with painting, after the usual Renaissance fashion; and Pelletier agrees with Horace in regarding the combined power of art and nature as

1 *Défense*, ii. 3. 2 *Ibid.* ii. 11.

necessary to the fashioning of a poet. His conception of the latter's office is not unlike that of Tasso and Shelley, "It is the office of the poet to give novelty to old things, authority to the new, beauty to the rude, light to the obscure, faith to the doubtful, and to all things their true nature, and to their true nature all things." Concerning the questions of language, versification, and the feeling for natural scenery, he agrees fundamentally with the chief writers of the Pléiade.

The greatest of these, Ronsard, has given expression to his views on the poetic art in his *Abrégé de l'Art Poétique françois* (1565), and later in the two prefaces of his epic of the *Franciade*. The chief interest of the *Abrégé* in the present discussion is that it expounds and emphasizes the high notion of the poet's office introduced into French poetry by the Pléiade. Before the advent of the new school, mere skill in the complicated forms of verse was regarded as the test of poetry. The poet was simply a *rimeur*; and the term "*poète*," with all that it implies, first came into use with the Pléiade. The distinction between the versifier and the poet, as pointed out by Aristotle and insisted upon by the Italians, became with the Pléiade almost vital. Binet, the disciple and biographer of Ronsard, says of his master that "he was the mortal enemy of versifiers, whose conceptions are all debased, and who think they have wrought a masterpiece when they have transposed something from prose into verse." [1] Ronsard's own account

1 Ronsard, vii. 310, 325.

of the dignity and high function of poetry must needs be cited at length: —

"Above all things you will hold the Muses in reverence, yea, in singular veneration, and you will never let them serve in matters that are dishonest, or mere jests, or injudicious libels; but you will hold them dear and sacred, as the daughters of Jupiter, that is, God, who by His holy grace has through them first made known to ignorant people the excellencies of His majesty. For poetry in early times was only an allegorical theology, in order to make stupid men, by pleasant and wondrously colored fables, know the secrets they could not comprehend, were the truth too openly made known to them.... Now, since the Muses do not care to lodge in a soul unless it is good, holy, and virtuous, you should try to be of a good disposition, not wicked, scowling, and cross, but animated by a gentle spirit; and you should not let anything enter your mind that is not superhuman and divine. You should have, in the first place, conceptions that are high, grand, beautiful, and not trailing upon the ground; for the principal part of poetry consists of invention, which comes as much from a beautiful nature as from the reading of good and ancient authors. If you undertake any great work, you will show yourself devout and fearing God, commencing it either with His name or by any other which represents some effects of His majesty, after the manner of the Greek poets... for the Muses, Apollo, Mercury, Pallas, and other similar deities, merely represent the powers of God, to which the first men gave several names for the diverse effects of His incomprehensible majesty." [1]

In this eloquent passage the conception of the poet as an essentially moral being, — a doctrine first enunciated by Strabo, and repeated by Minturno and others, — and Boccaccio's notion of

1 Ronsard, vii. 37 *sq*.

poetry as originally an allegorical theology, are both introduced into French criticism. Elsewhere Ronsard repeats the mediæval concept that poets

> "d'un voile divers
> Par fables ont caché le vray sens de leurs vers." [1]

It will be seen also that for Ronsard, poetry is essentially a matter of inspiration; and in the poem just quoted, the *Discours à Jacques Grévin*, he follows the Platonic conception of divine inspiration or madness. A few years later Montaigne said of poetry that "it is an easier matter to frame it than to know it; being base and humble, it may be judged by the precepts and art of it, but the good and lofty, the supreme and divine, are beyond rules and above reason. It hath no community with our judgment, but ransacketh and ravisheth the same." [2]

In his various critical works Ronsard shows considerable indebtedness to the Italian theorists, especially to Minturno. He does not attempt any formal definition of poetry, but its function is described as follows: "As the end of the orator is to persuade, so that of the poet is to imitate, invent, and represent the things that are, that can be, or that the ancients regarded as true." [3] The concluding clause of this passage is intended to justify the modern use of the ancient mythology; but the whole passage seems primarily to follow Scaliger [4]

1 Ronsard, vi. 311 *sq*.

2 *Essais*, i. 36, Florio's translation.

3 Ronsard, vii. 322. *Cf.* Aristotle, *Poet.* ix. 1-4; xxv. 6, 7.

4 *Poet.* iii. 24.

and Minturno.[1] It is to be observed that verse is not mentioned in this definition as an essential requirement of poetry. It was indeed a favorite contention of his, and one for which he was indebted to the Italians, that all who write in verse are not poets. Lucan and Silius Italicus have robed history with the raiment of verse; but according to Ronsard they would have done better in many ways to have written in prose. The poet, unlike the historian, deals with the verisimilar and the probable; and while he cannot be responsible for falsehoods which are in opposition to the truth of things, any more than the historian can, he is not interested to know whether or not the details of his poems are actual historical facts. Verisimilitude, and not fact, is therefore the test of poetry.

In Vauquelin de la Fresnaye may be found most of the Aristotelian distinctions in regard to imitation, harmony, rhythm, and poetic theory in general; but these distinctions he derived, as has already been said, not directly from Aristotle, but in all probability from Minturno. Poetry is defined as an art of imitation: —

> "C'est un art d'imiter, un art de contrefaire
> Que toute poësie, ainsi que de pourtraire."[2]

Verse is described as a heaven-sent instrument, the language of the gods; and its value in poetry consists in clarifying and making the design compact.[3] But it is not an essential of poetry; Aris-

1 *De Poeta*, pp. 44, 47.
2 *Art Poét.* i. 187.
3 *Ibid.* i. 87 *sq.*

totle permits us to poetize in prose; and the romances of Heliodorus and Montemayor are examples of this poetic prose.[1] The object of poetry is that it shall cause delight, and unless it succeeds in this it is entirely futile: —

> "C'est le but, c'est la fin des vers que resjouir:
> Les Muses autrement ne les veulent ouir."

As it is the function of the orator to persuade and the physician to cure, and as they fail in their offices unless they effect these ends, so the poet fails unless he succeeds in pleasing.[2] This comparison is a favorite one with the Italian critics. A similar passage has already been cited from Daniello; and the same notion is thus expressed by Lodovico Dolce: "The aim of the physician is to cure diseases by means of medicine; the orator's to persuade by force of his arguments; and if neither attains this end, he is not called physician or orator. So if the poet does not delight, he is not a poet, for poetry delights all, even the ignorant."[3]

But delight, according to Vauquelin, is merely the means of directing us to higher things; poetry is a delightful means of leading us to virtue: —

> "C'est pourquoy des beaus vers la joyeuse alegresse
> Nous conduit aux vertus d'une plaisante addresse."[4]

Vanquelin, like Scaliger, Tasso, Sidney, compares the poet with God, the great Workman, who made everything out of

1 *Art Poét.* ii. 261.
2 *Ibid.* i. 697 *sq.*
3 *Osservationi*, Vinegia, 1560, p. 190.
4 *Art Poét.* i. 744.

nothing.[1] The poet is a divinely inspired person, who, *sans art, sans sçavoir*, creates works of divine beauty. Vauquelin's contemporary, Du Bartas, has in his *Uranie* expressed this idea in the following manner: —

> "Each art is learned by art; but Poesie
> Is a mere heavenly gift, and none can taste
> The dews we drop from Pindus plenteously,
> If sacred fire have not his heart embraced.
>
> "Hence is't that many great Philosophers,
> Deep-learned clerks, in prose most eloquent,
> Labor in vain to make a graceful verse,
> Which many a novice frames most excellent."[2]

While this is the accepted Renaissance doctrine of inspiration, Vauquelin, in common with all other followers of the Pléiade, was fully alive to the necessity of artifice and study in poetry; and he agrees with Horace in regarding both art and nature as equally necessary to the making of a good poet. It is usage that makes art, but art perfects and regulates usage: —

> "Et ce bel Art nous sert d'escalier pour monter
> A Dieu."[3]

II. *The Drama*

Dramatic criticism in France begins as a reaction against the drama of the Middle Ages. The mediæval drama was formless and inorganic, without art or dignity. The classical

1 *Art Poét.* i. 19. *Cf.* Tasso, cited by Shelley, *Defence*, p. 42, "No one merits the name of creator except God and the poet."

2 Sylvester's *Du Bartas*, 1641, p. 242.

3 *Art Poét.* i. 149.

drama, on the other hand, possessed both form and dignity; and the new school, perceiving this contrast, looked to the Aristotelian canons, as restated by the Italians, to furnish the dignity and art which the tragedy of Greece and Rome possessed, and which their own moralities and farces fundamentally lacked. In the first reference to dramatic literature in French criticism, the mediæval and classical dramas are compared after this fashion; but as Sibilet (1548), in whose work this passage appears, wrote a year or so before the advent of the Pléiade, the comparison is not so unfavorable to the morality and the farce as it became in later critics. "The French morality," says Sibilet, "represents, in certain distinct traits, Greek and Latin tragedy, especially in that it treats of grave and momentous deeds (*faits graves et principaus*); and if the French had always made the ending of the morality sad and dolorous, the morality would be a tragedy. But in this, as in all things, we have followed our natural taste or inclination, which is to take from foreign things not all we see, but only what we think will be useful to us and of national advantage; for in the morality we treat, as the Greeks and Romans do in their tragedies, the narration of deeds that are illustrious, magnanimous, and virtuous, or true, or at least verisimilar; but we do otherwise in what is useful to the information of our manners and life, without subjecting ourselves to any sorrow or pleasure of the issue." [1] It would seem that Sibilet regards

1 Sibilet, *Art Poét.* ii. 8.

the morality as lacking nothing but the unhappy ending of classical tragedy. At the same time this passage exhibits perhaps the first trace of Aristotelianism in French critical literature; for Sibilet specifies several characteristic features of Greek and Latin tragedy, which he could have found only in Aristotle or in the Italians. In the first place, tragedy deals only with actions that are grave, illustrious, and for the most part magnanimous or virtuous. In the second place, the actions of tragedy are either really true, that is, historical, or if not true, have all the appearance of truth, that is, they are verisimilar. Thirdly, the end of tragedy is always sad and dolorous. Fourthly, tragedy performs a useful function, which is connected in some way with the reformation of manners and life; and, lastly, the effect of tragedy is connected with the sorrow or pleasure brought about by the catastrophe. These distinctions anticipate many of those found later in Scaliger and in the French critics.

In Du Bellay (1549) we find no traces of dramatic theory beyond the injunction, already noted, that the French should substitute classical tragedy and comedy for the old morality and farce. A few years later, however, in Pelletier (1555), there appears an almost complete system of dramatic criticism. He urges the French to attempt the composition of tragedy and comedy. "This species of poetry," he says, "will bring honor to the French language, if it is attempted," — a remark which illustrates the innate predisposition of the French for dramatic poetry.[1] He then proceeds to distinguish tragedy from comedy much in the same manner as Scaliger does six years later. It is to be remembered that Pelletier's *Art Poétique* was published at Lyons in 1555, while Scaliger's *Poetics* was published at the same place in 1561. Pelletier may have known Scaliger personally; but it is more probable that Pelletier derived his information from the same classical and traditional sources as did Scaliger. At all events, Pelletier distinguishes tragedy from comedy in regard to style, subject, characters, and ending in exact Scaligerian fashion. Comedy has nothing in common with tragedy except the fact that neither can have more or less than five acts. The style and diction of comedy are popular and colloquial, while those of tragedy are most dignified and sublime. The comic characters are men of low condition, while those of tragedy are kings, princes, and great lords. The conclusion of comedy is always joyous, that of tragedy is always sorrowful and heart-rending. The themes of tragedy are deaths, exiles, and unhappy changes of fortune; those of comedy are the loves and passions of young men and young women, the indulgence of mothers, the wiles of slaves, and the diligence of nurses.[2]

By this time, then, Aristotle's theory of tragedy, as restated by the Italians, had become part of French criticism. The actual practice of the French drama had been modified by the introduction of these rules; and they had played so important a

1 Pelletier, *Art Poét.* ii. 7. 2 *Ibid.*

part that Grévin, in his *Bref Discours pour l'Intelligence de ce Théâtre*, prefixed to his *Mort de César* (1562), could say that French tragedy had already attained perfection, even when regarded from the standpoint of the Aristotelian canons. "Our tragedies," says Grévin, "have been so well polished that there is nothing left now to be desired, — I speak of those which are composed according to the rules of Aristotle and Horace." Grévin's *Discours* was published the year after Scaliger's *Poetics*, but shows no indication of Scaligerian influence. His definition of tragedy is based on a most vague and incomplete recollection of Aristotle, "Tragedy, as Aristotle says in his *Poetics*, is an imitation or representation of some action that is illustrious and great in itself, such as the death of Cæsar." He shows his independence or his ignorance of Scaliger by insisting on the inferiority of Seneca, whom Scaliger had rated above all the Greeks; and he shows his independence of the ancients by substituting a crowd of Cæsar's soldiers for the singers of the older chorus, on the ground that there ought not to be singing in the representation of tragedy any more than there is in actual life itself, for tragedy is a representation of truth or of what has the appearance of truth. There are in Grévin's *Discours* several indications that the national feeling had not been entirely destroyed by the imitation of the classics; but a discussion of this must be left for a later chapter.

In Jean de la Taille's *Art de Tragédie*, prefixed to his *Saül le Furieux* (1572), a drama in which a biblical theme is fashioned after the manner of classical tragedy, there is to be found the most explicit and distinct antagonism to the old, irregular moralities, which are not modelled according to the true art and the pattern of the ancients. They are but *amères épiceries* — words that recall Du Bellay. But curiously enough, Jean de la Taille differs entirely from Grévin, and asserts positively that France had as yet no real tragedies, except possibly a few translated from the classics. Waging war, as he is, against the crude formlessness of the national drama, perfect construction assumes for him a very high importance. "The principal point in tragedy," he says, "is to know how to dispose and fashion it well, so that the plot is well intertwined, mingled, interrupted, and resumed,... and that there is nothing useless, without purpose, or out of place." For Jean de la Taille, as for most Renaissance writers, tragedy is the least popular and the most elegant and elevated form of poetry, exclusive of the epic. It deals with the pitiful ruin of great lords, with the inconstancy of fortune, with banishment, war, pestilence, famine, captivity, and the execrable cruelty of tyrants. [1] The end of tragedy is in fact to move and to sting the feelings and the emotions of men. The characters of tragedy — and this is the Aristotelian conception — should be neither extremely bad, such men as by their crimes merit punishment, nor perfectly good and holy, like Socrates, who was wrongfully put to death. Invented or allegorical

1 Robert, app. iii.

characters, such as Death, Avarice, or Truth, are not to be employed. At the same time, Jean de la Taille, like Grévin, is not averse to the use of scriptural subjects in tragedy, although he cautions the poet against long-winded theological discussions. The Senecan drama was his model in treating of tragedy, as it was indeed that of the Renaissance in general; and tragedy approached more and more closely to the oratorical and sententious manner of the Latin poet. Ronsard, for example, asserts that tragedy and comedy are entirely *didascaliques et enseignantes*, and should be enriched by numerous excellent and rare *sentences* (*sententiæ*), "for in a few words the drama must teach much, being the mirror of human life." [1] Similarly, Du Bellay advises poets to embellish their poetry with grave *sentences*, and Pelletier praises Seneca principally because he is *sentencieux*.

Vauquelin, in his *Art Poétique*, gives a metrical paraphrase of Aristotle's definition of tragedy: —

> "Mais le sujet tragic est un fait imité
> De chose juste et grave, en ses vers limité;
> Auquel on y doit voir de l'affreux, du terrible,
> Un fait non attendu, qui tienne de l'horrible,
> Du pitoyable aussi, le cœur attendrissant
> D'un tigre furieux, d'un lion rugissant." [2]

The subject of tragedy should be old, and should be connected with the fall of great tyrants and princes; [3] and in regard to the number of acts, the number of interlocutors on the stage, the *deus ex*

1 Ronsard, iii. 18 *sq*.
2 *Art Poet.* iii. 153.
3 *Ibid.* ii. 1113, 441.

machina, and the chorus, [1] Vauquelin merely paraphrases Horace. Comedy is defined as the imitation of an action which by common usage is accounted wicked, but which is not so wicked that there is no remedy for it; thus, for example, a man who has seduced a young girl may recompense her by taking her in marriage. [2] Hence while the actions of tragedy are "virtuous, magnificent, and grand, royal, and sumptuous," the incidents of comedy are actually and ethically of a lower grade. [3] For tragi-comedy Vauquelin has nothing but contempt. It is, in fact, a bastard form, since the tragedy with a happy ending serves a similar but more dignified purpose. Vauquelin, like Boileau and most other French critics after him, follows Aristotle at length in the description of dramatic recognitions and reversals of fortune. [4] Most of the other Aristotelian distinctions are also to be found in his work.

In the *Art Poétique françois* of Pierre de Laudun, Sieur d'Aigaliers, published in 1598, these distinctions reappear in a more or less mutilated form. In the fifth and last book of this treatise, De Laudun follows the Italian scholars, especially Scaliger and Viperano. He does not differ essentially from Scaliger in the definition of tragedy, in the division into acts and the place of the chorus, in the discussion of the characters and subjects of tragedy, and in the distinction between tragedy and comedy. [5]

1 *Art Poét.* ii. 459.
2 *Ibid.* iii. 143.
3 *Ibid.* iii. 181.
4 *Ibid.* iii. 189 *sq.*
5 Robert, app. iv.

His conception of tragedy is in keeping with the usual Senecan ideal; it should be adorned by frequent *sentences*, allegories, similitudes, and other ornaments of poetry. The more cruel and sanguinary the tragic action is, the more excellent it will be; but at the same time, much that makes the action cruel is to be enacted only behind the stage. Like Pelletier, he objects to the introduction of all allegorical and invented characters, or even gods and goddesses, on the ground that these are not actual beings, and hence are out of keeping with the theme of tragedy, which must be real and historical. De Laudun has also something to say concerning the introduction of ghosts in the tragic action; and his discussion is peculiarly interesting when we remember that it was almost at this very time, in England, that the ghost played so important a part in the Shakespearian drama. "If the ghosts appear before the action begins," says De Laudun, "they are permissible; but if they appear during the course of the action, and speak to the actors themselves, they are entirely faulty and reprehensible." De Laudun borrowed from Scaliger the scheme of the ideal tragedy: "The first act contains the complaints; the second, the suspicions; the third, the counsels; the fourth, the menaces and preparations; the fifth, the fulfilment and effusion of blood." [1] But despite his subservience to Scaliger, he is not afraid to express his independence of the ancients. We are not, he says, entirely bound to their laws, especially in the number

1 *Art Poét.* v. 6.

of actors on the stage, which according to classic usage never exceeded three; for nowadays, notwithstanding the counsels of Aristotle and Horace, an audience has not the patience to be satisfied with only two or three persons at one time.

The history of the dramatic unities in France during the sixteenth century demands some attention. That they had considerable effect on the actual practice of dramatic composition from the very advent of the Pléiade is quite obvious; for in the first scene of the first French tragedy, the *Cléopâtre* of Jodelle (1552), there is an allusion to the unity of time, which Corneille was afterward to call the *règle des règles*: —

> "Avant que ce soleil, qui vient ores de naître,
> Ayant tracé son jour chez sa tante se plonge,
> Cléopâtre mourra!"

In 1553 Mellin de Saint-Gelais translated Trissino's *Sofonisba* into French, and the influence of the Italian drama became fixed in France. But the first distinct formulation of the unities is to be found in Jean de la Taille's *Art de Tragédie* (1572). His statement of the unities is explicit, "Il faut toujours représenter l'histoire ou le jeu en un même jour, en un même temps, et en un même lieu." [1] Jean de la Taille was indebted for this to Castelvetro, who two years before had stated it thus, "La mutatione tragica non può tirar con esso seco se non una giornata e un luogo." [2] The unity of time was adopted by Ronsard about this same time in the following words: —

1 Robert, app. iii. 2 *Poetica*, p. 534.

"Tragedy and comedy are circumscribed and limited to a short space of time, that is, to one whole day. The most excellent masters of this craft commence their works from one midnight to another, and not from sunrise to sunset, in order to have greater compass and length of time. On the other hand, the heroic poem, which is entirely of a martial character (*tout guerrier*), comprehends only the actions of one whole year." [1]

This passage is without doubt borrowed from Minturno (1564):—

"Whoever regards well the works of the most admired ancient authors will find that the materials of scenic poetry terminate in one day, or do not pass beyond the space of two days; just as the action of the epic poem, however great and however long it may be, does not occupy more than one year." [2]

Minturno, it will be remembered, was the first to limit the action of the heroic poem to one year. In another passage he deduces the rule from the practice of Virgil and Homer; [3] but Ronsard seems to think that Virgil himself has not obeyed this law. We have already alluded to the influence of Minturno on the Pléiade. Vauquelin de la Fresnaye, who explicitly acknowledges his indebtedness to Minturno, also follows him in limiting the action of the drama to one day and that of the epic to one year: —

"Or comme eux l'heroic suivant le droit sentier,
Doit son œuvre comprendre au cours d'un an entier;
Le tragic, le comic, dedans une journee
Comprend ce que fait l'autre au cours de son annee:
Le theatre jamais ne doit estre rempli
D'un argument plus long que d'un jour accompli." [4]

1 Ronsard, iii. 19.
2 *Arte Poetica*, p. 71.
3 *Ibid.* p. 12; *De Poeta*, p. 149.
4 *Art Poét.* ii. 253.

The two last lines of this passage bear considerable resemblance to Boileau's famous statement of the unities three-quarters of a century later.[1]

Toward the end of the sixteenth century, then, the unity of time, and in a less degree the unity of place, had become almost inviolable laws of the drama. But at this very period strong notes of revolt against the tyranny of the unities begin to be heard. Up to this time the classical Italian drama had been the pattern for French playwrights; but the irregular Spanish drama was now commencing to exert considerable influence in France, and with this Spanish influence came the Spanish opposition to the unities. In 1582 Jean de Beaubreuil, in the preface of his tragedy of *Régulus*, had spoken with contempt of the rule of twenty-four hours as *trop superstitieux*. But De Laudun was probably the first European critic to argue formally against it. The concluding chapter of his *Art Poétique* (1598) gives five different reasons why the unity of time should not be observed in the drama. The chapter is entitled, "Concerning those who say that the action of tragedy must conclude in a single day;" and De Laudun begins by asserting that this opinion had never been sustained by any good author. This is fairly conclusive evidence that De Laudun had never directly consulted Aristotle's *Poetics*, but was indebted for his knowledge of Aristotle to the Italians, and especially to Scaliger. The five arguments which he formulates against the unity of time are as follows: —

1 Boileau, *Art Poét.* iii. 45.

"In the first place, this law, if it is observed by any of the ancients, need not force us to restrict our tragedies in any way, since we are not bound by their manner of writing or by the measure of feet and syllables with which they compose their verses. In the second place, if we were forced to observe this rigorous law, we should fall into one of the greatest of absurdities, by being obliged to introduce impossible and incredible things in order to enhance the beauty of our tragedies, or else they would lack all grace; for besides being deprived of matter, we could not embellish our poems with long discourses and various interesting events. In the third place, the action of the *Troades*, an excellent tragedy by Seneca, could not have occurred in one day, nor could even some of the plays of Euripides or Sophocles. In the fourth place, according to the definition already given [on the authority of Aristotle], tragedy is the recital of the lives of heroes, the fortune and grandeur of kings, princes, and others; and all this could not be accomplished in one day. Besides, a tragedy must contain five acts, of which the first is joyous, and the succeeding ones exhibit a gradual change, as I have already indicated above; and this change a single day would not suffice to bring about. In the fifth and last place, the tragedies in which this rule is observed are not any better than the tragedies in which it is not observed; and the tragic poets, Greek and Latin, or even French, do not and need not and cannot observe it, since very often in a tragedy the whole life of a prince, king, emperor, noble, or other person is represented; — besides a thousand other reasons which I could advance if time permitted, but which must be left for a second edition." [1]

The history of the unity of time during the next century does not strictly concern us here; but it may be well to point out that it was through the offices of Chapelain, seconded by the authority of Cardinal Richelieu, that it became fixed in the

1 Arnaud, app. iii.

dramatic theory of France. In a long letter, dating from November, 1630, and recently published for the first time, Chapelain sets out to answer all the objections made against the rule of twenty-four hours. It is sustained, he says, by the practice of the ancients and the universal consensus of the Italians; but his own proof is based on reason alone. It is the old argument of *vraisemblance*, as found in Maggi, Scaliger, and especially Castelvetro, whom Chapelain seems in part to follow. By 1635 he had formulated the whole theory of the three unities and converted Cardinal Richelieu to his views. In the previous year Mairet's *Sophonisbe*, the first "regular" French tragedy, had been produced. In 1636 the famous *Cid* controversy had begun. By 1640 the battle was gained, and the unities became a part of the classic theory of the drama throughout Europe. A few years later their practical application was most thoroughly indicated by the Abbé d'Aubignac, in his *Pratique du Théâtre*; and they were definitely formulated for all time by Boileau in the celebrated couplet: —

> "Qu'en un lieu, qu'en un jour, un seul fait accompli
> Tienne jusqu'à la fin le théâtre rempli." [1]

III. *Heroic Poetry*

It was the supreme ambition of the Pléiade to produce a great French epic. In the very first manifesto of the new school, Du Bellay urges every French poet to attempt another *Iliad* or *Æneid* for

1 *Art Poét.* iii. 45.

the honor and glory of France. For Pelletier (1555) the heroic poem is the one that really gives the true title of poet; it may be compared to the ocean, and all other forms to rivers. [1] He seems to be following Giraldi Cintio's discourse on the *romanzi*, published the year before his own work, when he says that the French poet should write a *Heracleid*, the deeds of Hercules furnishing the mightiest and most heroic material he can think of. [2] At the same time Virgil is for him the model of an epic poet; and his parallel between Homer and Virgil bears striking resemblance to the similar parallel in Capriano's *Della Vera Poetica*, published in the very same year as his own treatise. [3] Like Capriano, Pelletier censures the superfluous exuberance, the loquaciousness, the occasional indecorum, and the inferiority in eloquence and dignity of Homer when compared with the Latin poet.

It was Ronsard's personal ambition to be the French Virgil, as in lyric poetry he had been proclaimed the French Pindar. For twenty years he labored on the *Franciade*, but never finished it. In the two prefaces which he wrote for it, the first in 1572, and the second (published posthumously) about 1584, he attempts to give expression to his ideal of the heroic poet. In neither of them does he succeed in formulating any very definite or consistent body of epic theory. They are chiefly interesting in that they indicate the general tendencies of the Pléiade, and show Ronsard's own rhetorical prin-

1 *Art Poét.* ii. 8.
2 *Ibid.* i. 3.
3 *Ibid.* i. 5. *Cf.* Capriano, cap. v.

ciples, and his feeling for nature and natural beauty. The passage has already been cited in which he speaks of the heroic poem as entirely of a martial character, and limits its action to the space of one year. It has also been seen that for him, as for the Italians, verisimilitude, and not fact, is the test of poetry. At the same time, the epic poet is to avoid anachronisms and misstatements of fact. Such faults do not disturb the reader so much when the story is remote in point of time; and the poet should therefore always use an argument, the events of which are at least three or four hundred years old. The basis of the work should rest upon some old story of past times and of long-established renown, which has gained the credit of men. [1] This notion of the antiquity of the epic fable had been accepted long ago by the Italians. It is stated, for example, in Tasso's *Discorsi dell' Arte Poetica*, written about 1564, though not published until 1587, fifteen years after Tasso had visited Ronsard in Paris.

Vauquelin de la Fresnaye has the Pléiade veneration for heroic poetry; but he cannot be said to exhibit any more definite conception of its form and function. For him the epic is a vast and magnificent narration, a world in itself, wherein men, things, and thoughts are wondrously mirrored: —

> "C'est un tableau du monde, un miroir qui raporte
> Les gestes des mortels en differente sorte....

1 Ronsard, iii. 23, 29.

> Car toute poësie il contient en soyméme,
> Soit tragique ou comique, ou soit autre poëme."[1]

With this we may compare what Muzio had said in 1551: —

> "Il poema sovrano è una pittura
> De l'universo, e però in sè comprende
> Ogni stilo, ogni forma, ogni ritratto."

But despite this very vague conception of the epic in the French Renaissance, there was, as has been said, a high veneration for it as a form, and for its masters, Homer and especially Virgil. This accounts for the large number of attempts at epic composition in France during the next century. But beyond the earlier and indefinite notion of heroic poetry the French did not get for a long time to come. Even for Boileau the epic poem was merely the *vaste récit d'une longue action.*[2]

1 Vauquelin, *Art Poét.* i. 471, 503.
2 Boileau, *Art Poét.* iii. 161.

CHAPTER III

CLASSIC AND ROMANTIC ELEMENTS IN FRENCH CRITICISM DURING THE SIXTEENTH CENTURY

THE principle for which the Pléiade stood was, like that of humanism, the imitation of the classics; and the Pléiade was the first to introduce this as a literary principle into France. This means, as regards French literature, in the first place, the substitution of the classical instead of its own national tradition; and, secondly, the substitution of the imitation of the classics for the imitation of nature itself. In making these vital substitutions, Du Bellay and his school have been accused of creating once and for all the gulf that separates French poetry from the national life. [1] This accusation is perhaps unfair to the Pléiade, which insisted on the poet's going directly to nature, which emphasized most strongly the sentiment for natural scenery and beauty, and which first declared the importance of the artisan and the peasant as subjects for poetry. But there can be but little doubt that the separation of poetry from the national life was the logical outcome of the doctrines of the Pléiade. In disregarding the older French poets and the evolution of indigenous poetry, in formu-

1 Brunetière, i. 45.

lating an ideal of the poet as an unsociable and ascetic character, it separated itself from the natural tendencies of French life and letters, and helped to effect the final separation between poetry and the national development.

I. *Classical Elements*

It was to Du Bellay (1549) that France owes the introduction of classical ideas into French literature. He was the first to regard the imitation of the classics as a literary principle, and to advise the poet, after the manner of Vida, to purloin all the treasures of Greek and Latin literature for the benefit of French poetry. Moreover, he first formulated the aristocratic conception of the poet held by the Pléiade. The poet was advised to flee from the ignorant people, to bury himself in the solitude of his own chamber, to dream and to ponder, and to content himself with few readers. "Beyond everything," says Du Bellay, "the poet should have one or more learned friends to whom he can show all his verses; he should converse not only with learned men, but with all sorts of workmen, mechanics, artists, and others, in order to learn the technical terms of their arts, for use in beautiful descriptions." [1] This was a favorite theory of the Pléiade, which like some of our own contemporary writers regarded the technical arts as important subjects of inspiration. But the essential point at the bottom of all these discussions is a high

1 *Défense*, ii. 11.

contempt for the opinion of the vulgar in matters of art.

The *Quintil Horatian* (1550) represents, as has already been seen, a natural reaction against the foreign and classical innovations of the Pléiade. Du Bellay's advice, "Prens garde que ce poëme soit eslogné du vulgaire," — advice insisted upon by many of the rhetoricians of the Italian Renaissance, — receives considerable censure; on the contrary, says the author of the *Quintil*, the poet must be understood and appreciated by all, unlearned as well as learned, just as Marot was. The *Quintil* was, in fact, the first work to insist on definiteness and clearness in poetry, as these were afterward insisted on by Malherbe and Boileau. Like Malherbe, and his disciple Deimier, the author of the *Académie de l'Art Poétique* (1610), in which the influence of the *Quintil* is fully acknowledged, the author of the *Quintil* objects to all forms of poetic license, to all useless metaphors that obscure the sense, to all Latinisms and foreign terms and locutions.[1] Du Bellay had dwelt on the importance of a knowledge of the classical and Italian tongues, and had strongly advised the French poet to naturalize as many Latin, Greek, and even Spanish and Italian terms as he could. The *Quintil* is particularly bitter against all such foreign innovations. The poet need not know foreign tongues at all; without this knowledge he can be as good a poet as any of the *grœcaniseurs, latiniseurs, et italianiseurs en françoys*. This protest availed little, and Du

1 *Cf.* Rucktäschel, p. 10 *sq.*

Bellay's advice in regard to the use of Italian terms was so well followed that several years later, in 1578, Henri Estienne vigorously protested against the practice in his *Dialogues du Nouveau Langage françois italianisé*. As Ronsard and Du Bellay represent the foreign elements that went to make up classicism in France, so the author of the *Quintil Horatian* may be said to represent in his humble way certain enduring elements of the *esprit gaulois*. He represents the national traditions, and he prepares the way for the two great bourgeois poets of France, — Boileau, with his "Tout doit tendre au bon sens," and Molière, with his bluff cry, "Je suis pour le bon sens."

According to Pelletier (1555), French poetry is too much like colloquial speech; in order to equal classical literature, the poets of France must be more daring and less popular. [1] Pelletier's point of view is here that of the Pléiade, which aimed at a distinct poetic language, diverse from ordinary prose speech. But he is thoroughly French, and in complete accord with the author of the *Quintil Horatian*, in his insistence on perfect clearness in poetry. "Clearness," he says, "is the first and worthiest virtue of a poem." [2] Obscurity is the chief fault of poetry, "for there is no difference between not speaking at all and not being understood." [3] For these reasons he is against all unnecessary and bombastic ornament; the true use of metaphors and comparisons of all sorts is "to explain and represent things as they really are."

1 *Art Poét.* i. 3.

2 *Ibid.* i. 9.

3 *Ibid.* i. 10.

Similarly, Ronsard, while recognizing the value of comparisons, rightfully used, as the very nerves and tendons of poetry, declares that if instead of perfecting and clarifying, they obscure or confuse the idea, they are ridiculous. [1] Obscurity was the chief danger, and indeed the chief fault, of the Pléiade; and it is no small merit that both Ronsard and Pelletier perceived this fact.

The Pléiade exhibits the classic temper in its insistence on study and art as essential to poetry; but it was not in keeping with the doctrines of later French classicists in so far as it regarded the poetic labors as of an unsociable and even ascetic character. In this, as has been seen, Ronsard is a true exponent of the doctrines of the new school. But on the whole the classic spirit was strong in him. He declares that the poet's ideas should be high and noble, but not fantastic. "They should be well ordered and disposed; and while they seem to transcend those of the vulgar, they should always appear to be easily conceived and understood by any one." [2] Here Du Bellay's aristocratic conception of poetry is modified so as to become a very typical statement of the principle underlying French classicism. Again, Ronsard points out, as Vida and other Italian critics had done before, that the great classical poets seldom speak of things by their bare and naked names. Virgil does not, for example, say, "It was night," or "It was day," but he uses some such circumlocution as this: —

> "Postero Phœbea lustrabat lampade terras."

1 Ronsard, iii. 26 *sq.* 2 *Ibid.* vii. 323.

The unfortunate results of the excessive use of such circumlocutions are well exemplified in the later classicists of France. Ronsard perhaps foresaw this danger, and wisely says that circumlocution, if not used judiciously, makes the style inflated and bombastic. In the first preface to the *Franciade*, he expresses a decided preference for the naïve facility of Homer over the artful diligence of Virgil. [1] In the second preface, however, written a dozen years later, and published posthumously as revised by his disciple Binet, there is interesting evidence, in the preëminence given to Virgil, of the rapidity with which the Latinization of culture was being effected at this period. "Our French authors," says Ronsard, "know Virgil far better than they know Homer or any other Greek writer." And again, "Virgil is the most excellent and the most rounded, the most compact and the most perfect of all poets." [2] Of the naïve facility of Homer we hear absolutely nothing.

We are now beginning to enter the era of rules. Ronsard did not undervalue the "rules and secrets" of poetry; and Vauquelin de la Fresnaye calls his own critical poem *cet Art de Règles recherchées*. [3] In regard to the imitation of the classics, Vauquelin agrees heart and soul with the Pléiade that the ancients

> "nous ont desja tracé
> Un sentier qui de nous ne doit estre laissé." [4]

Nothing, indeed, could be more classical than his

1 Ronsard, iii. 9 *sq*.
2 *Ibid*. iii. 23, 26.
3 *Art Poét*. iii. 1151.
4 *Ibid*. i. 61.

comparison of poetry to a garden symmetrically laid out and trimmed. [1] Moreover, like the classicists of the next century, he affirms, as does Ronsard also, that art must fundamentally imitate and resemble nature. [2]

The imitation of the classics had also a decided effect on the technique of French verse and on the linguistic principles of the Pléiade. Enjambement (the carrying over into another line of words required to complete the sense) and hiatus (the clash of vowels in a line) were both employed in Latin and Greek verse, and were therefore permitted in French poetry by the new school. Ronsard, however, anticipated the reforms of Malherbe and the practice of French classic verse, in forbidding both hiatus and enjambement, though in a later work of his this opinion is reversed. He was also probably the first to insist on the regular alternation of masculine and feminine rhymes in verse. This had never been strictly adhered to in practice, or required by stringent rule, before Ronsard, but has become the invariable usage of French poetry ever since. Ronsard regards this device as a means of making verse keep tune more harmoniously with the music of instruments. It was one of the favorite theories of the Pléiade that poetry is intended, not to be read, but to be recited or sung, and that the words and the notes should be coupled lovingly together. Poetry without an accompaniment of vocal or instrumental music exhibits but a small part of its harmony or perfection; and while

1 *Art Poét.* i. 22 *sq.*

2 *Ibid.* i. 813. *Cf.* Ronsard, ii. 12.

composing verses, the poet should always pronounce them aloud, or rather sing them, in order to test their melody. [1] This conception of music "married to immortal verse" doubtless came from Italy, and is connected with the rise of operatic music. De Laudun (1598) differs from the members of the Pléiade in forbidding the use of words newly coined or taken from the dialects of France, and in objecting to the use of enjambement and hiatus. It is evident, therefore, that while the influence of the Pléiade is visible throughout De Laudun's treatise, his disagreement with Ronsard and Du Bellay on a considerable number of essential points shows that by the end of the century the supremacy of the Pléiade had begun to wane.

The new school also attempted to introduce classical metres into French poetry. The similar attempt at using the ancient versification in Italy has already been incidentally referred to. [2] According to Vasari, Leon Battista Alberti, in his epistle,

> "Questa per estrema miserabile pistola mando,"

was the first to attempt to reduce the vernacular versification to the measure of the Latins. [3] In October, 1441, the *Scena dell' Amicizia* of Leonardo Dati was composed and recited before the Accademia Coronaria at Florence. [4] The first two parts of this piece

1 Ronsard, vii. 320, 332.

2 The early Italian poetry written in classical metres has been collected by Carducci, *La poesia Barbara nei Secoli XV e XVI*, Bologna, 1881.

3 Carducci, p. 2.

4 *Ibid.* p. 6 *sq.*

are written in hexameters, the third in Sapphics, the fourth in sonnet form and rhymed. The prologues of Ariosto's comedies, the *Negromante* and the *Cassaria*, are also in classical metres. But the remarkable collection of Claudio Tolomei, *Versi e Regole de la Nuova Poesia Toscana*, published at Rome in 1539, marked an epoch in sixteenth-century letters. In this work the employment of classical metres in the vulgar tongue is defended, and rules for their use given; then follows a collection of Italian verse written after this fashion by a large number of scholars and poets, among them Annibal Caro and Tolomei himself. This group of scholars had formed itself into an esoteric circle, the Accademia della Nuova Poesia; and from the tone of the verses addressed to Tolomei by the members of this circle, it would seem that he regarded himself, and was regarded by them, as the founder and expositor of this poetic innovation. [1] Luigi Alamanni, whose life was chiefly spent at the Court of France, published in 1556 a comedy, *La Flora*, written in classical metres; and two years later Francesco Patrizzi published an heroic poem, the *Eridano*, written in hexameters, with a defence of the form of versification employed. [2]

This learned innovation spread throughout western Europe. [3] In France, toward the close of the fifteenth

1 Carducci, pp. 55, 87, etc.

2 *Ibid.* pp. 327, 443. *Cf.* Du Bellay, *Défense*, ii. 7.

3 For the history of classical metres in France, *cf.* Egger, *Hellénisme en France*, p. 290 *sq.*, and Darmesteter and Hatzfeld, *Seizième Siècle en France*. p. 113 *sq.*

century, according to Agrippa d'Aubigné, a certain Mousset had translated the *Iliad* and the *Odyssey* into French hexameters; but nothing else is known either of Mousset or of his translations. As early as 1500 one Michel de Bouteauville, the author of an *Art de métrifier françois*, wrote a poem in classical distichs on the English war. Sibilet (1548) accepted the use of classical metres, though with some distrust, for to him rhyme seemed as essential to French poetry as long and short syllables to Greek and Latin. In 1562 Ramus, in his *Grammar*, recommended the ancient versification, and expressed his regret that it had not been accepted with favor by the public. In the same year Jacques de la Taille wrote his treatise, *La Manière de faire des Vers en françois comme en grec et en latin*, but it was not published until 1573, eleven years after his death. His main object in writing the book was to show that it is not as difficult to employ quantity in French verse as some people think, nor even any more difficult than in Greek and Latin.[1] In answer to the objection that the vulgar tongues are by their nature incapable of quantity, he argues, after the manner of Du Bellay, that such things do not proceed from the nature of a language, but from the labor and diligence of those who employ it. He is tired of vulgar rhymes, and is anxious to find a more ingenious and more

1 Estienne Pasquier, in his *Recherches de la France*, vii. 11, attempts to prove that the French language is capable of employing quantity in its verse, but does not decide whether quantity or rhymed verse is to be preferred.

difficult path to Parnassus. He then proceeds to treat of quantity and measure in French, of feet and verse, and of figures and poetic license.[1]

The name most inseparably connected with the introduction of classical metres into France in the sixteenth century is that of Jean Antoine de Baïf. This young member of the Pléiade, after publishing several unsuccessful volumes of verse, visited Italy, and was present at the Council of Trent in 1563. In Italy he doubtless learnt of the metrical innovations then being employed; and upon his return, without any apparent knowledge of Jacques de la Taille's as yet unpublished treatise, he set about to make a systematic reform in French versification. His purpose was to bring about a more perfect unison between poetry and music; and in order to accomplish this, he adopted classical metres, based as they were on a musical prosody, and accepted the phonetic reforms of Ramus. He also established, no doubt in imitation of the Accademia della Nuova Poesia, the Académie de Poésie et de Musique, authorized by letters patent from Charles IX. in November, 1570.[2] The purpose of this academy was to encourage and establish the metrical and musical innovations advocated by Baïf and his friends. On the death of Charles IX. the society's existence was menaced; but it was restored, with a

1 *Cf.* Rucktäschel, p. 24 *sq.*, and Carducci, p. 413 *sq.*

2 This academy has been made the subject of an excellent monograph by É. Fremy, *L'Académie des Derniers Valois*, Paris, n. d. The statutes of the academy will be found on page 39 of this work, and the letters-patent granted to it by Charles IX. on page 48.

broader purpose and function, as the Académie du Palais, by Guy du Faur de Pibrac in 1576, under the protection of Henry III., and it continued to flourish until dispersed by the turmoils of the League about 1585. But Baïf's innovations were not entirely without fruit. A similar movement, and a not dissimilar society, will be found somewhat later in Elizabethan England.

II. *Romantic Elements*

Some of the romantic elements in the critical theory of the Pléiade have already been indicated. The new movement started, in Du Bellay's *Défense*, with a high conception of the poet's office. It emphasized the necessity, on the part of the poet, of profound and solitary study, of a refined and ascetic life, and of entire separation from vulgar people and pleasures. Du Bellay himself is romantic in that he decides against the *traditions de règles*, [1] deeming the good judgment of the poet sufficient in matters of taste; but the reason of this was that there were no rules which he would have been willing to accept. It took more than a century for the French mind to arrive at the conclusion that reason and rules, in matters of art, proceed from one and the same cause.

The feeling for nature and for natural beauty is very marked in all the members of the Pléiade. Pelletier speaks of war, love, agriculture, and pastoral life as the chief themes of poetry. [2] He warns

1 *Défense*, ii. 11. 2 *Art Poét.* i. 3

the poet to observe nature and life itself, and not depend on books alone; and he dwells on the value of descriptions of landscapes, tempests, and sunrises, and similar natural scenes. [1] The feeling for nature is even more intense in Ronsard; and like Pelletier, he urges the poet to describe in verse the rivers, forests, mountains, winds, the sea, gods and goddesses, sunrise, night, and noon. [2] In another place the poet is advised to embellish his work with accounts of trees, flowers, and herbs, especially those dignified by some medicinal or magical virtues, and with descriptions of rivers, towns, forests, mountains, caverns, rocks, harbors, and forts. Here the appreciation of natural beauty as introduced into modern Europe by the Italian Renaissance — the feeling for nature in its wider aspects, the broad landscape, the distant prospect — first becomes visible in France. "In the painting or rather imitation of nature," says Ronsard, "consists the very soul of heroic poetry."

Ronsard also gives warning that ordinary speech is not to be banished from poetry, or too much evaded, for by doing so the poet is dealing a deathblow to "naïve and natural poetry." [3] This sympathy for the simple and popular forms of poetry as models for the poetic artist is characteristic of the Pléiade. There is a very interesting passage in Montaigne, in which the popular ballads of the peasantry are praised in a manner that recalls the famous words of Sir Philip Sidney concerning

1 *Art Poét.* ii. 10; i. 9
2 Ronsard, vii. 321, 324.
3 *Ibid.* iii. 17 *sq.*

the old song of Percy and Douglas, [1] and which seems to anticipate the interest in popular poetry in England two centuries later: —

> "Popular and purely natural and indigenous poetry has a certain native simplicity and grace by which it may be favorably compared with the principal beauty of perfect poetry composed according to the rules of art; as may be seen in the villanelles of Gascony, and in songs coming from nations that have no knowledge of any science, not even of writing. But mediocre poetry, which is neither perfect nor popular, is held in disdain by every one, and receives neither honor nor reward." [2]

The Pléiade, as has already been intimated, accepted without reserve the Platonic doctrine of inspiration. By 1560 a considerable number of the Platonic dialogues had already been translated into French. Dolet had translated two of the spurious dialogues; Duval, the *Lysis* in 1547; and Le Roy, the *Phœdo* in 1553 and the *Symposium* in 1559. The thesis of Ramus in 1536 had started an anti-Aristotelian tendency in France, and the literature of the French Renaissance became impregnated with Platonism. [3] It received the royal favor of Marguerite de Navarre, and its influence became fixed in 1551, by the appointment of Ramus to a professorship in the Collège de France. Ronsard, Vauquelin, Du Bartas, all give expression to the Platonic theory of poetic inspiration. The poet must feel what he writes, as Horace says, or his reader will never be moved by his verses; and for

1 Sidney, *Defence*, p. 29.

2 *Essais*, i. 54.

3 *Cf.* the *Revue d'Hist. litt. de la France*, 1896, iii. 1 *sq.*

the Pléiade, the excitement of high emotions in the reader or hearer was the test or touchstone of poetry.[1]

The national and Christian points of view never found expression in France during the sixteenth century in so marked a manner as in Italy. There are, indeed, traces of both a national and a Christian criticism, but they are hardly more than sporadic. Thus, it has been seen that Sibilet, as early as 1548, had clearly perceived the distinguishing characteristic of the French genius. He had noted that the French have only taken from foreign literature what they have deemed useful and of national advantage; and only the other day a distinguished French critic asserted in like manner that the high importance of French literature consists in the fact that it has taken from the other literatures of Europe the things of universal interest and disregarded the accidental picturesque details. Distinct traces of a national point of view may be found in the dramatic criticism of this period. Thus Grévin, in his *Bref Discours* (1562), attempts to justify the substitution of a crowd of Cæsar's soldiers for the singers of the ancient chorus, in one of his tragedies, on the following grounds: —

"If it be alleged that this practice was observed throughout antiquity by the Greeks and Latins, I reply that it is permitted to us to attempt some innovation of our own, especially when there is occasion for it, or when the grace of the poem is not diminished thereby. I know well that it will be answered that the ancients employed the chorus of

1 Ronsard, iii. 28; Du Bellay, *Défense*, ii. 11.

singers to divert the audience, made gloomy perhaps by the cruelties represented in the play. To this I reply that diverse nations require diverse manners of doing things, and that among the French there are other means of doing this without interrupting the continuity of a story." [1]

The Christian point of view, on the other hand, is found in Vauquelin de la Fresnaye, who differs from Ronsard and Du Bellay in his preference for scriptural themes in poetry. The Pléiade was essentially pagan, Vauquelin essentially Christian. The employment of the pagan divinities in modern poetry seemed to him often odious, for the times had changed, and the Muses were governed by different laws. The poet should attempt Christian themes; and indeed the Greeks themselves, had they been Christians, would have sung the life and death of Christ. In this passage Vauquelin is evidently following Minturno, as the latter was afterward followed by Corneille: —

> "Si les Grecs, comme vous, Chrestiens eussent escrit,
> Ils eussent les hauts faits chanté de Iesus Christ....
> Hé! quel plaisir seroit-ce à cette heure de voir
> Nos poëtes Chrestiens, les façons recevoir
> Du tragique ancien? Et voir à nos misteres
> Les Payens asservis sous les loix sulutaires
> De nos Saints et Martyrs? et du vieux testament
> Voir une tragedie extraite proprement? " [2]

Vauquelin's opinion here is out of keeping with the general theory of the Pléiade, especially in that his suggestions imply a return to the mediæval mystery and morality

1 Arnaud, app. ii.
2 Vauquelin, *Art Poét.* iii. 845; *cf.* iii. 33; i. 901.

plays. The *Uranie* of Du Bartas is another and more fervid expression of this same ideal of Christian poetry. In the *Semaines*, Du Bartas himself composed the typical biblical poem; and tragedies on Christian or scriptural subjects were composed during the French Renaissance from the time of Buchanan and Beza to that of Garnier and Montchrestien. But Vauquelin's ideal was not that of the later classicism; and Boileau, as has been seen, distinctly rejects Christian themes from modern poetry.

Although the linguistic and prosodic theories of the Pléiade partly anticipate both the theory and the practice of later classicism, the members of the school exhibit numerous deviations from what was afterward accepted as inviolable law in French poetry. The most important of these deviations concerns the use of words from the various French dialects, from foreign tongues, and from the technical and mechanical arts. A partial expression of this theory of poetic language has already been seen in Du Bellay's *Défense et Illustration*, in which the poet is urged to use the more elegant technical dialectic terms. Ronsard gives very much the same advice. The best words in all the French dialects are to be employed by the poet; for it is doubtless to the number of the dialects of Greece that we may ascribe the supreme beauty of its language and literature. The poet is not to affect too much the language of the court, since it is often very bad, being the language of ladies and of young gentlemen who make a profession of fighting well rather than of speaking well. [1] Unlike Malherbe and his school, Ronsard allows a certain amount of poetic license, but only rarely and judiciously. It is to poetic license, he says, that we owe nearly all the beautiful figures with which poets, in their divine rapture, enfranchising the laws of grammar, have enriched their works. "This is that birthright," said Dryden, a century later, in the preface of his *State of Innocence and the Fall of Man*, "which is derived to us from our great forefathers, even from Homer down to Ben; and they who would deny it to us have, in plain terms, the fox's quarrel to the grapes — they cannot reach it." Vauquelin de la Fresnaye follows Ronsard and Du Bellay in urging the use of new and dialect words, the employment of terms and comparisons from the mechanic arts, and the various other doctrines by which the Pléiade is distinguished from the school of Malherbe. How these useless linguistic innovations were checked and banished from the French language forever will be briefly alluded to in the next chapter.

1 Ronsard, vii. 322.

CHAPTER IV

THE FORMATION OF THE CLASSIC IDEAL IN THE SEVENTEENTH CENTURY

I. *The Romantic Revolt*

It is a well-known fact that between 1600 and 1630 there was a break in the national evolution of French literature. This was especially so in the drama, and in France the drama is the connecting link between century and century. The dramatic works of the sixteenth century had been fashioned after the regular models borrowed by the Italians from Seneca. The change that came was a change from Italian classical to Spanish romantic models. The note of revolt was beginning to be heard in Grévin, De Laudun, and others. The seventeenth century opened with the production of Hardy's irregular drama, *Les Amours de Théagène et Cariclée* (1601), and the influence of the Spanish romantic drama and the Italian pastoral, dominant for over a quarter of a century, was inaugurated in France.

The logic of this innovation was best expounded in Spain, and it was there that arguments in favor of the romantic and irregular drama were first formulated. The two most interesting defences of the Spanish national drama are doubtless the

Egemplar Poético of Juan de la Cueva (1606) and Lope de Vega's *Arte Nuevo de Hacer Comedias* (1609). Their inspiration is at bottom the same. Their authors were both classicists at heart, or rather classicists in theory, yet with differences. Juan de la Cueva's conception of poetry is entirely based on the precepts of the Italians, except in what regards the national drama, for here he is a partisan and a patriot. He insists that the difference of time and circumstance frees the Spanish playwright from all necessity of imitating the ancients or obeying their rules. "This change in the drama," he says, "was effected by wise men, who applied to new conditions the new things they found most suitable and expedient; for we must consider the various opinions, the times, and the manners, which make it necessary for us to change and vary our operations." [1] His theory of the drama was entirely opposed to his conception of the other forms of poetry. According to this standpoint, as a recent writer has put it, "the theatre was to imitate nature, and to please; poetry was to imitate the Italians, and satisfy the orthodox but minute critic." [2] Lope de Vega, writing three years later, does not deny the universal applicability of the Aristotelian canons, and even acknowledges that they are the only true rules. But the people demand romantic plays, and the people, rather than the poet's literary conscience, must be satisfied by the playwright. "I myself," he says,

1 Sedano, *Parnaso Español*, viii. 61.
2 Hannay, *Later Renaissance*, 1898, p. 39.

"write comedies according to the art invented by those whose sole object it is to obtain the applause of the crowd. After all, since it is the public who pays for these stupidities, why should we not serve what it wants?" [1]

Perhaps the most interesting of all the expositions of the theory of the Spanish national drama is a defence of Lope de Vega's plays by one Alfonso Sanchez, published in 1618 in France, or possibly in Spain with a false French imprint. The apology of Sanchez is comprehended in six distinct propositions. First, the arts have their foundation in nature. Secondly, a wise and learned man may alter many things in the existing arts. Thirdly, nature does not obey laws, but gives them. Fourthly, Lope de Vega has done well in creating a new art. Fifthly, in his writings everything is adjusted to art, and that a real and living art. Lastly, Lope de Vega has surpassed all the ancient poets. [2] The following passage may be extracted from this treatise, if only to show how little there was of novelty in the tenets of the French romanticists two centuries later: —

"Is it said that we have no infallible art by which to adjust our precepts? But who can doubt it? We have art, we have precepts and rules which bind us, and the principal precept is to imitate nature, for the works of poets express the nature, the manners, and the genius of the age in which they write.... Lope de Vega writes in conformity with art, because he follows nature. If, on the contrary, the Spanish drama adjusted itself to the rules and laws of the

1 Menéndez y Pelayo, iii. 434.

2 *Ibid.* iii. 447 *sq.*

ancients, it would proceed against the requirements of nature, and against the foundations of poetry.... The great Lope has done things over and above the laws of the ancients, but never against these laws."

Another Spanish writer defines art as "an attentive observation of examples graded by experience, and reduced to method and the majesty of laws." [1]

It was this naturalistic conception of the poetic art, and especially of the drama, that obtained in France during the first thirty years of the seventeenth century. The French playwrights imitated the Spanish drama in practice, and from the Spanish theorists seemed to have derived the critical justification of their plays. Hardy himself, like Lope de Vega, argues that "everything which is approved by usage and the public taste is legitimate and more than legitimate." Another writer of this time, François Ogier, in the preface of the second edition of Jean de Schelandre's remarkable drama of *Tyr et Sidon* (1628), argues for intellectual independence of the ancients much in the same way as Giraldi Cintio, Pigna, and the other partisans of the *romanzi* had done three-quarters of a century before. The taste of every nation, he says, is quite different from any other. "The Greeks wrote for the Greeks, and in the judgment of the best men of their time they succeeded. But we should imitate them very much better by giving heed to the tastes of our own country, and the genius of our own language, than by forcing ourselves to follow step by step both their intention and their expression." This would

1 Menéndez y Pelayo, iii. 464.

seem to be at bottom Goethe's famous statement that we can best imitate the Greeks by trying to be as great men as they were. It is interesting to note, in all of these early critics, traces of that historical criticism which is usually regarded as the discovery of our own century. But after all, the French like the Spanish playwrights were merely beginning to practise what the Italian dramatists in their prefaces, and some of the Italian critics in their treatises, had been preaching for nearly a century.

The Abbé d'Aubignac speaks of Hardy as "arresting the progress of the French theatre"; and whatever practical improvements the French theatre owes to him, there can be little doubt that for a certain number of years the evolution of the classical drama was partly arrested by his efforts and the efforts of his school. But during this very period the foundations of the great literature that was to come were being built on classical lines; and the continuance of the classical tradition after 1630 was due to three distinct causes, each of which will be discussed by itself as briefly as possible. These three causes were the reaction against the Pléiade, the second influx of the critical ideas of the Italian Renaissance, and the influence of the rationalistic philosophy of the period.

II. *The Reaction against the Pléiade*

The reaction against the Pléiade was effected, or at least begun, by Malherbe. Malherbe's power or message as a poet is of no concern here; in his rôle of grammarian and critic he accomplished certain important and widespread reforms in French poetry. These reforms were connected chiefly, if not entirely, with the external or formal side of poetry. His work was that of a grammarian, of a prosodist — in a word, that of a purist. He did not, indeed, during his lifetime, publish any critical work, or formulate any critical system. But the reforms he executed were on this account no less influential or enduring. His critical attitude is to be looked for in the memoirs of his life written by his disciple Racan, and in his own *Commentaire sur Desportes*, which was not published in its entirety until very recently.[1] This commentary consists of a series of manuscript notes written by Malherbe about the year 1606 in the margins of a copy of Desportes. These notes are of a most fragmentary kind; they seldom go beyond a word or two of disapproval, such as *faible*, *mal conçu*, *superflu*, *sans jugement*, *sottise*, or *mal imaginé*; and yet, together with a few detached utterances recorded in his letters and in the memoirs by Racan, they indicate quite clearly the critical attitude of Malherbe and the reforms he was bent on bringing about.

These reforms were, in the first place, largely linguistic. The Pléiade had attempted to widen the sphere of poetic expression in French literature by the introduction

1 The *Commentaire* is printed entire in Lalanne's edition of Malherbe, Paris, 1862, vol. iv. The critical doctrine of Malherbe has been formulated by Brunot, *Doctrine de Malherbe*, pp. 105-236.

of words from the classics, from the Italian and even the Spanish, from the provincial dialects, from the old romances, and from the terminology of the mechanic arts. All these archaisms, neologisms, Latinisms, compound words, and dialectic and technical expressions, Malherbe set about to eradicate from the French language. His object was to purify French, and, as it were, to centralize it. The test he set up was actual usage, and even this was narrowed down to the usage of the court. Ronsard had censured the exclusive use of courtly speech in poetry, on the ground that the courtier cares more about fighting well than about speaking or writing well. But Malherbe's ideal was the ideal of French classicism — the ideal of Boileau, Racine, and Bossuet. French was to be no longer a hodgepodge or a patois, but the pure and perfect speech of the king and his court. Malherbe, while thus reacting against the Pléiade, made no pretensions of returning to the linguistic usages of Marot; his test was present usage, his model the living language.[1] At the same time his reforms in language, as in other things, represent a reaction against foreign innovations and a return to the pure French idiom. They were in the interest of the national traditions; and it is this national element which is his share in the body of neo-classical theory and practice. His reforms were all in the direction of that verbal and mechanical perfection, the love of which is innate in the French nature, and which forms the indigenous

1 *Cf.* Horace, *Ars Poet.* 71, 72.

or racial element in French classicism. He eliminated from French verse hiatus, enjambement, inversions, false and imperfect rhymes, and licenses or cacophonies of all kinds. He gave it, as has been said, mechanical perfection, —

> "Et réduisit la Muse aux règles du devoir."

For such a man — *tyran des mots et des syllabes*, as Balzac called him — the higher qualities of poetry could have little or no meaning. His ideals were propriety, clearness, regularity, and force. These, as Chapelain perceived at the time, are oratorical rather than purely poetic qualities; yet for these, all the true qualities that go to make up a great poet were to be sacrificed. Of imagination and poetic sensibility he takes no account whatsoever. After the verbal perfection of the verse, the logical unity of the poem was his chief interest. Logic and reason are without doubt important things, but they cannot exist in poetry to the exclusion of imagination. By eliminating inspiration, as it were, Malherbe excluded the possibility of lyrical production in France throughout the period of classicism. He hated poetic fictions, since for him, as for Boileau, only actual reality is beautiful. If he permitted the employment of mythological figures, it was because they are reasonable and universally intelligible symbols. The French mind is essentially rational and logical, and Malherbe reintroduced this native rationality into French poetry. He set up common sense as a poetic ideal, and made poetry intelligible to the average mind. The

Pléiade had written for a learned literary coterie; Malherbe wrote for learned and unlearned alike. For the Pléiade, poetry had been a divine office, a matter of prophetic inspiration; for Malherbe, it was a trade, a craft, to be learnt like any other. Du Bellay had said that "it is a well-accepted fact, according to the most learned men, that natural talents without learning can accomplish more in poetry than learning without natural talents." Malherbe, it has been neatly said, would have upheld the contrary doctrine that "learning without natural talents can accomplish more than natural talents without learning." [1] After all, eloquence was Malherbe's ideal; and as the French are by nature an eloquent rather than a poetic people, he deserves the honor of having first shown them how to regain their true inheritance. In a word, he accomplished for classical poetry in France all that the national instinct, the *esprit gaulois*, could accomplish by itself. Consistent structural laws for the larger poetic forms he could not give; these France owes to Italy. Nor could he appreciate the high notion of abstract perfection, or the classical conception of an absolute standard of taste — that of several expressions or several ways of doing something, one way and only one is the right one; this France owes to rationalistic philosophy. Malherbe seems almost to be echoing Montaigne when he says in a letter to Balzac: —

"Do you not know that the diversity of opinions is as natural as the difference of men's faces, and that to wish

1 Brunot, p. 149.

that what pleases or displeases us should please or displease everybody is to pass the limits where it seems that God in His omnipotence has commanded us to stop?" [1]

With this individualistic expression of the questions of opinion and taste, we have but to compare the following passage from La Bruyère to indicate how far Malherbe is still from the classic ideal: —

> "There is a point of perfection in art, as of excellence or maturity in nature. He who is sensible of it and loves it has perfect taste; he who is not sensible of it and loves this or that else on either side of it has a faulty taste. There is then a good and a bad taste, and men dispute of tastes not without reason." [2]

III. *The Second Influx of Italian Ideas*

The second influx of Italian critical ideas into France came through two channels. In the first place, the direct literary relations between Italy and France during this period were very marked. The influence of Marino, who lived for a long time at Paris and published a number of his works there, was not inconsiderable, especially upon the French concettists and *précieux*. Two Italian ladies founded and presided over the famous Hotel de Rambouillet, — Julie Savelli, Marquise de Pisani, and Catherine de Vivonne, Marquise de Rambouillet. It was partly to the influence of the Accademia della Crusca that the foundation of the French Academy was due. Chapelain and Ménage were

1 *Œuvres*, Lalanne's edition, iv. 91.
2 *Caractères*, "Des Ouvrages de l'Esprit."

both members of the Italian society, and submitted to it their different opinions on a verse of Petrarch. Like the Accademia della Crusca, the French Academy purposed the preparation of a great dictionary; and each began its existence by attacking a great work of literature, the *Gerusalemme Liberata* in the case of the Italian society, Corneille's *Cid* in the case of the French. The regency of Marie de Medici, the supremacy of Mazarin, and other political events, all conspired to bring Italy and France into the closest social and literary relationship.

But the two individuals who first brought into French literature and naturalized the primal critical concepts of Italy were Chapelain and Balzac. Chapelain's private correspondence indicates how thorough was his acquaintance with the critical literature of Italy. "I have a particular affection for the Italian language," he wrote in 1639 to Balzac. [1] Of the *Cid*, he says that "in Italy it would be considered barbarous, and there is not an academy which would not banish it beyond the confines of its jurisdiction." [2] Speaking of the greatness of Ronsard, he says that his own opinion was in accord with that of "two great savants beyond the Alps, Speroni and Castelvetro "; [3] and he had considerable correspondence with Balzac on the subject of the controversy between Caro and Castelvetro in the previous century. In a word, he knew and

1 *Lettres*, i. 413. The references are to the edition by Tamizey de Larroque, Paris, 1880-1883.

2 *Ibid.* i. 156.

3 *Ibid.* i. 631 *sq.*

studied the critics and scholars of Italy, and was interested in discussing them. Balzac's interest, on the other hand, was rather toward Spanish literature; but he was the agent of the Cardinal de la Valette at Rome, and it was on his return to France that he published the first collection of his letters. The influence of both Chapelain and Balzac on French classicism was considerable. During the sixteenth century, literary criticism had been entirely in the hands of learned men. Chapelain and Balzac vulgarized the critical ideas of the Italian Renaissance, and made them popular, human, but inviolable. Balzac introduced into France the fine critical sense of the Italians; Chapelain introduced their formal rules, and imposed the three unities on French tragedy. Together they effected a humanizing of the classical ideal, even while subjecting it to rules.

It was to the same Italian influences that France owed the large number of artificial epics that appeared during this period. About ten epics were published in the fifteen years between 1650 and 1665.[1] The Italians of the sixteenth century had formulated a fixed theory of the artificial epic; and the nations of western Europe rivalled one another in attempting to make practical use of this theory. It is to this that the large number of Spanish epics in the sixteenth century and of French epics in the seventeenth may be ascribed. Among the latter

1 These epics have been treated at length by Duchesne, *Histoire des Poèmes Épiques français du X VII Siècle*, Paris, 1870.

we may mention Scudéry's *Alaric*, Lemoyne's *Saint Louis*, Saint-Amant's *Moyse Sauvé*, and Chapelain's own epic, *La Pucelle*, awaited by the public for many years, and published only to be damned forever by Boileau.

The prefaces of all these epics indicate clearly enough their indebtedness to the Italians. They were indeed scarcely more than attempts to put the rules and precepts of the Italian Renaissance into practice. "I then consulted the masters of this art," says Scudéry, in the preface of *Alaric*, "that is to say, Aristotle and Horace, and after them Macrobius, Scaliger, Tasso, Castelvetro, Piccolomini, Vida, Vossius, Robortelli, Riccoboni, Paolo Beni, Mambrun, and several others; and passing from theory to practice I reread very carefully the *Iliad* and the *Odyssey*, the *Æneid*, the *Pharsalia*, the *Thebaid*, the *Orlando Furioso*, and the *Gerusalemme Liberata*, and many other epic poems in diverse languages." Similarly, Saint-Amant, in the preface of his *Moyse Sauvé*, says that he had rigorously observed "the unities of action and place, which are the principal requirements of the epic; and besides, by an entirely new method, I have restricted my subject not only within twenty-four hours, the limit of the dramatic poem, but almost within half of that time. This is more than even Aristotle, Horace, Scaliger, Castelvetro, Piccolomini, and all the other moderns have ever required." It is obvious that for these epic-makers the rules and precepts of the Italians were the final tests of heroic poetry. Similarly, the Abbé d'Au bignac, at the beginning of his *Pratique du Théâtre*, advises the dramatic poet to study, among other writers, "Aristotle, Horace, Castelvetro, Vida, Heinsius, Vossius, and Scaliger, of whom not a word should be lost." From the Italians also came the theory of poetry in general as held throughout the period of classicism, and expounded by the Abbé d'Aubignac, La Mesnardière, Corneille, Boileau, and numerous others; and it is hardly necessary to repeat that Rapin, tracing the history of criticism at the beginning of his *Réflexions sur la Poétique*, deals with scarcely any critics but the Italians.

Besides the direct influence of the Italian critics, another influence contributed its share to the sum of critical ideas which French classicism owes to the Italian Renaissance. This was the tradition of Scaliger, carried on by the Dutch scholars Heinsius and Vossius. Daniel Heinsius was the pupil of Joseph Scaliger, the illustrious son of the author of the *Poetics*; and through Heinsius the dramatic theories of the elder Scaliger influenced classical tragedy in France. The treatise of Heinsius, *De Tragœdiæ Constitutione*, published at Leyden in 1611, was called by Chapelain "the quintessence of Aristotle's *Poetics*"; and Chapelain called Heinsius himself "a prophet or sibyl in matters of criticism." [1] Annoted by Racine, cited as an infallible authority by Corneille, Heinsius's work exercised

1 *Lettres*, i. 269, 424. On the theories of Heinsius, see Zerbst, *Ein Vorläufer Lessings in der Aristotelesinterpretation*, Jena, 1887.

a marked influence on French tragedy by fixing upon it the laws of Scaliger; and later the works of Vossius coöperated with those of Heinsius in widening the sphere of the Italian influence. It is evident, therefore, that while French literature had already during the sixteenth century taken from the Italian Renaissance its respect for antiquity and its admiration for classical mythology, the seventeenth century owed to Italy its definitive conception of the theory of poetry, and especially certain rigid structural laws for tragedy and epic. It may be said without exaggeration that there is not an essential idea or precept in the works of Corneille and D'Aubignac on dramatic poetry, or of Le Bossu and Mambrun on epic poetry, that cannot be found in the critical writings of the Italian Renaissance.

IV. *The Influence of Rationalistic Philosophy*

The influence of rationalistic philosophy on the general attitude of classicism manifested itself in what may be called the gradual rationalization of all that the Renaissance gave to France. The process thus effected is most definitely exhibited in the evolution of the rules which France owed to Italy. It has already been shown how the rules and precepts of the Italians had originally been based on authority alone, but had gradually obtained a general significance of their own, regardless of their ancient authority. Somewhat later, in England, the Aristotelian canons were defended by Ben Jonson on the ground that Aristotle understood the causes of things, and that what others had done by chance or custom, Aristotle did by reason alone. [1] By this time, then, the reasonableness of the Aristotelian canons was distinctly felt, although they were still regarded as having authoritativeness in themselves; and it was first in the French classicists of the seventeenth century that reason and the ancient rules were regarded as one and inseparable.

Rationalism, indeed, is to be found at the very outset of the critical activity of the Renaissance; and Vida's words, already cited, "Semper nutu rationis eant res," represent in part the attitude of the Renaissance mind toward literature. But the "reason" of the earlier theorists was merely empirical and individualistic; it did not differ essentially from Horace's ideal of "good sense." In fact, rationalism and humanism, while existing together throughout the Renaissance, were never to any extent harmonized; and extreme rationalism generally took the form of an avowed antagonism to Aristotle. The complete rationalization of the laws of literature is first evident toward the middle of the seventeenth century. "The rules of the theatre," says the Abbé d'Aubignac, at the beginning of his *Pratique du Théâtre*, "are founded, not on authority, but on reason," and if they are called the rules of the ancients, it is simply "because the ancients have admirably practised them." Similarly, Corneille, in his discourse *Des Trois Unités*, says that the unity of time would be arbitrary and tyrannical if it were merely required by Aristotle's *Poetics*,

1 *Discoveries*, p. 80.

but that its real prop is the natural reason; and Boileau sums up the final attitude of classicism in these words: —

> "Aimez donc la *raison*; que toujours vos écrits
> Empruntent *d'elle seule* et leur lustre et leur prix." [1]

Here the rationalizing process is complete, and the actual requirements of authority become identical with the dictates of the reason.

The rules expounded by Boileau, while for the most part the same as those enunciated by the Italians, are no longer mere rules. They are laws dictated by abstract and universal reason, and hence inevitable and infallible; they are not tyrannical or arbitrary, but imposed upon us by the very nature of the human mind. This is not merely, as we have said, the good nature and the good sense, in a word, the sweet reasonableness, of such a critic as Horace. [2] There is more than this in the classicists of the seventeenth century. Good sense becomes universalized, becomes, in fact, as has been said, not merely an empirical notion of good sense, but the abstract and universal reason itself. From this follows the absolute standard of taste at the bottom of classicism, as exemplified in the passage already cited from La Bruyère, and in such a line as this from Boileau: —

> "La raison pour marcher n'a souvent qu'une voie." [3]

This rationalization of the Renaissance rules of poetry

1 *Art Poét.* i. 37.

2 *Cf.* Brunetière, *Études Critiques*, iv. 136; and Krantz, p. 93 *sq.*

3 *Art Poét.* i. 48.

was effected by contemporary philosophy, if not by the works and doctrines of Descartes himself, at least by the general tendency of the human mind at this period, of which these works and doctrines are the most perfect expressions. Boileau's *Art Poétique* has been aptly called the *Discours de la Méthode* of French poetry. So that while the contribution of Malherbe and his school to classicism lay in the insistence on clearness, propriety, and verbal and metrical perfection, and the contribution of the Italian Renaissance lay in the infusion of respect for classical antiquity and the imposition of a certain body of fixed rules, the contribution of contemporary philosophy lay in the rationalization or universalization of these rules, and in the imposition of an abstract and absolute standard of taste.

But Cartesianism brought with it certain important limitations and deficiencies. Boileau himself is reported to have said that "the philosophy of Descartes has cut the throat of poetry;" [1] and there can be no doubt that this is the exaggerated expression of a certain inevitable truth. The excessive insistence on the reason brought with it a corresponding undervaluation of the imagination. The rational and rigidly scientific basis of Cartesianism was forced on classicism; and reality became its supreme object and its final test: —

"Rien n'est beau que le vrai."

Reference has already been made to various disadvantages imposed on classicism by the very nature of its origin

1 Reported by J. B. Rousseau, in a letter to Brossette, July 21, 1715.

and growth; but the most vital of all these disadvantages was the influence of the Cartesian philosophy or philosophic temper. With the scientific basis thus imposed on literature, its only safeguard against extinction was the vast influence of a certain body of fixed rules, which literature dared not deviate from, and which it attempted to justify on the wider grounds of philosophy. These rules, then, the contribution of Italy, saved poetry in France from extinction during the classical period; and of this a remarkable confirmation is to be found in the fact that not until the rationalism of the seventeenth and eighteenth centuries was superseded in France, did French literature rid itself of this body of Renaissance rules. Cartesianism, or at least the rationalistic spirit, humanized these rules, and imposed them on the rest of Europe. But though quintessentialized, they remained artificial, and circumscribed the workings of the French imagination for over a century.

PART THIRD

LITERARY CRITICISM IN ENGLAND

LITERARY CRITICISM IN ENGLAND

CHAPTER I

THE EVOLUTION OF ENGLISH CRITICISM FROM ASCHAM TO MILTON

LITERARY criticism in England during the Elizabethan age was neither so influential nor so rich and varied as the contemporary criticism of Italy and France. This fact might perhaps be thought insufficient to affect the interest or patriotism of English-speaking people, yet the most charming critical monument of this period, Sidney's *Defence of Poesy*, has been slightingly referred to by the latest historian of English poetry. Such interest and importance as Elizabethan criticism possesses must therefore be of an historical nature, and lies in two distinct directions. In the first place, the study of the literature of this period will show, not only that there was a more or less complete body of critical doctrine during the Renaissance, but also that Englishmen shared in this creation, or inheritance, of the Renaissance as truly as did their continental neighbors; and on the other hand this study may be said to possess an interest in itself, in so far as it will make the growth of classicism in England intelligible, and will indicate that the formation of the classic ideal had begun before the introduction of the French influence. In neither case, however, can early English criticism be considered wholly apart from the general body of Renaissance doctrine; and its study loses in importance and perspicuity according as it is kept distinct from the consideration of the critical literature of France, and especially of Italy.

English criticism, during the sixteenth and seventeenth centuries, passed through five more or less distinct stages of development. The first stage, characterized by the purely rhetorical study of literature, may be said to begin with Leonard Coxe's *Arte or Crafte of Rhetoryke*, a hand-book for young students, compiled about 1524, chiefly from one of the rhetorical treatises of Melanchthon. [1] This was followed by Wilson's *Arte of Rhetorike* (1553), which is more extensive and certainly more original than Coxe's manual, and which has been called by Warton "the first book or system of criticism in our language." But the most important figure of this period is Roger Ascham. The educational system expounded in his *Scholemaster*, written between 1563 and 1568, he owed largely to his friend, John Sturm, the Strasburg humanist, and to his teacher, Sir John Cheke, who had been Greek lecturer at the University of Padua; but for the critical portions of this work he seems directly indebted to the rhetorical treatises of the Italians. [2] Yet his obligations to the Italian human-

1 *Cf. Mod. Lang. Notes*, 1898, xiii. 293.
2 *Cf.* Ascham, *Works*, ii. 174-191.

ists did not prevent the expression of his stern and unyielding antagonism to the romantic Italian spirit as it influenced the imaginative literature of his time. In studying early English literature it must always be kept in mind that the Italian Renaissance influenced the Elizabethan age in two different directions. The Italianization of English poetry had been effected, or at least begun, by the publication of Tottel's *Miscellany* in 1557; on this, the creative side of English literature, the Italian influence was distinctly romantic. The influence of the Italian humanists, on the other hand, was directly opposed to this romantic spirit; even in their own country they had antagonized all that was not classical in tendency. Ascham, therefore, as a result of his humanistic training, became not only the first English man of letters, but also the first English classicist.

The first stage of English criticism, then, was entirely given up to rhetorical study. It was at this time that English writers first attained the appreciation of form and style as distinguishing features of literature; and it was to this appreciation that the formation of an English prose style was due. This period may therefore be compared with the later stages of Italian humanism in the fifteenth century; and the later humanists were the masters and models of these early English rhetoricians. Gabriel Harvey, as a Ciceronian of the school of Bembo, was perhaps their last representative.

The second stage of English criticism — a period

of classification and especially of metrical studies — commences with Gascoigne's *Notes of Instruction concerning the making of Verse*, [1] published in 1575, and modelled apparently on Ronsard's *Abrégé de l'Art Poétique françois* (1565). Besides this brief pamphlet, the first work on English versification, this stage also includes Puttenham's *Arte of English Poesie*, the first systematic classification of poetic forms and subjects, and of rhetorical figures; Bullokar's *Bref Grammar*, the first systematic treatise on English grammar; and Harvey's *Letters* and Webbe's *Discourse of English Poetrie*, the first systematic attempts to introduce classical metres into English poetry. This period was characterized by the study and classification of the practical questions of language and versification; and in this labor it was coöperating with the very tendencies which Ascham had been attempting to counteract. The study of the verse-forms introduced into England from Italy helped materially to perfect the external side of English poetry; and a similar result was obtained by the crude attempts at quantitative verse suggested by the school of Tolomei. The Italian prosodists were thus, directly or indirectly, the masters of the English students of this era.

The representative work of the third stage — the period of philosophical and apologetic criticism — is Sir Philip Sidney's *Defence of Poesy*, published posthumously in 1595, though probably written about

1 The *Reulis and Cautelis of Scottis Poesie* by James VI. of Scotland is wholly based on Gascoigne's treatise.

1583. Harington's *Apologie of Poetrie*, Daniel's *Defence of Ryme*, and a few others, are also contemporary treatises. These works, as their titles indicate, are all defences or apologies, and were called forth by the attacks of the Puritans on poetry, especially dramatic poetry, and the attacks of the classicists on English versification and rhyme. Required by the exigencies of the moment to defend poetry in general, these authors did not attempt to do so on local or temporary grounds, but set out to examine the fundamental grounds of criticism, and to formulate the basic principles of poetry. In this attempt they consciously or unconsciously sought aid from the critics of Italy, and thus commenced in England the influence of the Italian theory of poetry. How great was their indebtedness to the Italians the course of the present study will make somewhat clear; but it is certainly remarkable that this indebtedness has never been pointed out before. Speaking of Sidney's *Defence of Poesy*, one of the most distinguished English authorities on the Renaissance says: "Much as the Italians had recently written upon the theory of poetry, I do not remember any treatise which can be said to have supplied the material or suggested the method of this apology." [1] On the contrary, the doctrines discussed by Sidney had been receiving very similar treatment from the Italians for over half a century; and it can be said without exaggeration that there is not an essential principle in

1 J. A. Symonds, *Sir Philip Sidney*, p. 157. *Cf.* also, Sidney, *Defence*, Cook's introduction, p. xxvii.

the *Defence of Poesy* which cannot be traced back to some Italian treatise on the poetic art. The age of which Sidney is the chief representative is therefore the first period of the influence of Italian critics.

The fourth stage of English criticism, of which Ben Jonson is, as it were, the presiding genius, occupies the first half of the seventeenth century. The period that preceded it was in general romantic in its tendencies; that of Jonson leaned toward a strict though never servile classicism. Sidney's contemporaries had studied the general theory of poetry, not for the purpose of enunciating rules or dogmas of criticism, but chiefly in order to defend the poetic art, and to understand its fundamental principles. The spirit of the age was the spirit, let us say, of Fracastoro; that of Jonson was, in a moderate form, the spirit of Scaliger or Castelvetro. With Jonson the study of the art of poetry became an inseparable guide to creation; and it is this element of self-conscious art, guided by the rules of criticism, which distinguishes him from his predecessors. The age which he represents is therefore the second period of the influence of Italian criticism; and the same influence also is to be seen in such critical poems as Suckling's *Session of the Poets*, and the *Great Assises holden in Parnassus*, ascribed to Wither, both of which may be traced back to the class of critical poetry of which Boccalini's *Ragguagli di Parnaso* is the type.[1]

1 *Cf.* Foffano, p. 173 *sq.* In Spain, Lope de Vega's *Laurel de Apolo* and Cervantes' *Viage del Parnaso* belong to the same class of poems.

The fifth period, which covers the second half of the seventeenth century, is characterized by the introduction of French influence, and begins with Davenant's letter to Hobbes, and Hobbes's answer, both prefixed to the epic of *Gondibert* (1651). These letters, written while Davenant and Hobbes were at Paris, display many of the characteristic features of the new influence, — the rationalistic spirit, the stringent classicism, the restriction of art to the imitation of nature, with the further limitation of nature to the life of the city and the court, and the confinement of the imagination to what is called "wit." This specialized sense of the word "wit" is characteristic of the new age, of which Dryden, in part the disciple of Davenant, is the leading figure. The Elizabethans used the term in the general sense of the understanding, — wit, the mental faculty, as opposed to will, the faculty of volition. With the neo-classicists it was used sometimes to represent, in a limited sense, the imagination, [1] more often, however, to designate what we should call fancy, [2] or even mere propriety of poetic expression; [3] but whatever its particular use, it was always regarded as of the essence of poetic art.

With the fifth stage of English criticism this essay is not concerned. The history of literary criticism in England will be traced no farther than 1650, when the influence of France was substituted for that of Italy. This

1 *Cf.* Dryden, ded. epist. to the *Annus Mirabilis*.

2 Addison, *Spectator*, no. 62.

3 Dryden, preface to the *State of Innocence*.

section deals especially with the two great periods of Italian influence, — that of Sidney and that of Ben Jonson. These two men are the central figures, and their names, like those of Dryden, Pope, and Samuel Johnson, represent distinct and important epochs in the history of literary criticism.

CHAPTER II

THE GENERAL THEORY OF POETRY IN THE ELIZABETHAN AGE

THOSE who have some acquaintance, however superficial, with the literary criticism of the Italian Renaissance will find an account of the Elizabethan theory of poetry a twice-told tale. In England, as in France, criticism during this period was of a more practical character than in Italy; but even for the technical questions discussed by the Elizabethans, some prototype, or at least some equivalent, may be found among the Italians. The first four stages of English criticism have therefore little novelty or original value; and their study is chiefly important as evidence of the gradual application of the ideas of the Renaissance to English literature.

The writers of the first stage, as might be expected, concerned themselves but little with the theory of poetry, beyond repeating here and there the commonplaces they found in the Italian rhetoricians. Yet it is interesting to note that as early as 1553, Wilson, in the third book of his *Rhetoric*, gives expression to the allegorical conception of poetry which in Italy had held sway from the time of Petrarch and Boccaccio, and which, more than anything else, colored critical theory in Elizabethan

England. The ancient poets, according to Wilson, did not spend their time inventing meaningless fables, but used the story merely as a framework for contents of ethical, philosophic, scientific, or historical import; the trials of Ulysses, for example, were intended to furnish a lively picture of man's misery in this life. The poets are, in fact, wise men, spiritual legislators, reformers, who have at heart the redressing of wrongs; and in accomplishing this end, — either because they fear to rebuke these wrongs openly, or because they doubt the expediency or efficacy of such frankness with ignorant people, — they hide their true meaning under the veil of pleasant fables. This theory of poetic art, one of the commonplaces of the age, may be described as the great legacy of the Middle Ages to Renaissance criticism.

The writers of the second stage were, in many cases, too busy with questions of versification and other practical matters to find time for abstract theorizing on the art of poetry. A long period of rhetorical and metrical study had helped to formulate a rhetorical and technical conception of the poet's function, aptly exemplified in the sonnet describing the perfect poet prefixed to King James's brief treatise on Scotch poetry. [1] The marks of a perfect poet are there given as skilfulness in the rhetorical figures, quick wit, as shown in the use of apt and pithy words, and a good memory; — a merely external view of the poet's gifts, which takes no account of such essentials as imag-

1 Haslewood, ii. 103.

ination, sensibility, and knowledge of nature and human life.

Webbe's *Discourse of English Poetrie* (1586) gives expression to a conception of the object of poetry which is the logical consequence of the allegorical theory, and which was therefore almost universally accepted by Renaissance writers. The poet teaches by means of the allegorical truth hidden under the pleasing fables he invents; but his first object must be to make these fables really pleasing, or the reader is deterred at the outset from any acquaintance with the poet's works. Poetry is therefore a delightful form of instruction; it pleases and profits together; but first of all it must delight, "for the very sum and chiefest essence of poetry did always for the most part consist in delighting the readers or hearers." [1] The poet has the highest welfare of man at heart; and by his sweet allurements to virtue and effective caveats against vice, he gains his end, not roughly or tyrannically, but, as it were, with a loving authority. [2] From the very beginnings of human society poetry has been the means of civilizing men, of drawing them from barbarity to civility and virtue. If it be objected that this art — or rather, from the divine origin of its inspiration, this more than art — has ever been made the excuse for the enticing expression of obscenity and blasphemy, Webbe has three answers. In the first place, poetry is to be moralized, that is, to be read allegorically. The *Metamorphoses* of Ovid, for example, will become, when so understood,

1 Haslewood, ii. 28. 2 *Ibid.* ii. 42.

a fount of ethical teaching; and Harington, a few years later, actually explains in detail the allegorical significance of the fourth book of that poem. [1] This was a well-established tradition, and indeed a favorite occupation, of the Middle Ages; and the *Ovide Moralisé*, a long poem by Chrétien Le Gouais, written about the beginning of the fourteenth century, and the equally long Ovidian commentary of Pierre Berçuire, are typical examples of this practice. [2] In the second place, the picture of vices to be found in poetry is intended, not to entice the reader to imitate them, but rather to deter sensible men from doing likewise by showing the misfortune that inevitably results from evil. Moreover, obscenity is in no way essentially connected with poetic art; it is to the abuse of poetry, and not to poetry itself, that we must lay all blame for this fault.

A still higher conception of the poet's function is to be found in Puttenham's *Arte of English Poesie* (1589). The author of this treatise informs us that he had lived at the courts of France, Italy, and Spain, and knew the languages of these and other lands; and the results of his travels and studies are sufficiently shown in his general theory of poetry. His conception of the poet is directly based on that of Scaliger. Poetry, in its highest form, is an art of "making," or creation; and in this sense the poet is a creator like God, and forms a world out of nothing. In another sense, poetry

1 Haslewood, ii. 128.
2 *Hist. Litt. de la France*, xxix. 502-525.

is an art of imitation, in that it presents a true and lively picture of everything set before it. In either case, it can attain perfection only by a divine instinct, or by a great excellence of nature, or by vast observation and experience of the world, or indeed by all these together; but whatever the source of its inspiration, it is ever worthy of study and praise, and its creators deserve preëminence and dignity above all other artificers, scientific or mechanical.[1] The poets were the first priests, prophets, and legislators of the world, the first philosophers, scientists, orators, historians, and musicians. They have been held in the highest esteem by the greatest men from the very first; and the nobility, antiquity, and universality of their art prove its preëminence and worth. With such a history and such a nature, it is sacrilege to debase poetry, or to employ it upon any unworthy subject or for ignoble purpose. Its chief themes should therefore be such as these: the honor and glory of the gods, the worthy deeds of noble princes and great warriors, the praise of virtue and the reproof of vice, instruction in moral doctrine or scientific knowledge, and finally, "the common solace of mankind in all the travails and cares of this transitory life," or even for mere recreation alone.[2]

This is the sum of poetic theorizing during the second stage of English criticism. Yet it was at this very time that the third, or apologetic, period was prepared for by the attacks which the Puritans directed against poetry, and especially the drama.

1 Puttenham, p. 19 *sq.* 2 *Ibid.* p. 39.

Of these attacks, Gosson's, as the most celebrated, may be taken as the type. Underlying the rant and exaggerated vituperation of his *Schoole of Abuse* (1579), there is a basis of right principles, and some evidence at least of a spirit not wholly vulgar. He was a moral reformer, an idealist, who looked back with regret toward "the old discipline of England," and contrasted it with the spirit of his own day, when Englishmen seemed to have "robbed Greece of gluttony, Italy of wantonness, Spain of pride, France of deceit, and Dutchland of quaffing." [1] The typical evidences of this moral degradation and effeminacy he found in poetry and the drama; and it is to this motive that his bitter assault on both must be ascribed. He specifically insists that his intention was not to banish poetry, or to condemn music, or to forbid harmless recreation to mankind, but merely to chastise the abuse of all these. [2] He praises plays which possess real moral purpose and effect, and points out the true use and the worthy subjects of poetry much in the same manner as Puttenham does a few years later. [3] But he affirms, as Plato had done hundreds of years before, and as a distinguished French critic has done only the other day, that art contains within itself the germ of its own disintegration; and he shows that in the English poetry of his own time this disintegration had already taken place. The delights and ornaments of verse, intended really to make moral doctrine more pleasing and less abstruse

1 Gosson, p. 34.
2 *Ibid.* p. 65.
3 *Ibid.* pp. 25, 40.

and thorny, had become, with his contemporaries mere alluring disguises for obscenity and blasphemy.

In the first of the replies to Gosson, Lodge's *Defence of Poetry, Musick, and Stage Plays*, written before either of the treatises of Webbe and Puttenham, are found the old principles of allegorical and moral interpretation, — principles which to us may seem well worn, but which to the English criticism of that time were novel enough. Lodge points out the efficacy of poetry as a civilizing factor in primitive times, and as a moral agency ever since. If the poets have on occasion erred, so have the philosophers, even Plato himself, and grievously. [1] Poetry is a heavenly gift, and is to be contemned only when abused and debased. Lodge did not perceive that his point of view was substantially the same as his opponent's; and indeed, throughout the Elizabethan age, there was this similarity in the point of view of those who attacked and those who defended poetry. Both sides admitted that not poetry, but its abuse, is to be disparaged; and they differed chiefly in that one side insisted almost entirely on the ideal perfection of the poetic art, while the other laid stress on the debased state into which it had fallen. A dual point of view was attempted in a work, licensed in January, 1600, which professed to be "a commendation of true poetry, and a discommendation of all bawdy, ribald, and paganized poets." [2] This Puritan movement

1 Lodge, *Defence* (*Shakespeare Soc. Publ.*), p. 6.

2 Arber, *Transcript of the Stat. Reg.*, iii. 154.

against the paganization of poetry corresponds to the similar movement started by the Council of Trent in Catholic countries.

The theory of poetry during the second stage of English criticism was in the main Horatian, with such additions and modifications as the early Renaissance had derived from the Middle Ages. The Aristotelian canons had not yet become a part of English criticism. Webbe alludes to Aristotle's dictum that Empedocles, having naught but metre in common with Homer, was in reality a natural philosopher rather than a poet; [1] but all such allusions to Aristotle's *Poetics* were merely incidental and sporadic. The introduction of Aristotelianism into England was the direct result of the influence of the Italian critics; and the agent in bringing this new influence into English letters was Sir Philip Sidney. His *Defence of Poesy* is a veritable epitome of the literary criticism of the Italian Renaissance; and so thoroughly is it imbued with this spirit, that no other work, Italian, French, or English, can be said to give so complete and so noble a conception of the temper and the principles of Renaissance criticism. For the general theory of poetry, its sources were the critical treatises of Minturno [2] and Scaliger. [3] Yet without any decided novelty of ideas, or even of expression, it can lay

1 Haslewood, ii. 28.

2 Sidney's acquaintance with Minturno is proved beyond doubt, even were such proof necessary, by the list of poets (*Defence*, pp. 2, 3) which he has copied from Minturno's *De Poeta*, pp. 14, 15.

3 Scaliger's *Poetics* is specifically mentioned and cited by Sidney four or five times; but these citations are far from exhausting his indebtedness to Scaliger.

claim to distinct originality in its unity of feeling, its ideal and noble temper, and its adaptation to circumstance. Its eloquence and dignity will hardly appear in a mere analysis, which pretends to give only the more important and fundamental of its principles; but such a summary — and this is quite as important — will at least indicate the extent of its indebtedness to Italian criticism.

In all that relates to the antiquity, universality, and preëminence of poetry, Sidney apparently follows Minturno. Poetry, as the first light-giver to ignorance, flourished before any other art or science. The first philosophers and historians were poets; and such supreme works as the *Psalms* of David and the *Dialogues* of Plato are in reality poetical. Among the Greeks and the Romans, the poet was regarded as a sage or prophet; and no nation, however primitive or barbarous, has been without poets, or has failed to receive delight and instruction from poetry. [1]

But before proceeding to defend an art so ancient and universal, it is necessary to define it; and the definition which Sidney gives agrees substantially with what might be designated Renaissance Aristotelianism. "Poetry," says Sidney, [2] "is an art of imitation, for so Aristotle termeth it in his word *μίμησις*, that is to say, a representing, counterfeiting, or figuring forth; to speak metaphorically, a

1 *Defence*, p. 2 *sq.*; *cf.* Minturno, *De Poeta*, pp. 9, 13.
2 *Defence*, p. 9.

speaking picture, [1] with this end, — to teach and delight." [2] Poetry is, accordingly, an art of imitation, and not merely the art of versifying; for although most poets have seen fit to apparel their poetic inventions in verse, verse is but the raiment and ornament of poetry, and not one of its causes or essentials. [3] "One may be a poet without versing," says Sidney, "and a versifier without poetry." [4] Speech and reason are the distinguishing features between man and brute; and whatever helps to perfect and polish speech deserves high commendation. Besides its mnemonic value, verse is the most fitting raiment of poetry because it is most dignified and compact, not colloquial and slipshod. But with all its merits, it is not an essential of poetry, of which the true test is this, — feigning notable images of vices and virtues, and teaching delightfully.

In regard to the object, or function, of poetry, Sidney is at one with Scaliger. The aim of poetry is accomplished by teaching most delightfully a notable morality; or, in a word, by delightful instruction. [5] Not instruction alone, or delight alone,

1 This ancient phrase had become, as has been seen, a commonplace during the Renaissance. *Cf., e. g.*, Dolce, *Osservationi*, 1560, p. 189; Vauquelin, *Art Poét.* i. 226; Camoens, *Lusiad.* vii. 76.

2 Sidney's classification of poets, *Defence*, p. 9, is borrowed from Scaliger, *Poet.* i. 3.

3 *Defence*, p. 11. *Cf.* Castelvetro, *Poetica*, pp. 23, 190.

4 *Defence*, p. 33. *Cf.* Ronsard, *Œuvres*, iii. 19, vii. 310; and Shelley, *Defence of Poetry*, p. 9: "The distinction between poets and prose writers is a vulgar error."

5 *Defence*, pp. 47, 51. *Cf.* Scaliger, *Poet.* i. 1, and vii. i. 2: "Poetæ finem esse, docere cum delectatione."

as Horace had said, but instruction made delightful; and it is this dual function which serves not only as the end but as the very test of poetry. The object of all arts and sciences is to lift human life to the highest altitudes of perfection; and in this respect they are all servants of the sovereign, or architectonic, science, whose end is well-doing and not well-knowing only.[1] Virtuous action is therefore the end of all learning; [2] and Sidney sets out to prove that the poet, more than any one else, conduces to this end.

This is the beginning of the apologetic side of Sidney's argument. The ancient controversy — ancient even in Plato's days — between poetry and philosophy is once more reopened; and the question is the one so often debated by the Italians, — shall the palm be given to the poet, to the philosopher, or to the historian? The gist of Sidney's argument is that while the philosopher teaches by precept alone, and the historian by example alone, the poet conduces most to virtue because he employs both precept and example. The philosopher teaches virtue by showing what virtue is and what vice is, by setting down, in thorny argument, and without clarity or beauty of style, the bare rule.[3] The historian teaches virtue by showing the experience of past ages; but, being tied down to what actually happened, that is, to the particular truth of things

1 Aristotle, *Ethics*, i. 1; Cicero, *De Offic*. i. 7.

2 This was the usual attitude of the humanists; *cf*. Woodward, p. 182 *sq*.

3 *Cf*. Daniello, p. 19; Minturno, *De Poeta*, p. 39.

and not to general reason, the example he depicts draws no necessary consequence. The poet alone accomplishes this dual task. What the philosopher says should be done is by the poet pictured most perfectly in some one by whom it has been done, thus coupling the general notion with the particular instance. The philosopher, moreover, teaches the learned only; the poet teaches all, and is, in Plutarch's phrase, "the right popular philosopher," [1] for he seems only to promise delight, and moves men to virtue unawares. But even if the philosopher excel the poet in teaching, he cannot move his readers as the poet can, and this is of higher importance than teaching; for what is the use of teaching virtue if the pupil is not moved to act and accomplish what he is taught? [2] On the other hand, the historian deals with particular instances, with vices and virtues so commingled that the reader can find no pattern to imitate. The poet makes history reasonable; he gives perfect examples of vices and virtues for human imitation; he makes virtue succeed and vice fail, as history can but seldom do. Poetry, therefore, conduces to virtue, the end of all learning, better than any other art or science, and so deserves the palm as the highest and the noblest form of human wisdom. [3]

The basis of Sidney's distinction between the poet and the

1 *Defence*, p. 18.

2 *Ibid.* p. 22. *Cf.* Minturno, *De Poeta*, p. 106; Varchi, *Lezzioni*, p. 576.

3 That is, the highest form of *human* wisdom, for Sidney, as a Christian philosopher, naturally leaves revealed religion out of the discussion.

historian is the famous passage in which Aristotle explains why poetry is more philosophic and of more serious value than history.[1] The poet deals, not with the particular, but with the universal, — with what might or should be, not with what is or has been. But Sidney, in the assertion of this principle, follows Minturno[2] and Scaliger,[3] and goes farther than Aristotle would probably have gone. All arts have the works of nature as their principal object, and follow nature as actors follow the lines of their play. Only the poet is not tied to such subjects, but creates another nature better than ever nature itself brought forth. For, going hand in hand with nature, and being enclosed not within her limits, but only by the zodiac of his own imagination, he creates a golden world for nature's brazen; and in this sense he may be compared as a creator with God.[4] Where shall you find in life such a friend as Pylades, such a hero as Orlando, such an excellent man as Æneas?

Sidney then proceeds to answer the various objections that have been made against poetry. These objections, partly following Gosson and Cornelius Agrippa,[5] and partly his own inclinations, he reduces to four.[6] In the first place, it is objected that a man might spend his time more profitably than by reading the figments of poets. But since teaching virtue is the real aim of all learning, and since poetry has been shown to accomplish this

1 *Poet.* ix. 1–4.
2 *De Poeta*, p. 87 *sq.*
3 *Poet.* i. 1.
4 *Defence*, pp. 7, 8.
5 *De Van. et Incert. Scient.* cap. v.
6 *Defence*, p. 34 *sq.*

better than all other arts or sciences, this objection is easily answered. In the second place, poetry has been called the mother of lies; but Sidney shows that it is less likely to misstate facts than other sciences, for the poet does not publish his figments as facts, and, since he affirms nothing, cannot ever be said to lie.[1] Thirdly, poetry has been called the nurse of abuse, that is to say, poetry misuses and debases the mind of man by turning it to wantonness and by making it unmartial and effeminate. But Sidney argues that it is man's wit that abuses poetry, and not poetry that abuses man's wit; and as to making men effeminate, this charge applies to all other sciences more than to poetry, which in its description of battles and praise of valiant men notably stirs courage and enthusiasm. Lastly, it is pointed out by the enemies of poetry that Plato, one of the greatest of philosophers, banished poets from his ideal commonwealth. But Plato's *Dialogues* are in reality themselves a form of poetry; and it argues ingratitude in the most poetical of philosophers, that he should defile the fountain which was his source.[2] Yet though Sidney perceives how fundamental are Plato's objections to poetry, he is inclined to believe that it was rather against the abuse of poetry by the contemporary Greek poets that Plato was chiefly cavilling; for poets are praised in the *Ion*, and the greatest men of every age have been patrons and lovers of poetry.

1 *Cf.* Boccaccio, *Gen. degli Dei*, p. 257 *sq.*; and Haslewood, ii. 127.
2 *Defence*, pp. 3, 41; *cf.* Daniello, p. 22.

In the dozen years or so which elapsed between the composition and the publication of the *Defence of Poesy*, during which time it seems to have circulated in manuscript, a number of critical works appeared, and the indebtedness of several of them to Sidney's book is considerable. This is especially so of the *Apologie of Poetrie* which Sir John Harington prefixed to his translation of the *Orlando Furioso* in 1591. This brief treatise includes an apology for poetry in general, for the *Orlando Furioso* in particular, and also for his own translation. The first section, which alone concerns us here, is almost entirely based on the *Defence of Poesy*. The distinguishing features of poetry are imitation, or fiction, and verse. [1] Harington disclaims all intention of discussing whether writers of fiction and dialogue in prose, such as Plato and Xenophon, are poets or not, or whether Lucan, though writing in verse, is to be regarded as an historiographer rather than as a poet; [2] so that his argument is confined to the element of imitation, or fiction. He treats poetry rather as a propædeutic to theology and moral philosophy than as one of the fine arts. All human learning may be regarded by the orthodox Christian as vain and superfluous; but poetry is one of the most effective aids to the higher learning of God's divinity, and poets themselves are really popular philosophers and popular divines. Harington then takes up, one by one, the four specific charges of Cornelius Agrippa, that poetry is a nurse of lies, a pleaser of fools, a

1 Haslewood, ii. 129. 2 *Ibid.* ii. 123.

breeder of dangerous errors, and an enticer to wantonness; and answers them after the manner of Sidney. He differs from Sidney, however, in laying particular stress on the allegorical interpretation of imaginative literature. This element is minimized in the *Defence of Poesy*; but Harington accepts, and discusses in detail, the mediæval conception of the three meanings of poetry, the literal, the moral, and the allegorical.[1] The death-knell of this mode of interpreting literature was sounded by Bacon, who, while not asserting that all the fables of poets are but meaningless fictions, declared without hesitation that the fable had been more often written first and the exposition devised afterward, than the moral first conceived and the fable merely framed to give expression to it.[2]

This passage occurs in the second book of the *Advancement of Learning* (1605), where Bacon has briefly stated his theory of poetry. His point of view does not differ essentially from that of Sidney, though the expression is more compact and logical. The human understanding, according to Bacon, includes the three faculties of memory, imagination, and reason, and each of these faculties finds typical expression in one of the three great branches of learning, memory in history, reason in philosophy, and imagination in poetry.[3] The imagination, not being tied to the laws of matter, may join what nature has severed and sever what nature has joined; and poetry, therefore, while restrained in the meas-

1 Haslewood, ii. 127.

2 Bacon, *Works*, vi. 204-206.

3 *Cf. Anglia*, 1899, xxi. 273.

ure of words, is in all things else extremely licensed. It may be defined as feigned history, and in so far as its form is concerned, may be either in prose or in verse. Its source is to be found in the dissatisfaction of the human mind with the actual world; and its purpose is to satisfy man's natural longing for more perfect greatness, goodness, and variety than can be found in the nature of things. Poetry therefore invents actions and incidents greater and more heroic than those of nature, and hence conduces to magnanimity; it invents actions more agreeable to the merits of virtue and vice, more just in retribution, more in accordance with revealed providence, and hence conduces to morality; it invents actions more varied and unexpected, and hence conduces to delectation. "And therefore it was ever thought to have some participation of divineness, because it doth raise the mind, by submitting the shows of things to the desires of the mind; whereas reason doth buckle and bow the mind unto the nature of things." [1] For the expression of affections, passions, corruptions, and customs, the world is more indebted to poets than to the works of philosophers, and for wit and eloquence no less than to orators and their orations. It is for these reasons that in rude times, when all other learning was excluded, poetry alone found access and admiration.

This is pure idealism of a romantic type; but in his remarks on allegory Bacon was foreshadowing the development of classicism, for from the time of

1 *Works*, vi. 203.

Ben Jonson the allegorical mode of interpreting poetry ceased to have any effect on literary criticism. The reason for this is obvious. The allegorical critics regarded the plot, or fable, — to use a simile so often found in Renaissance criticism — as a mere sweet and pleasant covering for the wholesome but bitter pill of moral doctrine. The neo-classicists, limiting the sense and application of Aristotle's definition of poetry as an imitation of life, regarded the fable as the medium of this imitation, and the more perfect according as it became more truly and more minutely an image of human life. In criticism, therefore, the growth of classicism is more or less coextensive with the growth of the conception of the fable, or plot, as an end in itself.

This vaguely defines the change which comes over the spirit of criticism about the beginning of the seventeenth century, and which is exemplified in the writings of Ben Jonson. His definition of poetry does not differ substantially from that of Sidney, but seems more directly Aristotelian: —

> "A poet, *poeta*, is... a maker, or feigner; his art, an art of imitation or feigning; expressing the life of men in fit measure, numbers, and harmony; according to Aristotle from the word *ποιεῖν*, which signifies to make or feign. Hence he is called a poet, not he which writeth in measure only, but that feigneth and formeth a fable, and writes things like the truth; for the fable and fiction is, as it were, the form and soul of any poetical work or poem." [1]

1 *Discoveries*, p. 73. On Jonson's distinction between poet (*poeta*), poem (*poema*), and poesy (*poesis*), see my article in *Modern Philology*, 1905, ii. 459, n.

Poetry and painting agree in that both are arts of imitation, both accommodate all they invent to the use and service of nature, and both have as their common object profit and pleasure; but poetry is a higher form of art than painting, since it appeals to the understanding, while painting appeals primarily to the senses. [1] Jonson's conception of his art is thus essentially noble; of all arts it ranks highest in dignity and ethical importance. It contains all that is best in philosophy, divinity, and the science of politics, and leads and persuades men to virtue with a ravishing delight, while the others but threaten and compel. [2] It therefore offers to mankind a certain rule and pattern of living well and happily in human society. This conception of poetry Jonson finds in Aristotle; [3] but it is to the Italians of the Renaissance, and not to the Stagyrite, that these doctrines really belong.

Jonson ascribes to the poet himself a dignity no less than that of his craft. Mere excellence in style or versification does not make a poet, but rather the exact knowledge of vices and virtues, with ability to make the latter loved and the former hated; [4] and this is so far true, that to be a good poet it is necessary, first of all, to be a really good man. [5] A similar doctrine has already been found in many critical writers of the sixteenth century; but perhaps the noblest expression of this conception of the poet's consecrated character and office occurs in

1 *Discoveries*, p. 49.

2 *Ibid.* p. 34.

3 *Ibid.* p. 74.

4 *Ibid.* p. 34.

5 *Works*, i. 333.

the original quarto edition of Jonson's *Every Man in his Humour,* in which the "reverend name" of poet is thus exalted: —

"I can refell opinion, and approve
The state of poesy, such as it is,
Blessed, eternal, and most true divine:
Indeed, if you will look on poesy,
As she appears in many, poor and lame,
Patched up in remnants and old worn-out rags,
Half-starved for want of her peculiar food,
Sacred invention; then I must confirm
Both your conceit and censure of her merit:
But view her in her glorious ornaments,
Attired in the majesty of art,
Set high in spirit with the precious taste
Of sweet philosophy; and, which is most,
Crowned with the rich traditions of a soul,
That hates to have her dignity prophaned
With any relish of an earthly thought,
Oh then how proud a presence doth she bear!
Then is she like herself, fit to be seen
Of none but grave and consecrated eyes." [1]

Milton also gives expression to this consecrated conception of the poet. Poetry is a gift granted by God only to a few in every nation; [2] but he who would partake of the gift of eloquence must first of all be virtuous. [3] It is impossible for any one to write well of laudable things without being himself a true poem, without having in himself the experience and practice of all that is praiseworthy. [4] Poets are the champions of liberty and the "strenuous enemies

1 *Works*, i. 59, n.
2 Milton, *Prose Works*, ii. 479.
3 *Ibid.* iii. 100.
4 *Ibid.* iii. 118.

of despotism"; [1] and they have power to imbreed and cherish in a people the seeds of virtue and public civility, to set the affections in right tune, and to allay the perturbations of the mind. [2] Poetry, which at its best is "simple, sensuous, and passionate," describes everything that passes through the brain of man, — all that is holy and sublime in religion, all that in virtue is amiable and grave. Thus by means of delight and the force of example, those who would otherwise flee from virtue are taught to love her.

1 *Prose Works*, i. 241. 2 *Ibid.* ii. 479.

CHAPTER III

THE THEORY OF DRAMATIC AND HEROIC POETRY

DRAMATIC criticism in England began with Sir Philip Sidney. Casual references to the drama can be found in critical writings anterior to the *Defence of Poesy*; but to Sidney belongs the credit of having first formulated, in a more or less systematic manner, the general principles of dramatic art. These principles, it need hardly be said, are those which, for half a century or more, had been undergoing discussion and modification in Italy and France, and of which the ultimate source was the *Poetics* of Aristotle. Dramatic criticism in England was thus, from its very birth, both Aristotelian and classical and it remained so for two centuries. The beginnings of the Elizabethan drama were almost contemporary with the composition of the *Defence of Poesy*, and the decay of the drama with Jonson's *Discoveries*. Yet throughout this period the romantic drama never received literary exposition. The great Spanish drama had its critical champions and defenders, the Elizabethan drama had none. It was, perhaps, found to be a simpler task to echo the doctrines of others, than to formulate the principles of a novel dramatic form. But the true explanation has already been suggested.

The sources of the dramatic criticism were the writings of the Italian critics, and these were entirely classical. In creative literature, however, the Italian Renaissance influenced the Elizabethans almost entirely on the romantic side. This, perhaps, suffices to explain the lack of fundamental coördination between dramatic theory and dramatic practice during the sixteenth and early seventeenth centuries. Ascham, writing twenty years before Sidney, indicated "Aristotle's precepts and Euripides' example" as the criteria of dramatic art; [1] and in spirit these remained the final tests throughout the Elizabethan age.

I. *Tragedy*

In Webbe's *Discourse of English Poetrie* we find those general distinctions between tragedy and comedy which had been common throughout the Middle Ages from the days of the post-classic grammarians. Tragedies express sorrowful and lamentable histories, dealing with gods and goddesses, kings and queens, and men of high estate, and representing miserable calamities, which become worse and worse until they end in the most woful plight that can be devised. Comedies, on the other hand, begin doubtfully, become troubled for a while, but always, by some lucky chance, end with the joy and appeasement of all concerned. [2] This distinction is said to be derived from imitation of the *Iliad* and the *Odyssey*; and in this, as well in

1 *Scholemaster*, p. 139. 2 Haslewood, ii. 40.

his fanciful account of the origins of the drama, Webbe seems to have had a vague recollection of Aristotle. Puttenham's account of dramatic development is scarcely more Aristotelian; [1] yet in its general conclusions it agrees with those in the *Poetics*. His conception of tragedy and comedy is similar to Webbe's. Comedy expresses the common behavior and manner of life of private persons, and such as are of the meaner sort of men. [2] Tragedy deals with the doleful falls of unfortunate and afflicted princes, for the purpose of reminding men of the mutability of fortune, and of God's just punishment of a vicious life. [3]

The Senecan drama and the Aristotelian precepts were the sources of Sidney's theory of tragedy. The oratorical and sententious tragedies of Seneca had influenced dramatic theory and practice throughout Europe from the very outset of the Renaissance. Ascham, indeed, preferred Sophocles and Euripides to Seneca, and cited Pigna, the rival of Giraldi Cintio, in confirmation of his opinion; [4] but this, while an indication of Ascham's own good taste, is an exceptional verdict, and in direct opposition to the usual opinion of contemporary critics. Sidney, in his account of the English drama, could find but one tragedy modelled as it should be on the Senecan drama. [5] The tragedy of *Gorboduc*, however, has one defect that provokes Sidney's censure, — it does not observe the unities of time and place.

1 Puttenham, p. 47 *sq.*

2 *Ibid.* p. 41.

3 *Ibid.* p. 49.

4 Ascham, *Works*, ii. 189.

5 *Defence*, p. 47 *sq.*

In all other respects, it is an ideal model for English playwrights to imitate. Its stately speeches and well-sounding phrases approach almost to the height of Seneca's style; and in teaching most delightfully a notable morality, it attains the very end of poetry.

The ideal tragedy — and in this Sidney closely follows the Italians — is an imitation of a noble action, in the representation of which it stirs "admiration and commiseration," [1] and teaches the uncertainty of the world and the weak foundations upon which golden roofs are built. It makes kings fear to be tyrants, and tyrants manifest their tyrannical humors. Sidney's censure of the contemporary drama is that it outrages the grave and weighty character of tragedy, its elevated style, and the dignity of the personages represented, by mingling kings and clowns, and introducing the most inappropriate buffoonery. There are, indeed, one or two examples of tragi-comedy in ancient literature, such as Plautus's *Amphitryon*; [2] but never do the ancients, like the English, match hornpipes and funerals. [3] The English dramas are neither true comedies nor truc tragedies, and disregard both the rules of poetry and honest civility. Tragedy is not tied to the laws of history, and may arrange and modify events as it pleases; but it is certainly bound by the rules of poetry. It is evident, there-

1 *Defence*, p. 28. This is the Elizabethan equivalent for Aristotle's *katharsis* of "pity and terror."

2 *Cf.* Scaliger, *Poet.* i. 7.

3 *Defence*, p. 50.

fore, that the *Defence of Poesy*, as a French writer has observed, "gives us an almost complete theory of neo-classic tragedy, a hundred years before the *Art Poétique* of Boileau: the severe separation of poetic forms, the sustained dignity of language, the unities, the *tirade*, the *récit*, nothing is lacking." [1]

Ben Jonson pays more attention to the theory of comedy than to that of tragedy; but his conception of the latter does not differ from Sidney's. The parts, or divisions, of comedy and tragedy are the same, and both have on the whole a common end, to teach and delight; so that comic as well as tragic poets were called by the Greeks *διδάσκαλοι*. [2] The external conditions of the drama require that it should have the equal division into acts and scenes, the true number of actors, the chorus, and the unities. [3] But Jonson does not insist on the strict observance of these formal requirements, for the history of the drama shows that each successive poet of importance has gradually and materially altered the dramatic structure, and there is no reason why the modern poet may not do likewise. Moreover, while these requirements may have been regularly observed in the ancient state and splendor of dramatic poetry, it is impossible to retain them now and preserve any measure of popular delight. The outward forms of the ancients, therefore, may in part be disregarded; but there are certain essentials which must be observed by the tragic poet in whatsoever age he may flourish. These are, "Truth of argument, dignity of persons,

1 Breitinger, p. 37. 2 *Discoveries*, p. 81. 3 *Works*, i. 69.

gravity and height of elocution, fulness and frequency of sentence." [1] In other words, Jonson's model is the oratorical and sententious tragedy of Seneca, with its historical plots and its persons of high estate.

In the address, "Of that Sort of Dramatic Poem which is called Tragedy," prefixed to *Samson Agonistes*, Milton has minutely adhered to the Italian theory of tragedy. After referring to the ancient dignity and moral effect of tragedy, [2] Milton acknowledges that, in the modelling of his poem, he has followed the ancients and the Italians as of greatest authority in such matters. He has avoided the introduction of trivial and vulgar persons and the intermingling of comic and tragic elements; he has used the chorus, and has observed the laws of verisimilitude and decorum. His explanation of the peculiar effect of tragedy — the purgation of pity and fear — has already been referred to in the first section of this essay. [3]

II. *Comedy*

The Elizabethan theory of comedy was based on the body of rules and observations which the Italian critics, aided by a few hints from Aristotle, had deduced from the practice of Plautus and Terence. It will, therefore, be

1 *Works*, i. 272.

2 *Cf.* Bacon, *De Augm. Scient.* iii. 13; and Ascham, *Scholemaster*, p. 130.

3 He seems also to allude to the theory of *katharsis* in the *Reason of Church Government*; *Prose Works*, ii. 479.

unnecessary to dwell at any great length on the doctrines of Sidney and Ben Jonson, who are the main comic theorists of this period. Sidney defines comedy as "an imitation of the common errors of our life," which are represented in the most ridiculous and scornful manner, so that the spectator is anxious to avoid such errors himself. Comedy, therefore, shows the "filthiness of evil," but only in "our private and domestical matters." [1] It should aim at being wholly delightful, just as tragedy should be maintained by a well-raised admiration. Delight is thus the first requirement of comedy; but the English comic writers err in thinking that delight cannot be obtained without laughter, whereas laughter is neither an essential cause nor an essential effect of delight. Sidney then distinguishes delight from laughter almost exactly after the manner of Trissino. [2] The great fault of English comedy is that it stirs laughter concerning things that are sinful, *i.e.* execrable rather than merely ridiculous — forbidden plainly, according to Sidney, by Aristotle himself — and concerning things that are miserable, and rather to be pitied than scorned. Comedy should not only produce delightful laughter, but mixed with it that delightful teaching which is the end of all poetry.

Ben Jonson, like Sidney, makes human follies or errors the themes of comedy, which should be

1 *Defence*, p. 28.

2 *Ibid.* p. 50 *sq.* *Cf.* Trissino, *Opere*, ii. 127 *sq.*; and Cicero, *De Orat.* ii. 58 *sq.*

"an image of the times,
And sport with human follies, not with crimes,
Except we make them such, by loving still
Our popular errors, when we know they're ill;
I mean such errors as you'll all confess
By laughing at them, they deserve no less." [1]

In depicting these human follies, it is the office of the comic poet to imitate justice, to improve the moral life and purify language, and to stir up gentle affections. [2] The moving of mere laughter is not always the end of comedy; in fact, Jonson interprets Aristotle as asserting that the moving of laughter is a fault in comedy, a kind of turpitude that depraves a part of man's nature. [3] This conclusion is based on an interpretation of Aristotle which has persisted almost to the present day. In the *Poetics*, *τὸ γελοῖον*, the ludicrous, is said to be the subject of comedy; [4] and many critics have thought that Aristotle intended by this to distinguish between the risible and the ridiculous, between mere laughter and laughter mixed with contempt or disapprobation. [5] The nature and the source of one of the most important elements in Jonson's theory of comedy, his doctrine of " humours," have been briefly discussed in the first section of this essay. It will suffice here to define a "humour" as an absorbing singularity of character, [6] and to note that it grew out of the concep-

1 *Works*, i. 2.
2 *Ibid.* i. 335.
3 *Discoveries*, p. 82.
4 *Poet.* v. 1.
5 *Cf.* Twining, i. 320 *sq.*, and Kames, *Elements of Criticism*, vol. i. chap. 7.
6 *Cf.* Jonson, *Works*, i. 67 and 31.

tion of *decorum* which played so important a part in poetic theory during the Italian Renaissance.

III. *The Dramatic Unities*

Before leaving the theory of the drama, there is one further point to be discussed, — the doctrine of the unities. It has been seen that the unities of time and place were, in Italy, first formulated together by Castelvetro in 1570, and in France by Jean de la Taille in 1572. The first mention of the unities in England is to be found, a dozen years later, in the *Defence of Poesy*, and it cannot be doubted that Sidney derived them directly from Castelvetro. Sidney, in discussing the tragedy of *Gorboduc*, finds it "faulty in time and place, the two necessary companions of all corporal actions; for where the stage should always represent but one place, and the uttermost time presupposed in it should be, both by Aristotle's precept and common reason, but one day, there [*i.e.* in *Gorboduc*] is both many days and many places inartificially imagined." [1] He also objects to the confusions of the English stage, where on one side Africa and on the other Asia may be represented, and where in an hour a youth may grow from boyhood to old age. [2] How absurd this is, common sense, art, and ancient examples ought to

1 *Defence*, p. 48; *cf.* Castelvetro, *Poetica*, pp. 168, 534.

2 *Cf.* Whetstone, *Promos and Cassandra* (1578), cited in Ward, *Dram. Lit.* i. 118; also, Jonson, *Works*, i. 2, 70; Cervantes, *Don Quix.* i. 48; Boileau, *Art Poét.* iii. 39. In the theory of the drama, Sidney's point of view coincides very closely with that of Cervantes.

teach the English playwright; and at this day, says Sidney, the ordinary players in Italy will not err in it. If indeed it be objected that one or two of the comedies of Plautus and Terence do not observe the unity of time, let us not follow them when they err but when they are right; it is no excuse for us to do wrong because Plautus on one occasion has done likewise.

The law of the unities does not receive such rigid application in England as is given by Sidney until the introduction of the French influence nearly three quarters of a century later. Ben Jonson is considerably less stringent in this respect than Sidney. He lays particular stress on the unity of action, and in the *Discoveries* explains at length the Aristotelian conception of the unity and magnitude of the fable. "The fable is called the imitation of one entire and perfect action, whose parts are so joined and knit together, as nothing in the structure can be changed, or taken away, without impairing or troubling the whole, of which there is a proportionable magnitude in the members." [1] Simplicity, then, should be one of the chief characteristics of the action, and nothing receives so much of Jonson's censure as "monstrous and forced action." [2] As to the unity of time, Jonson says that the action should be allowed to grow until necessity demands a conclusion; the argument, however, should not exceed the compass of one day, but should be large enough to allow place for digressions and episodes, which are to the fable what furniture is to a house. [3]

1 *Discoveries*, p. 83. 2 *Works*, i. 337. 3 *Discoveries*, p. 85.

Jonson does not formally require the observance of the unity of place, and even acknowledges having disregarded it in his own plays; but he does not favor much change of scene on the stage. In the prologue of *Volpone*, he boasts that he has followed all the laws of refined comedy,

> "As best critics have designed;
> The laws of time, place, persons he observeth,
> From no needful rule he swerveth."

Milton observes the unity of time in the *Samson Agonistes*: "The circumscription of time, wherein the whole drama begins and ends is, according to ancient rule and best example, within the space of twenty-four hours."

With the introduction of the French influence, the unities became fixed requirements of the English drama, and remained so for over a century. Sir Robert Howard, in the preface of his tragedy, *The Duke of Lerma*, impugned their force and authority; but Dryden, in answering him, pointed out that to attack the unities is really to contend against Aristotle, Horace, Ben Jonson, and Corneille. [1] Farquhar, however, in his *Discourse upon Comedy* (1702), argued with force and wit against the unities of time and place, and scoffed at all the legislators of Parnassus, ancient and modern, — Aristotle, Horace, Scaliger, Vossius, Heinsius, D'Aubignac, and Rapin.

1 *Essay of Dram. Poesy*, p. 118.

IV. *Epic Poetry*

The Elizabethan theory of heroic poetry may be dismissed briefly. Webbe refers to the epic as "that princely part of poetry, wherein are displayed the noble acts and valiant exploits of puissant captains, expert soldiers, wise men, with the famous reports of ancient times;" [1] and Puttenham defines heroic poems as "long histories of the noble gests of kings and great princes, intermeddling the dealings of gods, demi-gods, and heroes, and weighty consequences of peace and war." [2] The importance of this form of poetry, according to Puttenham, is largely historical, in that it sets forth an example of the valor and virtue of our forefathers. [3] Sidney is scarcely more explicit. [4] He asserts that heroic poetry is the best and noblest of all forms; he shows that such characters as Achilles, Æneas, and Rinaldo are shining examples for all men's imitation; but of the nature or structure of the epic he says nothing.

The second part of Harington's *Apologie of Poetrie* is given up to a defence of the *Orlando Furioso*, and here the Aristotelian theory of the epic appears for the first time in English criticism. Harington, taking the *Æneid* as the approved model of all heroic poetry, first shows that Ariosto has followed closely in Virgil's footsteps, but is to be preferred even to Virgil in that the latter pays reverence to false deities, while Ariosto has the advantage of the

1 Haslewood, ii. 45.
2 Puttenham, p. 40.
3 *Ibid.* p. 54.
4 *Defence*, p. 30.

Christian spirit. But since some critics, "reducing all heroical poems unto the method of Homer and certain precepts of Aristotle," insist that Ariosto is wanting in art, Harington sets out to prove that the *Orlando Furioso* may not only be defended by the example of Homer, but that it has even followed very strictly the rules and precepts of Aristotle. [1] In the first place, Aristotle says that the epic should be based on some historical action, only a short part of which, in point of time, should be treated by the poet; so Ariosto takes the story of Charlemagne, and does not exceed a year or so in the compass of the argument. [2] Secondly, Aristotle holds that nothing that is utterly incredible should be invented by the poet; and nothing in the *Orlando* exceeds the possibility of belief. Thirdly, epics, as well as tragedies, should be full of *περιπέτεια*, which Harington interprets to mean "an agnition of some unlooked for fortune either good or bad, and a sudden change thereof"; and of this, as well as of apt similitudes and passions well expressed, the *Orlando* is really full.

In conclusion, it may be observed that epic poetry did not receive adequate critical treatment in England until after the introduction of the French influence. The rules and theories of the Italian Renaissance, restated in the writings of Le Bossu, Mambrun, Rapin, and Vossius, were thus brought into English criticism, and found perhaps

1 Haslewood, ii. 140 *sq*.
2 *Cf*. Minturno, *Arte Poetica*, p. 71; and Ronsard, *Œuvres*, iii. 19.

their best expression in Addison's essays on *Paradise Lost*. Such epics as Davenant's *Gondibert*, Chamberlayne's *Pharonnida*, Dryden's *Annus Mirabilis*, and Blackmore's *Prince Arthur*, like the French epics of the same period, doubtless owed their inspiration to the desire to put into practice the classical rules of heroic poetry. [1]

1 *Cf.* Dryden, *Discourse on Satire*, in *Works*, xiii. 37.

CHAPTER IV

CLASSICAL ELEMENTS IN ELIZABETHAN CRITICISM

I. *Introductory: Romantic Elements*

It were no less than supererogation to adduce evidences of the romantic spirit of the age of Shakespeare. No period in English literature is more distinctly romantic; and although in England criticism is less affected by creative literature, and has had less effect upon it, than in France, it is only natural to suppose that Elizabethan criticism should be as distinctly romantic as the works of imagination of which it is presumably an exposition. As early as Wilson's *Rhetoric* we find evidences of that independence of spirit in questions of art which seems typical of the Elizabethan age; and none of the writers of this period exhibits anything like the predisposition of the French mind to submit instinctively to any rule, or set of rules, which bears the stamp of authority. From the outset the element of nationality colors English criticism, and this is especially noticeable in the linguistic discussions of the age. At the very time when Sidney was writing the *Defence of Poesy*, Spenser's old teacher, Mulcaster, wrote: "I love Rome, but London better; I favor Italy, but England more; I honor the Latin, but I worship the English."[1] It is this spirit which pervades what may be called the chief expression of the romantic temper in Elizabethan criticism, — Daniel's *Defence of Rhyme* (1603), written in answer to Campion's attack on rhyme in the *Observations in the Art of English Poesy*. The central argument of Daniel's defence is that the use of rhyme is sanctioned both by custom and by nature — "custom that is before all law, nature that is above all art."[2] He rebels against that conception which would limit

> "Within a little plot of Grecian ground
> The sole of mortal things that can avail;"

and he shows that each age has its own perfections and its own usages. This attempt at historical criticism leads him into a defence of the Middle Ages; and he does not hesitate to assert that even classical verse had its imperfections and deficiencies. In the minutiæ of metrical criticism, also, he is in opposition to the neo-classic tendencies of the next age; and his favorable opinion of *enjambement* and his unfavorable comments on the heroic couplet[3] drew from Ben Jonson an answer, never published, in which the latter attempted to prove that the couplet is the best form of English verse, and that all other forms are forced and detestable.[4]

1 Morley, *English Writers*, ix. 187.

2 Haslewood, ii. 197.

3 *Ibid.* ii. 217.

4 *Jonson, Works*, iii. 470. *Cf.* Gascoigne's comments on *enjambement*, in Haslewood, ii. 11.

II. *Classical Metres*

Daniel's *Defence of Rhyme* may be said to have dealt a death-blow to a movement which for over half a century had been a subject of controversy among English men of letters. In reading the critical works of this period, it is impossible not to notice the remarkable amount of attention paid by the Elizabethans to the question of classical metres in the vernacular. The first organized attempt to introduce the classical versification into a modern language was, as Daniel himself points out, [1] that of Claudio Tolomei in 1539. The movement then passed into France; and classical metres were adopted by Baïf in practice, and defended by Jacques de la Taille in theory. In England the first recorded attempt at the use of quantity in the vernacular was that of Thomas Watson, from whose unpublished translation of the *Odyssey* in the metre of the original Ascham has cited a single distich: —

> "All travellers do gladly report great prayse of Ulysses,
> For that he knew many mens maners, and saw many cities." [2]

This was probably written between 1540 and 1550; toward the close of the preceding century, we are told, a certain Mousset had already translated the *Iliad* and the *Odyssey* into French hexameters.

Ascham was the first critical champion of the use of quantity in English verse.[3] Rhyme, he says, was introduced

1 Haslewood, ii. 205.
2 *Scholemaster*, p. 73.
3 *Ibid.* p. 145 *sq.*

by the Goths and Huns at a time when poetry and learning had ceased to exist in Europe; and Englishmen must choose either to imitate these barbarians or to follow the perfect Grecians. He acknowledges that the monosyllabic character of the English language renders the use of the dactyl very difficult, for the hexameter "doth rather trot and hobble than run smoothly in our English tongue;" but he argues that English will receive the *carmen iambicum* as naturally as Greek or Latin. He praises Surrey's blank verse rendering of the fourth book of the *Æneid*, but regrets that, in disregarding quantity, it falls short of the "perfect and true versifying." An attempt to put Ascham's theories into practice was made by Thomas Blenerhasset in 1577; but the verse of his *Complaynt of Cadwallader*, though purporting to be "a new kind of poetry," is merely an unrhymed Alexandrine.[1]

In 1580, however, five letters which had passed between Spenser and Gabriel Harvey appeared in print as *Three proper, and wittie, familiar Letters* and *Two other very commendable Letters*; and from this correspondence we learn that an organized movement to introduce classical metres into English had been started. It would seem that for several years Harvey had been advocating the use of quantitative verse to several of his friends; but the organized movement to which reference has just

1 *Cf.* Haslewood, ii. p. xxii. The treatises of Gascoigne (1575) and King James VI. (1584) contain no reference to quantitative verse.

been made seems to have been started independently by Thomas Drant, who died in 1578. Drant had devised a set of rules and precepts for English classical verse; and these rules, with certain additions and modifications, were adopted by a coterie of scholars and courtiers, among them being Sidney, Dyer, Greville, and Spenser, who thereupon formed a society, the Areopagus, [1] independent of Harvey, but corresponding with him regularly. This society appears to have been modelled on Baïf's Académie de Poésie et de Musique, which had been founded in 1570 for a similar purpose, and which Sidney doubtless became acquainted with when at Paris in 1572.

From the correspondence published in 1580, it becomes evident that Harvey's and Drant's systems of versification were almost antipodal. According to Drant's system, the quantity of English words was to be regulated entirely by the laws of Latin prosody, — by position, diphthong, and the like. Thus, for example, the penult of the word *carpēnter* was regarded as long by Drant because followed by two consonants. Harvey, who was unacquainted with Drant's rules before apprised of them by Spenser in the published letters, follows a more normal and logical system. To him, accent alone is the test of quantity, and the law of position cannot make the penult of *carpēnter* or *majēsty* long. "The Latin is no rule for us," says Harvey; [2] and often where position and diphthong fall together,

1 *Cf.* Pulci, *Morgante Maggiore*, xxv. 117.
2 Haslewood, ii. 280.

as in the penult of *merchaŭndise*, we must pronounce the syllable short. In all such matters, the use, custom, propriety, or majesty of our speech must be accounted the only infallible and sovereign rule of rules.

It was not, then, Harvey's purpose to Latinize our tongue. His intention was apparently twofold, — to abolish rhyme, and to introduce new metres into English poetry. Only a few years before, Gascoigne had lamented that English verse had only one form of metre, the iambic. [1] Harvey, in observing merely the English accent, can scarcely be said to have introduced quantity into our verse, but was simply adapting new metres, such as dactyls, trochees, and spondees, to the requirements of English poetry.

Drant's and Harvey's rules therefore constitute two opposing systems. According to the former, English verse is to be regulated by Latin prosody regardless of accent; according to the latter, by accent regardless of Latin prosody. By neither system can quantity be successfully attempted in English; and a distinguished classical scholar of our own day has indicated what is perhaps the only method by which this can be accomplished. [2] This method may be described as the harmonious observance of both accent and position; all accented syllables being generally accounted long, and no syllable which violates the Latin law of position

1 Haslewood, ii. 5.

2 R. Ellis, *Poems and Fragments of Catullus translated in the original metres*, London, 1871, p. xiv. *sq*.

being used when a short syllable is required by the scansion. These three systems, with more or less variation, have been employed throughout English literature. Drant's system is followed in the quantitative verse of Sidney and Spenser; Harvey's method is that employed by Longfellow in *Evangeline*; and Tennyson's beautiful classical experiments are practical illustrations of the method of Professor Robinson Ellis.

In 1582, Richard Stanyhurst published at Leyden a translation of the first four books of the *Æneid* into English hexameters. From Ascham he seems to have derived his inspiration, and from Harvey his metrical system. Like Harvey he refuses to be bound by the laws of Latin prosody, [1] and follows the English accent as much as possible. But in one respect his translation is unique. Harvey, in his correspondence with Spenser, had suggested that the use of quantitative verse in English necessitated the adoption of a certain uniformity in spelling; and the curious orthography of Stanyhurst was apparently intended as a serious attempt at phonetic reform. Spelling reform had been agitated in France for some time; and in Baïf's *Etrennes de Poésie françoise* (1574), we find French quantitative verse written according to the phonetic system of Ramus.

Webbe's *Discourse of English Poetrie* is really a plea in favor of quantitative verse. His system is based primarily on Latin prosody, but reconciled with English usage. The Latin rules are to be followed when the English and

1 Stanyhurst, p. 11 *sq*.

Latin words agree; but no word is to be used that notoriously impugns the laws of Latin prosody, and the spelling of English words should, when possible, be altered to conform to the ancient rules. The difficulty of observing the law of position in the middle of English words may be obviated by change in spelling, as in the word *mournfùlly*, which should be spelled *mournfūly*; but where this is impossible, the law of position is to be observed, despite the English accent, as in *royālty*. Unlike Ascham, Webbe regards the hexameter as the easiest of all classical metres to use in English. [1]

Puttenham is not averse to the use of classical metres, but as a conservative he considers all sudden innovations dangerous. [2] The system he adopts is not unlike Harvey's. Sidney's original enthusiasm for quantitative verse soon abated; and in the *Defence of Poesy* he points out that although the ancient versification is better suited to musical accompaniment than the modern, both systems cause delight, and are therefore equally effective and valuable; and English is more fitted than any other language to use both. [3] Campion, like Ascham, regards English polysyllables as too heavy to be used as dactyls; so that only trochaic and iambic verse can be suitably employed in English poetry. [4] He suggests eight new forms of verse. The English accent is to be diligently observed, and is to yield to nothing save the law of position; hence the

1 Haslewood, ii. 69.
2 Puttenham, p. 126 *sp*.
3 *Defence*, p. 55.
4 Haslewood, ii. 167.

second syllable of *Trumpīngton* is to be accounted long. [1] In observing the law of position, however, the sound, and not the spelling, is to be the test of quantity; thus, *love-sick* is pronounced *love-sĭk*, *dangerous* is pronounced *dangerŭs*, and the like. [2]

III. *Other Evidences of Classicism*

With Campion's *Observations* (1602) the history of classical metres in England may be said to close, until the resuscitation of quantitative verse in the present century. Daniel's *Defence of Rhyme* effectually put an end to this innovation; but the strong hold which the movement seems to have had during the Elizabethan age is interesting evidence of the classical tendencies of the period. Ben Jonson has usually been regarded as the forerunner of neo-classicism in England; but long before his influence was felt, classical tendencies may be observed in English criticism. Thus Ascham's conservatism and aversion to singularity in matters of art are distinctly classical. "He that can neither like Aristotle in logic and philosophy, nor Tully in rhetoric and eloquence," says Ascham, "will from these steps likely enough presume by like pride to mount higher to the misliking of graver matters; that is, either in religion to have a dissentious head, or in the commonwealth to have a factious heart." [3] His insistence that it is no slavery to be bound by the laws of art, and the stress he lays on perfection of style, are no less classical. [4]

1 Haslewood, ii. 186.
2 *Cf.* Ellis, *op. cit.*, p. xvi.
3 *Scholemaster*, p. 93.
4 *Ibid.* pp. 118, 121.

Similar tendencies may be observed in the writers that follow Ascham. Harvey's strictures on the *Faerie Queene* were inspired by two influences. As a humanist, he looked back with contempt on mediæval literature in general, its superstitions, its fairy lore, and the like. As a classicist in art, he preferred the regular, or classic, form of the epic to the romantic, or irregular form; and his strictures may be compared in this respect with those of Bembo on the *Orlando* or those of Salviati on the *Gerusalemme*. So Harington attempts to make the *Orlando* chime with the laws of Aristotle, and Sidney attempts to force these laws on the English drama. So also Sidney declares that genius, without "art, imitation, and exercise," is as nothing, and censures his contemporaries for neglecting "artificial rules and imitative patterns." [1] So Webbe attempts to find a fixed standard or criterion by which to judge good and bad poets, and translates Fabricius's summary of the rules of Horace as a guide for English poetry. [2]

English criticism, therefore, may be said to exhibit classical tendencies from its very beginning. But it is none the less true that before Ben Jonson there was no systematic attempt to force, as it were, the classic ideal on English literature. In Spain, as has been seen, Juan de la Cueva declared that poetry should be classical and imitative, while the drama should be romantic and original. Sidney, on the contrary, sought to make the drama classical, while

1 *Defence*, p. 46. 2 Haslewood, ii. 19, 85 *sq*.

allowing freedom of imagination and originality of form to the non-dramatic poet. Ben Jonson was the first complete and consistent English classicist; and his classicism differs from that of the succeeding age rather in degree than in kind.

Bacon's assertion that poetry is restrained in the measure of words, but in all other points extremely licensed, [1] is characteristic of the Elizabethan point of view. The early critics allowed extreme license in the choice and treatment of material, while insisting on strict regularity of expression. Thus Sidney may advocate the use of classical metres, but this does not prevent him from celebrating the freedom of genius and the soaring heights of the imagination. There is nothing of these things in Ben Jonson. He, too, celebrates the nobility and power of poetry, and the dignity of the poet's office; but nowhere does he speak of the freedom of the imagination or the force of genius. Literature for him was not an expression of personality, not a creation of the imagination, but an image of life, a picture of the world. In other words, he effected what may be called an objectification of the literary ideal.

In the second place, this image of life can be created only by conscious effort on the part of the artist. For the creation of great poetry, genius, exercise, imitation, and study are all necessary, but to these art must be added to make them perfect, for only art can lead to perfection. [2] It is this insistence on art as a distinct element, almost as an end in itself, that distinguishes Jonson from

1 *Works*, vi. 202. 2 *Discoveries*, p. 78.

his predecessors; and nowhere is his ideal of art expressed as pithily as in the address to the reader prefixed to the *Alchemist* (1612): —

"In Poetry, especially in Plays,... the concupiscence of dances and of antics so reigneth, as to run away from nature, and be afraid of her, is the only point of art that tickles the spectators. But how out of purpose, and place, do I name art? When the professors are grown so obstinate contemners of it, and presumers on their own naturals, as they are deriders of all diligence that way, and, by simple mocking at the terms, when they understand not the things, think to get off wittily with their ignorance. Nay, they are esteemed the more learned, and sufficient for this, by the many, through their excellent vice of judgment. For they commend writers as they do fencers or wrestlers; who, if they come in robustiously, and put for it with a great deal of violence, are received for the braver fellows; when many times their own rudeness is the cause of their disgrace, and a little touch of their adversary gives all that boisterous force the foil. I deny not but that these men, who always seek to do more than enough, may some time happen on some thing that is good and great; but very seldom; and when it comes it doth not recompense the rest of their ill.... But I give thee warning, that there is a great difference between those that, to gain the opinion of copy [*i.e.* copiousness], utter all they can, however unfitly; and those that use election and a mean [1] [*i.e.* selection and moderation]. For it is only the disease of the unskilful to think rude things greater than polished; or scattered more numerous than composed." [2]

Literature, then, aims at presenting an image of life through the medium of art; and the guide

1 *Cf.* Scaliger, *Poet.* v. 3, where the highest virtue of a poet is said to be *electio et sui fastidium*; and vi. 4, where it is said that the "life of all excellence lies in measure."

2 *Works*, ii. 3; *cf. Discoveries*, pp. 22-27.

to art, according to Jonson, is to be found in the rules of criticism. Thus, for example, success in comedy is to be attained

"By observation of those comic laws
Which I, your master, first did teach the age;" [1]

and elsewhere, it will be remembered, Jonson boasts that he had swerved from no "needful law." But though art can find a never-failing guide and monitor in the rules of criticism, he does not believe in mere servile adherence to the practice or theory of classical literature. The ancients are to be regarded as guides, not commanders. [2] In short, the English mind was not yet prepared to accept the neo-classic ideal in all its consequences; and absolute subservience to ancient authority came only with the introduction of the French influence.

This is, perhaps, best indicated by the history of Aristotle's influence in English criticism from Ascham to Milton. The first reference to the *Poetics* in England is to be found in Ascham's *Scholemaster*. [3] There we are told that Ascham, Cheke, and Watson had many pleasant talks together at Cambridge, comparing the poetic precepts of Aristotle and Horace with the examples of Euripides, Sophocles, and Seneca. In Sidney's *Defence of Poesy*, Aristotle is cited several times; and in the drama, his authority is regarded by Sidney as almost on a par with that of the "common reason." [4] Harington was not satisfied until he

1 *Works*, iii. 297.
2 *Discoveries*, p. 7.
3 *Scholemaster*, p. 139.
4 *Defence*, p. 48.

had proved that the *Orlando* agrees substantially with Aristotle's requirements. Jonson wrote a commentary on Horace's *Ars Poetica*, with elucidations from Aristotle, in which

> "All the old Venusine [*i.e.* Horace], in poetry,
> And lighted by the Stagyrite [*i.e.* Aristotle], could spy,
> Was there made English;" [1]

but the manuscript was unfortunately destroyed by fire in 1623. Yet Jonson was aware how ridiculous it is to make any author a dictator. [2] His admiration for Aristotle was great; but he acknowledges that the Aristotelian rules are useless without natural talent, and that a poet's liberty cannot be bound within the narrow limits prescribed by grammarians and philosophers. [3] At the same time, he points out that Aristotle was the first critic, and the first of all men to teach the poet how to write. The Aristotelian authority is not to be contemned, since Aristotle did not invent his rules, but, taking the best things from nature and the poets, converted them into a complete and consistent code of art. Milton, also, had a sincere admiration for "that sublime art which [is taught] in Aristotle's *Poetics*, in Horace, and the Italian commentaries of Castelvetro, Tasso, Mazzoni, and others." [4] But despite all this, the English independence of spirit never failed; and before the French influence we can

1 *Works*, iii. 321; *cf.* i. 335, iii. 487.
2 *Discoveries*, p. 66.
3 *Ibid.* p. 78 *sq.*
4 *Works*, iii. 473.

find no such thing in English criticism as the literary dictatorship of Aristotle. [1]

1 The chapter on poetry in Peacham's *Compleat Gentleman* (1622) is interesting chiefly because of its indebtedness to Scaliger, who is called by Peacham (p. 91) " the prince of all learning and the judge of judgments, the divine Julius Cæsar Scaliger." This constitutes him a literary arbiter if not dictator. In the *Great Assises holden in Parnassus* (1645), Scaliger is proclaimed one of the lords of Parnassus, in company with Bacon, Sidney, Erasmus, Budæus, Heinsius, Vossius, Casaubon, Mascardi, Pico della Mirandola, Selden, Grotius, and others. The star of scholarship in criticism was passing northward; for the influence of the Dutch critics on Jonson and others, see my *Critical Essays of the Seventeenth Century*, Oxford, 1908, vol. i. pp. xvi-xviii.

CONCLUSION

It has been established, I think, that by the middle of the sixteenth century a unified body of poetic rules and theories had been developed in Italy, and then passed into France, England, Spain, Germany, Portugal, and Holland, and through Holland into Scandinavia; [1] so that by the beginning of the seventeenth century there was a common body of Renaissance doctrine throughout western Europe. Each country gave this system a national cast of its own, but the form which it received in France ultimately triumphed; and modern classicism therefore represents the supremacy of the French phase or version of Renaissance Aristotelianism. This critical system was first developed by the formal treatises on poetics during the Cinquecento, but it is a mistake to consider them as merely isolated monuments, or as furnishing the only ways in which poets, critics, and scholars approached the study of literature. They represent, in fact, but one of several critical heirlooms which Italy passed on to its foster-child France.

The humanists, as Professor Vossler has shown,[2] conceived of the nature of poetry in terms, first of theology, then of

1 For the influence of Heinsius and other Dutch critics in Sweden, *cf.* E. Wrangel, *Sveriges litterära förbindelser med Holland, särdeles under 1600-talet,* Lund, 1897.

2 *Poetische Theorien in der italienischen Frührenaissance*, Berlin, 1900, p. 88.

oratory, and finally of rhetoric and philology. This development, while apparently in the direction of an æsthetic interest in literature, was really tending toward an exclusive attention to external details, and, as an inevitable result of the growth of erudition, toward a loss of interest in poetry for itself as a creative art. The impassioned defences of poetry by Petrarch, Boccaccio, and Coluccio Salutati, in which its vital impulse was conceived to be at one with that of God himself, were succeeded by calmer studies in which poetry was given a place side by side with the other humanistic disciplines. "When I say letters (*litteras*)," says Ermolao Barbaro, "I mean philosophy which is conjoined with eloquence." [1] "The poet differs in no way from the orator," says Tiphernas, echoing Cicero, "except that he is permitted to roam about more freely, is somewhat more restricted in his numbers, and approaches more closely to music." [2] So that, while Humanism might during its progress emphasize this or that side of humanistic culture, it tended more and more to concern itself with the whole body of classical studies, and to consider them as forming a unity in themselves. The *studia sapientiœ* and the *studia eloquentiœ*, at first carefully distinguished from each other, tended more and more to merge in the single category of *studia litterarum*. [3] "The

1 *Angeli Politiani Opera*, Lugduni, 1539, p. 457.
2 K. Müllner, *Reden und Briefe italienischer Humanisten*, Vienna, 1899, p. 187.
3 *Cf.* V. Rossi, *Il Quattrocento*, Milan, n.d., p. 407 *sq.* (note on pp. 2, 3).

moderns," Vives justly complained, in his *De Causis Corruptarum Artium*, "confound the arts by reason of their resemblance, and of two that are very much opposed to each other make a single art. They call rhetoric grammar, and grammar rhetoric, because both treat of language. The poet they call orator, and the orator poet, because both put eloquence and harmony into their discourses." [1]

To this body of secular learning, — massed under the general head of *litteræ*, or *studia humanitatis*, or *eloquentia*, or *philologia*, according to the predominating interest of the period or the individual taste of the writer, — the chief opposition was represented by the two great mediæval survivals, the tradition of scholastic training and the tradition of chivalry. The defence of letters against the first was undertaken by the pedagogic treatises of the fifteenth and early sixteenth centuries. All the writers on humanistic education — the Italians, Leonardo Bruni, Æneas Sylvius Piccolomini, Maffeo Vegio, Battista Guarino, Jacopo di Porcia, the Frenchman Budæus, the Dutchman Erasmus, the German Sturm, the Spaniard Vives, the Englishmen Elyot and Ascham — not only explain, but also defend, the position of classical literature, and especially classical poetry, in the new scheme of teaching. It is the charges of paganism and immorality which chiefly confront them; and though they advance few, if any, original arguments in answering these

1 *Opera*, ed. Mayans, Valencia, 1785, vi. 64. For the significance of Vives as a critic, see the Italian translation of this book, p. 139, n.

charges, they emphasize the educative and refining influence of literary study, and indicate its value as nourishment for the young mind.

Similarly, the tradition of chivalry — the tradition of the active life *par excellence*, which found little place for culture — raised the question whether or not the study of letters is practically useless to the gentleman, whether it conduces to effeminacy, whether it unfits him for the martial or courtly life. The question was so often debated that Castiglione, in the *Cortegiano* (1528), could say that "as this controversy has already been long waged by very wise men, there is no need to renew it." But few Cinquecento treatises on the courtier, on the gentleman, on honor, on manners and courtesy, fail to discuss the relative merits of letters and arms as accomplishments for perfect manhood; and not a few separate tractates, such as Nifo's *De Armorum Litterarumque Comparatione* and Giacomini Tebalducci Malespini's *Della Nobiltà delle Lettere e delle Armi*, are devoted to the same theme. The controversy between Muzio, who espoused the cause of letters in his *Il Gentilhuomo*, and Mora, who espoused that of arms in his *Il Cavaliere*, is well known. But the consensus of opinion tended wholly in one direction. Castiglione and Guazzo might differ as to whether preëminence should be accorded to letters or arms, but they agreed fundamentally that both are essential to a complete man. The argument centred for the most part on the question of glory: did letters or arms bring the greater fame? So, in early days, when chivalry had been confronted by the conflict between arms and love, between the reward of chivalrous deeds (*ol pretz d'armas e de cavallairia*), on the one hand, and the delights of gallantry (*lo joy de dompnas e d'amia*), on the other, [1] it was the same question of honor, of glory, which was at stake; it was the same doubt as to the effeminizing effect of love on valor that agitated the chivalric mind. But humanism justified culture beyond all dispute as a gentle accomplishment. Loys le Roy, in his *Vicissitude*, showed the concurrence of letters and arms among all civilized nations; and William Segar, in his *Honor Military and Civil*, summed up the whole discussion by asserting that "the endeavor of a gentleman ought to be either in arms or learning, or in them both; and in my own poor conceit, hardly deserveth he any title of honor that doth not take pleasure in the one or the other." [2]

The poetics of the Cinquecento thus inherited, in theoretical form, a defence of classical poetry against the charges of paganism and immorality, a defence of the study of letters against the charges of effeminacy and practical uselessness, a defence of classical literature as an educative and refining force, a defence of literary study

1 *Cf.* the *tenzone* between Sordello and Bertran d'Alamanon, in C. de Lollis, *Vita e poesie di Sordello*, Halle, 1896, p. 174. The formal treatises on love during the Cinquecento are also not without interest for the history of criticism and poetic theory. Thus, for example, Equicola, in his *Libro di natura d'amore*, discusses at some length the treatment of love in classical, Tuscan, French, Provençal, and Spanish poetry — an early example of comparative criticism.

2 *Cf.* Einstein, *Italian Renaissance in England*, New York, 1902, p. 93.

in general, not as mere humanistic erudition, but as an accomplishment of gentlemen and courtiers, as an element in general culture. Moreover, the defence of the vernacular, tentatively begun in Dante's *De Vulgari Eloquentia*, was carried on to final victory by Bembo and his school, and the discussion was continued by a host of ardent advocates, such as Varchi and Muzio in Italy, Du Bellay and Henri Estienne in France, Juan de Valdés in Spain, and Cheke, Ascham, and Mulcaster in England.

Poetic theory had thus far been chiefly nourished upon the rhetorical and oratorical treatises of Cicero, the moral treatises of Plutarch (especially those upon the reading of poets and the education of youth), the *Institutiones Oratoriæ* of Quintilian, and the *De Legendis Gentilium Libris* [1] of Basil the Great. To these a vast body of classical criticism was added by the sixteenth century. Aldus, in 1503, published the works of the chief Greek rhetoricians. Giulio Cammillo elucidated Hermogenes; Robortelli, Longinus; and commentaries on the *Ars Poetica* of Horace appeared in great number. But the diffusion of Aristotle's *Poetics* was central in developing poetic theory and in furnishing a standard of judgment in criticism; and the

1 This work was very popular among the humanists. It was translated into Latin by Leonardo Bruni about 1405 (*cf.* Coluccio Salutati, *Epistola*, in *Scelta di Curiosità letterarie*, 1867, lxxx, 221), and is cited, *e.g.*, by Toscanella (Müllner, *op. cit.*, p. 194) and Æneas Sylvius (*Opera*, Basileæ, 1571, p. 983). Vives, as late as 1531, seems to rate it higher than Aristotle's *Poetics* (*Opera*, vi. 342).

outgrowth of the older humanistic heritage and of these new Aristotelian studies was that unified body of doctrine which may be summed up in the phrase "Renaissance poetics." The outworn criteria of *doctrina* and *eloquentia*, by which the humanists had tested all literary endeavor, were superseded by a thousand new ones, — probability, verisimilitude, unity, the fixed norm for each literary *genre*, and the like. Viewed from the standpoint of European criticism as a whole — for the same transformation was effected, not only in Italy, but in all the transalpine countries as well — the development may be summed up by saying that the ideal of classical imitation was merged into that of neo-classical rules. Imitation had been followed by theory, and theory by law.

The immediate problem of criticism was the application of this body of poetic theory to the body of creative literature, past and present. This was largely assisted by the literary controversies of the sixteenth century, such as those concerned with the *Orlando Furioso*, the *Gerusalemme Liberata*, the *Orbecche*, the *Divina Commedia*, the *Pastor Fido*. Even the personal polemics of the time — such as those of Caro and Castelvetro, Sigonio and Robortelli, Giraldi Cintio and Pigna, Aretino and Franco, Dolce and Ruscelli, Domenichi and Doni — were not wholly unfruitful in this respect. Poetic theory even entered the field of linguistic controversy, and so, for example, Varchi's distinction between the versifier and the poet in the *Ercolano* [1] is combated

1 B. Varchi, *Opere*, Trieste, 1859, ii. 150.

by Castelvetro in his answer to Varchi's dialogue. [1] No field of intellectual interest was untouched by it; it enriched the philosophic systems of Telesio, Campanella, and Bacon, among many others, and these show the century's advance in comparison with the paucity or confusion of ideas in regard to poetry in the earlier work of a Savonarola or a Vives.

The Italian academies swarmed with lecturers who elucidated verses of Petrarch, Bembo, Dante, Ariosto, Tasso, and the like; and though these academic discourses were for the most part trivial and futile, and chiefly concerned with the interpretation of external details, yet they could not fail to assist, in some measure, the assimilation of poetic theory, and, more important still, to foster (let us hope) that criticism which has its eyes directly on the poet's page. Of these the most characteristic are the *lezioni* (delivered before the Florentine and Paduan academies) and the minor treatises of Benedetto Varchi, who is in some respects the representative critic of the mid-Cinquecento. A master of poetic theory, he has also ideas of his own on the method and scope of criticism itself. In writing of critical prolegomena, "not only for works of philosophers, but of all other writers, both in prose and in verse," he discusses seventeen points, some absolutely necessary, others merely useful, which should be considered in the preliminary interpretation of any book: the name and the life of the author, the title of the book, whether it is legiti-

1 Varchi, *Opere*, 1859, ii. 217.

mate or not, its aim, its subject, its instrument, its office, its utility, its divisions, the order of the parts, under what form of philosophy it falls, its method of teaching, its proportion, its mode of language, and the like. [1] These are all concerned with externals; all, or nearly all, avoid or ignore the consideration of literature on its purely æsthetic side. Yet these, after all, are mere preliminaries; with what shall we concern ourselves, when we come to the work itself? Varchi tells us, in a brief but important fragment, *Qualità che si ricercano negli scrittori e negli scritti*; [2] and these qualities are four: ethical quality (*bontà*) and philosophic soundness (*dottrina*), with regard to the content of literature; eloquence (*eloquenza*) and art (*arte*), with regard to its treatment. Of these, says Varchi, the two first are nobler than the two last, since they deal with things as the latter do with words; the former give literature its instructive value, the latter its pleasure. But *bontà* and *dottrina* alone do not suffice, for the reason that all things are composed of form, which is the nobler part, and of matter, the less noble; and this form is given to literature by art, which in a sense also includes eloquence, and which alone tests the genius and judgment of a writer. Here, obviously, we are listening once more to the old humanistic catchwords, *doctrina* and *eloquentia*, matter and form, words and things, profit and pleasure, — remnants of classical phrase or mediæval jargon; we still feel the humanistic pedantry and formalism of the

1 Varchi, *Opere*, ii. 806. 2 *Ibid*. ii. 813.

Quattrocento, the older scholastic interest in the subtleties of definition.

This may perhaps appear more clearly when we consider how Varchi has put his ideas into practice. It is a favorite practice of his to use a few verses as the text of a philosophic discourse; a sonnet of Della Casa, for example, furnishes the pretext for a lecture on jealousy. [1] But his critical method may best be illustrated by the eight lectures on the *canzoni degli occhi* of Petrarch, read privately at the University of Florence during the spring of 1545. [2] In the first of these he follows in general the method he himself had laid down for all preliminary discussion. He concerns himself with six points: first, the genus to which the three *canzoni* belong, which, as he decides, is that species of rhetoric called "demonstrative or laudative;" secondly, the style of the poems, which is neither high nor low, but in the first *bassamente mezzano,* in the second *mediocremente mezzano,* in the third *altamente mezzano*; thirdly, the species or sort of poetry to which they belong, which is "lyrical," so called because originally intended to be sung to the lyre, "exegetic or narrative," because the poet speaks in his own person, and "mixed," because the versification is in part regulated and in part free; fourthly, their subject and aim, the subject being

1 Varchi, *Opere*, ii. 570. This *lezione* was translated into English in 1615 by Robert Tofte, under the title of *The Blazon of Jealousie*, with interesting marginal illustrations from contemporary English poetry.

2 *Op. cit.* ii. 439.

"natural," or concerned with the things of nature, and the poet's aim is to give praise and fame to Madonna Laura; fifthly, their similarities and dissimilarities; and, lastly, their structural dependence on one another.

All this scarcely touches the problem of true criticism, but in the succeeding lectures Varchi treats of the *canzoni* at closer range. His method is to consider one stanza after another, and to discuss its parts minutely. Thus, on the opening lines —

"Perchè la vita è breve,
E l'ingegno paventa all' alta impresa," etc., —

after pointing out that the poet here states his theme, he proceeds to make such comments as these:

"*La vita*, i.e. the space of human existence; *è breve*, i.e. short; *e l'ingegno*, i.e. my own; *paventa*, fears and trembles; *all' alta impresa*, i.e. considering the height of the subject, and how difficult it is to attempt praise of such beautiful eyes." [1]

Or on the verses —

"Quel che pensier non pareggia,
Non che l'agguagli altrui parlar, o mio" —

he comments:

"That is, the beautiful eyes of Madonna Laura; nor could a diviner circumlocution be used, nor expressed in lovelier words and more suitable terms; for *parlar*, which is a verb, corresponds with *pensier*, which is a noun, the present subjunctive *agguagli* with the present indicative *pareggia*, and *mio* with *altrui*. All this, we must believe, really indicates that things must be placed first, then conceits or thoughts... in the third place words or terms...

1 Varchi, *op. cit.* ii. 446.

and lastly, writing... since things are much truer than thoughts, thoughts than words, words than writing." [1]

It is inconceivable that such puerile interpretation could illuminate the text of Petrarch, or advance the cause of criticism; but beyond these verbal comments and scholastic distinctions Varchi, in these Petrarchan discourses, does not attempt to go. [2]

Yet these lectures, it must be remembered, were delivered three or four years before the outburst of interest in Aristotle's *Poetics* occasioned by the commentaries of Robortelli (1548) and Maggi (1550) and the Italian translation of Segni (1549); they antedate his own lectures on the theory of poetry by eight years. In order to comprehend clearly what the poetics of the Renaissance accomplished for criticism in a brief period of time, these lectures of 1553 have but to be compared with those of 1545. In the treatment of the lyric, the Cinquecento, being without the guidance of those definite theories and fixed laws which had been elaborated for dramatic and epic poetry, lost itself in details and pedantries. The old scholastic subtleties still follow Varchi in his discourse on "Poetics in General" and in the five on "Poetry," to which I have

1 Varchi, *op. cit.* ii. 448.

2 The following curious comment on these *lezioni*, to be found in one of Alfonso de' Pazzi's sonnets against Varchi (reprinted in the *Terzo libro dell' opere burlesche*, 1760, p. 338), is not without some justification: —

"Le canzoni degli occhi ha letto ii Varchi,
Ed ha cavato al gran Petrarca gli occhi."

Cf. Graf, *Attraverso il Cinquecento*, Turin, 1888, pp. 26, 64.

already given ample attention; [1] but a surer touch, a new attitude toward his material, indicate that a change of some sort had come. In one of these lectures, after stating that the *Giron Cortese* of Alamanni pleases him more than the *Orlando Furioso* (and a judgment so astounding must be taken into consideration when defining his position as a critic), he says:

> "To few, and perhaps to none, is it permitted to affirm: This or that man has erred, this or that thing is bad. Every one can say, many should indeed say: It seems to me that this or that man has erred, this or that thing does not seem to me good. It is conceded to every one to say: The figures of this or that sculptor or painter do not please me; but to very few indeed is it conceded to affirm: These figures are not good." [2]

This, in another form, is the old concept of the diversity *de gustibus*, but it is important as showing that theory had as yet not been crystallized into dogma. The orthodox neo-classic criticism, having transformed into laws the proper pleasure to be derived from each literary *genre*, was shaken by no such doubts. But early in the eighteenth century Marivaux gave expression to a point of view very much akin to that of Varchi. The critics of his day, according to Marivaux, might assert of a work of art, "That is worthless, that is detestable;" but such reasoning is itself worthless and detestable, since a man of taste may say of a book, "It does not please me," but "he will never decide that it is bad until after he has compared his own ideas

1 *Supra*, pp. 25, 34, 41, 50, etc.
2 *Opere*, ii. 691.

with those of others." [1] Here the doubt as to whether the code of poetics can afford the individual critic a fixed standard of judgment is a sign that the neo-classic structure is beginning to crumble; for it is upon the development of this very concept that criticism expended its chief effort in the century and three-quarters that separate Varchi from Marivaux.

The development in this respect is indicated in a lecture by Torquato Tasso on a sonnet of Della Casa, delivered more than a quarter of a century later before the Ferrarese Academy. [2] The method of Varchi's Petrarchan discourses is here followed, in first considering the style in which the sonnet is written, and then elucidating its various parts; though Varchi's jejune formulæ of the high, mediocre, and low styles are superseded by a more philosophical discussion of poetic style, based on the theories of Hermogenes, Demetrius Phalereus, and Cicero, and the puerile verbal exposition of Varchi gives place to a method that is not exclusively expository, but is based on Tasso's juster conception of the function of criticism. At the very outset he defines his position by contrasting the method of *imitation*, which judges works of art merely by their similarity or dissimilarity to some masterpiece in the same kind, and the method of *art*, whose higher function it is

"to investigate the reasons why this verse seems sweet, this one harsh; this one humble and plebeian, this one noble

1 G. Larroumet, *Marivaux, sa vie et ses œuvres*, Paris, 1894, p. 448.
2 Tasso, *Opere*, ed. Rosini, xi. 42 *sq*.

and magnificent; this one too careless, this one too highly colored; this one cold, this one bombastic, this one insipid; why here the movement and speed of the speech are praised, here the slowness and delay; here direct speech, here indirect; here the long period, here the short; and, in a word, why compositions please or displease: and having found the reasons of all these things, there form in the mind some that are universal, true, and infallible, gathered from the experience of many particulars; and it is the knowledge of these which Art more properly demands for itself."

Why works of art please or displease! the universal and infallible grounds of our pleasure and displeasure! — here are problems beyond the scope of Varchi's tentative and empirical method; here is a significant advance over Varchi's assumption of the individual basis of the pleasure or displeasure which poetry gives. Yet Tasso's own method is a compromise between the two which he defines; the method of imitation and that of art are alike necessary to the critic.

Here criticism is beginning to turn eyes upon itself, leaping from the two questions which had interested it most in the sixteenth century, "What is poetry?" and "What is the meaning of this or that poem?" to a third question, which it but vaguely apprehended: "What is criticism?" To say that this question was first neatly put and definitely discussed in the seventeenth century is to say that not until then did criticism become a self-conscious and organized art; and it is characteristic of this change of attitude that, while Horace and Vida had written "Arts of *Poetry*," it is literally an "Essay on *Criticism*" upon which Pope expended a kindred poetic skill. Writing some forty years after Boileau, he substituted a brief sketch of the history of criticism from Aristotle to Roscommon for the rapid survey of French poetry in the *Art Poétique*.

This new organization of critical method and critical theory was developed on the basis of Renaissance poetics. The body of rules and theories was the same, but the attitude toward them was gradually changing; and the history of this attitude gives us the history of criticism in the seventeenth and eighteenth centuries. At the beginning of the seventeenth century the intellectual ferment in Italy and Spain developed new theories of style, based on the rhetorical discussions of classical antiquity and the Renaissance. It was this ferment of thought which produced the ideal of "wit" which was derived through the French *esprit* from the Italian *ingegno*. A new terminology was being created, indicative of a change of interest from the materials of literature to the moods and faculties of the creative mind. Words like "fancy," "judgment," "wit," "humor," "taste," "the sublime," were acquiring new meaning and a higher vogue. But the rationalism of the classic spirit throttled this initial outburst, and it was not till the middle of the eighteenth century that the human mind, rather than literature itself, was systematically studied for the development of principles of criticism. Tasso, as we have seen, propounded the vital problem why poetry is pleasing to the human mind, but he attempts to find the answer in poetry itself.

With the growth of the rationalistic spirit the main interest of criticism was in fixing a reasonable standard of critical judgment. "Criticism, as it was first instituted by Aristotle," says Dryden, "was meant a standard of judging well; the chiefest part of which is to observe those excellences which should delight a reasonable reader." [1] This is no longer Tasso's problem why certain excellences please; there are in poetry excellences which ought to please the reasonable reader. La Bruyère goes still farther in asserting that for every reader there is one absolute standard of taste:

> "There is a point of perfection in art, as of excellence or maturity in nature. He who is sensible of it and loves it has perfect taste; he who is not sensible of it and loves this or that else on either side of it has a faulty taste. There is then a good and bad taste, and men dispute of tastes not without reason." [2]

Dryden's standard of judgment and La Bruyère's standard of taste are both the result of the application of reason to æsthetic pleasure. Yet the development of the ideal of taste [3] was dangerous to the rigid spirit of classicism. The recognition of the subjective basis of taste soon led to a contrast

1 *Works*, ed. Scott-Saintsbury, v. 112.

2 *Caractères*, "Des ouvrages de l'esprit." *Cf.* Shaftesbury, *Characteristicks*, London, 1711, iii. 154, 156.

3 On the early history of the term "taste" *cf.* Croce, *Estetica*, p. 194 *sq.*; Borinski, *Poetik der Renaissance*, p. 308 *sq.*; *Baltasar Gracian und die Hoflitteratur*, p. 39 *sq.*; and Farinelli's valuable review of the last in the *Revista critica de historia y literatura españolas*, vol. ii., 1896. *Cf.*, however, Addison, *Spectator*, No. 409, June 19, 1712, where Gracián's priority in the use of the term is accepted.

with those neo-classic rules which constituted the external element in art. Pope recognized that taste might give a grace beyond the reach of art; the concept of the *je ne sais quoi* [1] was formulated, to comprehend these elements of æsthetic pleasure not explicable by the rules of Renaissance poetics; and finally, Montesquieu, in his *Essai sur le Goût*, says that

> "art gives the rules, and taste the exceptions; taste discovers on what occasions art should submit to it, and on what occasions it should submit to art." [2]

It is natural to find, side by side with this evolution, a kindred development of interest in the subjective processes of art. [3] Montesquieu himself

1 This phrase had been employed as early as the sixteenth century, both in Italy and in France. Tasso uses it, and Mlle. de Gournay, the *fille d'alliance* of Montaigne, speaks of "l'amour, qui est je ne sçai quoy, doit sourdre aussi de je ne sçai quoy" (Doncieux, *Bouhours*, pp. 264, 265). Bouhours established its use in criticism in the seventeenth century, and was followed in the eighteenth by Marivaux, Montesquieu, Feijóo, and a host of others (*cf.* Croce, *Estetica*, p. 205 *sq.*; Larroumet, *Marivaux*, p. 498 *sq.*). From the time of Shaftesbury (*Characteristicks*, i. 147, etc.) it was also naturalized in England.

2 *Œuvres complètes*, Paris, 1834, p. 596.

3 John Morley (*Burke*, p. 19) gives to Burke's essay *On the Sublime and Beautiful* the credit of having first established the principle "that critics of art seek its principles in the wrong place, so long as they limit their search to poems, pictures, engravings, statues, and buildings, instead of first arranging the sentiments and faculties in man to which art makes its appeal;" but this contention, it is scarcely necessary to say, ignores a long line of antecedent speculations on the continent and even in England.

complains that the ancients regarded as positive qualities all the relative qualities of the soul; the Platonic dialogues are absurd, since they deal with the good, the beautiful, the agreeable, and the like, as positive realities:

> "The sources of the beautiful, the good, the agreeable, etc., are in ourselves, and to seek for their reasons is merely to seek for the causes of the pleasures of our soul. Let us examine then our soul, let us study it in its actions and its passions. Poetry, painting, sculpture, architecture, music, the dance, in fine, the works of nature and of art, can give pleasure to the soul; let us see why, how, and when they do so." [1]

The new science of æsthetics was to attempt, and in a sense to solve, this new problem; the romantic movement was to apply the fruits of those labors to literature and to literary criticism.

The attitude toward the body of Renaissance poetics had thus, during the seventeenth and eighteenth centuries, undergone a complete transformation. In the Renaissance itself, the humanistic period, with its ideal of classical imitation, was followed by a period of theorizing along the lines of the Aristotelian *Poetics*, and the results were before long hardened into fixed rules and dogmas of criticism. The neo-classical period regarded these rules, first from the attitude of "wit," then of reason, and finally of taste. When Hobbes, in the address prefixed to his translation of the *Iliad* (1675), says that "there be many men called *critics*, and *wits*, and *virtuosi*, that are accustomed to

1 *Œuvres complètes*, p. 587, and note.

censure the poets," [1] he has indicated the three classes of littérateurs who were to carry on these three phases of critical activity.

Imitation, theory, law; wit, reason, taste, — each in its turn became a guiding principle of criticism, until with the romantic movement all were superseded by the concept of the creative imagination. The first three represent, as it were, the stages through which Renaissance poetics passed in the process of complete codification; the last three represent the stages of its decline and death.

1 Spingarn, *Critical Essays of the Seventeenth Century*, Oxford, 1908, ii. 68; *cf.* i. p. xc *sq*.

APPENDICES

APPENDIX A

CHRONOLOGICAL TABLE OF THE CHIEF CRITICAL WORKS OF THE SIXTEENTH CENTURY

Date	Italy	Date	France	Date	England
1527	Vida: *De Arte Poetica.*			c.1524	Cox: *Rhetoric.*
1529	Trissino: *Poetica*, pts. i.-iv.				
1535	Dolce: transl. of Horace's *Ars Poetica.*				
1536	Pazzi: transl. of Aristotle's *Poetics.*				
1536	Daniello: *Poetica.*				
1539	Tolomei: *Versie Regole della Nuova Poesia.*	1545	Pelletier: transl. of Horace's *Ars Poetica.*		
1548	Robortelli: ed. of Aristotle's *Poetics.*	1548	Sibilet: *Art Poétique.*		
1549	Segni: transl. of Aristotle's *Poetics.*	1549	Du Bellay: *Défense et Illustration.*		
1550	Maggi: ed. of Aristotle's *Poetics.*			1553	Wilson: *Rhetoric.*
1554	Giraldi Cintio: *Discorsi.*	1554	Pelletier: *Art Poétique.*		
1559	Minturno: *De Poeta.*	1555	Morel: ed. of Aristotle's *Poetics.*		

CHRONOLOGICAL TABLE (*Continued*)

Date	Italy	Date	France	Date	England
1560	Vettori: ed. of Aristotle's *Poetics*.	1560	Pasquier: *Recherches*.	1567	Drant: transl. of Horace's *Ars Poetica*.
1561	Scaliger: *Poetics*.	1561	[Scaliger: *Poetics*.]	1570	Ascham: *Scholemaster*.
1563	Trissino: *Poetica*, pts. v., vi.			1575	Gascoigne: *Notes of Instruction*.
1564	Minturno: *Arte Poetica*.				
1570	Castelvetro: ed. of Aristotle's *Poetics*.	1565	Ronsard: *Abrégé de l'Art Poétique*.	1579	Gosson: *School of Abuse*.
				1579	Lodge: *Reply to Gosson*.
1575	Piccolomini: ed . of Aristotle's *Poetics*.	1572	Jean de la Taille: preface of *Saül*.	1580	Harvey and Spenser: *Letters*.
				c. 1583	Sidney: *Defence of Poesy* (publ. 1595)
1579	Viperano: *De Arte Poetica*.	1572	Ronsard: preface of *Franciade*.		
1586	Patrizzi: *Della Poetica*.			1585	James VI.: *Reulis and Cautelis*.
1587	T. Tasso: *Discorsi dell' Arte Poetica*.	1573	Jacques de la Taille: treatise on French classical metres.		
1588	Denores: *Poetica*.			1586	Webbe: *Discourse of English Poetrie*.
1597	Buonamici: *Discorsi Poetici*.	1598	De Laudun: Art *Poétique françois*.	1589	Puttenham: *Arte of English Poesie*.
1598	Ingegneri: *Poesia Rappresentativa*.	—	Vauquelin: *Art Poétique*.	1591	Harington: *Apologie of Poetrie*.
1600	Summo: *Discorsi Poetici*.				

APPENDIX B

SALVIATI'S ACCOUNT OF THE COMMENTATORS ON ARISTOTLE'S "POETICS."

THE following is Lionardo Salviati's account of the commentators on Aristotle's *Poetics* up to 1586. The passage is cited from an unpublished Ms. at Florence (Cod. Magliabech. ii. ii. II.), beginning at fol. 371. The title of the Ms. is *Parafrasi e Commento della Poetica d' Aristotile*; and at fol. 370 it is dated January 28, 1586.

DELLI INTERPRETI DI QUESTO LIBRO DELLA POETICA

Averroe primo di tutti quelli interpreti della Poetica che a nostri tempi sono pervenuti, fece intorno a esso una

Averroës.

breve Parafrasi, nella quale come che pure alcune buone considerationi si ritrovino, tutta via per la diversità e lontananza de costumi, che tra greco havea, e tra gli arabi poca notizia havendone, pochissima ne potè dare altrui. Appresso hebbe voglia

Valla.

Giorgio Valla di tradur questo libro in latino, ma o che la copia del testo greco lo ingannasse, o che verso di sè fusse l' opera malagevole per ogni guisa massimamente in quei tempi, egli di quella impresa picciola lode si guadagnò. Il che considerando

Pazzi.

poi Alessandro de Pazzi, huomo delle lingue intendente, et ingegnoso molto, alla medesima cura si diede, et ci lasciò la latina traduzzione, che in tutti i latini comenti fuorch' in quello del Vettorio si leggie. E per ciò che dotto huomo era, et hebbe copia di ottimi testi scritti a penua, diede non poca luce a questa opera, e più anche fatto havrebbe se da la morte stato non fusse sopravenuto. Ma Francesco Rubertello a tempi nostri, nelli studj delle lingue esercitatissimo, conoscendo che di maggior aviso li faceva mestieri, non solamente purgò il testo di molte macchie che accecato il tenevano, ma il primo fu ancora, che con distese dichiarationi, et con innumerabili esempli di poeti greci e latini, fece opera di illustrarlo. Vulgarizzollo appresso Bernardo Segni in questo nostro Idioma, et con alcune sue brevi annotationi lo diede in luce. E nella tradutione per alcune proprie voci che ai greci vocaboli ottimamente corrisposero, non se n' uscì anche egli senza commendazione. Ma con molto maggior grido et applauso, il comento del Maggio, chiarissimo filosopho, fu dal mondo ricevuto; perciochè havendo egli con somma gloria nella continua lettura della Philosophia i suoi anni trapassati, con l' ordine principalmente giovò a questo libro, e col mostrarne la continuatione et in non pochi luoghi soccorse il Rubertello. E se si fusse alquanto meno ardente contro di lui dimonstrato, nè così vago stato fusse di contrapporseli, sarebbe alcuna volta per avventura uscito fuor più libero il parer suo, e più saldo. A lato a quel del Maggio fu la latina traduzione et comento di Pier Vettori pubblicato, il quale essendo oltre ad ogni altro, delle antiche scritture diligentissimo osservatore, e nella cognitione delle lingue havendosi sì come io stimo a tempi nostri, il primo luogo guadagnato, hauta commodità, et in gran numero di preziosi et antichi esemplarj scritti a mano, in ogni parte, ma nella correzzione del testo spetialmente e nella traduzione, ha fatto sì che poco più avanti pare che di lume a

Robortelli.

Segni.

Maggi.

Vettoxi.

questo libro possa desiderarsi. Fu non di manco a

Castelvetro. questi anni di nuovo da un dotto huomo in questa lingua volgarizzato et esposto, et più a lungo che alcun altro che ciò habbia fin quì adoprato ancor mai. Questo sarà da me per tutto ovunque mi convenga nominarlo, il comento vulgare appellato, e per più brevità con quelle due prime lettere C. V. in questa guisa lo noterò. Nel qual comento hanno senza alcun fallo di sottilissimi avvedimenti, ma potrebb' essere, sì come io credo, più sincero. Perciò che io stimo, che dove egli dal vero si diparte, il faccia per emulazione per lo più per dimostrarsi di sottil sentimento e per non dire come li altri. È la costui tradutione, fuorchè in alcune parti dove egli secondo che io avviso volontariamente erra, tra le toscane la migliore. E sono le sue parole et in essa e nell' espositione molto pure, et in puro volgare fiorentino, quanto comporta la materia l' una e l' altra è dettata. Ultimamente la traduzzione, e con essa l' annotazione di

Piccolomini. Mgr. Alessandro Piccolomini sono uscite in stampa, il quale havendosi con molte altre sue opere d' astrologia e di filosofia e di rettorica parte composte, parte volgarizzate, non picciol home e molta riputazione acquistata, creder si può altrettanto doverli della presente faticha avvenire. Dietro a sì chiari interpreti non per emulatione, la quale tra me e sì fatti huomini

Salviati. non potrebbe haver luogo, ma per vaghezza che io pure havrei di dover ancor io, se io potessi a questa impresa, alcun aiuto arrecare dopo lo studio di dieci anni che io ci ho spesi, scendo, quantunque timido, in questo campo, più con accesa volontà, che con speranza, o vigore desideroso che avanti che venirmi gloria per false opinioni, sieno i miei difetti discretamente da savio giudice gastigati.

BIBLIOGRAPHY

This bibliography includes a list of the principal books and editions used in the preparation of the essay, and should be consulted for the full titles of works cited in the text and in the foot-notes.

I. SOURCES

Ascham, R. *The Scholemaster*, edited by E. Arber. London, 1870.

—— *The Whole Works*, edited by Rev. Dr. Giles. 3 vols. in 4 parts. London, 1864.

Aubignac, Abbé d'. *La Pratique du Théâtre*. 2 vols. Amsterdam, 1715.

Bacon, F. *Works*, edited by J. Spedding, R. L. Ellis, and D. D. Heath. 15 vols. Boston, 1863.

Batteux, C. *Les Quatres Poétiques d'Aristote, d'Horace, de Vida, de Despréaux*. Paris, 1771.

Berni, F. *Rime, Poesie Latine, e Lettere*, per cura di P. Virgili. Firenze, 1885.

Boccaccio, G. *Geneologia degli Dei*, trad. per G. Betussi. Vinegia, 1547.

—— *Vita di Dante*, per cura di F. Macrì-Leone. Firenze, 1888.

Bruno, G. *Opere*, raccolte da A. Wagner. 2 vols. Lipsia, 1830.

Butcher, S. H. *Aristotle's Theory of Poetry and Fine Art, with a Critical Text and a Translation of the Poetics*. London, 1895.

Carducci, G. *La Poesia Barbara nei Secoli XV e XVI*. Bologna, 1881.

Caro, A. *Apologia degli Academici di Bianchi di Roma contra M. Lodovico Castelvetro*. Parma, 1558.

Castelvetro, L. *Poetica d' Aristotele vulgarizzata et sposta*. Basilea, 1576.

—— *Opere Varie Critiche*, colla vita dell' autore scritta da L. A. Muratori. Milano, 1727.

Cook, A. S. *The Art of Poetry: The Poetical Treatises of Horace, Vida, and Boileau, with the translations by Howes, Pitt, and Soame*. Boston, 1892.

Dacier, A. *La Poétique traduite en François, avec des Rémarques*. Paris, 1692.

Daniello, B. *La Poetica*. Vinegia, 1536.

Dante Alighieri. *Tutte le Opere*, per cura di E. Moore. Oxford, 1894.

Denores, J. *Discorso intorno a que' Principii che la Comedia, la Tragedia, et il Poema Heroico ricevono dalla Philosophia*. Padova, 1587.

—— *In Epistolam Q. Horatij Flacci de Arte Poetica, ex quotidianis Tryphonis Gabrielij Sermonibus Interpretatio*. Venetiis, 1553.

—— *Poetica, nel qual si tratta secondo l' opinion d' Arist. della Tragedia, del Poema Heroico, & della Comedia*. Padova, 1588.

Donatus, A. *Ars Poetica*. Bononiæ, 1659.

Dryden, J. *An Essay of Dramatic Poesy*, edited by T. Arnold. Oxford, 1889.

Du Bellay, J. *Œuvres Choisies*, publiées par L. Becq de Fouquières. Paris, 1876.

Fracastoro, G. *Opera*. 2 vols. Genevæ, 1621.

Giraldi Cintio, G. B. *Scritti Estetici: De' Romanzi, delle Comedie, e delle Tragedie, ecc.* (Daelli's *Biblioteca Rara*, lii., liii.) 2 vols. Milano, 1864.

Gosson, S. *The Schoole of Abuse*, edited by E. Arber. London, 1868.

Haslewood, J. *Ancient Critical Essays upon English Poets and Poesy*. 2 vols. London, 1811–1815.
Ingegneri, A. *Della Poesia Rappresentativa*. Firenze, 1734.
Jonson, B. *Timber, or Discoveries made upon Men and Matter*, edited by F. E. Schelling. Boston, 1892.
—— *Works*, with Notes and Memoir by W. Gifford, edited by F. Cunningham. 3 vols. London, n. d.
Klette, T. *Beiträge zur Geschichte und Litteratur der Italienischen Gelehrtenrenaissance*. 3 parts. Greifswald, 1888–1890.
Le Bossu, R. *Treatise of the Epic Poem*, made English by W. J. Second edition. 2 vols. London, 1719.
Lionardi, A. *Dialogi della Inventione Poetica*. Venetia, 1554.
Luisino, F. *In Librum Q. Horatii Flacci de Arte Poetica Commentarius*. Venetiis, 1554.
Maggi, V., and Lombardi, B. *In Aristotelis Librum de Poetica Explanationes*. Venetiis, 1560.
Milton, J. *Prose Works*, edited by J. A. St. John. (Bohn's Library.) 5 vols. London, 1848.
Minturno, A. S. *L'Arte Poetica*. Venetia, 1564.
—— *De Poeta Libri Sex*. Venetiis, 1559.
Muzio, G. *Rime Diverse: Tre Libri di Arte Poetica, Tre Libri di Lettere in rime sciolti, ecc.* Vinegia, 1551.
Partenio, B. *Della Imitatione Poetica*. Vinegia, 1560.
Patrizzi, F. *Della Poetica: La Deca Istoriale, La Deca Disputata*. Ferrara, 1586.
Petrarca, F. *Opera quœ extant Omnia*. Basileæ, 1554.
Piccolomini, A. *Annotationi nel Libro della Poetica d'Aristotele*. Vinegia, 1575.
Pope, A. *Selecta Poemata Italorum, qui Latine Scripserunt*. 2 vols. Londini, 1740.
Puttenham, G. *The Arte of English Poesie*, edited by E. Arber. London, 1869.
Rapin, R. *Reflections on Aristotle's Treatise of Poesie* (transl.). London, 1674.

Robortelli, F. *In Librum Aristotelis de Arte Poetica Explicationes*. Florentiæ, 1548.

Ronsard, P. de. *Œuvres Complètes,* publiées par P. Blanchemain. 8 vols. Paris, 1857–1867.

Salviati, L. *Parafrasi e Commento della Poetica di Aristotile,* 370 folios, Cod. Magliabechiano, ii. ii. II. Ms.

—— *Trattato della Poetica, Lettura Terza,* 22 folios, Cod. Magliabechiano, vii. 7, 715. Ms.

Scaliger, J. C. *Poetices Libri Septem*. Editio Quinta. In Bibliopolio Commeliano, 1617.

Segni, A. *Ragionamento sopra le Cose pertinenti alla Poetica*. Fiorenza, 1581.

Segni, B. *Rettorica et Poetica d' Aristotele tradotte in lingua vulgare Fiorentina*. Vinegia, 1551.

Sidney, Sir P. *The Defense of Poesy, otherwise known as An Apology for Poetry,* edited by A. S. Cook. Boston, 1890.

Speroni, Sperone. *Opere*. 5 vols. Venezia, 1740.

Stanyhurst, R. *Translation of the First Four Books of the Æneid of P. Virgilius Maro,* edited by E. Arber. London, 1880.

Summo, F. *Discorsi Poetici*. Padova, 1600.

Tasso, B. *Delle Lettere: aggiuntovi il Ragionamento della Poesia*. 2 vols. Padova, 1733.

Tasso, T. *Opere, colle Controversie sulla Gerusalemme,* per cura di G. Rosini. 33 vols. Pisa, 1821–1832.

Trissino, G. G. *Tutte le Opere*. 2 vols. Verona, 1729.

Twining, T. *Aristotle's Treatise on Poetry, translated with Notes and two Dissertations on Poetical and Musical Imitation*. Second edition. 2 vols. London, 1812.

Varchi, B. *Lezzioni, lette nell' Accademia Fiorentina*. Fiorenza, 1590.

Vauquelin de la Fresnaye, J. *L'Art Poétique,* publié par G. Pellissier. Paris, 1885.

Vettori, P. *Commentarii in primum Librum Aristotelis de Arte Poetarum*. Florentiæ, 1560.

Webbe, W. *A Discourse of English Poetrie,* edited by E. Arber. London, 1871.
Woodward, W. H. *Vittorino da Feltre and other Humanist Educators: Essays and Versions.* Cambridge, 1897.

II. SECONDARY WORKS

Arnaud, C. *Études sur la Vie et les Œuvres de l'Abbé d'Aubignae, et sur les Théories Dramatiques au XVIIe Siècle.* Paris, 1887.
Aronstein, P. "Ben Jonson's Theorie des Lustspiels," in *Anglia* (1895), vol. xvii.
Baillet, A. *Jugemens des Savans sur les Principaux Ouvrages des Auteurs,* revûs par M. de la Monnoye. 8 vols. Amsterdam, 1725.
Borinski, K. *Die Poetik der Renaissance, und die Anfänge der litterarischen Kritik in Deutschland.* Berlin, 1886.
Bourgoin, A. *Les Maîtres de la Critique au XVIIème Siècle.* Paris, 1889.
Breitinger, H. *Les Unités d'Aristote avant le Cid de Corneille.* Deuxième édition. Genève et Bâle, 1895.
Brunetière, F. *L'Évolution des Genres dans l'Histoire de la Littérature.* Deuxième édition. Vol. i. Paris, 1892.
Brunot, F. *La Doctrine de Malherbe d'après son Commentaire sur Desportes.* Paris, 1891.
Canello, U. *Storia della Letteratura Italiana nel Secolo XVI.* Milano, 1880.
Cecchi, P. L. *T. Tasso, il Pensiero e le Belle Lettere Italiane nel Secolo XVI.* Firenze, 1877.
Cloetta, W. *Beiträge zur Litteraturgeschichte des Mittelalters und der Renaissance.* 2 vols. Halle, 1890–1892.
Comparetti, D. *Vergil in the Middle Ages,* translated by E. F. M. Benecke. London, 1895.

Croce, B. *Estetica come Scienza dell' Espressione e Linguistica generale.* Palermo, 1902.

De Sanctis, F. *Storia della Letteratura Italiana.* Sesta edizione. 2 vols. Napoli, 1893.

Di Niscia, G. "La Gerusalemme Conquistata e l' Arte Poetica di Tasso," in *Il Propugnatore* (1889), N.S. vol. ii. parts 1, 2.

Ebert, A. *Allgemeine Geschichte der Literatur des Mittelalters im Abendlande.* 3 vols. Leipzig, 1874–1887.

Egger, É. *Essai sur l'Histoire de la Critique chez les Grecs. Deuxième édition.* Paris, 1886.

—— *L'Hellénisme en France.* 2 vols. Paris, 1869.

Faguet, É. *La Tragédie française au XVIe Siècle.* Paris, 1894.

Foffano, F. *Ricerche Letterarie.* Livorno, 1897.

Gaspary, A. *Geschichte der Italienischen Literatur.* 2 vols. Strassburg, 1885–1888.

Hamelius, P. *Die Kritik in der Englischen Literatur des 17. und 18. Jahrhunderts.* Leipzig, 1897.

Jacquinet, P. *Francisci Baconi de Re Litteraria Judicia.* Parisiis, 1863.

Koerting, G. *Geschichte der Litteratur Italiens im Zeitalter der Renaissance.* 3 vols. Leipzig, 1878–1884.

Krantz, É. *L'Esthétique de Descartes, étudiée dans les Rapports de la Doctrine cartésienne avec la Littérature classique française au XVIIe Siècle.* Paris, 1882.

Langlois, E. *De Artibus Rhetoricœ Rhythmicœ.* Parisiis, 1890.

Lintilhac, E. *De J.–C. Scaligeri Poetice.* Paris, 1887.

——"Un Coup d'État dans la République des Lettres," in the *Nouvelie Revue* (1890), vol. lxiv.

Menéndez y Pelayo, M. *Historia de las Ideas Estéticas en España.* Segunda edición. 9 vols. Madrid, 1890–1896.

Müller, E. *Geschichte der Theorie der Kunst bei den Alten.* 2 vols. Breslau, 1834–1837.

Natali, G. *Torquato Tasso, Filosofo del Belle, dell' Arte, e dell' Amore.* Roma, 1895.
Pellissier, G. *De Sexti Decimi Sœculi in Francia Artibus Poeticis.* Paris, 1882.
Perrens, F. T. *Jérome Savonarole.* 2 vols. Paris, 1853.
Quadrio, F. S. *Della Storia e della Ragione d' ogni Poesia.* 5 vols. Milano, 1739–1752.
Quossek, C. *Sidney's Defense of Poesy und die Poetik des Aristoteles.* Krefeld, 1884.
Robert, P. *La Poétique de Racine.* Paris, 1890.
Rosenbauer, A. *Die Poetischen Theorien der Plejade nach Ronsard und Dubellay.* Erlangen, 1895.
Rucktäschel, T. *Einige Arts Poétiques aus der Zeit Ronsard's und Malherbe's.* Leipzig, 1889.
Schelling, F. E. *Poetic and Verse Criticism of the Reign of Elizabeth.* Philadelphia, University of Pennsylvania Press, 1891.
Solerti, A. *Vita di Torquato Tasso.* 3 vols. Torino, 1895.
Symonds, J. A. *Renaissance in Italy.* 7 vols. New York, 1888.
Teichmüller, G. *Aristotelische Forschungen.* 2 vols. Halle, 1869.
Tiraboschi, G. *Storia della Letteratura Italiana.* 9 vols. Firenze, 1805–1813.
Vossler, K. *Poetische Theorien in der italienischen Frührenaissance.* Berlin, 1900.
—— "Pietro Aretino's künstlerisches Bekenntnis," in *Neue Heidelberger Jahrbücher*, 1900, vol. x.

For further bibliographical information, see the Italian translation of this book (*La Critica letteraria nel Rinascimento, traduzione italiana del Dr. Antonio Fusco, con correzzioni e aggiunte dell' autore e prefazione di B. Croce*, Bari, 1905, pp. 337–347).

INDEX